breaking
TWIG

A Novel

Deborah Epperson

WRITE MONTANA * MONTANA

Breaking TWIG

by Deborah Epperson

Copyright © 2012 by Deborah Epperson

All rights reserved.

Email: breakingtwig@hotmail.com

ISBN-13: 978-1466463929
ISBN-10: 1466463929

Cover art by Erin Rankin
Cover design by Blue Heron Loft
Publisher: WRITE MONTANA Publishing

Acknowledgements

First, I want to give my sincere thanks to my Writer's Critique Group, a fantastic, eclectic group of women writers without whose help this novel would have never been completed.

Leslie Budewitz

Rena Desmond

Janet Fisher

Sami Rorvik

Debbie Burke

Christina Eisenberg

Marge Fisher

I would also like to thank the members of the Authors of the Flathead, especially Dennis Foley, Kathy Dunnehoff, Dr. Betty Kuffel, Tom Kuffel, and Carol Buchanan for their friendship, expertise, and support.

Miss Alice Cashen, my honors English teacher who said, "If you want to keep your sanity, never stop reading books." Smart lady!

My sincere thanks to Erin Rankin (cover designer), Roxanne McHenry (BumbleB Media, Inc.), and Tom Kuffel (print format designer) for your expertise and patience.

To Nathan, Tara, and Garrett, I give y'all my gratitude, my love, and any loose change you can find in the bottom of my purse. And to my BFFD (best friend forever dog) Jasmine, and our other four-legged family members, I give all the affection, tummy rubs, and jerky treats you will ever need.

This book is for my beloved late mother
Betty Pelt
the polar opposite of the mother in this novel.
Thank you, Momma, for showing me what a truly
kind, encouraging and loving person is.
We miss you.

"This above all: to thine own self be true, And it must follow, as the night the day, Thou canst not then be false to any man."
Shakespeare, Hamlet, act 1, scene iii

PROLOGUE

I must have been about five the first time Grandpa Eli told me the story of the Pickers and the Picks. He was sitting in his rocking chair on the back porch of the modest plantation house he'd built twenty years earlier. My imaginary friend, Claudia, and I were having a tea party under the shade of the weeping willow. A clump of purple flowers plucked from the wisteria vine trailing along the back picket fence served as our grapes, while half-a-dozen emerald leaves pilfered from a hothouse geranium represented mint cookies.

"Becky Leigh," he called. "Did I ever tell you the story of the Pickers and the Picks?"

"No, sir." I headed for the porch. "What are Pickers, Grandpa?"

"Pickers are mainly folks who are big on the outside, but small on the inside." He gave a push and the oak rocker resumed its familiar cadence. "Not necessarily tall and heavy big. Pickers are more like puffed up big."

I climbed into his lap, nestled into the crook of his shoulder. "Like popcorn puffs up when you cook it?"

"No, more like a sore that's got infected and is puffed up with mucus and poisons."

"That's yucky."

Grandpa laughed. "That's a true fact, Miss Becky."

"What do Pickers do?" I asked.

"Pickers hunt for someone who looks like easy pickin's."

"Easy pickin's? Do you mean like when Momma makes Papa and me pick dewberries along the railroad track instead of by Lost Mule Bog because she says it's easy pickin's along the tracks? But it's not really. It's just the bog is messier, and you know how she hates messes."

Grandpa stopped rocking. "Are you going to be quiet and let me finish my story, youngun?"

I covered my mouth to stifle a giggle. It was the funniest thing, my grandpa pretending to be mad at me. "Yes, sir. I'll be quiet."

The rocker started up again. "As I was saying, a Picker hunts for someone he thinks will be easy pickin's. That's usually someone smaller, younger, or weaker in some way. It can be someone whose only weakness is that he or she is a nice person."

I tapped Grandpa's shoulder. "How does a Picker change nice people into Picks?"

"Well, he screams and hollers at them. He makes them do things they know they shouldn't do. Champion Pickers are genuine experts at bullyin', intimidatin', and dominatin' gentler folks." The rocker stopped once more. "Do you understand anything I'm saying, Becky?"

"I think so. Maybe. Will I be a Picker or a Pick when I grow up, Grandpa?"

"Can't say for sure. Let's try an experiment." He helped me down and pointed to a line of ants marching across the porch floor. "Go stand by those ants."

I did as I was told.

"Now, Becky, I want you to stomp them ants as hard as you can."

"But why should I kill the ants, Grandpa? They're not hurting me."

"Because you can, girl. Because you can."

I began to stomp. I stomped the ants in the middle of the line, the ants in the back of the line, and all the ants at the head of the line. I stomped so hard my cat's dish vibrated across the floor, tumbled over the edge, and landed in the azalea bushes that circled the back porch. I didn't stop stomping until all the ants were either dead or beyond my reach.

Grandpa Eli motioned for me to come back. He put his hands on my shoulders and looked me straight in the eyes. "That's what Pickers do, Becky. They hurt other living things just because they can." Pulling me closer, he asked, "How did stomping those ants make you feel?"

I lowered my eyes. "Bad. I felt bad, but . . ."

"But what?"

"But when I was stomping them I felt . . ."

"You felt strong?"

I nodded, too ashamed to acknowledge my Picker-like feelings in words.

"How do you think the ants felt?"

"Terrible," I said. "And so will Pinecone when he sees his supper is gone."

"Don't you worry about that cat. He won't starve. But that's what happens when a Picker gets riled up. Lots of innocent folks get hurt too."

"Does this mean I'm gonna be a Picker when I grow up?"

"It's all up to you, child. You don't have to be a Picker or a Pick. You can choose to be nice to people and insist that they be nice to you."

I climbed back into his lap. "And if they're not nice to me?"

"If you stand up to the Pickers in this world, they'll leave you alone. Remember, they like easy pickin's."

"Have you ever been a Picker, Grandpa, or a Pick?"

"Sure. At certain times in life, most people are either a Pick or Picker. It usually takes a lifetime for folks to figure out they don't have to be either one."

"Grandpa, do you think a Picker, even a champion Picker that is, can ever change?"

"Maybe. With the passage of time and a heap of prayers, I think anyone can change."

I gave him a hug. "I think we should start praying for Momma right away."

Grandpa Eli smiled. "I think you're right, Becky Leigh."

*****

I did start praying. But after both my grandfather and my beloved Papa died, and after the only noticeable change in Momma — despite eight years of fervent prayers — was her new husband, I stopped. I let the tales of Pickers and Picks slip from my mind and forgot Grandpa Eli's warnings on the perils of becoming easy pickin's.

Not until one day in November of '63 did I recall the lessons of the porch. That was the morning Momma and her new husband, Frank, went to the Miller's house to watch President Kennedy's funeral, and the time I got caught slipping into my new stepbrother's room to borrow some paper. It was also the day a seventeen-year-old boy decided to teach a thirteen-year-old girl a lesson she wouldn't forget. That was the day I knew for sure I was a Pick.

CHAPTER 1

November 25, 1963

I never meant to interrupt the funeral of the President of the United States. When Johnny Santo found me crying behind our garage, I begged him not to tell anyone my new stepbrother, Donald, had raped me, but Anna Marie Santo had taught her son right from wrong. Johnny wasn't about to let such a wicked deed go unpunished.

He took me to Anna, our housekeeper and the lady who'd taken care of me since my birth thirteen years earlier. Despite my pleas not to, Anna insisted on calling my mother, Helen, and giving her the bad news. Momma doesn't like bad news, unless she's the one delivering it. But Anna sincerely believed my momma would want to be told about my assault. I knew she wouldn't. Momma wanted to watch President Kennedy's funeral. She'd bought a new dress for the occasion. I didn't think she'd appreciate her plans being disrupted because of me. I wasn't wrong.

Momma stood in front of Anna and me, hands on her hips, feet apart, and lips pulled back in a snarl that would send the meanest cur in Sugardale, Georgia running for its life.

"Stay out of the way, Frank," she said to her new husband. "I'll take care of this."

I wrapped my arms around Anna's waist. "Please don't let them take me."

Momma stomped her foot. "Becky Leigh Cooper, let go of Anna and get over here."

I'd never seen Momma so mad. And I'd seen her plenty mad plenty of times. Still, I refused to release my hold on the one person I felt could save me.

Momma grabbed for me, but I swung Anna around and all Momma caught was air.

Johnny pulled back his fist and headed for my mother. "Leave her alone, bitch."

She screamed, ducked behind her husband, and latched on to the back of his new shirt. "He's gonna hit me, Frank. Do something."

"Stop, you're choking me, Helen." Frank Wooten pulled at the front of his shirt with both hands. "For God's sake, let go." He reached back, got a handful of Momma's dress, and yanked hard enough to procure his release, ripping her dress in the process.

"Damn you, Frank, you tore my new dress."

Johnny's uncle, Alejandro Garza, stepped between him and Momma. Mr. Garza grabbed his nephew's wrist and pointed at the television. "They're burying Mr. Kennedy today, Johnny. They're burying the President of the United States. Show some respect."

"That's right, boy," Helen snapped. "Show some respect."

Johnny pointed at me. "Why don't you show some respect for your own daughter?" The fifteen-year-old turned to Frank. "That no-good son of yours raped Rebecca today."

Frank stood there staring, as if unable to comprehend the meaning of Johnny's words.

"Did you hear what I said, Mr. Wooten?" Johnny asked, his voice growing higher with each word. "Donald raped Rebecca. When I see the bastard, I'm going to kill him."

Anna grabbed her son's arm. "You mustn't say things like that."

"Donald hurt Rebecca, Mother. I can't let him get away with that."

"You hear that, Frank? He's threatening to kill your son." Helen shook her finger at Johnny. "You're going to jail, boy. You're going to jail for threatening Donald and for talking my girl into letting you poke around inside of her. If anyone raped Becky Leigh, it was you."

I let go of Anna, put my head down, and charged at my mother the way Floyd Nelson's goat had once charged him. In all the madness, I forgot that goat had ended up on Floyd's bar-b-que pit. I just knew Momma had threatened my best friend. I'd have never fought my mother for myself, but I'd fight the Devil for Johnny. It's funny how that works.

I hit Momma so hard we went sailing over the back of Anna's red leather armchair. The skirt of my dress flew over my head and for a moment, I couldn't see anything but green and beige checks.

Momma liked dresses with tight skirts because they showed off her figure best, so it wasn't a surprise her new dress had a tight skirt. But it was a complete shock to everyone when her skirt ripped from hem to waist. She screamed for Frank, and I felt two strong hands pick me up. I struggled to get down, but even though I was a teenager in years, size-wise I looked about nine. I didn't have a chance against Frank.

Mr. Garza helped Momma up and quickly stepped out of her reach. I didn't blame him. I've been caught in Momma's reach many times. It isn't a pleasant experience.

"Your boy has turned my own daughter against me, Anna," Helen yelled.

I tried to tell Momma it wasn't Johnny who turned me against her, but she was arguing with him and his mother and didn't hear me. No one heard me even though I was screaming.

"Johnny would never hurt Rebecca," Anna shouted. "She's like a sister to him. He found her crying and brought her here. I've taken care of this child since she was born."

"You've been my maid since she was born. I'm her mother. I take care of her."

"And how do you do that?" Johnny asked. "With whippings and making her work like a slave." He pointed at Frank. "Rebecca's father has been dead for only three months, and you've brought this man and his monster son into her home. You let them hurt her. You let them hurt her bad."

Frank was holding me on his hip the way one would hold a two-year-old. We looked at each other, our faces inches apart. He was there to support Momma. It was his son who'd raped me. Yet when I looked into Frank's blue eyes, I saw pain and confusion. The same pain and confusion I'd seen in my papa's eyes and in my own. Because of that, I couldn't hate him.

"Are you going to let Johnny speak to me that way, Frank?" Momma asked.

My new stepfather put me down, but held on to my shoulders preventing me from running to Anna again. "I think we should all calm down."

"That's a good idea," Mr. Garza said.

The two men looked at each other for a moment and then both nodded.

Grandpa Eli had warned me to be careful about drawing lines in the sand. "A line in the sand can become a rut. A rut can become a ditch, and a ditch can be worn down into a pit. There's not much difference between a pit and a grave, Miss Becky," he often advised.

But on this day, the battle lines were drawn. Like usual, Momma had drawn them, and her battle lines were always deep — pit deep, grave deep. With Momma, you were either on her side or you were on the wrong side.

She stood there, arms folded across her chest, glaring at Frank, giving him *the look.* Frank had known my mother only a few months before they'd married. I figured he hadn't experienced the look yet and felt like I should warn him about it. But then I remembered, he and I were on opposite sides of Momma's line.

"That's all you have to say about the matter, Franklin Wayne Wooten?" Momma asked, in her low, slow-down voice.

Now, I really felt sorry for Frank. When my momma gives you the look and calls out your whole name in her low, slow-down voice, you're gonna pay. She only uses all three weapons together when she thinks she's been betrayed somehow. When you betray my mother — in fact or just in her head — you pay for it. Maybe not right away. Momma often likes to study on the best way to make someone repent for what she considers to be sins against her. But sooner or later, everybody pays. I didn't figure Franklin Wayne Wooten would be an exception just because he and Momma had been married for only three weeks.

For a moment, everyone quit shouting and pointing fingers at each other. For a moment, I felt some hope that we might all survive the day. Then, my momma spoke.

"It's time we called Sheriff Tate," Helen said. "Roy will know what to do."

I knew what that meant. Sheriff Tate was a good friend to my mother. So good in fact, that whenever Papa went out of town, Roy Tate would make a special trip to our house each night to make sure Momma and I were safe. Yes, I knew if Sheriff Tate came, he'd believe Momma's version of the rape over my truth. No doubt about it. Before this day was over, I'd be getting a good whipping. Might as well get one for lying as to get one for telling the truth. Anyway, the most important thing to me was keeping Johnny safe and out of jail.

"I lied about the rape." This time, everyone heard me.

"You lied, did you? Did you hear that, Frank?" Momma asked.

"Rebecca told the truth." Johnny started forward, but his uncle held him back.

"What would you know about the truth, boy?" Helen asked. "You're just damn lucky she spoke up before I called Sheriff Tate or you'd be spending the night in jail."

Anna came to me. She took my face in her hands and asked, "Are you sure Donald didn't hurt you? Are you sure you're not just trying to protect my Johnny?"

The room grew silent. Everyone's attention focused on me. Most of the time, I think of myself as being invisible. Not invisible like a ghost, but like a souvenir plate from last year's vacation. At first, everyone is excited about seeing the plate, but then it's put on the bookcase and only taken down when it needs cleaning. Soon, the little plate is viewed as being more trouble than it's worth.

"I'm sorry I lied, Anna."

Momma grinned. "Told you she was lying."

Anna looked at me and then at Frank. Their eyes locked. It appeared to me as if Anna was sending Frank a message in eye code. I couldn't tell what the message was or whether my stepfather was receiving Anna's telepathic eye communication or not. I just wanted to leave before Momma changed her mind and called Sheriff Tate to come get Johnny.

"Can we go home, Frank?" I asked.

Frank looked at Momma. She shrugged. That could mean yes or no. Momma does that when she wants to test someone's loyalty to her, or to see if they're smart enough to come up with her answer on their own. I wondered if Frank knew he was being tested.

"I think we're done here," he said. "We'll talk more about this at home."

Momma nodded. Frank had passed the test.

*****

It took Mr. Garza and his two teen-age sons to hold Johnny back while Momma and Frank put me in the car. Anna came out and assured me I'd be safe with my own mother. I don't think she believed that was a true fact. I know I didn't. But Anna had been comforting me all of my life. She wasn't going to stop now when I needed her most.

Anna gave me a good-bye hug. "I'll see you tomorrow."

"No, you won't," Momma said. "You're fired."

It felt as if someone had hit me square in the chest. I couldn't breathe. I tried to climb over the front seat of our two-door car, but Momma pushed me back.

"I have worked for your family thirteen years," Anna said. "You can't fire me like this."

"I just did." Momma crossed her arms in front of her heartless chest and proceeded with her tongue-lashing of my beloved Anna. "I have long felt that Becky did not need to be around your kind. I've wanted to fire you for years, but her daddy refused to let me."

Anna's chin quivered. "Mr. Paul was afraid to leave Rebecca alone with you."

"Don't expect a good reference from me," Momma said as she got in the car.

Anna grabbed the door handle. "You owe me eight days pay, Helen."

It was the first time I'd ever heard Anna call my mother by her first name.

Momma pushed Anna back, slammed the door, rolled down the window a tad. "I don't owe you a damn thing. If you think I do, take it up with Sheriff Tate."

Anna knew as I did, she'd have a better chance at being named Miss Georgia than she would have of getting the money my mother owed her.

Frank started to drive off, but Anna ran in front of the car. He slammed on his brakes.

I went flying forward into the back of Momma's head.

"Damn you, Becky," she screamed, while slapping me back.

My head pounded. My face stung. But I couldn't focus on my pain because of my fear for Anna's safety.

"Go, Frank," Helen shouted. "Run over her if you have to, but just go."

Frank stared at Momma as if he was seeing her for the first time. "I can't run over her, Helen. Are you crazy?"

Relief filled my every pore. Not just to hear Frank's refusal to slaughter my dear Anna, but to hear that perhaps, he'd realized what I'd known all my life. My momma was crazy.

She touched his arm. "I didn't mean for you to actually run over her, Sugar. I only wanted you to frighten her a bit."

A tapping on Frank's window caught our attention. Anna motioned for him to roll down the glass.

"Don't do it, Frank," Helen said. "Let's get out of here."

To my surprise and Momma's dismay, Frank rolled down the window. Guess he was a braver man than I'd give him credit for being.

" Mr. Wooten," Anna begged. "Please don't let her hurt Rebecca."

"Let's go, Frank," Helen yelled.

Frank mumbled something about me being okay and eased the car forward. As he did, he glanced back at me. The expression on his face told me he hadn't a clue as to what Anna was talking about. But Momma did.

CHAPTER 2

Momma shoved me into our living room. "Sit down Becky Leigh and don't move. I'll be back." She stomped up the stairs.

I did as I was told. When Momma returned, she'd have Papa's favorite belt. Whipping me with it made the pain worse and the humiliation greater. Momma was clever in that way.

Donald strolled into the room, walked over, and leaned down. "I warned you about telling anyone, didn't I, moron?"

I looked up into the meanest eyes I'd ever seen. His hand darted toward me. I crossed my arms in front of my face.

"Donald, what the hell are you doing?" Frank asked as he slammed the front door.

I wiped the sweat off my top lip and started breathing again.

"Make this kid shut up, Daddy, before her lies cost me my football scholarship."

Helen entered the room. "Don't worry, Donald. She's going to shut up." She walked over to me, snapped Papa's belt twice. "You owe your new brother an apology."

A shameless grin spread across Donald's pitted face. "Yeah, you owe me an apology."

I looked to Frank, hoping for some kind of miracle intervention from him. He stood there in silence. I'd lied to save Johnny and stood ready to take a whipping for it, but I would not apologize to Donald for his raping me. Holding my trembling chin as high as possible, I marched over to the ottoman, bent over it, and waited.

"If that's the way you want it," Momma said.

The worst time in a whipping isn't the actual blow itself. It's the seconds between the hits. That's when you feel the sting of the first smack and know a second one is on the way. Then there's a third, a fourth, and a fifth. After the fifth blow, I stopped counting. By then, the pain all ran together.

"I'm going to whip you until you apologize to Donald. I can last longer than you can."

My tears made a puddle on the hardwood floor. I had complete faith in Momma's ability to outlast me. Summoning the last of my courage, I readied myself to die on that stool.

"Stop it, Helen. For God's sake, stop it."

I looked up then and saw Frank grab my mother's whipping arm.

"Stay out of this, Frank." She tried to pull her wrist out of his grip. "We agreed we'd each discipline our own kids. This doesn't concern you."

"The hell it doesn't." He released her arm, but snatched the belt from her hand.

Helen uttered some obscenities and moved away.

"You can get up now, Becky," Frank said.

I stood. My head swirled and my knees buckled.

My stepfather grabbed me. "Are you all right?"

Momma lit a cigarette. "She's okay. She's had worse."

Frank lifted my head. Our eyes met. I could see he felt sorry for me. I don't particularly like being pitied. But in this case, I thought it a generous gesture on his part. After all, I'd accused his son of a terrible crime and then recanted my charge.

I held his arm for support. "I'd . . . I'd like to go upstairs and take a bath."

"Sure," he said. "I'll run you some water. Maybe you should help her, Helen."

"She can take a bath by herself."

"Damn, Helen, this child almost fainted. She could pass out in the tub and drown."

Momma stared at me. "Do you need your mommie to give you a bath, little girl?"

"No, ma'am."

Frank looked at his wife and shook his head. In time, he'd learn what Papa and I had come to know. It's a waste of breath and energy to argue with my mother.

*****

Frank filled the claw foot tub. "I hope this isn't too hot for you, Becky."

I laid my nightgown and robe on the back of the commode. "I'm sure it's fine." It was only 2 p.m., but I was exhausted and longed for the forgetfulness found in sleep.

"Anything else you need, Ladybug?" he asked.

"No, sir, but why do you call me Lady-bug?"

"Because you're as cute as a bug. Like a ladybug, you're red on top and always working in the garden." He ruffled my hair. "If you don't like me calling you that, I'll stop."

"It's okay. Papa and Johnny always called me Twig."

Frank smiled. "Is that because you're so little?"

"Yes, sir, and because a twig has to be flexible to survive. Papa said a twig must bend or a bad wind will break it. He told me to think of myself as a twig."

My stepfather's smile faded. "Would you prefer me to call you Twig?"

"Ladybug is fine. Only Papa and Johnny call me Twig."

Frank nodded and reached for my hand. "I need to know what happened today."

"I'll tell you what happened," Helen said as she sashayed into the room. "Becky let Johnny get into her panties. When Donald caught them, she made up a lie about your son to protect that Mexican boy."

I stared at my feet, too embarrassed by Momma's vulgar lie to look at my stepfather.

"Helen, I want Becky to tell me what happened. I need to know the truth."

Momma stood behind Frank giving me the look. If I told the truth, she'd call me a liar and phone Sheriff Tate to go get Johnny.

Frank got down on one knee in front of me. "I know you're not accustomed to having a big teenage boy around, Becky. Donald hasn't had much experience with little girls either. Did his roughhousing get out of hand? Did he scare you? Is that what happened?"

I nodded. I didn't mind lying to Momma. She didn't care if I told the truth or not, as long as I said what she wanted to hear. But I felt real bad about lying to Frank. Then again, I doubted he wanted to hear that his son was a rapist.

Helen grinned. "What did I tell you, Frank? She's a liar. Always has been."

"I think she's confused. This is all new to her."

"Confused or not, I hope you see the trouble your lies have caused, Becky Leigh, not to mention interrupting my watching President Kennedy's funeral." Momma pointed her finger at me. "Don't think I've forgotten you ripped my new dress. I owe you a whipping for that."

Frank stood. "Helen, if you spank this child for tearing your dress, you'll have to spank me too. After all, I tore it first."

"Why are you coddling her? All you're doing is rewarding her for her lying ways." She stormed out of the bathroom.

"You'd better get your bath before the water gets cold," Frank said as he turned to leave.

I grabbed his arm. "Anna's husband passed away years ago, so she needs to work. Do you think Momma will let her come back to work here? She and Johnny are my only friends."

Frank shook his head. "I doubt it."

I hate crying in front of people.

He handed me a towel. "Tell you what, Ladybug, this is all new to me too. I could use a friend myself. How about you and I make a pact to become friends?" He extended his right hand and we shook on it.

After my stepfather left, I undressed and looked at myself in the full-length mirror hanging on the bathroom door. My front didn't look too bad, except for my red eyes. I used Momma's makeup mirror to see my backside. The red welts on my upper rear and lower back didn't surprise me. I'd seen them before. But in addition to the welts, my rear end and upper thighs were sporting nasty black and blue bruises. On my back, the faint outline of Donald's hand could be seen.

I used up all the hot water trying to get the smell and feel of Donald off of me. After my bath, I slipped into Momma's bedroom, stole some of her fancy hand lotion, and rubbed it all over my body. She owed me that much.

*****

Entering my room, I found Momma sitting on my bed holding my secret shoebox of special photographs. Behind her, spread out on the chenille bedspread, were the rest of my pictures.

"What are you doing with my pictures?" I asked.

"I'm sorting them for you." She stuck her hand into the box and grabbed a fistful of its contents. When she opened her fingers, tiny bits of paper resembling confetti fell back into the container. That's when I saw the scissors resting on the bed beside her.

I grabbed the box. "You cut up my pictures?"

"Only the ones with Johnny and Anna in them."

"No," I yelled as I sifted through the pieces. I dropped the box, ran to the bed, and searched through the remaining photographs.

She grinned. "You won't find any pictures of Johnny. I got them all."

I wanted to pull out every curly blond hair in her head. But then, my eyes spotted something behind her. On my vanity, stuck between the wood frame and mirror, was the last picture of Johnny. Momma followed my line of sight straight to the picture. The race was on.

She was a good foot taller than my 57 inches and had a longer stride. But I was quicker. She took one step toward the vanity. Coming around her left side, I slammed my entire 78 pounds into her. Momentum and surprise were on my side. She went sailing sideways, landing on my bed. She cussed and called my name, but I didn't look back. I snatched the picture off the vanity, held it close to my heart, and turned back toward the door, intent on making my escape.

Like a bullfrog, Momma hopped off the bed and landed smack dab between me and the open bedroom door. But I'd gone through too much that day to be defeated now.

I rushed to the window. In a heartbeat, I threw it open. I was halfway onto the second floor verandah when Momma grabbed my robe. I shed the housecoat and dove for the floor, knocking over a lawn chair in the process. A pried-up nail slit the tail of my gown.

Jumping up as fast as my aching body would permit, I celebrated my victory with a couple of dance steps. Then I remembered there were no stairs leading off the verandah.

"Damn." Normally, I hate cussing. But I felt justified in using profanity this once.

I conducted a quick assessment of my predicament. Momma was half-hanging out the window, motioning for me to come back inside and threatening me with more whippings if I didn't obey. I figured I'd get a whipping even if I did go back. But if she thought I'd hand over my last picture of Johnny, then she was truly, certifiably crazy.

There were two ways off the verandah — back through the house or skidding down a live oak tree that stood a good four feet from the railing. I'm a good jumper, so I figured my best shot at freedom was that tree. I could pounce off the railing and grab hold of a limb on my way down. If I missed, I'd hit the brick walkway below.

I remembered a story Grandpa Eli had once told me. As a prisoner of war in World War I, he'd endured four months of torture. He once said, "When a person suffers constant, severe pain, he ultimately reaches his pain threshold. After that, it doesn't matter how much more pain they heap upon you, Miss Becky, it's all the same."

I knew two things. First, Grandpa was a smart man. Second, I'd definitely reached my pain threshold. So if I hit those bricks, it couldn't hurt much more than it was hurting already.

Holding Johnny's picture in my teeth, I climbed upon the railing and was about to make my leap of faith when two arms wrapped around my waist.

Frank pulled me down. "Are you trying to break your neck, Becky?"

"Hold on to her," Momma yelled out the window. "I'm coming."

I squirmed every which way trying to get out of his embrace, but it wasn't my day.

"Calm down, Ladybug. What's the matter with you?"

I opened my mouth to plead with him. A draft caught my picture and it floated away.

"Grab the picture, Frank," Momma shouted as she joined us on the verandah.

He released me and I scrambled to get my photo. "That picture is mine."

Three sets of hands vied for the snapshot. My stepfather won.

"Give it to me," Momma demanded.

"No, give it to me," I begged. Momma and I jumped at his hand, but he held it higher than either one of us could reach.

"You two stop this nonsense." Frank's eyes narrowed. "What's this all about?"

Momma and I started talking at once.

"One at a time," he said. "Becky, you be quiet and let your mother speak."

My chin quivered. I'd played this scene before. Momma would tell her side of the story and that would be the end of it.

She threw me a sarcastic smile. "Since the Santo boy is no longer a part of Becky's life, I figured it best to be rid of anything that might remind her of him."

"Did you rip up all of Becky's pictures of Johnny?" Frank asked.

"I felt that was best." She held her hand out for the snapshot, but Frank turned to me.

"What do you think about that, Ladybug?"

For a moment, I couldn't get my mouth to work. Adults seldom asked for my opinion. In the past, whenever Momma and I'd argue, Papa would give into her to keep peace in the family. Later, he would apologize to me for not taking my side into account. But his apology didn't make me feel better. It just made me feel sorry for Papa.

If I told him I wanted the picture because Johnny was in it, I knew Momma would pitch a hissy fit. I decided on a different approach.

"That's the last photo Papa and I took with Grandpa Eli. He died two months later. That's why I want to keep the picture, Frank."

"I told you to call him Daddy Frank, didn't I?" Momma reached over intending on giving me a slap upside my head, but her husband grabbed her wrist.

"There's been enough hitting and slapping today, Helen." Frank looked at the snapshot. "I can't see the harm in letting her keep one picture."

"I do." Helen jerked her hand free. "And I don't appreciate you undermining my authority with my daughter. How would you like it if I did the same to you with Donald?"

"She's got a point, Becky."

My heart sank. I wished I had jumped off the verandah and spattered myself all over the bricks. "Are you going to give my picture to Momma?"

"Of course he is," she said.

Frank looked at Momma and then at me. He held up the photograph, ripped it in two, and handed her the smaller piece. He gave me the larger one.

I looked at mine. There was Grandpa Eli, Papa, and half of me. Momma got the other half of my image and all of Johnny's.

She promptly tore her part into little pieces. "Becky Leigh, when are you going to realize that I'm the boss?"

I gave her my meanest stare and made the dangerous decision not to let her have the last word. No, not today. I looked up at Frank, batted my eyes the way I'd seen Momma do, and in my most innocent voice asked, "Is that right, Daddy Frank? Is Momma the boss?"

CHAPTER 3

The next few weeks were hard on me. Momma and Donald found subtle ways of retaliating for what they perceived as my turning Frank against them. I tried not to be caught alone with either one of them, especially Donald. Frank told me to let him know if his son bothered me. I'm not normally a tattletale, but I made an exception in Donald's case. He soon hated me as much as I hated him.

The worse part of those weeks was getting up every morning and not finding Anna fixing my breakfast. I grieved for her as if she'd died. According to Momma, Anna and Johnny were dead to me.

Momma's friend, Betty Powell, hired Anna at twice the salary we'd paid her. My mother made up horrible lies about Anna and insisted she be fired. But Betty chose to find a new best friend rather than give up a reliable housekeeper who could cook. Momma said she never liked Betty anyway and decided a housekeeper was a waste of money. She told Frank that she and I would keep up the house and garden.

My stepfather got more and more upset each time Momma whipped me. So she devised a new strategy and offered me a deal I dared not refused. My new assignment consisted of doing the housework in such a way that she got the credit. As long as Frank remained under the illusion that Momma was a great housekeeper and cook, I'd be safe.

Preferring work to whippings, I accepted my secret mission with enthusiasm. Anna had taught me well. I had complete faith in my abilities as a housemaid and so did Momma. She actually complimented me on the way I ironed Frank's shirts.

Finding ways to see Johnny proved to be my biggest challenge. I attended the eighth grade at the junior high, and Johnny, a sophomore, went to Sugardale High. We communicated through his cousin, Emelda, who sat behind me in history class. She charged Johnny and me a nickel for every note we passed via her makeshift postal services. She soon became the richest kid in Sugardale Junior High.

Two weeks before Christmas, Frank announced that Donald would be spending the holidays in Tallahassee with his maternal grandparents. I shouted, "Hallelujah." It was truly an embarrassing, but sincere reaction.

Momma was disappointed. "This is our first Christmas together. How can you let him go, Frank?"

"His grandparents are getting old and they haven't seen Donald in a year," Frank said. "When my late wife, April, got cancer, I worked two jobs to pay the medical bills, plus took care of her. Her folks offered to let Donald live with them." He sighed. "I knew they'd spoil him, but what choice did I have?"

In truth, I think Frank wanted Donald to go. My stepfather spent fourteen hours a day learning how to run Papa's hardware and garden store and then played referee when he got home. I regretted my tattling added to his misery, but I was determined not to become Donald's Pick too. I saw in him the ability to become a champion Picker, especially if tutored by Momma.

At the bus station, Frank gave Donald some money and Momma told him to bring us all presents from Florida. She made me hug his neck.

As I did, I whispered, "The best present you can get me is to not come back." I knew I'd pay for my comment, but it still felt good.

*****

Frank entered the greenhouse. He watched as I tied a green ribbon around the last pot of scarlet poinsettias. "You've done a fine job as usual, Becky."

I smiled. I had a deep desire to please my stepfather, but not because I thought of him as a father figure. I didn't. Paul Cooper was my papa. Frank understood that. We were friends, good friends.

There were days when I think I would've died if Frank hadn't come around to cheer me up. Despite the cold or his own weariness, he'd sit in the front porch swing or in the back yard glider and talk to me. We'd often sit on the back porch and just rock — he in Grandpa Eli's rocker, me in Papa's. We had lots of swings and rockers at our house, and we needed every one of them.

Frank put the last of the poinsettias in the back of his Ranchero pickup. "Let's drop these off at the store and go Christmas shopping, Ladybug."

"Is Momma going?"

"Helen's going Christmas caroling with her Sunday school class."

I clapped my hands. "Sounds great to me."

Frank went to the garage, came back with the ax. "Let's stop and cut us a Christmas tree."

"Papa always got a tree from our nursery."

He slipped the ax behind the seat. "Haven't you ever been Christmas tree hunting?"

"No, sir."

"You don't know what you're missing." He gave my long hair a gentle tug. "A friend of mine owns property on Starview Mountain. We'll stop on our way back from Kirbyville and get a tree."

"We're going to Kirbyville?"

"Yep." Frank handed me a twenty-dollar bill. "You'll need some spending money."

I tried to give it back to him, but he wouldn't take it.

"All our employees are getting Christmas bonuses. No one works harder than you." Frank winked at me. "Besides, you might want to buy me a Christmas present."

That was a true fact. I wanted to get a gift for Anna, Johnny, and despite my feelings, I'd have to get Momma and Donald some token gift too. It'd be bad manners not to, and Papa had always insisted I practice good manners.

*****

Kirbyville lay some forty miles south of Sugardale and was about three times as big. The Plaza Mall consisted of three-dozen stores. We headed for the biggest one. I bought Johnny a pair of leather gloves and chose a peach sweater for Anna. It had a beaded flower on the left shoulder. The saleslady picked out a green and burgundy paisley scarf for Momma. Frank suggested I get her a sweater to match.

"Then I won't have enough money to buy you and Donald a gift," I argued.

Frank gave me another twenty dollars. "Let me know if you need more."

Since it was Christmas — and because I no longer had an excuse not to — I bought Momma a green ribbed turtleneck with *no* beading. Frank recommended a record for Donald. I made sure my stepbrother's gift came out of the extra dollars his daddy gave me, and not out of the money I'd earned.

For Frank, I chose a long-sleeve shirt in baby blue to match his eyes. He had the prettiest eyes I'd ever seen on a man or a woman. When he laughed, his eyes danced.

He offered to treat me to lunch. "You get a table while I put our packages in the truck."

I walked into the café and there sitting at a table for four was Anna and Johnny. I joined them. When Frank returned, the three of us held our breath until he pulled out the chair next to Anna's. At first, it felt a little awkward. But by the time we ordered, we were all laughing.

Frank entertained us with stories about his adventures at learning to manage Papa's hardware store after spending most of his life working construction. After swearing us to secrecy, Anna told us things about Betty Powell that even Momma didn't know. We couldn't eat for laughing so hard. Through it all, Johnny held my hand under the table.

I don't know if it was my delight at being with the three people I loved most or if it was just the magic of Christmas, but I wanted to sit there forever. In my mind's eye, I could see us four as a family. Frank's dark hair and deeply tanned skin were only a shade lighter than Anna and Johnny's. With my auburn hair and green eyes, I was the oddball. But according to my imagination, Frank and Anna could've adopted me. Then I wouldn't have been blood kin to Johnny. Thus, the strange, non-brotherly feelings I had for him would've been okay. We'd been enjoying ourselves for an hour when Ethel Johnson walked up.

"Fancy seeing you here, Frank. Hi Becky." She ignored Anna and Johnny.

Frank and I nodded. Her presence meant trouble for us.

Mrs. Johnson cast Anna a hateful look. "Where's your lovely wife, Frank?"

"Helen's out caroling. Becky and I thought we'd sneak over and buy her Christmas presents." He pushed back his chair. "Don't you tell her, Ethel. You'll spoil our surprise."

"I won't," she said as she turned to leave.

That biddy was lying through her teeth. I knew she'd phone Momma and tell her we were with Anna and Johnny. I wished Frank hadn't used the term, "Sneak over."

Like Momma, Ethel was the type to take such a phrase and run with it.

*****

Seeing Anna and Johnny was both an answered prayer and a resurrected heartache. Neither Frank nor I spoke during our trip home. I think he understood I needed time to brood over losing them again.

About eleven miles out of Sugardale, my stepfather turned onto a dirt road.

"Where are we going?" I asked.

"Starview Mountain. We need a Christmas tree. Remember?"

I shrugged.

Frank drove to the top of the mountain. "Come on. I've got something to show you."

I buttoned my coat and got out.

He led me to the edge of a cliff. Below, a gorge split the rock walls as if God himself had thrown a lightning bolt from Heaven. "That's Cascade Canyon down there."

"How far can we see, Frank? Is that Tennessee?"

"Maybe." He pointed to the left side of the canyon wall. "That's how the canyon got its name."

A large, triangular-shaped rock jutted out past the face of the stone cliff. A small river tumbled over it, throwing itself this way and that onto the boulders below, darkening each one it touched. Streamers of water framed by giant icicles snaked their way to the canyon floor. Some combined to create shallow pools, while others joined with Lazy Rock Creek as it meandered through the gorge.

Frank put his arm around me. "It's an awesome sight, isn't it?"

I smiled. Once more, he'd pulled me out of my misery.

"Got something else to show you," he said.

We walked down a dirt road, passed a line of cottonwoods, and came upon a stream. At one point, the stream widened to form an ice-covered pond. I put my foot on the ice.

Frank jerked me back. "It's still a little thin. We'll come back in January and go ice skating."

"I don't know how."

He squatted down in front of me. "You mean to tell me you've never chopped down a Christmas tree or gone ice skating?"

I shook my head.

"Your education is sorely lacking, Ladybug. It's lucky I found you when I did."

Frank's words were truer than he realized.

We chopped down a fine eight-foot tree. When we got in the truck, my stepfather handed me a present. "This is for you. Open it."

I untied the ribbon, tore off the paper, and found a brown notebook filled with blank pages. "What's this for?"

"It's a journal for writing things down."

"What kind of things?"

"Anything you want." Frank took the journal and flipped through the empty pages. "When my first wife, April, was dying, I kept my feelings locked up inside of me. I had to be strong for her." He ran his hand over the cover. "Some days, I thought I'd go crazy. A friend gave me a journal, and I started writing my feelings down."

"Did it help?"

"Yes. Writing my feelings down helped to get them off my mind. Don't ask me why." Frank pushed back my hair. "The past six months have been rough on you, Becky. Losing your daddy, Anna, and Johnny. Plus, you've been saddled with Donald and me. Maybe writing things down will help you too."

I didn't speak until he started the pickup. "Can I give you a hug?"

"I'd love a hug, Ladybug."

We hugged a good long time and I realized Frank needed that hug as much as I did. It was our first hug, but it wouldn't be the last.

CHAPTER 4

I was right about Ethel Johnson. Momma stormed out of the house as soon as we pulled into our driveway. She tried to blame everything on me, but Frank wouldn't let her.

"Becky was with me, Helen. If you've a problem with us having lunch with Anna and Johnny, you take it up with me."

"You know I've forbidden her from seeing the Santos."

Frank pulled the tree from the back of the Ranchero. "Anna worked for this family for thirteen years. You act like it never happened."

"I don't want Becky around them."

He sighed. "How do like our Christmas tree?"

Helen stomped her foot. "Don't change the subject."

My stepfather leaned the tree against the pickup. "Hell, what do you expect from me, woman? Must I call you every time I eat lunch somewhere? If so, then we've got a problem."

Momma backed off. I think she realized she had finally pushed Frank too far. Since the day they married, she'd been trying to control him the way she had controlled my Papa. But Frank's independent nature presented quite a challenge to her.

She never said another word about our lunch with Anna and Johnny, but every time I got near her, she'd pinch me. Next to whippings, Momma liked pinching her victims. I wore long sleeve shirts so Frank wouldn't see the bruises. I worried that he would leave us if he and Momma had another fight over me. While the thought of being rid of Donald delighted me, the idea of life without Frank did not.

*****

Donald came back and school started up again. So did cousin Emelda's postal services. One Saturday in late March, I came in from the greenhouse and found Momma in the kitchen.

"Go take a bath, Becky, before you get this clean floor dirty."

"Yes, ma'am." I didn't know why she was worried. I mopped the floors.

Donald saw me heading for the bathroom and ran in there before me. He came out in a few minutes, smiling. I should've figured something was up. I'd been waiting months for him to repay me for my comment at the bus station.

I filled the tub, got some towels, and started to undress when Momma came running into the bathroom.

"Sandy called. She's having a come-as-you-are party. I've got to bathe and wash my hair." She grabbed my towels. "Iron my pink blouse and gray slacks, Becky. Hurry or Sandy will think I've spruced up."

I'd almost finished with Momma's blouse when her scream ripped through the house. It scared me so much I dropped the iron. I ran upstairs and found her sobbing.

"Look at my hair," she said. "Look at my beautiful hair."

Momma's hair was as stiff as my ironing board. She tried to comb it, but it was like trying to comb cement.

"Did you do this, Becky Leigh?"

"No, ma'am."

She picked up the shampoo bottle, turned it over, and shook it. Nothing came out. "Someone put something in the shampoo."

"Donald was in here before me."

"Come here, Donald," Momma yelled.

When he saw my mother's hair, his face turned red with guilt. He ducked into his bedroom and managed to lock the door before she could get her hands around his neck.

Momma pitched a blue ribbon hissy fit. She pounded on Donald's door, cussed him out, and threatened to cut him up and use him as catfish bait. When she sent me to get the ax, I got halfway to the garage before turning back.

It occurred to me that if Momma hacked up Donald, she'd go to prison. I'd be rid of both of them. But Donald's death would hurt Frank something terrible. My good Cooper blood finally got the best of me. I telephoned my stepfather and suggested he get home before Momma decided to go get the ax herself.

When he saw Momma's hair, Frank threw a fit that rivaled hers. She and I huddled in her room while he went after his son. Donald blamed me, but Frank found an empty bottle of glue with a Tallahassee price sticker still on it. How stupid can one boy be?

Momma, Frank, and I spent the afternoon at Monsieur Henri's Hair Salon. Momma wore her curly blond hair touching her shoulders. To get out the glue, Monsieur Henri — Henry Nash — had to cut most of it off. Every snip of the scissors brought a flood of tears.

Frank ended up buying Helen the most expensive wig in the place. In one way or another, he and I always got stuck paying for Momma and Donald's meanness.

Frank took away his son's car and all his privileges. Donald seldom came out of his room. When he did, Momma went after him like an alley cat after a mouse. Her devotion to making my step-brother's life miserable left her with little time to aggravate me and Frank.

For a little while, we had some peace.

*****

Summer came and Johnny got a job at Ferrell's Drugs, two doors down from our store, Cooper's Hardware and Garden. Momma allowed me to work at our store as long as the housework didn't suffer. I must have inherited her gene for chicanery. I thought of dozens of ways to accidentally run into Johnny.

Donald planned to spend the summer visiting his cousins in Alabama, but Frank told him he was going to learn the hardware business. My stepbrother wanted to be a cashier, but his daddy had enough sense not to let the boy near the money.

"You need to start at the bottom," Frank said and handed his son a broom.

Donald had been a star football player and homecoming king. The role of janitor didn't fit his image of himself. After three weeks on the job, he'd broken so much merchandise, he owed the store more money than it owed him.

Reluctantly, Frank conceded defeat, called his sister, and told his son to pack. The highlight of my summer came when Dumb Donald — as I called him — boarded the bus for Alabama. Momma didn't bother seeing him off. She stayed home, cut up his collection of sports magazines, and threw the pieces in the trash.

In August, Donald moved to Athens to attend the University of Georgia. Momma bought a bottle of wine, poured me a quarter cup and we secretly toasted his leaving.

Frank seemed relieved. Donald's grades were bad, but he could play football. His Picker instincts served him well on the sports battlefield. The bully got a full athletic scholarship, which proved what I'd known all my life — there's no justice in this world.

*****

The fall of '64 and the following year were the closest we ever came to being a normal family. Donald preferred to spend his holidays with his new friends from college. Momma and Frank got along pretty well, and I bent over backwards to be nice to her. Most days, she acted pleasant enough, but occasionally her Picker ways got the best of her.

Papa had always told me, "Your momma could charm the snakes out of Ireland if she wanted to." He was right. She could get anything if she set her mind on it.

A beautiful woman on the outside, Momma's curly blond hair framed flawless pale skin and sea-green eyes. Her manicured hands deftly applied her makeup and arranged every curl for maximum appeal. But it was her tilted-head grins and throaty laughs that caused men to get all sweaty and just plain silly around her.

She needed only to giggle and Mr. Pryor would wrap up his best cut of meat for her. A smile from her cranberry-colored lips always netted her a free soda water at the gas station. Even Reverend

Murray had been seen pulling at his collar after Momma cast him one of her sideways grins. She delighted in passing out lots of smiles to everyone — to everyone except me. The only things she gave me were those same green eyes and the back of her hand.

Momma's favorite activities included getting her hair fixed, flirting with any man breathing, and showing off her handsome husband. One summer afternoon, she invited her friends over to help organize a church fundraiser for foreign missionaries. The ladies moseyed outside, stood on the back porch, and gawked at Frank as he and I worked in our garden.

"You've got a fine garden, Frank," Carol Hickman said.

The other ladies agreed.

My stepfather grinned and the women giggled. He threw a fifty-pound bag of potting soil over his bare shoulder and nodded at me. "Becky deserves the credit for this garden. I'm just the hired hand."

The women tossed me a quick smile before turning their attention back to him.

"I could use a hired hand at my house," Mrs. Burke said.

The women laughed. Several added, "Me, too."

Helen descended the porch steps like the queen she thought she was, holding a glass of tea and wearing a new scarf fashionably tied on the side. She strolled over to Frank, rubbed her hand across his naked back and cooed, "Sorry girls. Frank only works in my garden." She made him kiss her full on the mouth.

Frank's face turned red; he retreated to the garage. Momma and her friends snaked back into the house to enjoy the lemon cake I'd prepared earlier. Lucky me got stuck finishing the work.

Yes, my mother enjoyed being Mrs. Frank Wooten. She even convinced me she loved my stepfather. I should've known better.

CHAPTER 5

Momma had lots of rules. Don't tell anyone what went on at home. Never touch her things. If coming home early, I should call first. Two weeks into my junior year, Principal Lott dismissed school early because of a gas leak. I forgot to call Momma.

I went home, changed my clothes, and had started back downstairs when I heard a strange moaning coming from Momma's bedroom. I pushed her door open. "Momma, are you okay?" It's hard to say who was the most shocked — momma, the naked man under her, or me.

"Close the damn door, Becky," she yelled.

I did as I was told. Standing in the hallway, I tried to wrap my brain around the scene I'd witnessed. Frank's face flashed in my mind.

Momma came out wrapped in a sheet. "What are you doing here?"

"I live here."

"Don't get smart with me." She slapped me hard.

I tumbled down three steps before I could grab the banister and stop my fall. Pulling myself up, I wiped the blood off my mouth and pointed to my bedroom. "I want to go to my room."

"Go," she said.

I tried to slip past her.

She grabbed my arm. "Didn't I tell you to call first if you were coming home early?"

"I . . . I forgot."

She smacked me again.

I raised my free hand and pulled my head in like a turtle to fend off her next two blows.

The door to her room opened and the stranger stepped out, zipping up his trousers. Tall and skinny except for a paunch, he had a receding hairline and a small scar above his right eyebrow. He tried to button his shirt, but his shirttail caught in his zipper.

"Get to your room, girl." Momma turned to the man. "Don't forget your damn jacket."

Out my window, I watched her lover cut across our yard, get in a gray sedan, and speed away. Minutes later, she strolled into my room and offered me a glass of ice tea. "I brought you a drink, Sugar."

I wasn't thirsty, but I knew better than to refuse her hospitality. Papa always said, "When Helen starts calling someone 'Sugar,' he'd better watch his wallet." Momma wanted something from me, but it wasn't money.

"Now that you're sixteen, Becky, I think it's time we had a woman-to-woman talk." She sat down on my bed. "I love Frank, but sometimes love isn't enough."

I sipped my tea.

"You'll soon discover a woman has needs just like a man. If she doesn't get those needs met regularly, she wonders if she's still attractive. She starts to doubt herself as a woman." Momma pulled her cigarettes from the pocket of her pink, silk robe, lit one, and took a long drag. "Understand what I'm saying?"

"Doesn't Frank meet your needs?"

"He works all day. When he gets home, he showers, eats, and heads outside to that damn greenhouse." She took another drag. "When he finally comes to bed, he's asleep before I can kiss him goodnight."

"Can't you wake him?"

"Shouldn't have to." She walked over to my desk. "It's his duty to stay awake and tend to my needs."

I cringed as Momma rubbed out her cigarette on the back cover of Steinbeck's *Grapes of Wrath,* a gift from Grandpa Eli. "So your affair is Frank's fault?"

"This was a one-time fling, Becky. Get that through your thick head." She stuffed the half-smoked cigarette back into the package. "Children think their parents are perfect, but we're not, Sugar. We make mistakes sometimes."

I'd figured that out the time she broke my arm. "What do you want from me?"

"Are you going to tell Frank?"

I didn't answer.

"In my own way, I was trying to help him. He said we needed more insurance on this house. That fellow I was with sells insurance. I wanted to get us a better rate."

Did Momma think me that big a fool? Or was she so crazy she believed her own lie?

"So this is our little secret, right Sugar?" she asked.

"Yes, ma'am."

Momma headed for the door. "I'm going to take a bath. Make up my bed. Remember to change the sheets."

I waited until I heard the water running before slamming my door. That woman had no shame. I decided not to sit by her in church anymore in case God decided to strike her dead. He might miss and hit me.

*****

I could barely look at Frank that night, but Momma acted like her usual self. After washing the supper dishes, I headed upstairs.

"Aren't you going to help me in the greenhouse, Ladybug?" Frank asked.

"I would, but I have lots of homework tonight."

"Don't worry about it then. Just keep them grades up."

From the verandah, I watched him walk to the greenhouse. Momma was the biggest fool in Cascade County. I'd rather her beat me half to death than hurt Frank. I felt so bad that I decided to write Claudia a letter.

When we were young, Johnny and I played a game where we pretended to be different people. My favorite pretend person was a gal I named Claudia. She had the perfect family, always knew the right thing to say and do, and never lied or told half-truths like me. Folks listened to her; they respected her. She was nobody's Pick, nor was she a Picker. Whenever I wrote in the journal Frank gave me, I'd pretend I was writing to Claudia.

Dear Claudia,

You'll be shocked to hear I caught Momma in bed with another man. I know you wouldn't approve, but I agreed not to tell Frank. It would only hurt him and he'd leave us. I'm selfish enough to want him to stay. By remaining silent, I'm helping Momma perpetrate the lie that she loves him. She is incapable of love.

Donald and his college buddies spent the summer in Europe, drinking beer and chasing women. I've dreamed of visiting Paris to see the splendid buildings and beautiful gardens. Such a trip is wasted on that dummy.

It's not right. Momma gets to have a lover and a husband, and Donald gets to go to Europe. Frank works himself to death to support them. For his trouble, he gets an adulterous wife and a son who's a rapist. I work hard, do what I'm told, and yet I'm not allowed to see Johnny. That's the way it is between Pickers and Picks. Picks give and Pickers get.

Goodbye for now.
Your best friend,
Becky Leigh Cooper
P.S. Is life ever fair?

CHAPTER 6

The first Friday in October, I came home to an empty house — or so I thought. After pouring myself a glass of milk, I sneaked a couple of lemon bars from the cookie jar. When I turned around, Momma was standing there, Papa's belt in her raised hand.

She struck her first blow. "I warned you about seeing Johnny, didn't I?"

Momma hit me so hard, I dropped my milk and cookies. Glass shattered and crumbs scattered across the floor. I spun around, slammed into the screen door and fell out onto the back porch. I tried to get up, but she kicked me in the ribs. My head hit the edge of Papa's rocker. A stabbing pain sliced through me.

"How long have you been seeing him, Becky Leigh?"

I rose to my knees. "Just a little while . . ."

"Liar!" Her fist smashed into the right side of my face.

Down I went. Blood streamed from my head. Each time I tried to get up, she knocked me down. Finally, I rolled onto my side, pulled my knees up, and folded my hands over my head in a futile attempt to protect myself.

With both hands, Momma swung Papa's belt. Then she grabbed the broom and whacked me with the handle. "I'll teach you to defy me." She continued beating me until the broom handle broke. "Clean up the kitchen and then go to your room."

My head throbbed and my ribs stung. I struggled to breathe. Yet somehow, I managed to clean up the mess. I considered calling Johnny to come get me, but he'd moved to Kirbyville to work and attend junior college. Besides, if he showed up, someone might end up dead.

I dragged myself upstairs, put on my pajamas, crawled into bed. I washed the blood off my face with tears. It was hours before God granted me the relief sleep brings. A tapping on my door woke me.

"Are you awake, Ladybug?"

I didn't answer Frank. He couldn't see me like this.

A squeak of the door hinge announced his entrance. Light from the hall split the blackness of my room. The mirror on my dresser reflected his movements as he placed a tray on my nightstand.

"Helen said you were sick. I brought you some soup."

"I'm not hungry."

"Try a little, Ladybug. Can you sit up and eat a bite?"

"No."

"How about if I helped you?" Frank pushed his hand against my back.

My body jerked. A yelp escaped my lips before I could stop it.

"What's the matter with you, Becky?"

"Nothing. Go away."

"Not until I see what's the matter." Frank turned on the light.

I pulled the sheet over my head, but he yanked it back.

"Damn, Ladybug, what happened to you?"

"Where's Momma?"

"She's gone to a baby shower." He helped me sit up. "How did you get that cut on your forehead?"

"I fell . . . down the stairs."

"Then why did your mother tell me you were sick? Let me see your back." He pulled up the back of my pajama top. "What the hell? Helen did this, didn't she?"

"Yes. Momma found out I've been seeing Johnny. Leave it alone, Frank, or you'll make matters worse."

"Make matters worse? Have you seen your face?"

I shook my head.

He retrieved my hand mirror and held it up in front of me. "Look."

A right eye swollen half-shut. A puffy cheek stained blue-black. Dried blood caked over a two-inch gash along my hairline. "It's not so bad," I said.

Frank shook his head, threw the mirror down, and walked into the hall. He returned a few minutes later. "I called Doctor Condray. He'll meet us at the clinic. That cut needs stitches." He wrapped my chenille robe around me.

My stepfather refused to listen to my protest. He picked me up, carried me to his truck, and away we went into the darkness.

*****

When we returned, Helen met us at the front door. "Where have you two been?"

Frank pushed her aside, led me to the sofa. "I took Becky to the doctor's."

"What kind of lie is she spreading now?" Momma asked.

"Becky said she fell down the stairs, but I know you beat her."

"I just gave her a well-deserved whipping. She's been seeing Johnny behind my back."

"You didn't whip her, you beat her." Frank pushed up my bangs. "She had to have stitches in her head."

She shrugged. "That's not so bad."

"It's not as bad as the concussion or the broken arm you gave her before. Is that what you mean, Helen?"

"I don't know what Becky told you, but —"

"She didn't tell me anything. Dr. Condray did."

"He had no damn right to tell you that," she shouted.

Frank rubbed his temple. "You're right. Heaven forbid I know the truth."

"If she hadn't disobeyed me, she wouldn't have got a whipping." Helen crossed her arms. "Whatever she got, she deserved."

"How can you call yourself a mother?"

"I don't appreciate your tone, Frank."

"Your mother and I need to talk, Becky. Can you make it upstairs by yourself?"

I nodded.

"I'm not discussing this matter anymore." She turned, started to walk away.

Frank grabbed her arm. "We're going to talk. About this and a whole lot more."

*****

I stood in the doorway watching Frank pack. "Are you going on a business trip?"

"Nope," he said without looking at me.

I knew that he was leaving Momma, but couldn't bring myself to say the words. Apparently, neither could he. If no one said the words out loud, perhaps they wouldn't come true. I sat down on the bed next to his suitcase.

Frank turned away, went next door to the bathroom.

While he was gone, I sifted through the half-packed case. Underwear, socks, pajamas, three dress shirts. On the doorknob, two pair of slacks and a pair of jeans hung on wooden hangers.

He returned, tucked his toothbrush, deodorant, and shaving kit into the pocket in the lid of his suitcase, and then retrieved a blue shirt from his closet.

"I bought you that shirt for Christmas."

Frank flashed a quick smile. "That's why it's my favorite."

"We went Christmas shopping in Kirbyville and had lunch with Anna and Johnny. On the way home, we chopped down a nice big Christmas tree. Remember?"

"I remember."

"You promised to teach me to ice skate, but you didn't. I guess you never will."

He stopped packing and looked at me. "Helen and I may be separating, Becky, but you and I will still be friends."

"You know that's not true. If you leave Momma, she'll never let me see you. You know how she is." I slid off the bed and walked over to the window. "I told you taking me to the doctor's would make things worse."

"Don't blame yourself. Helen and I have had problems for some time now. Truth be told, I've been thinking about leaving for over a year." Frank plopped down on the bed. "I kept hoping she'd change, but I see now that's never going to happen."

"But you're not just leaving her, you're leaving me too."

"You're the reason I've stayed this long, Ladybug. I thought that I could protect you, but apparently I can't."

"Take me with you," I begged.

"I'd like to, but that's not possible. You're Helen's child and you're underage. Besides, I don't have a home to go to."

"Where are you going to live?"

"At my office for now." He ran his hands through his hair. "I'll need to find a job before I get a more permanent place."

"A job? Aren't you going to run the store?"

"The store belongs to Helen. I doubt she'll want me to stay on as manager."

"But think of all the hard work and long hours you've put into the store, Frank. You've doubled the business in only three years." I grabbed my side.

He picked up his cufflinks, watch, and tie clasp from the dresser. "You should be resting, Becky. Doctor Condray said your ribs were bruised."

"And he said that stinky ointment he gave us needed to be applied to my back twice each day. Who's going do that? Momma won't."

Frank sighed. "I'll come by before work and after supper."

"Don't bother," I yelled and stormed out of the room.

*****

I paced my bedroom floor. When Frank left, Momma would be furious and blame me for everything. I couldn't take another beating tonight. I packed a small bag, grabbed a jacket, and sneaked down the stairs. Once outside, I climbed into the back of Frank's pickup, curled up in the left hand corner near the cab, pulled a tarp over me. My side felt like something had ruptured. But if I could make it to Kirbyville and find Johnny, I'd be okay. He'd help me escape my crazy mother. The truck door opened, slammed, and the engine started. The Ranchero peeled out of the driveway.

*****

The full moon had an iridescent white ring around it. Grandpa Eli called such a halo circled moon a liar's moon. Figuring it would be safer to travel as a boy, I slipped on my jacket, turned the collar up, and pushed my hair up under a blue knit cap. I walked down the center of the highway, following the white stripe that would lead me to Johnny and freedom.

I'd thought they'd be more traffic on a Friday night. Even so, when a car finally did come by, I hid behind a tree. But I couldn't walk the forty miles to Johnny's. By the time the third car came along, I'd gathered enough courage to accept a ride from a chicken farmer from Canton. He gave me a ride as far as the all-night diner just north of Kirbyville. I sat down at the end of the counter, away from the other customers.

The waitress sauntered over. "What'll it be?"

"Glass of milk, please."

"What happened to you, boy?" she asked.

My disguise seemed to be working. "I fell down some stairs," I said in my lowest voice.

She smiled. "Sure you did."

While waiting for my milk, I thought about Frank. When we arrived at the store, I'd waited until he went inside before leaving my hiding place. Standing in the darkness, I'd peered through the window and watched him slump into his chair. He looked weary, depressed, defeated. Momma had won. Frank and I were homeless and she had everything. Everything, but no one. Maybe in some small way, my stepfather and I had won after all. If Momma had one weakness, it was she hated being alone.

The waitress returned with the milk and handed me a piece of chocolate pie.

"I didn't order pie."

"You like chocolate pie, don't you?"

"Yes, but —"

"Don't worry, it's on the house." She leaned in close and whispered, "I've fallen down those same damn stairs a few times myself."

My benefactor looked around six feet tall, in her mid-forties, and model thin. She wore her frosted hair in a French twist and had hazel eyes that half-closed when she smiled.

She pointed to a three-inch scar on her left forearm. "Courtesy of my ex-husband. But I got even."

"How?"

"I shot the bastard." She handed me a fork. "It didn't kill him, but it put the fear of God into him. He hasn't come around in two years." She picked up a pot of coffee. "I'm Rita. If you need anything, just holler."

CHAPTER 7

I'd never thought about shooting Momma. I had on occasion wished she'd die or disappear. My fantasies involved death by accident or natural causes. Murder had never entered the picture.

I finished the last of my pie and motioned for my check.

"I'll take that." A hand reached over my shoulder and snatched the ticket from Rita.

I turned. "What are you doing here, Frank?"

"Looking for you, Becky."

"Becky?" Rita asked. "You're a girl?"

"I figured it was safer to pretend to be a boy."

"Well, you really fooled me." She pointed at Frank. "Is he the one?"

"No, he's my stepfather."

The waitress looked Frank over real good. "Are you sure he's not the one who hurt you?"

Frank's head snapped back. "Do I look like the sort of man who'd beat a child?"

"Can't go by looks." She brushed a wisp of hair behind her ear. "I'm Rita. You want coffee?"

"Sure." Frank took the stool beside me. "What do you want to eat, Ladybug."

"I had some pie."

"You need more than pie," he said as Rita poured his java. "A couple of grilled cheese sandwiches, fries with gravy, and another glass of milk, please."

She smiled. "Coming right up."

I waited until Rita left before asking Frank how he'd found me.

"Helen called and said you'd run away. She wanted to call Sheriff Tate, but I told her I'd find you and bring you home."

"I'm not going home."

"If you don't, Tate will be knocking down Johnny's door before morning." Frank took a sip of coffee. "That is where you're headed, isn't it?"

"Yes, sir."

"Didn't you realize that would be the first place they'd look for you?"

I didn't answer. When I left Sugardale, my plan had seemed so logical. I'd find Johnny, tell him what happened, and we'd leave the state tonight. By the time Momma discovered I'd run off, Johnny and I would be in Tennessee.

"It's lucky I decided to stop for coffee," Frank said. "Hitchhiking can be dangerous, especially for a girl."

"Living with Momma can be dangerous." I hid my face in my hands. "I can't take any more of her."

Frank put his arm around me. "Let's eat, Ladybug. Then we'll figure out what to do."

*****

"Rita sure seems nice," Frank said when we climbed into his truck.

I nodded.

He started the engine, then eased onto the highway, and headed south.

"Where are we going?"

Frank grinned. "Since we're this close, we might as well visit Johnny."

"You're taking me to see Johnny?"

"We can't stay long. Helen will call Sheriff Tate if I don't get you back soon."

"Thank you, Frank." Seeing Johnny might give me the courage to face going home.

*****

Ten minutes later, we entered Kirbyville. I spotted Johnny's car at the Dairy Freeze.

"You're sure that's Johnny's black Mustang?" Frank asked.

"I'm sure."

He pulled into the crowded parking lot. "You stay here. I'll get him."

"Why can't I go too?"

He pointed to my face. In my eagerness to see Johnny, I'd forgotten about the bruises. "We'd better tell Johnny I fell down the stairs."

"What is this aversion you and your mother have to telling the truth?" Frank asked.

I lowered my head. "I don't want Johnny to get mad and do something crazy."

"Your intentions are good, Ladybug, but the truth always comes out. Lying just makes it worse." Frank brushed back my hair. "Besides, Johnny wouldn't believe that story anymore than I did. I'll be right back."

It seemed like a dang eternity before my stepfather returned. "Where's Johnny?" I asked.

Frank slammed his door. "He's not here."

"But there's his car."

"Maybe he let someone borrow it. I don't know."

"I'll go find him." I opened my door and started to get out, but Frank grabbed my arm.

"No, we have to go now, Becky. Close the door."

"But I haven't seen Johnny yet." Laughter suddenly filled the air. A group of young people exited the Dairy Freeze.

"There's Johnny." I started to get out, but Frank stopped me.

"Becky —"

"Johnny's here, Frank. He's right there . . ."

Johnny leaned against his car. A pretty brunette sauntered up next to him, wrapped her arms around his neck and whispered something in his ear. They laughed, and then kissed.

I looked at my stepfather. "I guess Momma and I aren't the only liars in the family."

"I'm so sorry, Ladybug. I wanted to leave before you saw them."

"Like you said, the truth always comes out." I stepped out of the truck.

"Come back, Becky. You don't want to do this."

Ignoring my stepfather's warning, I walked toward the crowd. Pain, humiliation, and pure rage surged through me. My whole body shook. I stopped about a dozen feet from Johnny and his friend.

At first, no one noticed me. Then one of the girls asked, "Who's that?"

"I don't know," a tall blond replied. "What happened to her face?"

"Hello, Johnny," I said, hating the tremor in my voice.

Johnny stopped kissing the girl and looked up. "Rebecca!" He straightened up so fast, he knocked the brunette into the arms of the guy behind her.

"Surprised to see me?" My eyes shifted from him to his girlfriend, then back to him.

He pointed at her. "This isn't what you think. She doesn't mean anything to me."

The girl slapped Johnny's arm. "What do you mean by that crack? Who's the chick with the messed up face?"

"She's my fiancée."

"Fiancée? Since when?"

Johnny and the girl started arguing. I turned and walked away. I was almost to the Ranchero when he caught up with me.

"Let me explain, Honey," he begged. "I didn't know you were coming. If I'd known —"

"Then you wouldn't have got caught cheating. Right?"

"I'm not cheating. Not really. She's in one of my classes."

"I see. You couldn't come to Sugardale this weekend because your homework assignment was to kiss your classmates."

He grasped my arm. "I stayed to work overtime to make extra money for us."

Johnny had given me a ring, a dainty silver flower with a diamond chip in the center. I took it off and put it in his hand.

"Don't do this, Twig."

I got into the truck, slammed the door. "Can we go now, Frank?"

"Wait, Mr. Wooten." Johnny motioned for me to roll down my window.

I hesitated, then rolled it down halfway. Part of me wanted to run away, but a bigger part of me longed for Johnny to say the words that would build a bridge across the dark chasm he'd created between us. The truth or a good lie would do as long as it paved my way back to the boy I'd loved all my life.

"What happened to you?" Johnny asked.

"Momma found out we've been seeing each other." I pulled back my bangs to show my stitches. "I ran away from home tonight. I thought we could elope. Reckon you're too busy."

He reached inside, touched my shoulder. "That kiss didn't mean anything to me. I love you."

"It meant something to me." I pushed his hand away. "Momma claims men can't be trusted. Apparently, she's right."

Johnny grabbed the window with both hands. "You know Helen's crazy."

I started rolling up the window. "I don't ever want to see you again, Johnny Santo." My words were a lie, but the ounce of pride I had left demanded they be spoken. "Let's go, Frank."

"Give me another chance," Johnny yelled as we pulled out of the parking lot.

Using the side mirror, I watched Johnny grow smaller and smaller until the black night swallowed him.

CHAPTER 8

A light rain began to fall as Frank and I headed home. He told me it was okay to cry, but I was too numb. The picture show in my mind kept repeating the same two scenes in perfect tempo with the windshield wipers — Momma beating me with the broom, and Johnny kissing the brunette. Frank stopped at our store. He told me to wait in the pickup, but for once, I didn't do as I was told.

The whistle of the train drew me to the tracks. At first, I could only hear the clickity-clack of its wheels. Then it rounded a distant curve and I saw the light — big, bright, and warm. The light cleaned away the darkness before it. If I joined my body with the light, maybe I could be clean and bright too. The movie running in my mind would be turned off forever. I walked up the embankment and climbed onto the tracks.

"Get off the damn tracks, Becky," Frank screamed. He ran toward me, but slipped and fell on the wet grass. "Please get off."

My stepfather had been trying to save me all night. First, from Momma's anger and later, from Johnny's betrayal. It seemed like Frank spent half his time trying to save me. Trying and failing. Still, he wouldn't give up. Now, he wanted to save me from the light, but the light is too fast.

"Ladybug, don't do this." He struggled to get on his feet. "Don't do this to me, Becky!"

The fear in his voice penetrated my frozen brain. Frank would witness my body's joining with the white light and be haunted by that picture every day of his life. He'd feel responsible. Wouldn't Momma like that — me dead, and Frank tortured by guilt. How could I justify hurting my one true friend? Stepping off the tracks, I half-walked, half-slid down the soggy embankment.

Frank pulled me into his arms. "Don't ever do that again, Ladybug. I love you. I couldn't bear losing you like that."

I saw a movie once about an ancient Greek named Achilles. He was invincible except for his heel. Everyone who fought him died. One day, a really smart man just pulled a plug out of Achilles' heel. Everything inside of the Greek hero drained out onto the sand.

When Frank said he loved me, he pulled the plug out of the internal wall I'd built to hold back all my misery. I started sobbing right there by the railroad tracks. He sat down in the wet grass, pulled me into his lap, and rocked me. Only Frank knew how much rocking soothed my soul. Oblivious to the rain, we rocked back and forth in time with the clickity-clack of the train's wheels as they rolled past. That train traveled miles down the line before I ran out of tears.

"Why would Johnny do this to me?" I asked between sobs. "We've loved each other forever. Planned on getting married."

"Men do crazy things sometimes, Becky. We do things without thinking them through. If it seems right at the moment, we just jump in."

"Is that what happened between you and Momma?"

Frank nodded. "I should have got to know Helen better."

"But then you wouldn't have married her."

"Probably not."

"Then we wouldn't be friends."

He hugged me. "That's why I am glad I married her."

Frank was lying for my sake. He would've been fine without me. But what would've happened to me without him?

"Do you believe that Momma is all bad?" I asked.

"I don't think anyone is all bad."

I wiped my cheek. "But she is hard to love, isn't she?"

"Yes, Ladybug, at times she's very hard to love." Frank kissed the top of my head. "It's late. We'd better get home."

I buried my face in his chest. "I can't take another whipping tonight."

"I'm moving back." He lifted my face, looked me in the eyes. "I won't let Helen lay a finger on you. She'll have to kill me first."

A shiver ran through me. As far as I knew, Momma had never killed anyone, but I figured that if push came to shove, she could.

*****

It'd quit raining by the time we got home. I sat in the truck listening to the shouting coming from inside the house. I couldn't make out the words, but knew Momma and Frank were arguing about me. My hand kept reaching for the door handle. Every instinct in my body urged me to skedaddle, but I'd promised Frank I'd wait in the pickup until he returned.

The shouting stopped suddenly. I hung my head outside the window trying to hear any noise coming from the house. Total quiet. The only thing more frightening than two adults fighting is the silence that follows. Your imagination goes wild. In my mind, I saw Momma stabbing Frank with a butcher knife.

Frank was usually calm in a crisis. But if this night could drive me to contemplate suicide, maybe it had driven him over the edge too. Momma had a Picker's knack for pushing people beyond their limit. What if she'd tried to work her Picker ways on Frank tonight? Perhaps she'd stopped screaming because she was dead. In a fit of justified rage, Frank might have strangled her.

It seemed plausible to me that one or both of them could be lying in a puddle of blood, gasping for their last breath. Should I go check on them? I could call an ambulance. I needed to go in, but my legs wouldn't move. The deeper the silence grew, the heavier my limbs became. All I could do was hold my exploding head, rock, and try to muster my courage.

*****

I stood on our front porch and studied the four-inch strip of painted wood that separated the outside world from the insanity that resided inside. I'd never paid much attention to the threshold before except to sweep it or step over it. But tonight, its significance was indisputable. It was the boundary between comfort and pain, safety and danger, perhaps even between life and death.

The outside light was off. Even so, the darkness of the porch provided more safety than the lights inside could ever offer. For never in my sixteen years had Momma struck me, kicked me, or hurt me while I stood on the front porch or in the front yard. The possibility that someone might witness such an attack made her nervous. Right now, one of the neighbors could be peering out their window watching me. If still alive, Momma would know that too. As long as I remained on the front porch, I was safe.

But what about dear Frank? Was he hurt? Bleeding? Did he need my help to bind up any wounds Momma might have inflicted? If he'd killed Helen, he'd need my help to hide her body. Where would we bury her? The north side of the greenhouse would be best.

"Please, God," I whispered, "don't let Frank be dead." I should've said the same prayer for Momma's sake, but I couldn't. I didn't desire my mother's death, but if forced to choose between her survival and Frank's, I would pick Frank. That realization heaped a large measure of sadness upon my soul.

The front door swung open. Momma stood there, her blond hair piled high in a topknot. A fresh coat of crimson polish decorated her nails and a matching tint of war paint graced her lips. If she'd been dressed in her new teal suit instead of her floral nightgown and fuzzy slippers, I'd have sworn she was on her way to church. No blood stained her garments. But if Frank was alive, where was he? Why hadn't he returned to the pickup?

"Are you going to stand out there all night, Becky Leigh?" She stepped back to give me room to enter the house. The light from the hallway spilled out onto the front porch.

I didn't move. After several attempts, I managed to ask, "Where's Frank?"

"Right here, Ladybug."

I turned around to find my stepfather coming around the side of the house. He must have come out the back door. I blinked back tears of relief. "Are you all right?"

"I'm fine," he said. "I asked you to wait in the truck."

"It got really quiet. I was afraid something might have happened."

"We haven't killed each other . . . yet," Momma said.

"Your mother is kidding. You always did have a flare for the dramatic, Helen."

She lit her cigarette. "Since everyone seems bent on running off tonight, maybe I should dash off to Hollywood. You two would sure like that, wouldn't you?"

"There's no call for sarcasm," Frank said. "Remember our agreement."

"What agreement?" I asked.

"I'll let your stepfather answer that. After all, he's the man in charge." She blew little smoke rings at Frank. "Isn't that right, Sugar?" She turned and walked into the living room.

"What's Momma talking about, Frank?"

"Go inside, Becky. It's cold and we're both soaked."

I took a deep breath and stepped over the threshold. Frank closed the door behind us. Here I was again, on the dangerous side of that door.

"Better get those wet clothes off, Ladybug. Take a hot shower and get ready for bed."

"Maybe you should help her, Frank," Helen called from the living room. "What about it, Becky? Do you need Daddy Frank's help in getting those wet clothes off?"

The side of my face that wasn't black and blue redden as the heat of humiliation flashed over me.

Frank's face darkened; his jaw tightened. "Pay her no mind. She's been drinking."

I nodded. Momma often said disgraceful things to me, but this tirade had been aimed at my stepfather because he dared to help me. It shamed me to know I carried her blood. If I could, I'd find a leech and train it to suck all her Picker blood from my veins, leaving only my papa's good Cooper blood.

*****

The clock read half-past two by the time I crawled into bed. My head throbbed and my body ached, but the pain in my heart kept the sandman at bay. Every time I closed my eyes, a picture of Johnny kissing the brunette flashed across my mind. As I grabbed a tissue, I saw the doorknob turn. "Frank?"

"Nope, it's me," Helen said, closing the door behind her.

My neck muscles tensed. "Where's Frank?"

"Taking a shower. Don't worry. I'm sure he'll check on his *Ladybug* before coming to bed. Did he tell you about our arrangement?"

I pulled the quilt up under my chin. "No."

"He will. Just ask him." She snickered as she wiped off one of my tears. "Are you crying because you're happy to be home, Sugar?"

I knew better than to answer that question.

Helen stood. "There's no use crying unless it can do you some good. A few, well-timed tears can be a useful tool. Otherwise, crying is a waste of time and energy." She walked to the door. "By the way, stay off the damn railroad tracks. If I wanted you dead, I'd kill you myself." She slammed the door behind her.

She hadn't come to check on the injuries she'd inflicted. Her sole purpose had been to inform me that Frank would be paying a high price for helping me. She knew such knowledge would hurt more than any pinch, slap, or kick ever could.

It seemed like forever before a sliver of light invaded my room. "Come on in, Frank."

I turned on my bedside lamp. "I've been waiting for you."

"You should be asleep, Ladybug."

"What's this arrangement you made with Momma?"

"Don't worry about it. You get to sleep."

"I want to know what it is."

"We'll talk tomorrow, Becky. It's late and I'm tired."

I pointed to the jar of medicine. "Too tired to put that stinky salve on my back?"

"Certainly not." Frank retrieved the jar from the dresser. "Do you want to sit up or be on your stomach?"

I rolled over on my stomach. With great care, Frank pulled up the back of my pajama top. I flinched when he first applied the creosote-smelling balm.

"I'm trying to go easy."

"That stuff is cold. While you're doctoring my back, tell me about this arrangement you made with Momma. Okay?"

"There's not much to it. I told her I'd come home, but wouldn't abide her being mean to you." He reached for more salve. "She agreed to stop hitting you."

"Why did you tell her about me standing on the railroad tracks?"

"You weren't standing on the tracks, Becky. You were waiting for the train to run over you. Helen needed to realize how far she's pushed you."

He pulled down my top and I sat up. "There's a towel on the vanity bench. Are you mad at me, Frank?"

"No, go to sleep." He wiped his hands on the towel. "I'll put this in the laundry."

"Are you sure you're not mad?"

He came over, pushed back my bangs, and inspected the stitches. "I could never be mad at you. I just want you to be happy . . . and safe."

I gave him a hug. "I see what Momma's up to. After all these years, she's finally figured out how to make you her Pick."

"What are you talking about? What's a Pick?"

I gave him an abbreviated history lesson on Picks and Pickers. "Momma's going to try to play us against each other."

"That's ridiculous, Becky."

"No, it's not. You've got to leave, Frank, before it's too late."

He stood. "The only place I'm going is to bed."

I reached for his hand. "Trust me. You need to go now."

Frank ran his hand over his face. "Earlier tonight you were begging me to stay."

"It's different now. Before, Momma was angry with just me. Now, she figures you've betrayed her too. I know her. You have to leave before she finds a way to punish you also."

"It won't be like that. I agreed to give our marriage another chance. Helen says I owe her that much." He let out a deep sigh. "She's probably right."

"You see how she has gone and messed up your thinking, Frank? Trust me, you don't owe her anything." I considered telling him about the insurance salesman, but decided not to. If I did, I might end up having to call an ambulance after all.

Frank kissed the top of my head and turned off the lamp. "Get some rest, Ladybug, and don't worry about me."

As soon as he left, I turned on the lamp. Despite my exhaustion, I had to figure a way to save my stepfather. Once Momma got her hooks into a Pick, she never let go. If Frank wouldn't leave, then I'd have to. But where would I go? Not to Johnny's, that's for sure.

Tears started rolling again. Reaching under my pillow, I pulled my fuzzy stuffed cat from its hiding place. Johnny had bought it for me because it was the spitting image of a kitten Grandpa Eli had once given me. I'd named my toy kitty Pinecone in honor of his real life twin.

"What am I going to do, Pinecone?" I asked as I slipped my hand around the back of the kitty's neck.

With a little help from me, Pinecone shook his head.

I told my furry friend about Johnny and the brunette. "I can't believe he could betray us like that, can you?"

Again, the cat shook his head.

I pulled my kitty to my heart and we cried. After a while, I wiped my tears off my cotton-stuffed friend. "We can't worry about that traitor anymore. We have to think of a way to get Frank out of Momma's vindictive clutches."

Pinecone agreed.

The memory of the train and how warm and inviting its light had looked came back to me. But the train only came through Sugardale twice a week.

I recalled a story from the *Sugardale Gazette* about a young woman who'd killed herself by slicing her wrists. Several fat blue veins lay just under my skin. I'm very skilled with a butcher knife, having cut up dozens of chickens in my life.

"It'll be rather messy, won't it?"

Pinecone nodded.

"Momma will probably make Frank clean it up, won't she?"

My kitty agreed.

I decided to end my life in the upstairs bathtub. It was a deep, old claw-footed thing. I didn't want the blood to overflow the tub and make a big mess for Frank. I'd have to get a butcher knife from the kitchen. Might need to sharpen it too. After all, I didn't want to saw my veins open. No use in adding extra pain.

There were a few letters I wanted to write before my demise. One to Frank to tell him not to blame himself for my suicide. Another one to Johnny so he'd know how he broke my heart. If he felt any guilt, it would serve him right. And dear Momma deserved a letter. I wanted her to know I'd beaten her this time. She wouldn't have Frank or me to pick on anymore for I was certain he'd leave her after my death. My last letter would be to Claudia. She'd be disappointed in me, but knowing the pain I've endured, maybe she'd forgive me.

It occurred to me that killing oneself involved a lot of work. "Pinecone," I said, scratching his fuzzy head, "I'm too tired to kill myself tonight. We'll have to wait until tomorrow. Okay?"

Pinecone nodded. He was always such an agreeable kitty.

CHAPTER 9

The intruder stood over me; his hand covered my mouth. "Be quiet," he ordered.

I nodded. My uninvited guest removed his hand and switched on the milk-glass lamp sitting on my nightstand. I covered my eyes to shield them from the unexpected light. Peeking through separated fingers, I asked, "What do you want, Johnny Santo?"

He didn't answer. Instead, he stuffed my robe against the bottom of the bedroom door to keep the light from escaping into the hall. Then Johnny tiptoed over, sat down on my bed.

"Why the hell are you here?" I asked.

"It's not like you to cuss, Rebecca." He reached for my hand. "I've been coming over here every night for the past five nights. Where've you been?"

"Not that's any of your business, but the doctor said I should stay home from school for awhile." I jerked my hand away. "Momma was worried that people would ask questions about my bruises, so Frank took us to Atlanta for a few days. He thought we could all use a little vacation."

Johnny frowned. "A vacation with Helen? Sounds more like a nightmare."

"Oh, it was tolerable enough. Momma went shopping most everyday with her old friend, Eva Whitcomb."

Johnny edged closer. "Eva Whitcomb? Isn't she the rich lady who's had a bunch of husbands?"

I nodded and picked at a loose thread in Grandma Cooper's old quilt. "Why are you here? I told you goodbye at the Dairy Freeze."

"I want to explain about Lynn."

"There's nothing to explain." I could've gone all my life without knowing the name of that brown-hair hussy.

"Don't you want to know why I kissed her?"

"Nope." Chalk up another bald-face lie for me. I longed to know everything, but my wounded pride prevented me from asking.

Pride is a tricky emotion to navigate. If you don't show any, people ask, "Where's your pride, girl?" And if you do have pride, those same folks remind you, "Pride goes before a fall." No matter which side of pride you come down on, you can find yourself in a lot of trouble. It's like Momma in a way. No matter which way you jump, she's gonna get you.

"Let me explain," he pleaded.

I crossed my arms. "Did you ever notice how the name Lynn rhymes with the word sin? Lynn . . . sin. Sin . . . Lynn."

Johnny scratched his head. "She's a nice girl, Rebecca."

"Then sneak into her house and bother her instead of me." I fell back and pulled the quilt over my head. Johnny tugged at the cover, but I held tight. It's amazing how strong a girl can be when she's crazy-mad.

"You really want me to leave?" he asked.

"Figured that out on your own, did you?"

"Don't be sarcastic. You sound like your mother."

I yanked the covers back and sat up. "I don't sound like Momma. How can you say such a hurtful thing?"

"I'm sorry." He brushed his hand across the fading bruises on my face. "She got you good this time, didn't she?"

"That's nothing. You should've seen my back."

Johnny's right hand balled into a fist. He slammed it against the palm of his left hand.

"I'm gonna kill the goddamn bitch."

"You shouldn't take the Lord's name in vain, Johnny."

He grabbed my hands. "I thought you didn't believe in God."

"I might be wrong. I was wrong to believe you loved me."

"No you weren't. I do love you. It's just ..."

"Just that she's prettier than me?"

"She's not prettier than you, but she's available and you're not."

I yanked my hands away. "What do you mean?"

"Thanks to your mother, we seldom get much time together. It's not enough. I need more."

"Me, too, but she's always watching me. It'll be worse now." I hugged my pillow.

"What are we going to do, Johnny?"

"Does this mean you forgive me?"

"Have you been cheating on me all along?"

"I swear I haven't. That was the only time." He slicked back his dark hair. "Two guys from work came over. We had a few beers and then went to get something to eat. The Dairy Freeze was crowded so Lynn and her friends asked if they could share our table."

"And you just had to let them. Right?"

"I wanted to be polite."

"Next you'll be telling me you weren't really kissing her, you were just inspecting her tonsils for biology class."

He rubbed his thumbs across the back of my hands. "I'm sorry. I love you. Forgive me."

Johnny was the only boyfriend I'd ever had and I'd never known him to lie to me. Still, I couldn't help but wonder if he was telling the truth. The first time I visit him just happens to be the first time he's kissing another girl? Humph!

I remembered Momma's yarn about how she bedded the insurance man to get a better rate for Frank. Johnny's tale wasn't much better, but there was one big difference. I wanted to believe his story.

"Do you believe me?" he asked.

Grandpa Eli had often told me that the real truth was seldom what we thought it was. "Most of the time," he said, "people choose to believe a story because it fills their need. At other times, they're afraid not to believe it. Then right or wrong, that belief becomes their truth."

I'd never understood grandpa's words until tonight. Although my brain didn't accept Johnny's story, my heart begged me to believe it. I chose to listen to my heart.

"Yes, Johnny, I believe you. What are we going to do now?"

"You still want to elope?"

I threw my arms around his neck. "More than ever, but how —"

"Leave everything to me," he whispered. "Just be ready next Sunday night."

*****

It started raining as we returned home from Sunday night prayer meeting.

"Damn," Helen said, pushing back a limp curl. "This rain is making my hair fall."

"They predicted we'd get some rain from the hurricane that battered South Carolina this afternoon." Frank closed the front door. "Looks like they were right."

"My next beauty shop appointment isn't until Wednesday. What am I going to do with this hair until then?"

"That's the problem with hurricanes, Helen. They're so damn inconvenient."

"Oh that's cute, Frank, real cute."

Frank headed for the stairs. "I'm going to bed."

"Don't you want to wait for me?" Helen asked.

"If it rains all night, the new greenhouse might flood. I need to get up early to keep an eye on things." He looked over the rail at her. "I'm tired. I'm going to sleep."

"Seems you're tired a lot these days. Maybe you should see a doctor," Helen yelled. "What the hell you looking at, Becky?"

"Nothing, Momma, I was just thinking."

"Imagine that. Our little Becky is thinking. Should I break out the champagne?"

My jaw tightened, but I held my tongue. I couldn't afford a fight with Momma tonight.

"I was thinking maybe Henry Nash could move your appointment to Monday."

"It's Monsieur Henri. Can't you remember anything?" She stood in front of the large gilded mirror that hung over her Queen Anne credenza. "Mondays are busy, but he might fit me in." She smiled at herself and twirled a golden curl around her finger. "I am a good customer, aren't I?"

"Yes, ma'am." My momma seemed to be developing a keen interest in Henry Nash. As far as I could tell, Mr. Nash didn't return such interest — at least not yet. Henry was likable enough, but he wasn't half as handsome as Frank.

Except for Johnny, my stepfather was the best-looking man in Sugardale. His blue eyes, dark hair, and the small dimple in his chin caught the eye of many of our female customers. To me, Frank had the rugged good looks of a lumberjack, the soul of a poet, and more patience than that fellow in the Bible had. I didn't know any lumberjacks or poets personally, but I'd heard tales and read books about them. Momma was a fool to treat Frank so bad.

She walked over to the phone table, picked up the receiver and started dialing.

"Isn't it sort of late to be calling someone?" I asked.

Momma slammed down the receiver. "Are you spying on me?"

I shook my head.

"You'd better not be. I'll kick your lazy ass up between your shoulders if you ever do. Now go to bed." She picked up the receiver and started dialing again.

I was halfway up the stairs when it occurred to me tonight would be the last time I'd ever see my mother. For some strange reason, I went back downstairs. She was talking on the phone.

"Momma?"

She cupped her hand around the mouthpiece and whispered, "Hold on a minute, Henry." Momma looked at me. "Didn't I tell you to get in bed?"

"I just wanted to tell you . . . goodnight."

"Goodnight. Now go to bed." She turned back to the phone. "You still there, Henry?"

I had no regrets about leaving her. None at all. I started up the stairs.

"Becky Leigh," she called.

I swiveled around. Momma stood in the living room doorway, the phone in her right hand, the receiver pressed against her shoulder. "Ma'am?"

She tilted her head, gave me a smile. "Sweet dreams, Sugar. Don't let the bedbugs bite."

"Sweet dreams to you too, Momma." Why did she have to pick tonight to be nice to me? There should be a law. If you're mean to your kids, you've got to be mean to them all the time. This business of being hateful one minute, nice the next, and then hateful again was just too dang confusing. But it didn't matter. I was leaving, and I sure wasn't going to miss her.

CHAPTER 10

Our plan had seemed so simple. We'd meet behind the greenhouse at midnight Sunday and walk to Bragg Road where Johnny's car would be parked. We'd drive the fifty-eight miles to the Tennessee line. Once across, we'd get a motel room and sleep a few hours. First thing in the morning, we'd get a marriage license and get hitched. Tennessee didn't require a waiting period or blood test, and Johnny had bought a fake driver's license for me that said I was eighteen. After the wedding, we'd drive to Texas. Johnny's relatives in San Antonio would put us up until we could get jobs and an apartment.

I'd brought sandwiches and cookies, had pinned my hair up under a ball cap, and worn one of Frank's old jackets. Anyone passing us would think we were two guys. Neither one of us had planned for a driving rain courtesy of a hurricane named Ida. A few miles across the Tennessee line, we came upon a fishing camp and rented a cabin to wait out the storm.

Johnny sat our suitcases by the foot of the bed. "I'm sorry, Honey. I'd planned on something nicer for our first night together."

"It's not so bad," I said, surveying our tiny cabin.

Johnny frowned. "The cabins near the river are larger, but the owner said they might flood if this rain keeps up."

"This is fine." I inspected the contents of the eight-foot counter that served as the cabin's kitchen. "There are a couple of pots and a hot plate. Do they sell groceries here?"

"I saw some canned goods and bread." Johnny opened the door of the old round-top icebox, pulled a metal ice tray from the freezer. "Do you want some groceries?"

"You'll have to get out in the rain again."

"Might as well go while I'm wet. I'll get some soup to go along with the sandwiches you brought."

"Okay. I'll unpack while you're gone."

"I won't be long." He kissed me. "Don't run off."

I laughed. "You mean don't float away, right?" I loved the way Johnny teased me. It was a subtle, witty kind of rub that reminded me of Grandpa Eli's humor.

As soon as Johnny left, I unpacked and began sprucing up our cabin. I washed the dust off a couple of white ironstone plates and bowls and set the yellow-topped chrome table for two. The two dining chairs were covered in a matching lemon-colored vinyl. The vinyl on one chair was torn on the edge. Gray cotton hung down on the rusting metal leg. I pushed the stuffing back in as best I could and mentally designated it as my chair. I found an etched-glass kerosene lamp and a box of matches. I sat it in the middle of the table to serve as our centerpiece.

A gosh-awful orange and blue flowered throw covered the bed. I snatched it off, folded it, and laid it on the floor behind a worn olive-green tweed chair. A cocoa-brown blanket covered white cotton sheets and two feather pillows.

I folded the blanket back halfway, lit the lamp, and turned off the overhead light. The scene I'd set wasn't too bad. The gentle radiance of the lamp cast a muted glimmer over the entire room. A picture of the Last Supper hung over the bed. The wavering flame reflected off the protective glass as if to bless our haven from the storm.

Johnny returned and was as pleased with my decorating as I was. "This is great. It's so romantic." He pulled me into his arms and kissed me hard.

I pushed him away. "You're getting me wet."

"Sorry."

"You'd better take a hot shower, Johnny."

"Okay. I'll shower while you heat the soup." He blew me a kiss. "You want to take a shower with me, Twig?"

"What?"

"Do you want to take a shower with me? We can wash each other's back."

I held up a can of tomato soup.

He nodded and closed the bathroom door.

Looking around the room, I could see how the dim light and turned-down bed might give Johnny the wrong impression. It hadn't been my intention to create a romantic atmosphere. I'd simply tried to make the cabin more presentable by hiding the ugly.

*****

"Blow out the lamp, Rebecca, and come to bed."

I pulled back the curtain. "Get some sleep. I'll keep watch in case the rain stops."

"Even if it stopped raining right now, it'd be awhile before the roads were passable."

"I still think I should keep watch."

Johnny patted the bed. "Oh come on, Twig. I'm cold. I need you to warm me up."

"Put on your pajamas."

"I sleep in my shorts. I don't own any pajamas."

"I'll buy you some for a wedding present."

Johnny got out of bed and sat down across the table from me. "Are you afraid to come to bed with me, Rebecca?"

"I'm not afraid." I pushed the curtain back again. "This rain isn't letting up. What if it doesn't stop soon?"

"Quit worrying so much about your mother. If we can't get out, Helen can't get in."

"She'll send Sheriff Tate after us."

"He has no jurisdiction here. We're safe, Rebecca. Come to bed with me."

I hugged my knees. "You seem to forget, we're not married yet."

Johnny got up, retrieved something from his suitcase, and climbed back into bed. "Come here. I want to show you something."

"Show me what?"

"I've got a present for you. Come see."

I sat on the bed opposite him. He handed me a blue velvet box. "What's this?"

"Open it."

I lifted the lid. Inside was a ring, a delicate, filigree silver band. "It's beautiful."

"It belonged to my Grandmother Santo. My grandfather had it made for her for their twenty-fifth anniversary. She left it to my father, who left it to me." Johnny slid it on my finger. "I want you to have it as your wedding ring. How does it fit?"

"It's a little big," I said, twirling the ring slowly around my knuckle.

"Don't worry. When we get to Texas, my aunts will fatten you up."

I handed the ring back to him. "You'd better keep this until the wedding."

Johnny got out of bed, opened the night-stand drawer, then banged it shut.

"What are you looking for?" I asked as he inspected the end table on my side. He was naked except for his underwear and I struggled to keep my focus off the bulge in the front of his briefs.

Grandpa Eli and I once caught Tommy Nipp and his two brothers skinny-dipping at Jayhawker Pond. When the boys saw us, they climbed out on the opposite bank. Grandpa and I cackled until our sides ached as their pale rear-ends ran for the woods. Tommy turned around once, but his hands were cupped over his tallywacker so I didn't get to see it. Grandpa assured me I wasn't missing much since Tommy was only nine at the time.

Then there was that thing with Donald. He'd shoved me face down into his bedspread. All my efforts had gone into gasping for air while the knife-like pain ripped through me.

Johnny picked up a book from the top of the old knotty pine chest-of-drawers. "Here it is. I knew they'd have one."

"Have one what?"

"A Bible. I knew they would have a Bible. Never rented a motel room that didn't."

"When did you rent a motel room?"

"When I went to Texas last year with my cousin."

I crossed my arms. "Your cousin? Is this cousin named Lynn by any chance?"

"You know Segundo and I took my mother to Texas last year." Johnny climbed back into bed. "If I wanted to be with Lynn, I'd be with Lynn. But

I'm here, in this run-down fish camp, and I'm ready to marry you."

"You make it sound like you're doing me a favor." I started to get off the bed, but he pulled me back.

"What are you afraid of, Rebecca?"

"Nothing. Let me go." I struggled to get away, but Johnny held tight.

"Tell me what you're afraid of," Johnny whispered.

I grew still.

He turned me around to face him. "Please tell me, Twig. You can tell me anything."

I threw my arms around his neck. "I'm afraid we'll get caught."

"No, we won't."

"I'm afraid your aunts won't like me."

"Yes, they will. They know Mother thinks of you like her own daughter."

"I'm afraid you'll . . . you'll stop loving me once we're married."

"Why would I do that?" he asked.

"Momma and Papa stopped loving each other after they married. The same thing happened between Momma and Frank."

Johnny pushed my bangs out of my eyes. "Don't you see a pattern there?"

"Yes. Couples stop loving each other after they're married."

"Only when one member of that couple is Helen. Then the question isn't why did Frank and your daddy stop loving her, it's how did they fall for her in the first place?" He ran his hand down his arm. "I don't see how God Almighty could love your mother, Rebecca."

Johnny made a good point about Papa and Frank. But I didn't think the Lord had a choice. The Reverend Murray often cited a Bible verse that said the Lord loved the vilest of sinners. I figured even Momma was covered under that scripture.

"Hold this," Johnny said, handing me the Bible. He placed his right hand on the Good Book and raised his left hand. "I, John David Santo, take Rebecca Leigh Cooper to be my wedded wife."

"What are you doing, Johnny?"

"I'm saying my wedding vows. To have and to hold, from this day forward —"

"We can't marry ourselves. Can we?"

"I'm trying to be romantic, Twig."

I laid the Bible down. "Romantic or not, this isn't a legal marriage."

"Yes, it is." He handed the Bible back to me. "When two people promise themselves to each other, it's called a common-law marriage. And it's legal."

"Then how come I've never heard of it?" I passed the Lord's Word back to Johnny.

"People don't do it much anymore, but it's still legal," he said. "My civics teacher said so. It started back in the old days when there weren't enough preachers or judges to go around. Folks couldn't wait forever to get married, could they?"

"Reckon not." Johnny's explanation made perfect sense.

"We truly love each other and want to get married, don't we?"

"That's what I want more than anything."

He took hold of my hands. "We can have a common-law marriage tonight and a regular ceremony tomorrow. Okay?"

"Let me think a minute." I'd once heard Momma and Mrs. Weeks talking about a skinny woman who lived with Mr. Eason in a trailer house behind his machine shop. Momma said it was rumored that the lady couldn't have children. Mrs. Weeks commented it was probably a good thing since the woman was Mr. Eason's common-law wife. I wasn't sure what that meant at the time.

"Do you promise we'll get a license and get married by a preacher soon, Johnny?"

"The first town we come to. I promise."

I picked up the Bible. "Okay. Let's get married."

*****

"What's wrong now, Twig?" Johnny asked an hour later.

I scooted farther back in the vinyl chair. "Nothing."

Johnny got out of bed and came over to the table. "Then why are you sitting here instead of lying in bed with your husband?"

I shrugged. "I'm not sleepy."

"I'm not sleepy, either." He started kissing my neck and rubbing my back.

"That tickles."

"Come to bed with me, Twig. Come warm me up."

"You're hot enough." In all of our secret meetings, Johnny and I had never gone further than rubbing each other's back.

"It's your job to cool me off."

"Is that what this common-law marriage thing was really all about? Just a trick to get me into bed with you?"

Johnny sat down on the end of the bed. "I thought you knew me better."

The look on my new husband's face was similar to that of a scolded puppy. "I'm sorry."

I moved to his side. "I'm just nervous . . . about . . . about doing it."

He kissed me. "It won't be like it was with Donald."

I jumped up, ran to the window, and tried to blink back the tears welling up in my eyes. "I don't want to talk about Donald."

Johnny pulled me back onto the bed. "We need to discuss what happened or it'll always be hanging there between us."

I began to cry.

He pulled me into his lap. Whispering words of comfort, Johnny rocked me until I was all cried out. "One day, I'll kill that bastard for what he did to you. That's a promise."

I felt a chill, but didn't try to talk him out of his ominous pledge. We were on our way to Texas. With any luck, we'd never see Donald again.

As Johnny wiped away my tears, I asked, "It'll be good between us, right?"

He nodded. "We don't have to do anything until you want to."

"What I want is to be a good wife to you. I just don't know how to . . ."

"I can teach you."

"Have you had lots of practice?"

The corners of his mouth twitched. "Just a little."

"How much is a little?" I asked without a smile.

"A couple of times."

I knew Johnny had been with other girls. My gut told me it was more than twice.

Neither one of us were virgins. The fact that he'd willingly given up his innocence while mine was stolen from me made little difference now.

"Do you love me? Really, truly love me?"

He kissed the top of my head. "I love you, Twig. Always have. Always will."

I didn't need to hear anything more. "Blow out the lamp, Johnny."

CHAPTER 11

It rained all the next day and most of the following night. On the second day, the owner of the fishing camp, Mr. Kellum, knocked on our door at first light to tell us the roads were open again. The Conasauga River was rising. Mr. Kellum offered to discount our bill if Johnny helped him move furniture from the cabins near the river to a storage building on higher ground.

I'd cleaned the tiny cabin, repacked our suitcases twice, and studied Johnny's maps until I'd committed to memory every highway, back road, and pig trail that we'd travel down on our journey to our new life together in Texas. With no work left to do, I decided to write a letter to Claudia. I got my journal and sat down at the table.

Dear Claudia,

You'll be happy to hear that I've escaped Sugardale and Momma forever. I know you wouldn't approve, but Johnny and I ran off and got married. It wasn't a regular marriage. There was no preacher, judge, or witnesses. It's called a common-law marriage.

We'd planned on getting married in Chattanooga, but got caught up in the flooding from Hurricane Ida. Not wanting to spend our first night together in sin, we put our hands on the Bible and pledged ourselves to each other in front of a picture of Jesus and his disciples. Johnny assures me a common-law marriage is legal. I've never known him to lie to me except about his kissing Lynn. I'm certain it was mostly her fault.

Goodbye for now.
Your best friend,

Becky Leigh Cooper
P.S. Johnny said that one day he'd kill Donald for raping me. Do you believe that?

I slipped my journal into the suitcase just as someone knocked on the door. My new husband had forgotten the key again.

"Just a minute," I yelled. I unlocked the door and pulled it open.

"Hello, Becky Leigh."

I scooted back until the kitchen counter stopped my retreat. "You can't be here. This is Tennessee. You don't belong here."

Sheriff Tate ducked as he entered our little home. "If anyone doesn't belong here, Missy, it's you." He removed his Stetson, glanced around the room. "If this is the best Santo can provide, then it's a good thing Helen sent me after you."

I folded my arms across my chest. "There's nothing either you or Momma can do. Johnny and I are married now."

The sheriff chuckled, pulled out a chair, and sat down at the table. "That so? Let me see your marriage license."

I eased down across from Momma's foot soldier. "We're common-law married. You can't say it isn't legal, because it is."

Sheriff Tate laughed. "Is that all it took for him to get you into bed? I thought you were smarter than that."

I jumped up. "I'm not scared of you. You have no jurisdiction in this matter."

He slammed his fist down hard on the chrome table. "You'd better be scared of me, and I have all the jurisdiction I need standing behind you."

I turned. Behind me stood another lawman. His uniform was navy blue instead of gray like those the Cascade County deputies wore.

Sheriff Tate stood. "Let me introduce you two. This is Sergeant Walter Sparks of the Tennessee State Highway Patrol. He's been married to my cousin, Darlene, for twenty years now."

"Closer to twenty-five years," Sparks said.

Tate nodded. "This is Becky Cooper, the young lady kidnapped by the Mexican boy."

"I wasn't kidnapped."

"Santo is eighteen, an adult in the eyes of the law, and you're a minor. When an adult takes someone's minor child across the state line without parental consent, it's kidnapping as far as we're concerned." Tate slicked back his thinning hair and resettled the Stetson on his head. "In this case, I think we can add rape to the list of charges. Don't you, Walter?"

"Sounds good to me, Roy."

It was if an iceberg had instantly encased my body. I stood frozen, unable to move, think, or breathe. Finally, involuntary reflexes took over and forced me to suck a long gulp of air into my burning lungs. "Where's Johnny? What have you done with him?"

I ran past the Tennessee lawman, splashed through the puddles surrounding our cabin, and ended up in the middle of the muddy parking lot. It took a moment for my eyes to adjust to the sunlight. Sheriff Tate's deputy stood next to a Cascade County patrol car. Parked next to it was a dark blue Ford with a Tennessee Highway Patrol logo on its doors. Johnny's Mustang was where he'd parked it. The Kellums watched from their front porch.

"Where's Johnny?" I yelled.

"He's on his way back to Sugardale," the deputy said.

Sheriff Tate grinned. "Don't worry, Becky, you'll see Johnny again. You'll have to testify at his trial."

I sank down into the soaked earth, not caring that all eyes were on me. Sheriff Tate would deliver me to Momma and to a beating too terrible to imagine. But that meant little to me now. What had I done to Johnny? I wrapped my muddy hands around my waist and rocked.

* * * * *

One of Tate's deputies took Johnny to jail, while the other drove the Mustang back to Sugardale. Sheriff Tate brought me home. I'd begged Momma to let me see Johnny, but she'd refused. Frank offered to check on him for me. When my stepfather returned, he was furious. Johnny had been given a good working over. Tate claimed he'd resisted arrest and his deputies had to use force. Frank and I knew they'd beaten Johnny just for the hell of it. Momma said the boy got what he deserved. I wondered if she'd asked Sheriff Tate to hurt Johnny.

Momma stared out the front window. "You need to rake this yard, Becky."

"Please don't let them do this to Johnny, Momma." I took a step closer to her. "It was my idea to run away."

Frank cleared his throat. "Helen, you can't send that boy to prison for something you know he didn't do."

"If he ends up in prison, it'll be a judge and jury sending him there." She released the curtain, strolled over to the television and turned it on.

I ran over to the TV and pushed the off button. Momma shoved me away, turned it back on. I fell against the couch, bounced up, and headed for the television again.

She put her arm out to stop me. "If you touch my TV again, I'll knock the teeth out of your head."

Frank stepped between us, turned off the television. "Your soap operas can wait."

Helen stomped back to the window. "I blame you for this, Frank. You're always coddling Becky. Did you encourage her to run away with Johnny?"

"Don't blame Frank, Momma. He didn't know. It's all my doing. Punish me if you like, but not him or Johnny."

"Don't worry. I'm planning something special for you."

Frank crossed the room in three steps. He got right up in Momma's face. "You're not laying a hand on her, Helen. Do you understand me? Never again are you going to hit her."

Momma took a drag off her cigarette and blew the smoke into my stepfather's face. "You can't tell me how to discipline Becky." She started to take another drag, but Frank wrapped his hand around hers, entombing her fist and the lit smoke inside his own grasp. His jaw flexed, sweat popped out on his forehead. Momma's eyes grew big. When Frank finally loosened his grip, Momma yanked her hand free. Her smothered cigarette fell to the floor.

I caught a faint whiff of seared flesh as Frank walked past me. "Are you okay?"

Ignoring my question, he trudged over to the phone, picked up the receiver, held it out to

Momma. "Call Tate. Tell him you're dropping the charges against Johnny."

Helen picked up her pack of cigarettes. "Damn. Go get me a carton of cigarettes, Becky."

"Nobody's going anywhere until this is settled," Frank said.

She crushed the empty package. "I need a smoke."

Frank shook the receiver at her. "Then I suggest you make the call."

"Doesn't it bother you, Frank, to know Johnny talked Becky into sleeping with him?"

"Johnny didn't talk me into anything. I love him and we're married."

Momma laughed. "Roy told me how you claimed to be common-law married. It was embarrassing. How could you be so stupid?"

"I'm not stupid. There is such a thing as a common-law marriage, isn't there, Frank?"

My stepfather put the receiver back on its hook. "Yes, Ladybug, but it's more involved than just running off and claiming you're married."

I shook my head. "I don't care what anyone thinks. As far as I'm concerned, Johnny and I are married."

"You hear that?" Helen asked. "If Johnny is set free, they'll run away again. We might not find them in one piece next time." She jabbed her finger at me. "Running off in the middle of a hurricane. It's a wonder you didn't drown or something."

"I'd rather drown than live with you." I started to run out of the room, but Frank grabbed me. "I hate her."

"Don't say that, Ladybug."

"It's true." I wrapped my arms around his waist and started crying.

Frank eased my arms from around his body, wiped my tears away, and walked over to stand behind Momma. He put his hands on her shoulders. "I know you were worried about Becky being out in that storm. I was scared too."

She looked up at him. "I do care about her."

"I know." He pulled her around into his arms and began rubbing her back.

I didn't know what to think or to feel. For a long time now, I'd thought of Frank as belonging to me, not to Momma. He hated her as much as I did. Didn't he? Not in my wildest imagination could I believe he still had feelings for her. He had to be playing her, the way she so often played us. He was being nice to soften her up.

"Now, Helen," he said, "they're not the first young couple to run off to get married, and they won't be the last. April and I did the same thing when we were just seventeen."

Momma pulled away. "That doesn't make it right."

"That's true, and I could give them both a swift kick in the behind." Frank looked at me. "Do you realize how frightened we were? Anna almost drove herself crazy with worry."

I pulled at my ponytail. "Johnny left his mother a note."

"That's more than we got from you," Helen said.

I'd wanted to leave a letter for Frank, but couldn't risk Momma finding it. When we got to Texas, I'd planned to call him at work to let him know I'd escaped her clutches. Then he'd be free to leave her too. But instead of freeing us both, I'd managed to put Frank in the middle again and get Johnny thrown in jail. Maybe I was stupid.

Right now, Momma's anger was directed at Johnny. She knew I'd rather her kill me then have her destroy Johnny's life and, consequently, Anna's too. My mother was so clever, so deserving of the title of Champion Picker of Cascade County.

"Becky, I want you to promise your mother that if she gets Johnny out of jail, you won't run off anymore," Frank said.

"I promise I won't run off again."

"That will not do." She turned to Frank. "Becky doesn't give a damn about any promise she makes me. She'll stand there all day and lie to my face if she thinks it'll help that boy."

Momma was right. She and I had lied to each other so much, it was now second nature to us. It'd take the Lord Almighty to unravel the truth between us. I doubted He felt we were worth his efforts any longer. Even in Hell, I'd still be stuck with Momma.

"What does Becky have to do to convince you she won't run away again?" he asked.

Momma sashayed over to the door, tilted her head, and played with one of her curls.

I could almost see the devious little wheels in her head turning, trying to find the best way to box me into a corner.

"She has to promise she'll never run away with Johnny or anyone. And she must swear on her daddy's grave, she'll never try to kill herself again."

"Okay," I said. "I swear."

"I'm not finished," Momma said. "Becky has to make this promise to you, Frank."

"Why to me?"

"Because Becky would cut out her tongue before breaking a solemn promise to you."

I knew two things. First, to save Johnny from prison, I'd have to give Frank my true word I'd never run away or try to harm myself again. Second, I was certain Momma had sold her soul to the Devil in exchange for a multitude of talents and ways to torment me. How could I fight the Devil, especially when the Lord had grown weary of all my lying, sinful ways?

I gave Frank my word. Momma picked up the phone and called the sheriff's office. My stepfather and I listened as she spun her silver tale.

"Margie, this is Helen Wooten, I heard you were in a little fender bender last week. Just wanted to call and make sure you were okay, Sugar."

It wasn't necessary for us to hear the other side of the conversation. Nobody's opinion mattered except for my mother's.

"I'm glad you're all right," Helen said. "By the way, can I talk to Sheriff Tate? Or has that rascal slipped off and gone fishing?"

Margie must have said something funny because Momma laughed.

"Roy, this is Helen. Sugar, we need to get together to discuss this thing with Becky and Johnny before it gets out of hand. What are you doing right now that's more important than meeting me . . . in private, of course?"

Frank flinched at Momma's suggestion of a private meeting. The image of her riding the naked insurance salesman popped into my head. I knew how far she'd go to get what she wanted from a man. I hoped Frank didn't, but suspected he might.

*****

It was half-past midnight when Momma returned from her meeting with Sheriff Tate. She staggered in, fell against the deacon's bench, got a run in her nylons.

"Shit . . . these hose are brand new." The odor of whiskey, cigars, and after-shave blended with her perfume. "The cost of these stockings is coming out of your allowance."

"I don't get an allowance." I scrambled backwards to stay out of her slapping range.

She plopped down in Papa's old recliner. "Frank gives you money. The least you can do is to buy . . . buy me some new hose."

"What happened, Momma? Is Johnny out of jail?"

She slipped off her heels. "Where's Frank?"

"In the greenhouse." I ventured closer to her. "What did Sheriff Tate say?"

"That damn greenhouse. I'm going to burn it down. Then Frank will have . . . time for me." She pushed her bangs out of her eyes and giggled. "Maybe I should paint myself green, tape leaves to my body . . . change my name to Rose. What do you think?"

The swinging door between the kitchen and the dining end of the living room opened. Frank entered.

I stood between him and Momma, not sure who I was protecting. It didn't take very much imagination to see that Sheriff Tate and Momma had shared more than conversation and supper.

"Did Helen get Johnny released?" Frank asked.

I shrugged. "She's drunk."

He squatted down in front of Momma, pushed her hair back, and patted her cheeks.

"Bring me a damp cloth, Becky."

I did as I was told.

He wiped her face and arms off. "Helen, can you hear me? What happened?"

"I hear you."

"Is Tate going to release Johnny?"

Momma put her arms around Frank's neck. "Why don't you care for me, Sugar? You worry about Becky . . . about Johnny . . . the store. Why don't you worry about me?" She tried to kiss him, but he pulled back. "We had some good times in the beginning, didn't we?" She rested her head on his chest and started crying.

Frank sighed and patted her back. He looked so tired. Trying to mediate the running feud between Momma and me was sucking the life out of him.

The phone rang. I jumped. Anyone calling this late had to be the bearer of bad news.

It rang again. "I'll get it," I said, my voice quivering.

"No," Frank said, "I'll get it." He eased Helen back into the recliner. Her head fell limp against the headrest. She'd fallen asleep. He smoothed the damp cloth over her forehead. The phone rang again and he answered it.

"Hello. Yes, this is Frank."

I sat down on the ottoman, trembling, and listening for a clue as to the caller's identity.

Frank hung up the phone, walked over to the davenport and sat down. "Please come here, Ladybug."

I eased down beside him. "Who was on the phone?"

"Anna."

I latched onto Frank's arm. "Johnny's dead, isn't he? They killed him."

"No, Becky." Frank pried my hand loose. "Johnny's fine."

"Are you sure?"

"I'm sure. Calm down, Ladybug."

"I can't." I rested my head on Frank's shoulder. "I'm scared."

He kissed my head. "Do you want to know why Anna called?"

"Yes, sir."

"To thank your mother for getting Johnny released."

"He's free? Johnny's free?"

"Not yet, but he will be soon. The charges against him will be dropped in exchange for his enlisting in the military."

"Why should he enlist? He has a college deferment."

"Apparently, Helen and Sheriff Tate visited Cordell Varner, the county attorney, tonight. The three of them decided this plan would be best for everyone."

"Why didn't Momma drop the charges?"

"It's too late for that. Johnny's lawyer figures this is the best deal he'll get."

I jumped up. Momma was snoozing away in Papa's chair, a look of contentment on her smeared painted face. "It's her fault. She didn't go over to Mr. Varner's to help Johnny. She went to make sure he got sent as far away from me as possible."

Frank slowly rubbed the back of his neck. "Probably, but Ladybug, you and Johnny are partly responsible for this mess."

"What do you mean? Are you taking her side?"

"I'm not taking anyone's side, Ladybug, but how many times did I tell you to be patient? If you'd waited until you were eighteen, this story would've had a happy ending."

"But I couldn't wait. I ran away so we could both be free of Momma."

Helen stirred. "Where are you, Frank?"

"I'm here, Helen."

"I did good tonight, didn't I? I got Johnny set free like you wanted."

Frank nodded.

Helen grinned. "Are you proud of me?"

"Sure," he whispered as she nodded off again.

I grabbed his arm. "How can you be proud of her? Don't you know what she did?"

"Whatever Helen did, it was because I asked her to. Remember, I sent her to Tate."

"You are too nice, Frank. Momma takes advantage of that."

"We all take advantage of people we care about now and then. Helen's just better at it than most."

I hugged my stepfather. "I don't want her to hurt you anymore."

"I appreciate your concern, Ladybug, but it's my job to take care of us. Remember that, okay?"

"Okay."

Frank squeezed my hand. "I don't want us to ever mention what Helen did or didn't do tonight. Do you understand?"

"Why do you want to protect her?"

"You weren't here, Becky. These last few days were hard on all of us, including Helen."

"You said Momma cared about me, but I don't believe it."

"When you have a child, you'll understand." He smoothed back my hair. "There's no greater agony than not knowing if your child is safe."

"Frank," Helen called, "I'm tired. Help me to bed."

He went to her. "Put your arms around my neck."

She was quick to obey. "I don't feel well. Stay with me tonight . . . please."

He hesitated briefly, then picked her up. "Sure."

She sighed and unveiled a lazy grin.

"Lock up and go to bed, Ladybug." Frank started up the stairs. Momma's arms were wrapped around his neck; her chin rested on his shoulder.

I stood at the bottom of the staircase, looking up at Frank's back and Momma's face.

Her eyes popped open. A twisted smirk split her face. She waved and then winked. Damn her hide. She'd given another Oscar-caliber performance and Frank and I had bought it.

Three days ago, everything had seemed simple. I'd been so sure Johnny and I would make good our escape. Now, I'd lost the little I had. Because of me, Momma had been given the chance to play the role of concerned parent and obedient wife. Frank's guilt over sending her to Sheriff Tate and his parental sympathies made him even more vulnerable to her hooks. And Anna would be stuck with bills from her son's attorney.

Worse of all, I'd lost Johnny. Instead of college, he faced military service and the possibility of being sent to Vietnam. If Momma's wish to see him dead came true, I'd have only myself to blame.

Momma claimed she and I were alike in many ways. Until today, I'd denied her allegation. Now I knew she'd told the truth. When it came to ruining people's lives, I was most definitely my mother's daughter.

CHAPTER 12

Frozen grass crunched beneath our boots. Icicles of various lengths hung off the canyon ledges next to a trickle of water slipping over the triangular-shaped rock. The harshness of the coldest winter in thirty years echoed the bitterness fermenting in me. I headed for the truck, leaving Frank alone to admire the wonders of Starview Mountain. Climbing into the cab, I practiced what I'd say to him.

Two months had passed since Johnny's departure and the agony of not being allowed to tell him goodbye still lingered. I'd only asked for a few minutes with him. Despite my pleas and Frank's requests on my behalf, Momma had refused to grant permission. My only tangible memento of the day was a brief note Johnny wrote to me. Anna gave it to Frank personally to pass on to me. Otherwise, I'm sure I'd have never received it.

In the note, Johnny promised to write, swore he'd come back for me, and pledged his everlasting love. It was now mid-December and I'd yet to get one letter. Still, I clung to his promise as if it was a lasso hanging over a pit of rattlesnakes.

The driver's door opened and Frank got in. "It's colder than frog titties out there."

I forced a smile.

He started the engine and turned on the heater. "What did you want to talk about?"

"Why do you love this pickup so much?"

"Before my first wife died, she made me promise to use some of her life insurance money to buy a new pickup. I didn't want to, but it seemed important to April. I think of it as a present from her." Frank patted the dash of the red and white '62 Ranchero. "I got an automatic so it'd be easier for Donald to drive, but he doesn't like trucks. We never had much in common except for loving his mother."

For the first time, I saw Frank as someone other than my friend and protector. He had secret heartaches of his own to deal with. How unfair for me to burden him with mine. But what choice did I have? For a long time we sat in silence, each lost in our own memories.

Frank turned off the truck. "What's on your mind, Ladybug? Why did you want to come out here?"

"You love this place so. Why don't you buy it?"

"I would if Mr. Parr would sell it. He keeps hoping his children will want it someday."

"Why wouldn't they?"

"His son is a doctor in Boston, and his daughter married an engineer from California. They seldom visit." Frank laughed. "They think Georgia is all peach trees and rednecks."

At that moment, I knew exactly how April must have felt. I'd have given my eyeteeth to been able to give Starview Mountain to Frank. "Maybe Mr. Parr will change his mind and sell it to you."

"Perhaps." Frank reached for my hand. "You didn't bring me here to talk about trucks and land. What's the matter, Ladybug?"

"I am . . . I am going to . . . I am pretty sure . . ."

"Are you pregnant, Becky?"

I didn't answer.

Frank pushed the seat back. "I heard you throwing up this morning."

"Do you think Momma heard?"

"I don't know. Helen's a heavy sleeper."

Momma and Frank's reconciliation hadn't lasted very long. Donald had come home for the Thanksgiving holidays and brought his college roommate, Bruce, with him. On Friday, Momma dragged Frank off to look at new cars. I stayed home to pot a batch of poinsettias for our store. Around noon, Donald and Bruce came in the greenhouse to tease me about Johnny.

They predicted Johnny would get killed in Vietnam. The more upset I became, the more they taunted me. Donald asked me how I liked my honeymoon and dared his friend to grope me. After backing me into a corner, Bruce proceeded to accept the dare. Donald stood there laughing, drinking beer, and urging his buddy on. I was hysterical — crying, screaming, begging them to leave me alone — when Frank walked in. He picked up a rake and went after them. Donald knocked out a panel in the greenhouse wall. He and Bruce jumped through it and high-tailed it down the street.

The boys, as Momma called them, didn't return until after midnight. Frank sat waiting for them on the front porch with their suitcases. He told them to go back to college and suggested Donald visit his grandparents at Christmas.

Helen had hated Donald since the day he'd put glue in her shampoo. But for some reason, she spoke up for him. I suppose tormenting me wasn't a major offense in her book. She told Frank he was too hard on the boys. Frank responded by moving into Grandpa Eli's old bedroom. She begged him to come back to her bed, but he refused. He told her I was the only reason he wasn't leaving for good.

The way she stared at me, if looks could kill, I'd have been dead.

"Momma can't find out, Frank. She'll kill me for sure."

He chuckled. "She'll pitch a fit, but Helen won't kill you."

My eyes begin to sting. "You still don't understand her. She'd rather tell the neighbors I fell and broke my neck than to have them know I'm carrying Johnny's baby."

"How can I help you, Ladybug?"

"You have to release me from my promise not to run away."

"I can't do that."

"You have to. I've got to get away before she finds out."

"And go where, Becky Leigh? You don't have any other family." Frank started up the truck and turned the heater on high again. "Have you told Johnny?"

"Johnny's cousin, Emelda, gave me his address. I wrote to him before Thanksgiving, as soon as I missed my . . . as soon as I knew. I haven't heard a word from him since he left."

"Don't get upset. He'll write as soon as he can. The first few months you're in the Army, they barely give you time to catch your breath, much less write home."

I hung my head so my hair would hide my face.

"Don't cry, Ladybug."

"I'm not crying. You know I hate crying."

"Yeah, I know." Frank pulled me into his arms.

"What's going to happen to me?"

He kissed the top of my head. "You'll be fine. We'll get through this together."

"How? I'm not giving up Johnny's baby."

"I didn't expect you would." Frank wiped the tears from my face. "My sister in Alabama always wanted a daughter."

"Momma might kill me, but I doubt she'd adopt me out."

Frank laughed. "That's not exactly what I meant."

"What then?"

"Three of Christina's sons are grown and have left home. Only her youngest is left, and he's graduating next May." Frank pushed my hair out of my eyes. "I bet she'd be tickled to have you stay with her."

"What about her husband?"

"Barney lets my sister run the house as she sees fit. He loves gardening, but couldn't get his boys interested in it. I'm sure he'd appreciate your help."

"And I would help him, Frank. I'd earn my keep."

"I've no doubt about that." He handed me his handkerchief. "Blow your nose."

"What about Momma?"

Frank rubbed the back of his neck. "School lets out for Christmas next week. I'll tell her I want us all to visit my sister over the holidays. When it's time to come home, we'll tell her about the baby. Since there'll be other people around, maybe Helen won't explode."

I shook my head. "I wouldn't bet my life on that."

*****

Helen pulled a lipstick from her purse. "I don't know why Frank insists we go to Alabama for Christmas. Donald will be in Florida. We could have a fine holiday right here."

"I thought you liked Donald now."

She rolled her eyes. "I swear, Becky Leigh, you're so dense sometimes. I hate that boy worse than a cat hates a bath."

"Then why did you take up for Donald at Thanksgiving?"

"That's my business." Momma gave her lips a fresh coat of cherry red, then smacked them twice. "Haven't you ever heard of killing your enemy with kindness?"

"You plan on killing Donald?"

"I haven't decided what I'm going to do to him. But he owes me for ruining my hair and that debt will be paid." She dropped the lipstick into her purse, snapped the bag shut, and turned to me. "You hide and watch, Sugar. Hide and watch and learn."

Normally, I'd feel sorry for anyone who had the misfortune of finding themselves caught in Momma's crosshairs. But in Donald's case, I made an exception. Despite Reverend Murray's sermons on turning the other cheek, I hoped Momma would think of something awful to do to Donald. That thought probably generated another black mark next to my name in God's record book. But one more wasn't going to make Hell any hotter.

Helen grabbed the keys to her new powder-blue Thunderbird, a Christmas present to herself. "Let's go, Becky. I don't want to be late."

"I still don't understand why we have to go to Brockton to see a new dentist."

"I told you, Doctor Varholt is booked up. We really need to get our teeth cleaned before Christmas." She opened the front door. "I hear Doctor Nixon is good. Come on."

I didn't move. "I told Celia Lundy I'd help her wrap Christmas presents today."

"Call her and say you can't come. I'll wait in the car. Hurry up."

I'd made up the story about Celia in hopes that Momma would let me stay home, but she'd called my bluff. I picked up the receiver and dialed the number for our store. Agnes Shaver, Frank's secretary, answered.

"Mrs. Shaver, may I speak to my stepfather, please?"

"Frank is in a meeting with representatives from the new pottery supplier, Becky. He's not very happy with them."

Frank was an understanding man, but when it came to business, he could be a bear. He insisted on a quality job and excellent service from his employees and suppliers.

"Please tell him Momma is taking me to the dentist in Brockton."

"To Brockton? Why Brockton?"

"Momma believes Doctor Nixon is a really good dentist."

"I've heard some things about him."

"What've you heard?"

"Just some rumors. I have to go, Becky. I'll give Frank your message."

"Thank you, ma'am." As I hung up the phone, I wondered about the rumors and decided to call Mrs. Shaver again. But then, Momma started honking the horn. I knew better than to keep her waiting.

*****

Helen flipped down her visor. "I'm glad we have this chance to talk, aren't you?"

"Yes, ma'am," I said, adding another lie to my ever-growing list. Brockton was a half-hour drive west of Sugardale and Momma had been bending my ear since we'd pulled out of the driveway. Mostly, her yammering was gossip. How the blue topaz ring Mr. Mercer got his wife was really just blue glass, and how Betty Powell wanted to be friends again now that Anna had moved back to Texas.

"We don't get many chances to do things together. Mother-daughter things."

I stared out the passenger window. "No, ma'am." I stopped short of adding, "Thank God."

"Stop patting your foot so hard, Becky. You're shaking the damn car."

Whenever I'm nervous, I get an almost uncontrollable urge to rock or swing. Being cooped up in a car with Momma made me anxious. My stomach felt like a boy scout was using my intestines to practice his knot tying.

Helen cracked her window a bit. A thin stream of frigid air seeped into the car. She undid her top two buttons and pushed apart the sides of her turquoise cotton blouse.

I pulled my coat together.

"We've had a rough year, Becky. I may have gone overboard on the whipping I gave you last autumn. But a child who deliberately lies to her mother deserves to be punished. Doesn't she?"

Momma had a knack for asking damned-if-you-do and damned-if-you-don't questions. I gave her as dubious a nod as I could get away with.

"I'm glad you agree." She rolled down her window a tad more. "A mother's primary responsibility is to do what she thinks is best for her child. It's a difficult task, especially when she's the sole parent."

"You were never alone. You had Papa and Frank."

"You could wrap your daddy around your little finger, and Frank never loved you like I'd hoped he would."

"Frank cares about me."

"Sure he does, but he's never acted like a father to you. He just wants to be your friend. A true father knows love must be balanced with discipline."

"Maybe Frank figured since you were so quick to hand out the discipline, he'd be the one to give out the love."

Helen's knuckles paled as she gripped the steering wheel tighter. "What a mean thing to say. I don't know where you learned such cruelty."

I looked out my window, rolling my eyes as I listened to her ramble on about how much she cared about me. I might not be the smartest squirrel in the tree, but I know a nut when I see one. And my momma was nuts if she thought I was buying her fake declarations of affection.

She rolled her window up and turned the heater on high. "A child belongs to its mother because she gave the child life. The mother must do what she thinks is best."

Who was she trying to convince? Herself or me? I wanted to ask her if she had any cheese to go with the bologna she was trying to feed me, but didn't dare ask while in slapping range. She turned the heater on, then off, then on again, as if unable to decide whether she was hot or cold. Maybe she'd caught the flu bug that was going around.

"Do me a favor, Becky."

Here it comes, the true reason for this mother knows best speech. "What kind of favor?"

"Stop tapping your damn finger on the arm rest. You're gonna drive me crazy."

In my opinion, that would be a short trip.

*****

Helen pulled up in front of the dentist's office. "We're here."

Dr. Nixon's office was at the edge of town in a small building that had obviously once been someone's home. The house was painted yellow and trimmed in a milky white.

"Aren't the decorations pretty?" Momma asked.

I nodded. On one side of the walkway, a snowman waved to us. The other side of the yard presented a nativity scene with Mary, Joseph, and the baby Jesus lying in a manger. A split-rail fence laden with fat, multi-colored bulbs surrounded the snow-frosted yard. The last remnants of the day's brilliance muted the radiance of the Christmas lights, causing an eerie glow to settle over the otherwise beguiling scene.

I couldn't shake the feeling that something was out of place. Then I noticed the window boxes. Dead tendrils of last summer's flowers hung down the sides of the boxes. Stems that once propped up fragrant blossoms were now bare twigs reaching up past the clinic's windows, resembling prison bars. I wondered why, when everything else was so neat, the window boxes had been left as a testimonial of sorts to death. The muscles in my shoulders tightened.

"I guess we should get out," she said.

I waited for Momma to open her door, but she sat staring at the dentist's office. Her hand moved to the door handle, back to the steering wheel, then back to the handle. She never liked going to the dentist much. She wasn't afraid. It was more of a control issue. It's hard to be in charge when a stranger is shoving his hand into your mouth.

"Let's get our teeth cleaned after Christmas, Momma."

"You should wear your hair pulled away from your face." She pushed my hair behind my ears. "You look like you're twelve instead of sixteen. If you pulled the sides of your hair up, you'd look more your age. I could show you how."

"I like my hair the way it is."

She frowned. "If Frank made the suggestion, you'd try it."

"Are we going to the dentist or not?"

Her attention turned back to the office. "I suppose. We're here. Might as well get it over with." She got out of car and slammed the door.

Momma was behaving especially peculiar today. During breakfast, she'd raved about my biscuits. I'd been baking the same biscuits for three years without a single compliment from her. She was up to something. When I got home, I'd alert Frank.

Grandpa Eli had always told me to listen to my heart. But it's hard to hear anything when Momma's yelling, "Get out of the car, Becky Leigh."

Once on the porch, she lit a cigarette, smoked half of it, flicked it into the snow.

She slipped her arm around me. "Don't worry, Sugar. I'll take care of you."

A chill brushed the back of my neck.

CHAPTER 13

I heard voices. A man and a woman arguing. At first, I thought the voices were in my head. Then I realized it was Momma and Frank. As usual, they were arguing about me. I opened my eyes just a sliver. Frank sat bent over in a gray, straight-back chair, elbows on his knees, his chin resting on his fists. On the opposite side of the strange room, Momma stood staring out a window, smoking a cigarette.

"How could you do this, Helen?" Frank asked.

"Was I supposed to let her throw away her future because of one stupid mistake?"

She sucked on the cigarette, then blew smoke at the ceiling. "I never dreamed it'd turn out like this. That damn dentist was supposed to know his business."

Frank stood. "It was her decision to make, not yours."

"How can she decide what's best for her? She's sixteen and crazy in the head for that Mexican boy. She tried to kill herself over him. Killing yourself over a man. That's plain crazy."

I wanted to touch my stomach, to touch the place where my baby slept, but my arms wouldn't move. Had we been in an accident on the way home from the dentist? Was I paralyzed? Why couldn't I remember?

Frank ran his hand across his face. "I had it all worked out. My sister in Alabama agreed to take care of Becky until the baby came."

"And then what? Do you really believe she would've given it up?"

My nose twitched as the smoke drifted over the bed. I tried to make sense of my stepfather's words. I guessed his sister had changed her mind about my staying with her.

Momma crushed her cigarette out on the windowsill. "There's not one damn ashtray in this room."

"You're not supposed to smoke in here."

"We all do things we're not supposed to do, don't we, Frank? Like you helping her keep this secret from me."

"Just how did you find out?"

"That's my business." Helen turned back to the window. "Becky's young. She'll get over this. Trust me, I know."

"The doctors say she might never —"

"What the hell do they know?" Momma asked. "Besides, maybe she's better off."

I might never what? Never move my arms again? Never walk again? I wished Momma would quit interrupting Frank. She always hogged the conversation.

He eased back into the straight-back chair. "What is it, Helen? What makes you claw at people until you strip them of everything decent? Until you strip them to the bone?"

She pulled the window blind up all the way. A sunbeam spotlight shot across the room high-lighting my stepfather. "You know the saying, Frank, monkey see . . . monkey do. We're all monkeys doing what we've been taught."

"Who taught you to be such a predator?"

She whirled around to face him. "My daddy, of course. Didn't you know daddies have the most influence on their girls? Just look at

Becky. She lives in the garden because her daddy lived there."

"Gardening is good for the soul," Frank said. "But you wouldn't know about that."

She laughed. "If you're trying to say I don't have a soul, then you're right."

"You admit it?"

"I had a choice once, to have a soul or to survive. I chose to survive." She lit another cigarette, blew the smoke out the side of her mouth. "If Becky lives, it'll be because of what she's learned from me, not anything you or her daddy taught her."

If I lived? I must be worse off than I thought. I didn't feel too bad. My arms wouldn't move and my throat felt as if I'd drank a glass of cotton, but I wasn't in much pain. I tried to remember what had happened. I recalled the dentist saying he needed to put me to sleep to pull a bad tooth, a tooth that didn't hurt. Then, there was the matter of the dream. In it, Dr. Nixon's assistant had spilled something red all over her clean white uniform. Strawberry punch? Red paint, perhaps?

Helen lowered the blind. A shadow crept across the room. "I'm going to get something to eat. Do you want anything?"

"I can't believe you, Helen," Frank said. "I knew you were a shrew, but don't you have any morals? Any conscience?"

"You'd better look to your own house before you start pointing fingers at me."

"What does that mean?"

"Who do you think told me about the dentist?" Helen asked. "Your son."

He jumped up. "You can't blame this on Donald. He's away at school. This was your own doing."

"What do you think he's been doing at college? With the lousy grades he gets, it's sure not studying."

Frank glared at Momma, as if daring her to say another word against his son. But my mother had never met a man she was afraid of, or one she couldn't destroy if she so desired.

"What did you say, Frank? I didn't hear you."

"I don't believe a word out of your lying mouth."

"That's because you don't want to face the truth about Sonny Boy. You never have." She crushed out her cigarette. "You remember last spring when he needed $200 for a class trip? That money was for Dr. Nixon. Donald got some girl from South Carolina pregnant and took her to visit our incompetent dentist."

"How would you know that?"

She grinned. "I've got my sources." Helen jabbed her finger at Frank. "And she wasn't the only gal he knocked up. There was a waitress who worked in a café near the university —"

"Stop it!" Frank slicked back his hair with both hands. "You're lying."

Helen grabbed the door handle. "Ask him if you dare. Or ask the girls. No telling how many young women Donald has left in Dr. Nixon's inept hands." She flung open the door and fled the room.

Frank watched the door close. Like the lid of a coffin in a late-night vampire movie, the door closed slowly, with a low creaking sound. He sank down onto the straight-back chair again, closed his eyes, and wrapped his hands around his head as if trying to keep his brain from falling out.

I knew how he felt. My own brain bounced around in my skull trying to make sense of Momma's words. What did Dr. Nixon have to do with Donald? Why would my stepbrother bring his girlfriends all the way to Brockton just to see a dentist? Then, like the pieces of a horrible jigsaw puzzle, it all came together — Momma, my baby, and the red-stained white uniform.

*****

A week later, Frank stood in the open doorway of my hospital room. "May I come in, Ladybug?"

I managed a small nod.

"I brought some flowers from the green-house." He held up a silver vase packed with burgundy poinsettias, pink rosebuds, baby's breath, and maidenhair fern. He put the arrangement on the table opposite my hospital bed. "Is here okay?"

"That's fine."

Frank placed the straight-back chair beside my bed and sat down. "And how are you feeling today?"

"What is today?" I asked. "Is it Christmas yet?"

"It's Christmas Eve."

"No wonder the nurses are anxious to get me moved. They don't want me to mess up their Christmas dinner tomorrow."

One of the doctors had told me I was being transferred to a place called Havenwood. He called it a sanitarium, a fancy word for insane asylum. Momma told them I'd killed my baby and had tried to kill myself because a Mexican boy raped me.

Frank told the doctors Momma was lying. He explained how she'd taken me to see Dr. Nixon and how the dentist anesthetized me, and then botched an illegal abortion. But the educated and righteous chose to believe that champion Picker, Momma. After all, Dr. Nixon was an upstanding citizen of Brockton. I was an unlucky teenager from out-of-town who'd carried the illegitimate child of a pepper-belly rapist. Any young woman from a well-to-do white family might be tempted to kill herself under similar conditions.

I pulled the blanket up under my chin. "Is Momma here?"

"I see they untied your hands." Frank began massaging the red marks on my wrist.

"I suppose Christmas got the best of them. Plus, they knew you were coming and weren't in the mood for another fight."

My hands had been tied to the bedrails for most of my hospital stay. Supposedly, for my own good. Standard procedure when dealing with a patient who'd attempted suicide. Frank untied my hands on three occasions and pleaded for them to remain unbound, but rules are rules. In the end, he'd only succeeded in getting himself banned from the hospital until today. The strangers in white who now controlled my destiny had allowed today's visit because of my impending transfer.

"Is Momma coming?" The murdering witch hadn't come by since the day I woke up. Frank claimed she was too ashamed to face me, but I knew better. She feared I would kill her if the opportunity presented itself. She was right.

Frank reached for my other wrist. "Helen is cooking Christmas dinner, as if everything was normal. I think she's lost her mind."

I grabbed his sleeve. "You'd better not go feeling sorry for her."

"I won't. I just think all the despicable things she's done have caught up to her and the guilt is driving her crazy."

"Don't you believe it for one minute." I tightened my grip on his arm. "This is another act, another performance designed to get you to forgive her." I leaned back against my pillow. "It's time you realized I know Momma better than anyone."

"I see that now." Frank placed my hand against his cheek. "If I'd listened before, I wouldn't have failed you. I should've taken you away the day you told me about the baby."

I yanked my hand away. "Yes, you should have."

He went to the window and stood with his back to me. He raised his hand and wiped something off his face. I knew he felt guilty for failing to save my baby and me from Momma's lunacy. But I had no pity for him or for myself. I'd ignored the pleadings of my heart when it tried to warn me something was wrong and had allowed Momma to escort me into that murderer's lair. I'd underestimated her again. The last time I did that, Johnny paid the price. This time, our baby paid for my mistake with its life.

Frank swiveled around. "I wonder how Helen found out about the baby."

"I figured that out. Momma must have intercepted my letters to Johnny. She said he hadn't written to me because he never loved me. I bet she got hold of his letters to me too."

"I'd wager Roy Tate had a hand in getting them for her. I'll get the letters for you, Becky. Helen will give them to me or —"

"Don't waste your time, Frank. Momma's too smart to keep any incriminating evidence. She's burned them by now."

Frank rubbed the back of his neck. "Those things Helen said about Donald. Do you think they were true?"

"It all fits. Remember Thanksgiving, when Momma took up for Donald? She wanted to get on his good side to get information from him on illegal abortions. She planned my baby's murder for weeks."

Frank came and stood by my bed. "I've got an appointment next week with another lawyer. I'll find a way to get you out of Havenwood. I promise."

"Don't make promises you can't keep. A new lawyer will tell you the same thing the others did. A stepfather has no legal standing, not like the mother."

"She's not a mother to you."

"Legally she is. And legally, I'm crazy. So the law says she can put me away."

He shook his head. "It's not right, Ladybug. If they'd only listen to the truth."

"People don't care about what's right or true. They never did. They only care about what's convenient. It wasn't convenient for Momma to have an illegitimate, half-Mexican grandchild."

"Becky, I can't —"

"Let it be, Frank. If I go home, I'll kill her."

For a time neither one of us spoke. Then Frank asked, "What do you want me to do?"

"With me gone, Momma will turn her wickedness on you. My advice is to run. Run like a hound from Hell was after you because she will be."

CHAPTER 14

"Your stepfather is here, Miss Cooper."

"Tell him to leave," I said without looking up. After five months in Havenwood, I could easily recognize Nurse Bridger's monotone voice. It was the one constant in this spittoon of a place where the virtues of remaining calm were often touted, but seldom followed.

I marveled at her ability to remain composed despite the wailing, screaming, and throwing of objects by my fellow prisoner-patients. At first, I'd thought her unflappable nature stemmed from her role as a medical professional, but later I realized it sprung from her resolve to shut everything and everyone out.

"Why didn't you tell me today was your birthday?" she asked.

I looked up. In her early forties, Nurse Bridger might be considered attractive, but definitely not pretty. She had cocoa eyes, braided dark blond hair piled into a bun, and an extra twenty pounds on her five-feet-six frame. The monotony of her speech and a small mole above her right eyebrow distinguished her from the other paid misfits in our floundering Havenwood family.

"Would you have baked me a cake?"

"No."

I smiled. Others might not appreciate Nurse Bridger's straight-to-the point answers, but I did. In this outhouse of human remains, she served as my hero. I longed to duplicate her ability to walk through the day doing what she must to survive, while permitting no one and nothing to touch her. She sailed down the river of life unimpeded by those drowning around her. With a little luck, perhaps I too could cut out all emotions and just exist.

Bridger crossed her arms. "Mr. Wooten is waiting, Miss Cooper."

Every Sunday for five months, Frank had made the 90-mile round trip from Sugardale to Havenwood, and every Sunday I'd refused to see him. But still, he came.

"Please tell him to go home." I resumed my reading.

Nurse Bridger snatched the book out of my hands. "If you're going to pretend to read, you should consider turning a page now and then." She flipped the page and handed me the book. "I don't get paid to deliver messages. You can tell him to leave or he can sit on the patio until he comes to his senses and realizes you are not worthy of his loyalty."

*****

Frank sat on a cement bench that had cherubs carved into each leg. For reasons beyond my understanding, cherubs were the decorations of choice in this den of demons. The chubby angelic creatures were on sconces in the hall, above every door, and on murals in a room that served as an interrogation chamber during the week and the chapel on Sunday. I couldn't escape their prying eyes even when I peed, for their images were infused into the bathroom wallpaper. The decorator had been either a lover of irony or a profoundly sick bastard.

"Hello, Frank."

He jumped up. "Becky . . . you startled me." He took two steps toward me, put his arms out, and then stopped. After a moment's hesitation, he hugged me.

I stiffened. In the past, Frank's embrace had comforted me, but now his touch — or anyone else's — agitated me.

"How have you been, Becky? You look. . ."

"I look like shit."

Frank's eyes widened. "When did you start cussing?"

I shrugged.

"Don't they feed you?"

I shrugged again. My weight had dropped from 116 to 101 pounds. Dark circles under my eyes testified to countless nights with little sleep.

"When did you cut your hair?" he asked.

I ran my hand through my cropped mane. "A couple of weeks ago. Somebody got head lice so they chopped off everyone's hair."

"It'll grow back," he said. "Besides, it'll be cooler now that summer's on the way."

Same old Frank, still trying to find a silver lining in every freaking cloud.

"Didn't you get my messages telling you not to come?" I asked.

"I figured those were made up by the staff."

"They were from me. You're wasting your time here."

Ignoring my comment, he pointed to two packages wrapped in shiny green paper secured with peach ribbons. "Happy seventeenth birthday, Ladybug."

I ran a finger over the glossy ribbon. "Don't call me Ladybug. Ladybug is dead."

He frowned. "Don't say that."

"How's the store? How's Momma?"

"Business is good. Helen's been nervous and upset since you left."

"She's never come to see me. Not once. I hoped it was because she was dead."

Frank rocked back on his heels. "I hate to hear you talk like that, Becky."

"Then don't come anymore," I said in a tone sharper than I'd intended. "What's Momma telling the neighbors? Did she tell them I'm here?"

He snickered. "Helen tell the truth? Not likely. She told everyone you're in Alabama caring for my sick sister."

"That sounds like her."

He dropped down onto the bench. "I moved out of the house the day you came here."

"Momma's alone?"

"Yes."

I laughed. "No wonder she's so nervous. Momma never could handle being alone. She has to have an audience. Someone to pick on. I once overhead Grandpa Eli tell Papa that Momma didn't like being alone because it forced her to see the truth about herself."

Frank nodded. "So that's why Helen is so desperate to get me back."

I joined him on the bench. "What do you mean by desperate?"

"Helen offered to put the store in my name if I'd move home and pretend we're a couple again."

"Take it," I said. "Take it and anything else you can get."

Frank picked at the peach ribbon. "I don't want to live in the same house with her after what she did to you. I want a divorce."

I grabbed his arm. "If you divorce Momma, she won't let you visit me."

He sighed. "That's why I haven't pushed for it."

"Take the store, Frank. Take everything you can from her."

"Don't talk like that, Becky. You sound like Helen."

"That's because I'm her daughter. I tried to fight it, but it's no use."

"You're not at all like her."

"Momma's black blood is inside of me. We might as well use it to our advantage." I squeezed his arm. "Who's taking care of Papa's garden if you're not there?"

"I send a guy from the store over to weed and mow."

I stood. "That's not enough. Papa's garden requires a lot of work, especially in the spring. I thought I could depend on you, Frank."

"But you told me to leave Sugardale and Helen."

I pulled at the little hair I had left. "Did I say that? It's hard for me to remember things. It's those damn pills they make us take."

"Don't worry, Becky. I'll be here for as long as it takes. I owe you that much."

"You owe me more than that, damn you. You promised to protect me and my baby."

Frank shoulders slumped. "It's true. I failed you again."

"You can make it up to me by moving home, caring for Papa's garden, and taking the store and the house from Momma."

He stood, walked to the edge of the patio, and started pacing. "Helen might agree to sign over the store, but never the house."

"She would if you threaten to tell everyone she had her own grandbaby killed and had me locked away for her crime." I walked over to Frank. "Momma will do anything to keep up appearances, to stay perched on her pedestal. We can use that against her."

"You're talking about blackmail, Becky. That's the kind of stunt Helen would pull."

"Exactly. That's why she always wins." I took Frank's face in my hands, forcing him to look at me. "I need to know Papa's garden is being taken care of. I have to beat her this once."

"This doesn't seem right."

I slipped my arms around his waist. "Do this for me and I'll forgive you for everything."

Frank hugged me tight. "Will you promise to see me when I visit?"

"Yes," I whispered.

"I don't like it, but I'll do it for you . . . if you're sure it's what you want"

"I'm sure." A bell rang twice. "That's the signal to return to our rooms."

We untangled ourselves and Frank retrieved the presents he'd brought. "The top one is a couple of journals. The big box is a pretty robe for my pretty Ladybug."

I accepted the gifts and forced a smile for his sake.

*****

I buttoned my jacket and kicked at a pile of leaves. From this corner of the asylum grounds, one could see the houses in town and smell the smoke from their chimneys. On the porches, the flags of summer had been replaced with pumpkins, corn stalks, and cardboard monsters in anticipation of Halloween. The scent of burning leaves hitched a ride on a gust of wind headed our way. I wished for a broomstick that could fly over the eight-foot fence that separated us certified loony birds from the alleged sane.

"What's wrong?" Frank asked. "For the last two visits you've hardly said a word."

"Nothing."

He cupped his hands and blew on them. "Something is troubling you."

I shrugged.

"Is someone giving you a hard time? Nurse Bridger, perhaps?"

I picked up a limb and used it to scatter more leaves.

Frank ripped the stick out of my hand, tossed it aside. "Dammit, Becky. I can't help you if you won't talk to me."

"We've walked too far. I can't hear the bell ring from here." I ran toward the main building, not stopping until I reached the patio.

Frank caught up with me. "What are you afraid of?"

"Nothing. You ask too many questions. I've got to go in now."

He studied me. "You'd tell me if something was wrong, wouldn't you?"

I nodded. "I'll try to save the plant." My stepfather had brought me a half-dead miniature rosebush from Papa's garden. Frank had received permission to place the wounded plant in the Havenwood solarium. I didn't want him to leave it, but he reminded me of the deathbed promise I'd made my papa — a promise to take care of his garden. Working in the garden comforted me. I suspected that was the real reason Frank had brought the sad little plant.

What I really needed was a rocking chair, but the shrewd Havenwood Gestapo had denied my request. If I got a rocking chair, the other patients would want one too. Personally, I couldn't imagine any place that needed rocking chairs more.

Frank kissed my cheek. "I'll see you next Sunday."

"Okay." I hated Sundays. Hated for Frank to see me like this, yet hated his leaving even more. He kept promising me that one day soon, I'd leave with him. But after ten months in this abyss, my hopes were dying faster than Papa's rosebush.

*****

May 1, 1968, my eighteenth birthday had finally arrived. I looked around my room. My bed was made, the trashcan emptied, and my suitcases packed. I'd said goodbye to the few souls I considered friends and thanked the cook for the combination birthday-going home cake she'd made for me. The only thing left to do was finish my letter to Claudia.

As usual, Nurse Bridger entered my room without knocking. "Mr. Wooten is downstairs, Miss Cooper."

"I'll be down when I finish this letter."

She frowned. "It's not polite to keep such a nice gentleman waiting."

"If I didn't know better, Nurse Bridger, I'd think that you have a crush on my stepfather."

"Don't try to be clever, Miss Cooper. You haven't the gift."

I smiled at my quick-witted adversary. Nurse Bridger and I'd begun our battle of wits the day I arrived. It was the only bright spot in my sixteen months of incarceration in this pristine purgatory. Early on, I'd noticed her discreet yet undeniable interest in Frank. She often lectured me on how fortunate I was to have such a devoted stepfather, yet failed to pity me for having a mother who never visited.

I couldn't resist one last jab. "Are you upset because I'm going home with Frank or because you're not?"

Nurse Bridger locked her arms across her chest. "You may be leaving us today, Miss Cooper, but I wouldn't be so flippant about it." She walked out into the hall before turning to face me. "Chances are, you'll be back."

"Never," I yelled and slammed the door. I willed my hands to stop shaking so I could finish my letter to Claudia.

Dear Claudia,

You'll be glad to hear I'm finally leaving this snake pit called Havenwood. I turned eighteen today and am now considered an adult. They can't keep me locked up anymore. I know you wouldn't approve, but I'm going home to Sugardale, even though Momma still lives there. Frank tried to talk me into going somewhere else. He's fearful of what seeing Momma will do to me. He's trying to protect me, but I must keep my pledge to care for Papa's home and garden. Momma always said Papa's death was mainly my fault. She could be right.

You must promise never to divulge the horrible things that have happened here. Nobody would believe it. They'd say I was crazy and the Pickers-in-white would lock me away again. Only you and I will ever know the truth. Can you live with that? I've managed to live with Donald's secret all these years, so I'll just add these to the pile. I must admit the load is getting heavy.

Frank is waiting. Goodbye for now.

Your best friend,

Becky Leigh Cooper

P.S. Is it possible to become the thing you hate?

CHAPTER 15

The squeak of the back door signaled Frank's return from work. He came into the dining room where I was setting the table for his evening meal.

"Is Helen gone?" he asked.

"Yes."

He sighed. "Thank God."

My feelings echoed his. Momma had left that morning to attend a weeklong Bible retreat in Memphis with ladies from the church. In truth, I think she wanted time away from us too. I'd been home from Havenwood for over a year and had yet to speak one word to the woman who, as far as I was concerned, had killed my baby. I did her laundry, cooked her meals, and cleaned up after her in silence. When she attempted to talk to me, I ignored her. I spent most of my time upstairs in my room, working in Papa's garden, or with Frank.

He wasn't much better company for Helen. Any conversation he had with her was polite, but short. Before he moved back in, Frank added a backyard staircase to the verandah making it possible for him and me to reach the second floor without going through the house. He moved his study up to Grandpa Eli's old bedroom and turned his downstairs office unto a bedroom for Momma. Frank informed her that the upstairs was off limits to her. The only real connection she had with him was their evening meal, which I served to them in the dining room. I ate alone in the kitchen.

It made Momma angry that I'd talk to Frank, but not to her. Once, when I refused to answer a question, she raised her hand to slap me. But I gave her a look that said if she struck me, it would be the last thing she ever did. She never raised her hand to me again.

It's strange how time switches things around. Now Momma was the one who needed to be on guard. She'd convinced the doctors I was crazy and should be locked away. If I killed her now, I'd have the perfect defense — insanity. She realized this and thus, kept her distance.

I'd thought of using Momma's fear of me as a tool to make her my Pick. Let her see how it felt to be constantly bullied and berated. Given time, I could become a champion Picker too. After all, I'd sat at the feet of the master for over nineteen years. But to be a Picker or a Pick, a person must care about something — something that could be lost. I'd already lost everything important to me. Johnny, my baby, any hope for the future. Momma called me the zombie. For once, she spoke the truth. The only thing that got me out of bed each morning and kept me sane was my pledge to care for Papa's home and garden. That and taking care of Frank.

After showering, Frank came into the kitchen, carrying his bowl and silverware. "Mind if I join you, Becky?"

"I don't mind." I put a placemat down opposite mine and he pulled out the chair and sat. "It was too hot to turn on the oven today. Hope you don't mind po-boy sandwiches and leftover soup."

Frank smiled. "Anything is fine with me."

Momma would've complained. She expected an entrée, two vegetables, bread, and dessert for supper. Anything less was an incomplete meal. But Frank was easy to please.

It would've been easy for Momma to have kept Frank's affection and thus, kept him in her bed. She'd predicted I'd come between them and her prediction came true. But even now, she couldn't see she'd been the one who put me there. Her need for control and her campaign to annihilate me ended up destroying the last fragments of her marriage to Frank.

We were three people alone, living in the same house, pretending to the world we were a family. Our life together was a sham, designed to keep the neighbors and our customers happy.

I stayed to care for Papa's house and garden. Frank stayed to look after me. Momma stayed because she'd rather live a lie than have her friends know the truth about her dead marriage.

"Watch out, Frank, this soup is hot." I filled his bowl.

He bent over the steaming mixture of potatoes and ham. "It smells delicious."

The heat from the soup caused the scent of his aftershave to waft upwards. The aroma of spice and musk filled my senses. Frank always smelled so good to me. I halved his sandwich, placed it and his favorite banana peppers on a plate, and poured two large glasses of ice tea. I added a slice of lemon to my drink and a slice of lime to his. Frank preferred limes.

He lifted the top of the po-boy roll to find slices of roast beef, sugar-cured ham, and smoked turkey topped with lettuce, tomato, and sweet purple onion. A honey-mustard dressing — Granny Cooper's secret recipe — coated the insides of the bun. He took a bite. "Delicious." He pushed a stray piece of lettuce back into his mouth.

I smiled. The only pleasures in my life came from working in the garden and finding ways to help Frank. He'd saved my life in more ways than one. Because of that and his never failing kindness to me, I desired to please him.

"Is that all you're going to eat?" he asked.

I'd allotted a small bowl of soup and half a sandwich for myself. "I'm not hungry."

Frank put down his sandwich and reached for my hand. "I wish you'd eat more."

"I made a lemonade pie for dessert. I'll have a piece later."

He nodded. Between bites, Frank told me about a combination hardware–nursery store for sale in Kirbyville. "It's a nice store, bigger than our store here. Lots of growth potential." He took a sip of tea. "The owner wants to retire and will help with the financing. Opportunities like this don't come along every day, Becky."

"How would you run two stores in two different towns?"

He wiped his mouth. "I've been thinking about that. I've got some ideas I'd like to discuss with you later."

"Okay."

After supper, Frank dried the dishes. I almost wished Momma could've been there to see it. She didn't believe in a man helping in the kitchen. According to her, that was woman's work. Of course, she was seldom the woman doing the work.

After the dishes were done, Frank asked me to wait in the living room while he retrieved some books from his truck. When he returned, he placed the books on the coffee table. "We'll get to these in a bit."

He sat down on a footstool beside my chair, wiped his palms on his jeans, and then rubbed the back of his neck. His nervousness amused me. He seemed more like a man trying to find the courage to propose marriage, than he did a man wanting to discuss a business venture. There was a boyish charm to his obvious discomfort.

Frank had the prettiest eyes I'd ever seen, and the sapphire-colored shirt he wore made his eyes seem even bluer. Black hair accented by a gentle wave and deeply tanned skin combined to complete a most attractive package.

He licked his lips, undid the top button of his shirt, and wiped his hands again. "Is it hot in here, Becky?"

"Very."

I turned on the ceiling fan while Frank opened the door so we could catch the evening breeze. We resettled ourselves and I waited for him to muster his courage.

He took hold of my hands. "Listen to everything I've got to say before you speak."

I nodded.

"I want to buy the store in Kirbyville."

"Okay, Frank, but how —"

"Please let me finish. I want to sell the Sugardale store and buy the one in Kirbyville."

I'd never thought about selling Papa's store. I pulled my hands from his.

"I've given this a lot of thought," he said. "There's a nice two bedroom apartment above the Kirbyville store. I want us to move there."

"What about Momma?"

"Helen can live here." Frank picked up the books he'd brought in. "These catalogs are from the Kirbyville Community College. You could go to school there."

Papa and I had talked about my going to college. "You'll be the first Cooper to be a college graduate," he'd promised. But that promise, along with his promise to take me to Paris, died when he was killed in a car accident in August of '63.

It had been a scorcher of a day. I'd begged Papa to go get Johnny and me some ice cream. Papa wanted to wait until we'd finished the weeding, but I'd pleaded until he finally gave in. A truck ran a stop sign and plowed into his car. Johnny and I heard the screeching of tires and the sound of metal on metal. We ran down the street to the accident. Papa was leaning against the steering wheel, the horn blaring, his face covered in a mixture of blood and Neapolitan ice cream. Johnny said I fainted. Momma said Papa's death was my fault because I'd pestered him into going for ice cream. I never ate another bite of ice cream.

At the hospital, I spoke with my father before he died. He made me promise to take care of his house and garden and reminded me that I was the last Cooper. A Cooper never breaks her word to another Cooper. That promise helped me survive Havenwood, but it tied me to Sugardale tighter than chains ever could.

Frank shoved the books into my lap.

"I can't go to college. I never finished high school."

He picked up a thick yellow book. "This book tells how to study for a GED test. If you pass the GED test this summer, they'll give you a high school diploma. Then you could start college in the fall."

"But what if I can't pass the test?"

Frank put his hand on my arm. "You'll pass, Becky. You're smart, and I'll help you study for it."

"Do you really think I'm smart?"

"You're the smartest, most hard-working woman I've ever known."

Woman. Frank had referred to me as a woman. I leaned forward and hugged him. "Thank you," I whispered.

He held me for a full minute before pulling back. "Then you'll go? You'll move with me to Kirbyville?"

"Momma couldn't take care of the house and garden. She doesn't know how."

"I don't care what Helen does. She can take care of herself or find some other sucker and get married again."

"You plan to divorce Momma?" The ugly thought of Papa's home left in my mother's hands or those of a stranger disturbed me greatly.

"You bet. Our marriage has been dead for years."

"I know, but . . ."

"But nothing, Becky. It's time to bury the dead and move on with our lives."

I stood and walked into the hallway, hoping to catch a breeze. Frank didn't know what he was asking of me. Maybe I was the one confused. "If we lived together, what would I do?"

Frank's eyes lit up. "You could do lots of things. Go to college, help at the store, learn to drive my truck."

The thought of Frank teaching me to drive his truck struck me funny. I laughed.

He grabbed me with both hands. "You laughed. You haven't laughed in years."

Frank was right. For the first time in over two years, I'd felt something deep enough to laugh about it. We hugged until it became embarrassing. As we untangled ourselves, I asked the question lingering in the back of my mind. "Frank, would we be...lovers?"

He staggered backwards, almost tripping over the footstool. "Why would you ask that?"

Fire rose in my cheeks, but I pushed on. "You're a man in his prime, and I know you're lonely. Momma says when a man takes care of a woman, he has a right to expect something in return."

Frank rubbed the back of his neck. "I want you to be happy, that's all. You don't owe me anything more."

Frank's declaration calmed my fears, but produced something akin to disappointment at the same time. "I'm not pretty enough for you?" Did those words come out of my mouth?

"You're beautiful, Becky. A man would be a fool not to want you." He brushed the back of his hand across my cheek

Blue eyes locked with green and held. For a moment, I thought Frank was going to kiss me. For a moment, I wanted him too.

He went into the kitchen and came back with two large glasses of ice water. He handed me one and drank the other in one continuous gulp. "We've never had that kind of relationship. I'm years older than you and I'm your stepfather to boot."

An audacious courage surged through me. "We've never looked upon each other as father and daughter, have we?"

He sat down on the coffee table. "No. I wanted to be a father to you, but I couldn't see you in that way."

"That's okay," I said, hating the quiver in my voice. "I never expected you to love me."

Frank's head jerked back. "I didn't say I didn't love you, Becky. I just couldn't see you as a daughter because you have old eyes."

"Old eyes?"

He motioned for me to sit down in front of him. "After April died of cancer, Donald and I were alone. It didn't seem like we were a family anymore and I missed that."

"I felt the same after Papa died."

Frank nodded. "I missed the sound of a woman's voice, the smell of perfume, the softness of a female's touch." He scooted closer to me. "When I married Helen, I hoped the four of us could become a family."

I looked at the floor. I'd done little to help make Frank's dream come true. My disdain for Donald had quickly blossomed into hate. But I had good reason to despise his son.

"When I saw you for the first time, Becky, I thought you were such a pretty little thing. I knew you'd have no trouble wrapping me around your fingers." Frank ran his palm across the back of my hand. "But when I looked into your green eyes, I didn't see a little girl. I saw eyes that looked so sad and full of pain that they looked like they belonged to someone who had lived a hard eighty years. That's why I could never think of you as a daughter. I couldn't get past your old eyes."

"I . . . I understand."

"Becky, I care about your happiness more than anything."

"And I care about you too. You're my only friend." I squeezed Frank's hand. "Where does this leave us?"

"In Kirbyville, I hope."

I walked out into the hall again. Crickets chirped their evening serenade. I felt Frank's eyes boring into my back. "I'm sorry, but I can't go with you."

He grabbed me and spun me around. "You have to go. I can't leave you with Helen."

"I promised to look after things here. I can't leave the care of Papa's garden to Momma. She'd destroy it just to torment me."

"Your father would've never asked you to stay if he'd known what terrible things she would do to you." Frank pulled me into his arms. "He'd want you to leave this place and go with me. I know he would."

I wanted to believe Frank. But just as he couldn't get past my old eyes, I couldn't find a way out of my pledge to Papa. "I don't want to lose you, Frank, but I won't leave my home." I pulled away, returned to the living room, sat down in Papa's recliner.

Frank stood in the doorway, his eyes filled with desperation. "If the only way to get you away from Helen is to sell this damn house, then that's what I'll do."

I jumped up. "You can't sell this house."

"Yes, I can. You begged me to blackmail Helen into signing both the store and house over to me. Remember? I did what you asked. Legally, I own this house."

"This is my house, mine and Papa's." I wrapped my arms around my waist, started to rock. "Why would you do this to me?"

"For your own good, Ladybug."

"I won't let you sell Papa's house." I lunged at Frank, but he was too quick.

He grabbed my hands, twirled me around, and locked his arms around my chest.

"Calm down, Becky."

I leaned back against his shoulder. "Please don't do this."

"Everything will be fine." Frank turned me around to face him. "I sprung this on you too fast. You just need time to think. Promise me you'll consider everything I've said."

"Okay." I did need time. Time to think of a way to get him to change his mind.

He held me for a couple of minutes before letting me go. "The geraniums need repotting. When I get back from the greenhouse, we'll have some pie." He kissed my forehead. "I can't go on living like we have been. It's too hard. Too lonely." He turned and headed outside.

I hated the loneliness as much as Frank did. Nevertheless, I knew I'd have to find a way to stop him from selling Papa's house.

CHAPTER 16

Frank had been in the greenhouse for three hours, long enough for me to devise a game plan. I reviewed the metamorphic changes taking place in me. There was only one way to get him to change his mind, only one way to keep Papa's home. I had to become a Picker and make Frank my Pick. For once in my life, I had to take control.

I'd manipulate him into doing my will just as Momma had manipulated Papa and me. The idea of my resorting to her conniving ways made me queasy, but what choice did I have? Frank seemed determined to save me despite my protest. Still, I vowed to be a nicer Picker to him than Momma had been to me.

Shouts, threats, and intimidation were her tools of the trade. My way would be kinder, gentler, and more effective. A grateful smile, a gentle touch, and a genuine sense of caring would bind a Pick closer than slaps, slurs, and screams ever could. A judicial use of my chosen arsenal mixed with a measured dose of sex would make Frank a most willing Pick.

My plan was simple, but brilliant. I would seduce Frank and then convince him he didn't want to sell Papa's house. That would be the easy part. He already cared for me and he was lonely. But to keep him in line, I needed a long-range plan. I decided to let Frank come to me on Fridays. He could touch me, taste me, and deposit his loneliness inside my broken womb. I wouldn't let him kiss me on the mouth however. That part of myself I'd hold in trust in case Johnny returned. Frank would want to kiss me full on the lips, and he'd want to come to me more than once a week. But in the end, he'd accept my terms. What choice would he have?

A box containing an emerald silk robe — a birthday gift from Frank — lay on my bed. It had a deep v-neck, long sleeves, and stopped three inches above my knees. The cuffs and neckline were accented with a soft French lace dyed to match. A detachable tie belt held the little robe together. Frank had given me the robe when I was in Havenwood. Tonight, I'd wear it for the first time. Hopefully, it'd make me more enticing to him. I'd use his gift to help make him my Pick. Momma would've loved the irony of it all.

Standing naked in front of the bathroom mirror, I checked my body for flaws. My breasts were a tad bit large in proportion to the rest of my body, but that could prove a plus in this case.

After showering and washing my hair, I slipped the silk robe on without drying off first. The dampness of my skin helped bind the cloth closer to my form. My long auburn hair contrasted nicely with the green. I pulled a few strands over my shoulders, let them fall across my breasts, and watched the outline of my bosom grow more distinct.

The back door slammed shut. I nervously counted Frank's footsteps as he climbed the stairs. He'd have to pass the bathroom to get to his bedroom. With precise timing, I opened the bathroom door and ran smack into him.

"Watch out there, Becky."

"Sorry. I didn't hear you come in. Did you get the geraniums repotted?" I took two steps back to allow him a better view.

"Most of them. I've still . . . still got . . ."

Frank's sudden stuttering indicated he'd definitely noticed me.

I locked my arms behind my back, forcing my breasts to push up and out. "You've still got what?"

"I've still got a dozen left to do, but I'll finish them tomorrow."

I smiled. "And I'll help you."

"You took a shower," he said, stating the obvious.

"It's so hot. I thought a shower would cool me off." I turned sideways to allow his roving eyes to take in my profile. "I saved some hot water so you could shower too."

"That's a good idea. Isn't that the robe I bought you?"

"Sure is." I ran my hand down the sleeve. "It's so soft and cool. Feel how cool it is."

He reached out to touch my sleeve, but I grabbed his hand, and placed it on my shoulder. "Feel here, Frank. Even the lace is soft." I rubbed his hand back and forth from my shoulder to the top of my breast. "It feels good, doesn't it?"

He nodded and I released his hand. He hesitated a moment before removing it.

I pranced out into the middle of the wide hallway, held out the bottom of my robe, and twirled in a slow circle. "How does it fit?"

"It fits fine, Becky." His eyes focused on my face, then drifted slowly downward.

"You've got a good eye." I ran to him, threw my arms around his neck, and kissed his cheek. "It's the nicest present I ever got." I hugged him tight, letting the dampness of my body seep into his shirt.

Frank stiffened, relaxed, and then slid his arms around my waist.

"I can't imagine my life without you," I whispered.

He pulled me tighter against him.

We held each other a long time, saying nothing, soaking in the warmth of another human's touch. I don't think he realized his right hand had slipped down to rest on my hips. If I kissed him full on the lips now, I'd have my Pick. But I couldn't do it. I'd never kissed any man on the lips except Johnny.

"Why don't you take your shower now, Frank?"

"Yeah ... sure," he said, his voice deep and wavering. He broke his hold and pulled back. "What are you going to do?"

"I'm going to cut us a piece of pie." I reached up and tweaked his nose in an effort to dispel the awkwardness of the moment.

Frank laughed, pivoted and headed for the bathroom. We traded smiles as he closed the door.

*****

The shower was still going when I returned. Slipping into Frank's bedroom, I opened the windows, turned the candlestick lamp next to his bed on low, and flipped on the small oscillating fan sitting on the walnut dresser. A ladderback chair set sandwiched between the dresser and its matching chest-of-drawers. I parked myself in it and waited.

The door between Frank's bedroom and the bathroom opened. He switched off the bathroom light, strode into his room wearing only a towel tied around his waist. He was busy brushing his wet hair and walked right past me.

"Here's your pie, Frank."

The man jumped four inches. "Damn, you scared me. What are you doing here?"

I crossed my legs. "I brought your pie, silly."

His attention went to my legs. "I thought we'd... we'd meet downstairs."

I uncrossed my legs, got up slowly, and walked over to him. "Taste this." I shoved a forkful of pie into his mouth.

He swallowed. "Great, but Becky, you shouldn't —"

"Lemonade pie tastes better after it sets a spell, don't you agree?" I offered him more.

He accepted another bite and nodded.

I took a small taste. "I cut a big piece so we could share. Do you mind?"

"That's fine. Why don't you get us some milk while I get dressed?"

"Okay, but I want to talk to you first." I laid the saucer of pie on the dresser, took Frank's hand, and led him to the padded cedar chest at the foot of the bed. "Sit down, please."

"Let's talk downstairs. First, I need to get dressed."

"And I need to say this now. I've seen you in a towel before, Frank."

He hesitated and then sat.

I retrieved the chair from the corner and placed it directly in front of him. "Please listen carefully and don't speak until I finish."

"Okay."

I sucked in a deep breath and blew it out. The fate of Papa's house depended on my next words. Tonight, I'd find out if I'd inherited any of

Momma's picker abilities. I handed Frank a photograph. "Do you remember this?"

He studied the picture. "Yes, it's the picture I tore the day you claimed Donald . . . the day Helen fired Anna Santo."

"Yes," I said, relieved he'd decided not to interject Donald into our conversation. "Momma tore up all my pictures of Johnny that day. This one was taken the day Grandpa Eli, Papa, Johnny, and I won the blue ribbon for our roses at the state fair. You stopped Momma from ripping it up. Do you remember?"

"Yes. I tore Johnny's picture off."

"But you saved most of it for me."

"It seemed important to you."

"It was." I pointed to my image. "When you split the picture, you tore my image in half."

He handed me the photo. "I'm sorry."

"If you sell this house, you'll be tearing me in half for real."

"I know you love this house, but it's not good for you here. You deserve more of a life than this."

"We both deserve more of a life, and I've come up with a plan that gives us everything we want."

"What kind of plan?"

I'd watched Momma play Papa enough times to know a champion Picker starts by giving her Pick a compliment. Then, she sprinkles in some guilt before going for the kill.

"You've worked hard building up our business, Frank. I hate to see you lose it."

"I wouldn't be losing it, I'd be selling it."

"Can you put a dollar amount on all the time and energy you've put into the store?"

"Probably not, but the Kirbyville store is a great deal."

"And we shouldn't pass it up. We should buy it."

Frank shook his head. "I can't have both stores."

"We can if you'll listen to me." Frank looked at me as if I'd lost my mind, but I pushed on. "Instead of expanding the Sugardale store as we've been planning to do, we use that money as a down payment on the store in Kirbyville. The present owner can carry the note for the rest."

"I can't be in two places at the same time, Becky."

"You don't have to. Gordon Zagat does a good job managing the store when you're out of town, doesn't he?"

"Gordon does a great job."

"Doesn't the Kirbyville store have a manager?"

"The owner says Neil Abbott is an excellent manager."

"There's our answer. We hire excellent managers and divide our time overseeing both stores. It's only an hour's drive to Kirbyville. It's a good plan, isn't it?"

He stroked the side of his face. "That might work."

"It will work." I reached for his hand. "I haven't been much help to you since I returned from Havenwood, have I?"

"Yes, you have, but I wish you'd get out more. It'd do you good to mix with people again."

"You're right. I just needed this past year and a half to get myself together. You can't imagine how horrible that place was."

Frank squeezed my hand. "I'll never forgive myself for letting them put you there."

"It doesn't matter now. That nightmare is over and I'm ready to take my place beside you. Let's buy the other store. With the help of two good managers, we could make Cooper's Hardware and Garden better than ever."

He grinned. "We could, couldn't we?"

"Yes, and we could still live here."

Frank went to stand near the window. "It's a good plan, business wise, but I can't stay in this house any longer. And I can't leave you alone with Helen."

"Why do you suddenly hate Papa's house so much?"

"I don't hate this house. It's a great house, but we need to get on with our lives. We can't do that living here."

I went to Frank. "You haven't heard the best part of my plan yet. Please let me finish before you rip out my heart."

"I don't want to hurt you, but my mind is made up about getting us out of here."

"Listen to the rest of my plan." I placed my hands on his bare chest. "The problem isn't this house or Momma. The problem is the twelve feet."

"The twelve feet? What are you talking about?"

I took a deep breath, rallied my Picker strength, and made Frank an offer I hoped he couldn't refuse. "The twelve foot hallway that separates our bedrooms."

Frank retreated backwards. "I don't know what you mean."

"You're right when you say we need to get on with our lives. We need to get on with our lives together."

"You're talking crazy, Becky. Hell, I'm still legally married to your mother. She sleeps right downstairs."

"And she's been sleeping downstairs for years. As you said, your marriage to her has been plumb dead for ages. We all know that, including Momma."

"Even so, your mother —"

"Momma goes to Monsieur Henri's three times a week. Do you really think it's only her hair that's getting done?"

"You mean Helen and Henry Nash have something going on?"

"Sure, and he's not the only lover she's had. I can't believe this comes as a surprise."

Frank rubbed the back of his neck. "Henry is, but I knew long ago Helen was running around on me. I chose to ignore it. I guess the whole county has been laughing at me for years."

"Momma's always discreet. She picks men who have more to lose than she does if the word gets out. That's how she controls them."

Frank didn't speak. Could he have another reason for wanting to divorce Momma and leave Sugardale?

"Are you seeing someone, Frank?"

"No ... not anymore. When I was living at the store, Agnes Shaver stopped by a few times after she got her divorce. Helen and I hadn't shared a bed in over a year. I just wanted someone to talk to, but one thing led to another."

"Is that why she quit and moved to Valdosta?"

"No. Her brother offered her a better job." Frank leaned back against the windowsill. "It didn't mean anything to either one of us. We were just lonely."

"I'm glad to hear that because I know in my heart that you and I were fated to be more than stepfather and stepdaughter. You know that too. Don't you?"

Frank stared at me, but didn't deny my words. "You're nineteen and I'm . . . old."

"I'm going on twenty, and all the girls I went to school with are either married or engaged. Many of them are pregnant or have kids already. And you're not old. You're just experienced. Besides, I look at you through old eyes, remember?" I moved closer to him. "I like what I see very much."

Surprise washed over his face.

Desperation breeds boldness. I backed up a few feet, summoned all my courage, and slipped off my robe. "Do you like what you see?"

His gaze wandered from my face to my feet and back up again, making strategic stops along the way. "This won't work."

"Yes, it will. We can buy the Kirbyville business. I can take classes at the college and help at the store. We'll still have this house, and the city apartment will be our special place." I moved toward him. "We can have it all."

"Kirbyville is hardly a city," he said as his eyes focused on my breasts.

I laughed. "It's bigger than Sugardale." I ran the back of my hand down the side of his face.

"Together, we can have it all, and we'll never be lonely again."

Frank swallowed twice. "Put on your robe, Becky, before things go too far."

I stepped close enough to feel his breath on my skin. "It's your decision. If you want to split us up and break my heart in the process, then put this robe back on me." I handed him the green silk. "I'll go back across the hall and never bother you again."

Frank ran his tongue over his lips. He reminded me of a hungry kid in a candy shop trying to decide what to sample first.

I slid my arms around his neck and nibbled on his earlobe. His hands found the small of my back. The heat of his rising desire warmed me through the towel. I planted short, eager kisses on his neck and whispered, "Make me happy, Frank. Make us both happy. Love me . . . please."

CHAPTER 17

Frank made a hard thrust deep inside of me. With that thrust, he finished with me, but didn't move. He relaxed his arms causing my 114 pounds to have to bear more of his weight. I could feel his heart lying on top of mine, beating in syncopated rhythm with his pulsating manhood as it spewed his seeds across the barren wasteland where Johnny's child once lay growing.

Finally, Frank rolled to my side. He kissed my neck, ran his hand across my chest, down my stomach to my knees, then back up as if checking for damage. Did he think he'd broken me somehow? He pulled me close. His arm became my pillow. A kiss on my cheek and a lazy smile showed his satisfaction with me for a job well done.

Frank looked at me with eyes bright, but tender. I knew the gleam in his eyes stemmed as much from gratitude as it did from sated desire. By giving him a chance to save me from more unhappiness, I'd given him a chance to be my hero. A long-buried truth brought to life in one of Grandpa Eli's lesson-stories floated across my mind.

Grandpa had once said, "If a woman makes a man feel like her hero, he'll move heaven and hell to please her."

As I watched Frank dozing, I vowed to take Grandpa's words to heart. I'd make Frank my hero, my hero Pick. In time, he'd give me Papa's house. Then no one could ever take it away.

Perhaps the best gift I'd given Frank was the opportunity for his own redemption. He'd been trying to save me for years. Trying and failing. He'd failed to save me from Momma's beatings, failed to protect my baby, and failed to keep me out of Havenwood. My deep sadness wounded him greatly. Now, he'd found a way to make us both happy.

Frank rested only minutes before reaching for me again. His left hand wandered up and down my body. Gentle, but calloused fingers traced the invisible trail of cool air emanating from the oscillating fan. The fan sucked in air tinged with the fragrance of the yellow jasmine bushes that danced beneath the bedroom window.

It wasn't the fault of the little fan that it failed to cool my warm body or Frank's hot passions. Indeed, the gentle machine put forth a most valiant effort. But skin rhythmically moving across other skin produces friction, and friction produces heat.

Frank eased inside of me again. This time, his thrusts were more controlled. He stoked the fire between us, letting it rise and fall with the exuberance of a refinery flare. In the final moments of our primal exchange his labors were so intense, I feared he might spontaneously combust, incinerating us both.

Momma would come home from her Bible retreat and find only the ashes of two people lying on Frank's bed. Surprisingly, that thought held some appeal to me. She'd always wanted matching urns to put on the fireplace mantel. Now, she'd have something to put in them. My ashes in one and Frank's in the other. But I quickly dismissed the fantasy. After all, who would take care of Papa's garden if both Frank and I were decorating Momma's mantel?

*****

It was almost midnight when I stepped into the front of the claw foot tub. Frank had suggested we take a shower together. I didn't see the danger at the time and agreed. But as he stepped in behind me, a tremor washed over me. I suddenly realized it was one thing to share a man's bed, but quite another to share his bath.

In the bedroom, the light had been muted and had conspired with me to obscure my real intent from Frank. The bright, artificial glare of the coverless bathroom lights would show me no such mercy. It wasn't my body I feared showing him, but rather, my face. Facial expressions had been known to betray a person's true feelings, and I was just a novice Picker.

As the warm water sprinkled down on me, my tensions trickled down the dark drain along with the sweat and physical remains of our earlier joinings. Frank stood behind me, massaging my scalp and neck. He continued down my back, massaging, then washing, then massaging again.

"Close your eyes and lean your head back," he said. His fingers crept through my hair as he continued his mission of washing then rinsing. "You can open your eyes now, Becky." Frank spun me around and lifted my chin. "Is it okay?"

My pulse quickened. In this room the last thing I wanted was direct eye contact with Frank.

Until tonight, this bathroom had provided me the sanctuary that can only be found in a room that has a door that has a lock. This was where I'd run to in a naive attempt to feel clean again the day Donald's sin ripped through my body and killed my innocence. This was also where I'd cried for my lost, yet still beloved, Johnny. And this room, with its cold, cracked linoleum floor, was where I often came at night, to hold myself and rock, and grieve for my dead unborn and all the babies that would never grow inside of me.

In this room, there was only the truth. If Frank looked into my eyes now, he would see my deceit. He'd know I seduced him not out of love, but out of a desperate desire to make him my Pick so I could get Papa's house.

"Becky, did you hear me?" Frank asked. "Is the water temperature okay?"

"It's fine." I looked out the small window above the tub. My eyes moved past the gravel driveway to a group of mimosa trees lining the western border of our property. Their feathery limbs silhouetted against a moonlit sky swayed in the wind. They reminded me of marionettes on stilts, shooing away demons or signaling a warning no one would heed.

"Now the front," he said.

Frank's words brought my attention back to his hands. He scrubbed the bar of soap back and forth across the washrag, looked at me and grinned. The soapsuds grew until he seemed satisfied. "Okay, honey, where do you want me to start?"

I held out my hand. "I can wash myself."

He laughed. "Yeah, but where's the fun in that?" He rubbed the cloth across my left shoulder. "Might as well start at the top."

I turned my attention back to the window. As Frank moved the washcloth across my shoulder, I concentrated on making my mind a blank. I'd almost succeeded when his hand moved to my breast. He moved the lathered cloth in circles starting from the outside and creeping toward my nipple. He finished with the left breast, then moved to the right.

My stomach felt as if I'd swallowed a dozen moths and they were frantically seeking their freedom. My eyes darted across the blank wall above the window trying to find anything that would take my attention off Frank's hands as he moved the cloth across my stomach and down my legs.

At the top left corner of the window there was a crack. It started at the header and moved up the wall, throwing off smaller cracks in its wake. An army of nails had tried to force the wall to stand at attention. But with the passage of time and the erosion of the foundation beneath it, the sheetrock cracked and settled wherever it could find support. The wall, once so fresh, pristine, and strong, was ugly now.

My eyes drifted back to the window. A white curtain rod ran its entire width. It hung there, serving no purpose, providing no protection from prying eyes. It simply waited for someone to hang a nice curtain on it so it could be pretty again. So it could complete the destiny for which it was created. For years, the rusting little rod had been waiting for someone to come along who would recognize its potential.

Everything in my life was cracked and broken. Like the little rod, I too had been waiting for someone to make me feel pretty and useful again. I'd been waiting for someone to rescue me. Frank had to be my savior. There was no one else.

He slipped the cloth between my legs. I gasped and tilted back on my heels. He guided my hands to his shoulders. "Hold on to me, Becky. I won't let you fall."

He pulled me into his chest. My arms pushed up around his neck. While his left hand burrowed deeper between my thighs, his right explored my back and hips.

"Stop, Frank," I whispered, but he didn't hear me. "Frank . . . stop."

He stepped back, his face clouded with confusion. "Don't you like my bathing you?"

"Sure," I said, while avoiding his eyes. "But the hot water will be gone soon and you haven't washed."

He smiled. "Turnabout is fair play."

Droplets of water ricocheted off my skin and onto his. I realized my Pick expected me to bathe him.

"We'd better rinse you off first." Frank twirled me around, pushed me under the spray.

As his hands doused me with lukewarm water, my mind scrambled to find a way out of my impending task.

He guided my hands to the chrome, added-on rod that carried water from the spout of the old tub up to a showerhead bolted into the wall. "Hold on here, Becky."

I gripped the pipe with both hands. The bottom of the tub was slippery, but I wasn't afraid of falling. Frank was behind me. He'd catch me.

"My first wife was sick for a long time," Frank said as he ran his hands up and down my arms. "We liked to take baths together, but long baths left April feeling weak. So we switched to showers."

When I was nine, Momma insisted I take classes at Miss Tilton's School of Proper Etiquette. Miss Tilton guaranteed any graduate of her school would always know the proper thing to say under any circumstances. But here I was, standing naked in a shower with a man intent on reminiscing about the bathing habits of his late wife, and I couldn't think of a word to say. Momma should ask for a refund.

"I think that'll do it," Frank said. "Now you can wash me."

Having failed to come up with a good excuse not to take my turn as washer, I shrugged and said, "Okay." Maybe it wouldn't be as brazen an act as it seemed. After all, we were lovers now. Might as well practice playing the part.

I squeezed the soap too hard causing it to slide out of my hand and drop between my feet. As I bent to retrieve it, my hips brushed against Frank's groin. A kaleidoscope of shadowed faces — Donald's and the Pickers-in-white — exploded inside my brain. I screamed, shoved Frank down, and fell out of the tub.

He tried to stand, but slipped and fell again. "What the hell is the matter?" he shouted as he finally got his feet under him.

I crawled across the floor, snatched up my robe, and slipped it over my wet body.

Frank stepped out of the tub and headed for me.

"Don't," I yelled and waved him away.

But he didn't stop. Instead, he helped me up. "What's wrong, Becky?"

"Nothing. Go away." I recognized the look of bewilderment in his eyes and the confusion in his voice. It was the same look and sound that came from me whenever Momma whipped me for no other reason than because she could.

"Why you're shaking like a bird lost in a hurricane. What did I do wrong?" he asked.

"Nothing's wrong. I just . . . wanted... a cup of tea."

Frank took my face in his hands. "No one screams like that because they want tea." He studied me for a moment. "Hell, I forgot you've had no experience with men."

I pulled away. "Yes, I have. I was married once. Johnny and I were married, no matter what Momma says."

"A two day, common-law marriage hardly qualifies you as being experienced."

"Don't forget about Donald." The words slipped out before I realized it.

Frank stepped back. His breathing deepened. "You said he . . . didn't rape you."

I headed for the door.

"You said Donald's roughhousing scared you. You told us —"

"I told you and Momma what you wanted to hear." I turned to face him. "But you knew the truth, Frank. You knew Donald raped me."

The hiss of the shower filled the white room. For the first time in almost seven years, I'd repeated my accusation. Now the word hung there between us, spinning on some invisible thread, spinning a web of truth around Frank from which he couldn't escape.

"I'm going to make some tea. Do you want some?" I asked.

He didn't answer. He stood trapped by the bonds of one little word — raped.

At the bottom of the stairs, I glanced back. Frank stood at the top of the landing. Water dripped from his body onto the floral carpet runner that accented the staircase. For the first time, I allowed my eyes to take in all of his nakedness.

I thought such a sight would embarrass me. Instead, a strange warmth seeped through me as I stared at the forty-year-old man standing there in the only suit God ever gave him. Hard work and daily exposure to the Georgia sun had left him trim, tanned, and tempting fodder for any woman who had a certain hunger, the one polite society insisted she deny or risk being labeled tramp or whore.

Momma's friends used to tease her about how young Frank looked. He could pass for thirty, while Momma's face owned every one of her thirty-seven years. I now understood why our female customers always wanted Frank to wait on them and tended to buy more hardware supplies than they'd ever use. I felt a twinge of jealousy.

My words had slashed Frank's heart. I regretted leaving him for I knew how deep a cut could run when you're alone. I started up the stairs. He turned and walked away. The bathroom door slammed. I didn't follow.

*****

I filled the kettle with water, set it on the stove, but didn't turn on the gas. Instead, I walked out onto the back porch and sat down in Grandpa Eli's old rocking chair. Momma had made the job of being a Picker look so easy. I leaned back, closed my eyes, and rocked.

"You shouldn't be in the night air with your hair wet, Ladybug."

I smiled, but didn't open my eyes. Frank had called me by his pet name for me. He couldn't be too mad.

"Tell me what happened that day," he said.

I stopped my rocking and looked up. The darkness of the porch hid his face from me. "Trust me. You don't want to know."

He got down on his knees in front of me. "I have to understand how my son could do something so vile."

"Hearing the details won't explain why Donald raped me." I tried to kiss Frank's forehead, but he pulled away.

He stood with his back to me, his arms wrapped around a porch column. I didn't have to ask him what he was feeling. I knew the thoughts bombarding his heart and mind because I'd spent many evenings hugging that same post. He was trying to hold on to his sanity, praying for this to be a nightmare, and hoping he'd wake up soon.

Which Frank should I answer? Frank, the friend? Frank, the lover? Or Frank, the Pick? The Pick I needed in order to keep my home. If my words cut too deep, he might leave. Picks had been known to revolt. Some Picks get so numb, they can no longer feel the needles their Picker sticks into them. Such Picks are useless to themselves, to others, and to their Master Picker. Since my return from Havenwood, I'd become such a Pick.

I went inside, turned on the burner beneath the kettle, and set out two mugs with teabags. I played with my teabag, dunking it up and down as if the hot water was already present. The screen door slammed. Frank sat down opposite me. The whistle of the kettle stopped my game. I filled our cups and dunked the little bag for real. Frank didn't move.

"Now, Becky," he said. "Tell me now."

"It'll only hurt you."

He jumped up, stepped to the back door, and slammed his fist against the doorframe. Blood ran down his arm.

I snatched up a kitchen towel and tried to wrap his hand, but he pulled it away.

"I asked Donald if he raped you. He denied it repeatedly. I swear to you, I didn't know." Frank slid to his knees in front of me. "Can you forgive me?"

He wrapped his arms around my waist just as I had wrapped mine around Anna's. She hadn't been able to save me from Momma that day in '63. Now years later, I couldn't save Frank from the truth about that damn day either. And I couldn't forget Momma's prophetic words.

The day after the rape, after Frank left for work, Momma warned me never to say anything against my new stepbrother. "If Frank leaves me because of what you said about Donald, I'll kill you, Becky Leigh."

That was the first time my mother had actually threatened to end my life. Even so, it was her threats against Johnny that scared me the most.

"Keep your mouth shut and those skinny legs of yours together because I ain't having any half-breed Mexican brats running around here," she'd warned. "I know plenty of fellows who'd kill that boy if I asked them to real nice."

I never took her threats lightly. But even though I'd kept my silence, Momma still almost managed to kill us. She got Johnny sent to Vietnam, and she let that butcher dentist cut on me. She made good on her threat to kill our baby.

I'd never mentioned the rape again until tonight. In the beginning, I'd understood why Frank didn't believe me. We hardly knew each other then. But after all we'd been through together, I'd come to think that he must have realized the truth by now. Granted, my belief wasn't based upon logic. It was simply my deep-seated need to have someone I loved and trusted believe in me.

An irrational sense of betrayal seized me as I looked down at the man who'd both saved and betrayed me. Should I forgive him for not believing me? Could I forgive him? I patted his head. "Everything's okay, Frank." Lying kept getting easier for me.

I pulled away, went into the living room, and turned the television on then off. A half-empty pack of cigarettes lay on the end table by Momma's chair. I picked it up.

"Put those nasty things down, Becky."

I threw the pack at Frank. "Watch out. You're beginning to sound like Momma."

"That's not funny." He crumpled up the pack and tossed it on the end table. "I know you're upset. You have a right to be angry."

"Gee, thanks. Thanks for granting me the right to be angry because your son raped me."

Frank rubbed the back of his neck. "It's late, let's finish this tomorrow."

"We'll finish it now," I yelled. "One way or another, we'll finish this tonight."

"Calm down, Becky."

"Don't tell me to calm down. I hate that."

He threw up his hands. "I don't know what you want from me. I know you want this house, but I still believe getting you away from here would be the best thing to do."

"You're trying to save me again. Every time you do, I end up having to forgive you for something."

Frank shook his head. "All the lies and the pain. How can we ever get past them?"

"We get past them by taking one last hard look at everything. All the painful secrets come out tonight. Then we put them behind us and go on with our plan."

He stared at me, his blue eyes wide and questioning. "Where do we start?"

"You once asked me what happened at Havenwood. Now, you've asked me about Donald. I'm ready to tell you if you still what to know."

He hesitated for a moment, then said "I need to know . . . right?"

"Yes. But the truth isn't pretty." I walked over to him. "Do you think you're up to it?"

CHAPTER 18

I reached behind my chest-of-drawers, retrieved my journal, went back downstairs, and handed it to Frank. "Everything you need to know starts on page thirty-two."

He stared at the notebook for a couple of minutes then handed it back to me. "I can't read it, Becky. I'm sorry."

"If I can live through it, dammit, you can read about it." I pushed the journal into his hands and sat down in front of him. "Start with the letter to Claudia."

"Who's Claudia?"

"An imaginary friend from when I was a kid. I'll tell you about her some other time."

Frank nodded. He turned to page thirty-two, paused a moment, then began to read.

Dear Claudia,

You'll be heartbroken to hear Momma pushed me into a bottomless pit called Havenwood. She told the doctors I'd killed my baby and had tried to kill myself. They chose to believe her lies instead of my truth. I wasn't surprised. After all, Momma is a champion Picker.

One night, two Pickers dressed in white came into my room. I tried to fight them, but they knew Donald's tricks. A Pick turned on her stomach cannot see her enemy. She can't strike the Picker, whose hands bear down on her back, pushing her down so that the only thing that hears her scream is her own bed. A bed has no mouth to tell. It has no arms to slap the Pickers away. After awhile, I gave up the fight and accepted my place

as their Pick. Then they rolled me over and began
again. They told me I was lucky because they could
have their choice of Picks in this house of Hell. I
would've gladly passed the honor to someone else
if I could've.

In time, the Pickers-in-white grew weary of
me. There were new faces on the floor and fresh
meat to be explored. Thus, they moved on. But I
knew that in another room, a fresh Pick lay on her
stomach, her cries for help muffled by her own bed
linens. But I remained silent and continued my
quest to be invisible, lest the Pickers notice me
again. I never talked about my role as their Pick.
Not to others. Not to Frank. Not even to my own
self, except in the dreams and screams that came
when I slept.

Like Momma, the Pickers-in-white were
champions. And like her, they left me with nothing.
Not my pride. Not my sanity. Not even the ability to
mourn for my dead child. For I was numb. I could
no longer see the stars in the night sky or hear the
whistle of the wind or feel the beating of my own
heart.

Frank laid the journal on the coffee table,
rested his elbows on his knees. "Now I know why
you screamed in the shower. I remind you of
Donald and the others."

"No, you don't. It's just that when my hips
brushed up against you that way, I saw their faces.
For a moment, I was back in Havenwood."

Frank covered his face with his hands.
Tears slipped through his fingers and fell on my
book. He had denied the truth about Donald, and
for that he was paying a high price. Truth denied

and then acknowledged is twice as bitter, twice as cruel.

I forced Frank to look at me. "When I look at you, I see a good man, a true friend, and a most welcomed lover." I wiped his tears away with the arm cover of Momma's new davenport. "Turn the page and read on."

He shook his head. "I can't bear to read anymore about how they hurt you, especially since I did nothing to stop it."

"You didn't know what was going on and I couldn't tell you. I was too ashamed and too afraid." The logic of my explanation wasn't enough to ease his pain and guilt. I picked up the journal, turned the page, and began to read out loud.

Dear Claudia,

You'll be distressed to hear that no one tried to save me. Not the doctors. Not the nurses. Not even the one who mopped the floors. In all fairness, I must admit I was beyond their reach.

Johnny didn't come. Momma didn't come. No one came for me except Frank, and I was beyond his reach too. But unlike the others, he would not give up. He didn't ask me to tell him what he needed to do. For Frank saw that I hadn't the strength to help him help me. He spent his time, his money, and his mind trying to find a way to reach me in the dark pit that had swallowed me. Like Grandpa Eli, Frank knew that there wasn't much difference between a pit and a grave. He knew if he couldn't pull me out of the pit, it would indeed become my grave.

In the fall of the year after the murder of my unborn child — for that is how I now divide time — Frank brought me the only thing that could possibly save me. He brought me one of Papa's roses. Not just the stems, but the whole bush. Like me, the bush was ugly. Like me, it was wounded. And like me, that bush — which had been so tenderly planted in life by Papa — was dying. Somehow, Frank realized that if I could save Papa's rosebush, then maybe I could save myself.

Frank helped me when no one else would or could help me. Together, we saved Papa's rosebush and in doing so, we saved me. Perhaps we even saved Frank, for Momma's deceit and his role — however unwittingly played — in causing my dilemma had bludgeoned his soul. Frank and I were victims together. We were Momma's Picks and wounded souls together. And it was together, we saved ourselves.

I closed the journal, laid it on the coffee table, and held out my arms to Frank. He pulled me to his chest. I'd shared the truth with him and he'd finally believed it. I'd told him about Picks and Pickers, but he hadn't seen them in himself or in me. Even now, Frank couldn't discern my transformation from Pick to Picker. He didn't realize I was slowly molding him to be my Pick. We often see the sins in others, but fail to acknowledge those same sins in ourselves or in our loved ones.

He took hold of my hands. "What do you want me to do, Becky?"

I'd waited all evening to hear those words. Now, hopefully, we could stop looking backwards and start our journey forward together. Only this time, I'd be the one who'd control our destiny.

"I want us to live in Papa's house and have both stores. You can have everything, Frank, including me."

He showered my hands with kisses. When he tried to kiss my lips, I jerked my head back.

"Why won't you let me kiss you?" Frank asked.

"You can kiss me, but not on the lips."

"That's the best place, Honey."

"I disagree." I moved over to sit by him on the sofa.

"But why not, Becky?"

"When I was in Havenwood, the nurses told us kissing on the lips spread germs."

"I'm willing to risk a few germs," he said.

"Maybe, but I'm not." Frank would require additional details or he'd continue his quest to kiss me on the mouth. "When you're told something enough times, a part of you starts to believe it. It doesn't matter if it's true or not, it only matters that you believe it." I stroked his cheek. "I'll make it up to you. I promise."

I placed a throw pillow behind my neck and leaned back on Momma's new davenport. The day it came, she informed me I wasn't allowed to sit on it because I might soil it with dirt from the garden. I ran my hand over the blue velvet upholstery. "What do you think of Momma's new sofa?"

"It's too damn expensive."

I snickered. "Well, it's only money. Your money."

"Our money," Frank said. "From now on, everything is ours."

Frank's words delighted me. My Pick was coming along nicely. To reward him, I eased my foot inside his open robe and began to rub his bare chest.

"I believe, Becky, you made me a promise a moment ago. Something about kissing."

"I always keep my promises."

Frank leaned forward. Hope had replaced the sadness in his eyes. "What do you promise me? If I give you the house, my heart, and everything else, what will you give me?"

"I promise to make you happy and to make sure you're never lonely again." I untied his robe, pushed it back, ran my hands over his shoulders. I didn't pledge undying love because I didn't think our situation required it on my part. "And I promise you one more thing, Frank."

"What?" he asked, powerless to mask the eagerness in his voice.

I untied the belt on my robe, taking my sweet time to allow him the opportunity to enjoy his anticipation of things to come. I slipped off the silk wrapping to reveal my gift to him, "There are a lot better places to kiss me than on my lips."

He cupped a breast in each hand. "I think you may be right."

I smoothed back his hair. "Sure, I'm right. I'm always right." Even though I wasn't proficient in the art of being a Picker, I knew one thing for certain. The primary lesson a Pick must learn is that his Master Picker is always right. This strict rule is the cornerstone of the Picker-Pick relationship. I made a mental note to subtly remind Frank of this rule at opportune times during the next few days. After all, that is how Picks and children learn, by having a Picker repeatedly tell them who and what they are.

I tried to imagine Momma's reaction when she returned home and learned I'd seduced Frank. The role of Picker was definitely more pleasant than that of Pick. I sighed and patted him on his head.

Suddenly, my body began to shake. Was it my vision of Momma or convulsions causing tremors to wash over my entire physical being? Neither. My trembling stemmed from the fact that Frank's hot mouth and curious tongue had reached their final destination. In years past when he and Momma still shared a bed, I'd often hear strange sounds coming from their room. Now, I knew why.

I struggled to keep my mind on Picker business while my body continued its involuntary response to Frank's extraordinary maneuvers. A Picker-in-training must remember that everything moves forward for the advancement of one major goal. My goal was to own Papa's house. So, I had to decide how much of myself to give to my new Pick.

Earlier, I'd thought about limiting our physical mergers to Friday nights, thus reducing the possibility of his growing tired of me. But in light of present happenings, I decided to make myself available to Frank as often as he desired. In all probability, that would involve a lot of time and considerable sacrifice on my part. But I needed to bind him so close to me that nothing could rip him out of my grasp.

Frank must become addicted to me. I'd heard of numerous twelve-step programs where addicts could get help fighting their particular addictions. But I knew of no plan that specialized in stopping a man from desiring a willing female, even if she was a Picker.

If I had to make the sacrifice of offering my body for tantalization and exploration by Frank's eager mouth and experienced hands, then so be it. In doing so, I'd advance my goal of gaining control of my Pick.

Even right now, as Frank and I christened Momma's new, blue velvet davenport, my body seemed impatient for that most intimate joining which, with any luck, would soon follow. Perhaps, Frank wasn't the only hungry child in that candy shop.

CHAPTER 19

Frank closed the deal on the Kirbyville store the day before Momma returned home. She liked the idea of owning two stores until Frank informed her he'd cancelled her credit at her favorite dress shop and had limited the amount she could charge at other local businesses. With great patience, he explained the necessity of putting most of the profits back into the stores so we could build up inventory and pay down debts. He gave her an allowance, which along with her annuity from Papa's estate added up to $600 monthly.

Momma pitched a conniption fit. Frank reminded her $600 was a month's wage for many folks, but that made no difference to Miss Spend-thrift. To shut her up, he agreed to review the situation in three months and consider increasing her allowance.

I wanted to tell Momma that Frank and I were lovers, but he preferred we keep our new relationship secret. He still struggled with the fact that he was legally married to her and worried about the difference in our ages. Neither detail concerned me.

I wanted to see Momma's face when she learned Frank belonged to me now. Even though she'd lost him years before due to her spitefulness and lies, she'd still be upset. She might not want him, but she wouldn't want me to have him either. She'd play the wounded wife scenario, lament her betrayal, and warn us we'd burn in Hell for our sins against her. That's when I'd pull out my list and read the names of all her known lovers. Frank and I might end up in Hell, but Momma would be right there with us.

Vengeance! That's what I wanted. But how could I hurt Momma without wounding and embarrassing Frank? It wasn't that he still had feelings for her. He didn't. In fact, sometimes it seemed he hated her more than I did. But Frank lacked the one personal quality Pickers like Momma and I had in common — the desire for revenge.

In the end, I agreed to keep our affair secret. My wish to please Frank was greater than my need for payback. Maybe I wasn't made in Momma's likeness after all. My soul might yet be saved from eternal damnation.

*****

What a difference a few months can make. For over two years, I'd walked through each day without delight or hope. But because of my new relationship with Frank, I found myself laughing and daring to dream again.

Frank had always been a visionary, one of those rare individuals who could look at something and recognize its potential. He'd worked a miracle with Papa's store. Grandpa Eli had always taken care of the business. In the three years between my grandpa's death and Frank's taking over, the store — under Papa's supervision — had lost money.

Papa was a lousy businessman, but a great gardener. He loved to feel the earth crumble in his hands and watch seeds he'd planted sprout and bloom. He'd passed on to me his reverence for life and his ability to see the beauty buried in a pot of dirt. But after losing Johnny and our baby, I'd pushed all life-affirming emotions to the dark recesses of my mind, allowing fear, despair, and downright hate to take their place. Frank planted a new seed of hope in me and doggedly tended it until it blossomed.

Under Frank's tutelage, I spent the summer of '69 studying for and passing my GED test. In late August, a letter from Kirbyville Community College confirmed my acceptance. Momma and I were surprised. Frank was ecstatic. He organized a party in my honor at the Kirbyville store. There was cake and punch for every employee, customer, and anyone who happened to wander by. For someone who'd spent most of her life trying to remain invisible, the attention was overwhelming. The only thing stopping me from flying up the stairs and taking refuge in our apartment was the smile on Frank's face every time he looked at me.

The party should have been for Frank. For me, going to college was a lost dream. But he found my dream and returned it to me on a silver platter. And when fear and self-doubt stopped me from reaching for it, he forced that platter into my hands.

Momma considered a party for me a waste of money, but she came anyway to see the new store. She liked it. It was bigger, fancier, and grossed more money than the Sugardale store. She insisted on seeing the apartment.

"You and Frank spend a lot of nights here, Becky Leigh. What do you do to pass the time?"

"We work on store business or watch TV." At Frank's urging, I'd started talking to Momma again. No long conversations, just short phrases like, "Pass the salt," or "Betty called." Simple statements of fact were my contribution to family harmony.

Momma turned the television on and off a couple of times as if checking to see if it worked. "I thought you didn't like watching TV. You never watched much at home."

"People change, Helen," Frank said as he entered the room.

She glanced at us and laughed. "If you say so, Sugar."

"How's Henry, Momma?"

"Henry's fine. Why do you ask?"

"I think you know." Momma was too smart not to catch my drift. If she started trouble about Frank and me spending time together, I had enough ammunition to annihilate her and her lover. After all, Henry had a business reputation to protect too.

"I'd better head home so you two can get back to the party or whatever else you had planned for the afternoon," she said.

"But there's something you should know, Momma."

"If you're going to tell me you two are lovebirds, Becky, you're a little late. I'm not blind or stupid like some members of this family."

"Don't start, Helen," Frank warned.

Momma laughed. "I'll make you a deal. You two keep the money coming in and leave Henry and me alone. In return, you can play house with my blessing, as long as you're discreet. For the sake of the business, we'll continue our happy family routine whenever we're in public, and we'll all live happily ever after. Okay?"

Damn her hide. I wanted to shock her, to embarrass her. I should've known it wouldn't happen. How can you humiliate someone who's incapable of feeling shame? I stared out the window while Frank and Momma discussed the finer points of the agreement, including a raise in her monthly allowance.

As she started to leave, Momma said, "I think I liked it better when you weren't talking to me, Becky."

There's no pleasing some people.

*****

I couldn't sleep. My classes at the junior college started the next day. Frank and I had stayed at the apartment. The idea was to get a good night's sleep so I'd be alert for my first day of class.

Throwing back the covers, I padded across the room and picked up the alarm clock. Frank kept it on the far side of the room so he had to get up to turn off the alarm. Once up, he never went back to bed, or rather he never went back to sleep. He liked making love in the morning. I preferred to do so at night. We compromised by doing both.

The green numerals glowed in the dark. Half past two. Only three hours until time to get up. After we made love, I'd cook breakfast while Frank showered. Then I'd tidy up the kitchen and take my bath while he read the morning paper. At 7 a.m., Frank would open the store. Half an hour later, I'd go downstairs, put on a fresh pot of coffee, and head for the greenhouse. That was pretty much our routine whenever we stayed at the apartment unless one of us decided to join the other in the shower. Then breakfast ended up being a donut instead of pancakes or omelets.

I climbed back into bed and snuggled up to his back. "Frank, are you awake?"

"No," he whispered.

"You must be awake, you're talking."

"I talk in my sleep."

"Can you answer questions in your sleep?"

"Not if it's about waiting another year to start college."

I gave him a shove and sat up.

Frank pulled himself up and turned on the lamp. "We've had this discussion a dozen times, Becky."

"You didn't agree with me before."

"And I'm not going to agree now either. Let's go to sleep."

"It makes more sense to wait. I'm needed at the stores."

Frank wrapped his arm around my bare shoulders. "I know you're afraid, but what's the worst that could happen?"

"What if the teachers ask me questions I can't answer?"

"Then they'd tell you the answers. That's their job."

I pushed his arm away. "I'm glad you find this funny." My career as a Picker wasn't going very well. How could I manipulate someone who agreed with me most of the time? And I learned not to make a fuss over anything. If I did, Frank got it for me. If I made a suggestion concerning the stores, he ordered it done. I found it hard to practice Picker ways against a man so dedicated to making me happy.

"It's a big campus. What if I can't find my class?"

Frank put his arm around me again. "If you want, I'll walk you to your first class. I'll even carry your books."

I laughed. "Johnny always carried . . ." How did I let that name slip out? "I'm sorry."

"Don't feel sorry. You two were special friends. You'll never forget that."

I leaned into him. "How is it you understand me better than I understand myself?"

He smiled. "Because, my young friend, I have the wisdom of time on my side."

I slipped my hand under the sheet and ran my fingers up his inner thigh. "I forgot you're such a decrepit old man."

Frank captured my dancing fingers. "Watch it, lady, you'll get something started."

"That's what I'm trying to do." I kissed his neck and proceeded down his chest.

He stroked my hair as my tongue flicked across his right nipple, then moved to his left.

Frank pushed me back. "You're trying to change the subject."

My lover knew me too well.

"Do you think about Johnny a lot, Becky?"

I shrugged.

"It's okay if you do. You loved him and he loved you."

"I don't know about that. He forgot about me soon enough."

"What do you mean?"

"Johnny's cousin, Emelda, came into the store last week. She said he married a gal he met while in the service. They live in Texas near Anna and are expecting a baby."

Frank eased down onto his right side. "Why didn't you tell me about this before?"

I laid down facing him. "It didn't seem important."

"No wonder you've been so sad this week."

"I'm not sad … not really. I'm happy for him. Johnny wanted children. I would never be able to give them to him."

Frank pulled the sheet over my shoulders. "The doctors weren't positive you couldn't have children. They said it might be hard for you —"

"If I could have a baby, I'd had one by now." I rolled over, giving Frank my back. That damn dentist messed up my insides so much that the chances of my being able to get pregnant were almost nonexistent. When the doctors first gave me the prognosis, I held out some hope. But after the visits from the Pickers-in-white and months of sharing Frank's bed, I knew I'd never have a child.

I convinced myself everything had worked out for the best. I might've been as bad a mother as Helen. No child deserved that. Yes, everything happened for the best. That was my new truth. What I told myself whenever I saw a pregnant woman or a new baby.

Frank put his arm over me. His breath warmed my neck. We lay in silence, watching shadows skip across the ceiling and walls. Shadows formed by the dim glow of a table lamp, the fluttering of curtains pushed around by an oscillating fan, and memories too powerful to be exorcised by weary minds.

"How can I take away the pain, Becky?"

"Tell me you love me."

"I love you."

"Tell me you'll always love me."

"I'll always love you."

I turned on my back and looked at Frank. "Promise me you'll never leave me."

"I'm not going anywhere, Becky."

I smiled. That's all I ever wanted. To know someone loved me and would always be there. That's not too much to ask for, is it?

Frank drew me closer to him and kissed my cheek.

A late afternoon shower had left the air muggy, but the little fan made the night's heat tolerable. An unexpected breeze caught the sheer curtains and took them for a ride halfway to the ceiling. My mind jumped back to the night I seduced Frank.

Like tonight, our first night together had been filled with recollections of painful memories, debates over what was best for me, and the acknowledgement of emotional and physical needs. Frank had faced the hard truth that his son had raped me.

Now, I had to admit an unwelcome truth. I'd been saving my kisses for a man who was never coming back to me. In Texas, another woman slept in Johnny's arms and carried his child. My dream of being his wife and the mother of his children would never come true.

Frank began stroking my brow, pushing beads of sweat off my forehead and into my damp hair.

Something else had happened the night I seduced Frank. After the tears had been shed, old secrets revealed, and passions sated, we'd made plans for a new beginning. Tomorrow would mark another new start for me. Becky Leigh Cooper was going to be a college student. I felt scared, but excited, and I wanted Frank to have something new too. For a long time, he'd desired something I couldn't give him until now.

"Kiss me, Frank."

Without hesitation, he kissed my forehead, my cheeks, my chin, and even the bridge of my nose. Frank kissed every inch of my face except my lips. I'd trained my Pick well, but now I no longer cared about Picks and Pickers for I was content, not happy necessarily, but content.

"You can kiss me on my mouth, Frank."

He pushed up on his elbow. "Are you sure? What about germs? I thought you were afraid."

I slid my hand around his neck, pulled his mouth close to mine. "I'm tired of being afraid. Kiss me."

Frank did as he was told. He kissed me until our lips ached.

*****

The Thanksgiving table looked beautiful. Grandma Cooper's lace tablecloth provided the perfect backdrop for the shimmering china, crystal goblets, and polished silverware. In an antique copper pot, miniature English ivy served as a bed for a centerpiece created from Indian corn, miniature gourds, and chrysanthemums in cream, gold, and burgundy. I'd done a great job. While the guests droned on about their plans for the waning days of 1970, I sat wondering why I'd agreed to host this farce.

Coy Charlotte, Donald's default wife, had insisted we have a traditional Thanksgiving dinner. I call her his default wife because Donald never intended on marrying the girl.

While I was at Havenwood, Donald injured his leg in a car wreck. The resulting surgery ended his football career and his dream of playing pro ball. Frank paid for his son's last year of college, but the boy didn't appreciate it. By Christmas of '67, Donald had flunked out of school and had gotten Charlotte pregnant.

Instead of getting an abortion, Charlotte Welch told her parents, who insisted Donald marry their daughter. Frank agreed, but good-time Donnie didn't care much for the notion of being a husband and a father. Charlotte's good reputation and an illegitimate baby meant little to him.

Mr. Welch, however, was concerned about both his daughter's reputation and his own. A man of considerable wealth and influence, Ben Welch owned the biggest Chevrolet dealership in North Georgia. He sat on advisory panels to the governor, several charity committees, and the local draft board. The irate father told Donald that, while his injured leg might keep him out of pro football, it wouldn't keep him out of Vietnam.

Mr. Welch's vow to get Donald drafted, along with the nightly television pictures of boys his age slogging through the bug-infested jungles of Vietnam, convinced Frank's no-good son to walk down the aisle. Little Amy was born on May 4, 1968, three days after I came home from Havenwood. In December of '69, Kim was born. After his marriage, Donald went to work selling used cars at his father-in-law's dealership.

When Frank told me Donald had become a father, it made me sick. Everything I'd ever wanted Donald got instead. I dreamed of seeing France, but he went. I longed to have a child, while my stepbrother got to become a parent against his wishes. Frank would've laid down his life for his son. And Momma? I'm alive in spite of her best efforts to kill me. Life is so unfair. It never brought me anything good except Frank.

I'd agreed to host this dinner because it meant so much to him. Since learning about my rape, Frank had struggled to find a balance between his love for his granddaughters and his disgust with Donald for what he'd done to me.

The morning had gone smoother than I'd expected. Helen and Charlotte talked about fashion and the girls. The men watched TV and I stayed in the kitchen, happy to do all the cooking. Stuffing a dead turkey held more appeal to me than watching Donald cram my special crab-stuffed mushroom caps into his big mouth.

I'd cleaned the house, cooked the food, and now I had to listen to my stepbrother brag about what a terrific salesman he was. To prove his point, Donald pulled out his key chain and showed us a medallion he'd received from Ben Welch Chevrolet for selling the most used cars in October.

I glanced around the room to see if the others were as bored with Donald's boasting as I was. Momma sat at one end. To her right was Charlotte, the default wife. Seated next to her and across from me was Donald, the rapist. Henry Nash had parked himself on my right. Momma had insisted her lover be included in our family gathering. She'd introduced him to Charlotte as an old family friend. The children lay sleeping on a pallet in front of the sofa.

Frank sat to my left at the head of the table. He wore many hats this day. Patriarch. Grandfather. Father of my rapist. Momma's legal husband and friend to her paramour. And finally, he was my protector and the keeper of my heart.

We were an odd lot. Yet to any stranger walking through the door, we looked like the typical, loving family. Momma had said this would be an interesting day. I think perverted would've been a more apt description.

Eleven-month-old Kim woke up and started crying.

"Can't you make that brat shut up?" Donald asked. "I'm trying to talk."

Charlotte tapped her fork against her plate. "And I'm trying to finish my pie. She'll get tired of crying soon and fall asleep."

I pushed back my chair. "I'll get her."

Amy stirred. I tucked her blanket around her, rubbed her back, and she quieted. Kim wrapped her chubby arms around my neck. I sat down in the rocker and proceeded to rock her, humming a lullaby Anna had sung to me when I was a child. Frank smiled. I could read the love in his face as clearly as I could see the hate in Donald's scowl.

The baby snuggled her cheek next to mine. I closed my eyes and slipped my hand up the back of her shirt. The scent of talcum powder, the warmth of smooth skin, and her whispered breaths in my ear delighted my senses. This was my idea of Heaven — a rocking chair, a baby in my arms, and Frank watching over us.

CHAPTER 20

The moment I stepped out of the van, I realized what I'd missed. I took a deep breath, letting the salty air fill my lungs. Slipping off my shoes, I ran toward the surf. Warm sand scrunched beneath my feet and pushed up between my toes.

At the water's edge, I stopped. I'd never been to the ocean before, and the vastness of the Atlantic demanded the kind of reverence normally reserved for grand cathedrals or national monuments. Waves of turquoise charged at me, crashing into the sand at the last possible moment lest their mighty force devour me. White foam circled my ankles as the waves retreated to their mother the sea to regroup for another attack.

Beneath my feet, wet sand deserted me, but I wasn't afraid. As soon as the sand ran way, thousands of identical grains rushed in to take their place. A cool breeze softened the heated assault of the late May sun.

"What do you think, Becky?" Frank asked.

"I love it. Don't you?" Before he could answer, I kissed him.

A wide smile captured his face. "I should have brought you here before."

"That's for sure." I jumped into his arms. He swung me around until we became so dizzy we fell down laughing.

Frank loomed above me. "I take it you like your present, Miss College Graduate."

"It's amazing."

He helped me sit up, moved behind me, and put his arms around me. "You deserved a break after all the work you've done the past two years."

Two years. It seemed impossible anyone's life could change as much as mine had in just two years. I'd turned twenty-one the first of May and graduated junior college with honors two weeks later. Both stores were doing better than either Frank or I ever dreamed possible, and we had plans to start a wholesale division soon. We envisioned flats of bedding plants stamped with the Cooper logo going out to all the major nurseries in the South. Papa and Grandpa Eli would've been proud.

Helen spent most of her time concentrating her efforts on teasing and tantalizing Henry Nash. She claimed she loved him. Frank, the eternal optimist, believed her. I didn't. But as long as she didn't intrude into my life with Frank, I didn't care.

When I looked in the mirror, I hardly recognized the young woman staring back at me. Red hair fell to her shoulders instead of halfway down her back and a few extra pounds had been added in the right places. The glimmer of happiness in her eyes and the hint of confidence in her voice fascinated me. It's amazing what a girl can do when she has one person in her life that loves and believes in her unconditionally.

I leaned back against Frank, relishing the tide's dampness as it seeped into my shorts. "We both deserved a break. I wouldn't have been able to accomplish anything without you."

I swiveled around, kissed him again. A trace of desperation fueled our feelings due to the stepfather-stepdaughter public charade we played in order to maintain the illusion of respectability. The possibility of having our secret lives revealed added an aura of intrigue to our relationship and to Momma and Henry's as well.

Helen thrived on the deception, spending hours dreaming up elaborate ways to secretly rendezvous with Henry. She viewed it as a challenge — her imagination and intellect pitted against the curiosity of nosey neighbors. She claimed to know the secrets of most everyone in Sugardale, information gathered from her liaisons with Sheriff Tate and Henry. Hairdressers are like bartenders. People tell them secrets they wouldn't discuss with their pastor. Momma assured us that if anyone unearthed the skeletons in our closets and thought to disclose the information, she could blackmail them into changing their mind. Frank said Momma should've been a spy for the CIA because she would have never been held back by a conscience. She took his comment as a compliment.

The cries of hungry gulls interrupted our necking. Frank stood up and held out his hand. "Let's go find the beach house I rented."

I brushed the sand off my shorts. "Is it far?"

"Shouldn't be. The real estate agent said it was near the fishing pier."

"Let's get some groceries so I can cook supper."

"You're on vacation, Honey. I'll take you out for supper."

"Let's go out tomorrow. I've something special in mind for tonight."

Frank grinned. "Okay, but I will want a second helping."

I kissed his forehead and whispered, "You always do."

*****

I shoved the last of the clean dishes into the cupboard and slammed the door shut.

"I don't want to talk about this."

Frank pulled a barstool out from beneath the counter that divided the kitchen and living room. "I've given the matter a lot of thought."

"Really? Just how long have you been thinking about getting rid of me, Frank? Since we got to the beach? Since the last time we made love on that damn mountain you fancy so much?"

"Don't be silly and don't cuss. It doesn't become you."

I rinsed out the dishrag, folded it in half, and laid it over the faucet. "Haven't you heard? I'm twenty-one now. I can do anything I damn well please. Drink, cuss, or make a fool of myself." I snatched up the dishrag and wadded it up in my hand. "I made a fool of myself over you long ago, didn't I?"

"If you would calm down a minute, Becky, you'd see that I'm right."

I threw the rag at Frank's head. He ducked. The cloth hit the pale blue wall behind him. It left a damp impression on the sheetrock before falling down onto the end table and knocking over a jar of seashells. The tiny shells scattered across the gray linoleum. I headed for the patio.

"Just a minute, Becky." As he stepped forward to intercept me, Frank's bare foot came down on the sharp little shells. "Shit." He hopped toward the bar. "Dammit," he yelled as his other foot crushed another batch of wayward shells. He reached the barstool and found refuge. Thin trails of blood trickled across the bottom of his feet as he plucked the tiny barnacles from his skin. "My sandals are by the bed. Will you get them for me, please?"

I didn't move.

He stopped pulling shells and glared at me. "Will you get my damn shoes?"

"You shouldn't cuss, Frank. It doesn't become you." I ground my flip-flop into the slick floor covering, did a quick about-face pivot, and was awarded with a shrill squeak. Thanks to Momma's tendency to throw breakable objects at me, I'd learned early in life that one should never be barefooted during a fight. If Frank thought picking seashells out of his feet was bad, he should try prying slivers of glass out of a bare foot. I yanked open the patio door and stepped out onto the deck.

"You can be just like Helen sometimes," he shouted.

"You should know, Mr. Wooten. You've screwed both of us," I screamed before jerking the sliding door closed.

*****

I spent most of the afternoon out on the deck, going inside only when Frank went for a walk. I locked myself in the bathroom intent on soaking my troubles away.

Around suppertime, he knocked on the bathroom door to ask if I wanted to go get something to eat. He begged me to unlock the door, urged me to be reasonable.

I ignored his pleas. How could he think about food while our life together deteriorated by the minute? There was only one answer. Frank no longer loved me.

Tears burned my cheeks as I watched him speed away in Momma's new Dodge van. Deep down, I knew he would never leave me stranded, but I still checked the bedroom to make sure his clothes were there.

I spent my time alone doing what most women do when faced with a similar situation — vacillate between wondering what I'd done wrong and cussing the man. Frank had been the one who'd insisted I go to college. Now, he was using my degree as an excuse to send me away.

Momma had warned me about trusting any man completely, even one as nice as Frank. But I'd considered the source of the advice and had done the exact opposite. I should've known better. Any man who could talk my mother into trading in her fancy Thunderbird for a Dodge van — even one with a backseat that folds down into a bed — has got to be slicker than Crisco.

By the time Frank returned, I'd convinced myself he was nothing better than a snake oil salesman, and I exited our rented love nest before he could change my mind. I wandered up and down the beach for hours before going back.

*****

Frank was mad. It wasn't the sort of mad a person gets when his favorite record gets broken or the kind of rage that swells up inside of you when you slam the car door on your own finger. This brand of anger pours over you when someone you care about gives you a bad scare.

"I didn't mean to worry you, Frank."

"Didn't you?" he asked. "Where the hell have you been?"

"I went for a walk along the beach." I pointed at the starfish-shaped clock hanging above the wicker sofa. "It's only half past nine."

"I searched the beach for you, Becky."

"I met some folks on the pier and tried my hand at crabbing. I caught three big —"

"I checked the damn pier twice."

"We must have missed each other somehow."

Frank stood there, his head bobbing up and down like the plastic dog Johnny's cousin once had on the back dash of his '63 Chevy.

"I didn't mean to stay gone so long. I lost track of time."

"I should've given you a watch for graduation instead of a trip to the beach." He headed for the deck.

I trailed after him. "I'm sorry."

Frank pounded the top rail with his fist. "Hell, Becky, I didn't know what happened to you. I thought someone got you or maybe you did something stupid."

"Something stupid? Like what?"

He gave me a sideways glance. "You know what I mean."

I started to proclaim my ignorance, but the words froze in my throat. "You thought I killed myself? Drowned myself, maybe?"

"You tried to end your life once before. Remember?"

"I was a kid. A silly, angry kid who thought she was alone in the world." I tugged at the sleeve of his shirt. "How could you think that about me after all we've been through?"

Frank swung around. "You accused me of wanting to be rid of you just because I believe you should continue your education. How could you think that about me?"

I had no more of an answer for him than he had for me. If this were a movie, this would've been the scene where Frank and I suddenly realized how foolish we'd been. We'd beg each other's forgiveness, pull our yearning bodies together, and make wild, impatient love right here on the deck. The stars would be bright. A full moon would reflect off thunderous waves whose powers would seem impotent compared to the passionate tide rolling over us. And of course, the man walking his dog along the beach would magically disappear.

But this wasn't a movie. Only a handful of stars and a three-quarter moon lighted the night's sky. In addition to the man with the dog, several couples walked hand-in-hand along the water's edge, just as Frank and I had done the past five nights. But tonight, we stood six feet apart, not touching, not talking, and not knowing how to get beyond our mutual disappointment with each other and with ourselves.

A woman's scream penetrated the salty ocean air. A man pulled a reluctant female into the surf. At first glance, it looked as though she was fighting him, but then a wave washed over them and a gush of shared laughter flooded the shoreline. Free of her captor's embrace, the woman ran giggling down the beach, stopping now and then to make sure her gentleman friend was following. The sound of their laughter tickled the night air long after the darkness swallowed their forms.

Frank stood with his hands on the rail, his focus on the sea. My mind searched for the words to make things right between us. His refusal to accept my apology worried me. I surveyed the deck. Chairs, tables, loungers, but no rocker. How can people furnished a house and not include at least one dang rocking chair? Even a hammock would've sufficed.

"Everyday I think about two things, Becky," Frank said, while keeping his eyes on the waves. "I think about what my life would be like without you. There'd be no laughter, no love, no balance. There'd be only work."

I placed my hand on top of his. "I feel the same. That's why my moving —"

He pulled his hand away, walked to the end of the deck, and turned to face me. "You didn't let me finish."

"I'm sorry. Go ahead," I urged, despite the knot in my gut.

"Like I said, every day I wonder what I'd do without you. I also wonder what you'd do if you weren't stuck in Sugardale with me."

"I'm not stuck. I want to be with you. I can't do anything without you, Frank."

"That's not true, Becky. You're stronger than you think. You need to see the wonderful things the world can offer a smart, pretty girl like you. Things you'll never find if you stay in Sugardale . . . or with me."

"You can show me new things."

"You should be with people your own age, people whose curiosity and energy match your own."

"Please don't start with the age thing again. It doesn't matter."

"It does." He walked over and put his hands on my shoulders. "You're at the beginning of your life. I'm halfway through mine. If you'd stop looking at yourself through Helen's eyes, you'd see how special you are."

"I'm not as stupid as Momma thinks I am. But Frank, I'm not as strong as you believe, either." I stopped to wipe away unwanted tears. "I'm a good gardener, a competent cook, and a pretty fair bookkeeper. That's all I am, but it's enough for me."

"It shouldn't be, Becky. There's much more waiting for you if you'd take a chance." Frank smoothed back a lock of my hair. "I bet if you went one semester, you'd like the university so much you wouldn't want to come back."

"And when you lose that bet, I'll be the one who pays." I grabbed the railing and watched as the Atlantic continued its unrelenting attack on the defenseless beach, each wave sweeping grains of sand from the shoreline as it retreated into dark waters. "You always think the best of everyone, Frank. But there are people like Momma and Donald out there, people waiting for easy pickin's like me to come along."

"You can't hide from the world behind me. It's time you took a chance on life."

"I took a chance when Johnny and I ran off together. Look at all I lost. Johnny, my baby, my freedom." I wiped more tears away. "I can't take any more. Please don't make me."

"I want you to be happy, to have the best life possible. You won't find it in Sugardale."

"I'm happy . . . with you." Sobbing, I wrapped my arms around his waist. "I'm happy with you. Please let me . . . just . . . be happy."

Frank sighed and pulled me into his chest. "Don't cry, Becky. It kills my soul to see you cry." He patted my back. "Okay. Don't cry. We'll do things your way for now."

*****

The next day, we said goodbye to our beachfront hide-a-way and headed for home. On our way to the beach, we'd dropped Helen off at Eva Whitcomb's house in Atlanta. Today, we'd pick her up and arrive back in Sugardale looking like the typical American family returning from vacation.

Eva and Momma had been good friends for over twenty years. Twice divorced and widowed once, Mrs. Whitcomb had — according to Momma — more money than one person could spend in a lifetime. So several times a year, Momma visited Eva to help her spend it.

Henry had gone to Palm Beach to visit his wealthy Aunt Velma and planned to stop by Eva's on his way back. When Momma informed Eva about the peculiarities of our family relationships, she voiced no objection. It seemed she lived a secret Bohemian life of her own — respectable socialite by day, party girl at night.

As he turned into the Whitcomb's tree-lined driveway, Frank cast me an anxious glance. "I hate this part."

I knew what he meant. Eva's maid would usher us inside the marbled floor entry and escort us into a large living room filled with expensive antique furniture and Persian rugs. I'd sit down on the edge of the least expensive-looking chair, pull my arms in close, and pray I didn't accidentally break some collectible worth more than my year's salary.

Frank would stand at the back wall, arms crossed, body tense, until Momma and her friend decided we'd had enough time to appreciate the opulence of our surroundings. Then dressed in their newest attire, the ladies would call down to us from the curved balcony overlooking the vaulted chamber. In one hand, Momma would be holding a champagne glass. Bags filled with designer clothes and accessories gleaned from Eva's closets would be clutched in her other hand. Normally, Momma wouldn't think of accepting hand-me-downs, but Eva's donations were different. Most had been worn only once or twice; many still had price tags on them; all were ridiculously expensive.

Helen would wave and then descend the curved staircase looking like the grand lady of the manor. This was the life she felt she'd been born to live, the life circumstances had stolen from her.

Frank and I accepted our parts in the ritual so we could have time alone together away from Sugardale. We did manage to attend a couple of out-of-state hardware conventions without setting nosey tongues to wagging. But we dared not risk more than a couple of weekends a year.

As we pulled up in front of the house, the massive oak doors opened up, and Helen came storming out. Frank was barely out of the van when she reached him.

"Here," she said, shoving designer bags at him. "My suitcases are in the hall." She came around to my side and opened the passenger door. "Move, Becky Leigh."

I slipped between the front bucket seats and made my way to the back. Eva Whitcomb came out wearing a simple caftan and no makeup. I barely recognized the woman. She opened the van door, leaned her head against Momma's, and whispered something.

Momma shook her head vigorously. Eva continued to whisper. I strained to hear what she was saying, but failed to catch a single word. Frank opened the backdoors of the van. He paused for a moment. Our eyes locked. I had a sinking feeling that whatever was happening with Momma would end up causing trouble for us. Frank's clenched jaw and raised right eyebrow indicated he shared my concern. He shoved Momma's suitcases up against the back of the seat and slammed the doors shut.

CHAPTER 21

I waited until the last car left the parking lot of Monsieur Henri's Hair Salon. As I pushed open the salon door, a trio of bells jingled.

"We're closed," Henry Nash called from the back room.

"It's me, Mr. Nash. Becky Cooper."

The curtained door between the two rooms parted and Momma's estranged lover entered carrying a bottle of shampoo in each hand. "What a nice surprise. How've you been?"

"Fine," I said, adding another lie to the pile.

"How's Frank?"

I sat down in a swivel chair. "He's okay."

"I saw him over at the bank yesterday. He looked tired."

"He's been working very long hours. We're trying to get a wholesale department going."

I didn't feel it helpful to explain that Frank and I spent extra time at the store because of Momma's foul mood. Since her breakup with Henry two weeks prior, she'd been feeling miserable and had made life hell for everyone who crossed her path.

"Helen has told me about the expansion. Sounds good." Henry set the bottles down next to the shampoo bowls. "How is your mother?"

"Momma's fine." Another lie.

"I've been worried about her. Every time I call, she hangs up on me." Henry walked to the front door and flipped the OPEN sign to CLOSED. "Did she send you?"

"No, sir. I needed my hair trimmed."

"I trimmed your hair before you went on vacation."

"I'm thinking about changing the color," I said, adding lie number four to the list.

I try to keep a count of my daily lies. On a good day, I tell five or less. Ten was about normal. At fifteen fibs, I'd promise myself to do better. When the number of falsehoods reached twenty, I turned the counting over to God.

According to Reverend Murray, the Lord keeps a true record of everyone's transgressions. Heaven's Holy library must have an entire room dedicated to my family — the Cooper-Wooten Journey to Purgatory Room. I imagine there are shelves of thick, leather-bound journals documenting every excruciating detail of our sinful acts in permanent ink. Momma and I are in a race to see who can fill the room up first. Because of her eighteen years head start, she holds the lead, but I'm fast closing the gap.

My true purpose for visiting Henry was to get him and Helen back together. Then Frank and I could get on with our normal, twisted lives.

Henry picked up my ponytail and examined my hair. "I've got customers who'd kill to have hair like yours." He sat down at the beauty station next to mine. "What's the real reason you dropped by?"

I shrugged. Even though Henry had been an integral part of my family's charade for several years, I knew little about him. His family had owned the local funeral home for four generations before selling it in the early sixties. Henry lived in a garage apartment next to his ancestral home, one of the oldest and grandest houses in Sugardale. Being the only mortuary in town had to be a lucrative enterprise. Sooner or later, you get everyone's business.

Henry's mother had died of pneumonia the past winter. His only living relative, Aunt Velma, resided in Palm Beach, Florida. Velma's late husband had made millions in the early days of the oil industry. According to my mother, Henry's aunt had three times the money Eva Whitcomb had. In this instance, I believed Momma. When it came to sniffing out who had money and who didn't, she had the nose of bloodhound.

"Did Helen tell you that I'm moving to Florida?" Henry asked.

I nodded. "She's awfully mad at you, Mr. Nash."

"Call me Henry." He swiveled his chair around to face me. "I can imagine how mad Helen is."

"No, you can't. You should hear some of the things she's saying about you."

"Let me guess," he said. "She's saying I'm deserting her. I don't love her anymore. I'm the lowest son-of-a-gun who ever walked the earth. Is that about right?"

"Pretty much, except her language is a lot stronger."

He laughed. "In all her ranting and raving, did Helen mention I asked her to move to Palm Beach with me?"

"Why would you do that?"

"Because I love her." Henry went to the back room and returned with a green velvet box. "I bought this ring in Florida." He opened the box. Tucked down in the center was a diamond solitaire. "I couldn't wait to get to Eva's to ask Helen to marry me."

My eyes grew wide, my mouth fell open, all coherent thought processes stopped.

Henry snapped the box closed. "You are looking at me like you think aliens stole my brain."

"Are you sure they haven't?"

Henry slipped the box into his shirt pocket. "I hope you're better at selling flowers, Becky, than you are at trying to sell me on Helen. That is why you're here, isn't it?"

"She's driving Frank and me plum crazy, Mr. Nash . . . I mean Henry." It's such a relief to be able to tell God's honest truth now and then.

He patted my shoulder. "Helen can be a double handful when she wants to be."

"Then why do you want to marry her?"

Henry turned and faced the large mirror that covered the wall in front of the beauty station. He stared at his likeness for several minutes, as if trying to find the answer to my question in his own reflection. "Have you ever wondered why I turned my back on my family's business and took up hairdressing for a living?"

"A lot of people wondered about that, especially after your daddy died and you sold the funeral parlor to the Levin brothers. Most people thought it was a downright shame you didn't carry on your family's tradition."

Henry's mouth tightened into a thin strip of lip; his eyes squinted half-closed, making the tiny lines around his hazel eyes deepen. "Do you think I was wrong? Was it selfish of me to want to do what made me happy instead of carrying on the family business?"

Our eyes met briefly. My last statement, however factual, had caused him considerable pain. That's one of the dangers of being honest after dining on lies every day. You tell one truth, and your mind hungers to tell more. Next thing you know, you're telling some poor fellow more truth than he ever wanted to hear. Momma might be right when she says the telling of what she calls, "Peanut lies," is truly an act of kindness.

"Don't ask me," I said. "After all, I'm the third generation to work in my family's company."

"Do you work there because you want to? Or because you feel you must?"

I glared into Henry's probing eyes. "Why are you asking me such a silly question? Grandpa Eli started the business. Papa took over when Grandpa died, and now it's my turn. With Frank's help, I'm going to see that the Cooper name is never forgotten. I have to make my papa proud of me."

"Don't you think your daddy would be proud of you anyway?"

I watched Henry Nash watching me. How much had Momma told him about me?

I slipped out of the chair. "I'd best be going."

"Your father would be very proud of you, Becky, even if you didn't work in the store."

"Right before Papa died, I promised him I'd take care of the house and store."

Henry stood. "You were a child when Paul died, Becky. No one expected you to keep such a promise."

"I can't break my promise to Papa, Mr. Nash. That wouldn't be right."

"It's Henry. Remember?"

"Okay," I said and walked toward the door.

"You want to know why I became a hairdresser instead of an undertaker?"

I turned around.

"Because the only time my mother laughed was when she went to the beauty parlor."

"I don't understand. I seem to remember her smiling."

"Smiling, yes, but never laughing. Growing up in our house, you learned early on that life had to be taken seriously. My father thought spontaneous laughter was a sign of disrespect. His father taught him that, just as his grandfather had taught his son. When you spend decades working with the dead, your heart shrinks. If it didn't, you'd go crazy. Bodies come in twisted, torn, abused, and diseased. A mortician's job is to put all the pieces together again so families can say their last goodbyes." Henry eased down upon a black vinyl-covered stool. "Even the women of our family were taught that laughter was unseemly for folks who made their living off the dead."

I pulled out the manicurist's chair and sat down.

"When I was a young boy, I would accompany my mother to the beauty parlor every Saturday morning. The ladies there would talk about husbands and kids and dresses that didn't fit anymore. Someone would tell a joke and everyone would laugh, including my mother." Henry rubbed his fingers across his forehead. "Her laugh was like music, Becky. A sweet, delicate melody played on some angel's golden harp. At least, that's what it sounded like to a five-year-old boy."

"That's real nice, Henry."

He nodded. "When I turned twelve, my father decided I needed to learn the family business. Instead of spending Saturdays with mother, I went to the funeral parlor to help my daddy." Henry walked over to the counter, picked up a brush, and started cleaning it with a wide-tooth, tortoise-shelled comb. "If a funeral was scheduled that day, my job was to escort the grieving family into a room where they could view the body of their loved one in private. The people would cry and moan and pray. Sometimes, one of the women folk would wrap her arms around my neck, sob, and ask questions like, 'Why did this happen to my child? Why my husband?'" Henry stopped cleaning the brush and looked back at me. "Hell, Becky, I was only a boy. How was I supposed to know why death takes some people and leaves others?"

I couldn't answer Henry's question any more than he could've answered the heartbroken relatives. A knot started to form in my stomach. I wanted to run away so I wouldn't have to see the anguish on Henry's face, wouldn't have to hear the sorrow in his voice. As a boy — trapped between the dead and the inconsolable — Henry must have felt the same desire to escape.

"What did you do on the days when there were no funerals?" I asked, in an attempt to change the subject.

Henry started cleaning the brush again. "I had to help prepare the dead for embalming. My job was to wash the body."

As he explained the steps in preparing the deceased for burial, Henry raked the comb through the bristles. The longer he talked, the harder he scraped the brush. The knot in my stomach tightened.

"Damn." Henry held up the comb. Two teeth were broken. "This was one of my best combs." He threw the ruined tool into the wastebasket. "I'm sorry, Becky, I didn't mean to go into such detail."

"That's okay. It didn't bother me." Another smile, another lie. "I better go now."

"But I haven't told you how I became a hairdresser yet."

"That's right, you haven't." I sank back down into the chair. My surprise visit to Henry's wasn't turning out the way I'd imagined it would. I'd come to convince him to stay in Sugardale, not to hear his life story. But my Southern upbringing wouldn't permit me to just walk out. Under certain conditions, lying and adultery might be considered forgivable offences, but deliberate rudeness to an adult — outside of your immediate family — was an inexcusable breech of good manners. Even a sinner like me could be polite.

"When I graduated high school," Henry said, "I wanted to go to college. My father said he could teach me everything about the funeral business. When I told him I planned to do something else with my life, he kicked me out. I moved to Atlanta, worked as a night watchman, and took classes at Georgia Tech during the day. I wanted to be an engineer, until the day I walked into a beauty college. The laughter reminded me of the happy times spent with Mother at the beauty shop." Henry rolled his stool closer. "I went in for a cheap haircut, but came out with a new career."

"What did your parents think?"

"Mother supported me. She'd send me money when she could. My father hated it."

"That must have been hard on you."

"It was harder on Mother, and I regretted that the most." Henry walked over and closed the Venetian blind that covered the front window.

"After I got my beautician's license, I worked for a while before returning to beauty school to get my instructor's certification."

"How did you end up back in Sugardale?"

"Mother broke her leg, I came home to visit her and Aunt Velma convinced me mother needed me. The beauty parlor here was for sale so I bought it."

"So you moved home?"

"Not at first. Father had a fit. If I'd been an engineer or even a damn barber, he might have come around. He accused me of moving home to embarrass him." Henry crossed his arms. "That wasn't the reason, but I admit the thought of thumbing my nose at him held some appeal. I suppose that sounds mean to you."

"Not really," I said. "I've felt that way numerous times."

He laughed. "You and Helen have gone a few rounds."

"You don't know the half of it, Henry."

"I know more than you think." His face turned serious again. "I know it's mostly Helen's fault. She's rode you hard all your life, hasn't she?"

Henry's candor and empathy surprised and confused me. Was it possible he knew Momma better than I'd suspected? It's an odd feeling, realizing someone knows more about you than you know about him. "What happened with your father?" I asked, in a subtle effort to turn the conversation back to his life.

"He wouldn't allow me to move home. He viewed my refusal to work in the family business as a personal betrayal. But Mother surprised us both. She said if I couldn't live in my father's house, she'd wouldn't either."

"Your mother left your daddy?"

"Almost. She agreed to stay after he let me move into the garage apartment." Henry sat down again. "I never planned to spend my life in Sugardale. I only stayed to care for Mother. Now that she's gone, I want to chase my dream again."

"What's your dream, Henry?"

"To move to Palm Beach, start with one salon and expand that to three shops. After that, I want to start a beauty school so I can teach others the secrets I learned while watching Mother and her friends get their hair done."

"What secrets?"

"Women don't come into the shop to get their hair fixed and their nails polished. They come because they want to feel better. They want to feel pretty." Henry pointed to the front door. "Women walk through that door with their heads hung low, looking like they have just run over their kid's puppy. After an hour in my shop, they leave smiling, their heads held high, and there's a speck of hope in their eyes. My goal is to make every woman feel like she's beautiful, inside and out. It's a small thing, but it's my talent, my gift. I like to make women happy, even if it's only for a few hours."

"You certainly make Momma happy."

He reached for my hands. "She makes me happy too. That's why I want her with me."

I looked at Henry's hands. They were smooth and pale instead of calloused and tanned like Frank's and Papa's. But they were strong hands just the same.

"Momma can be cruel. She's a habitual liar."

"We've all done our share of lying in the past. You, me, Frank. We've all lied to keep our personal lives secret. As for hurting others, we've done that too, haven't we?"

"I suppose. But Momma is the champion liar of all times."

Henry grinned. "Helen does have a way of bypassing the truth better than anyone I know. That's her talent, a talent honed during her horrible childhood in West Virginia."

"West Virginia? Momma isn't from West Virginia. She grew up on a Kentucky horse ranch. She had a wonderful childhood. She went to a private school and had a black pony named Coal." I pulled my hands out of Henry's. "The only sadness in her life came when her mother and the Major were killed in a train accident."

"The Major?"

"He was Momma's daddy. Everyone called him that because he had been a major in World War One. After his death, the ranch was sold to pay bills, and Momma moved to Atlanta. That's where she met Eva and Papa."

"Helen told you she was raised in Kentucky?" Henry asked.

"Yes. Papa told me that too. He'd have known if Momma was lying."

"Can you tell when your mother is lying, Becky?"

"Sure. If her mouth is open for any reason other than eating or brushing her teeth, it's a good bet she's lying."

Henry laughed. "I see your point, but I've found a better way to tell when Helen is being truthful."

"How?"

"When Helen is telling the truth, especially a truth she'd rather not tell, her right thumb twitches."

"I've never noticed that." I did not attempt to hide my skepticism.

"That's because Helen holds her cigarette in her right hand. But if you look close, you'll see her thumb twitch whenever she's telling the truth."

"It must not twitch often."

Henry laughed again. "No, not often. Your mother is a challenge for sure. But I manage to pull the truth out of her sometimes."

I'd always wondered what Momma saw in Henry Nash. He was nice-looking enough, but not handsome like Papa and Frank. A couple of inches taller than her, Henry had a smaller frame than her previous lovers did — at least those I knew about. I figured the only thing he and Helen had in common was their shared adoration for her honey-gold curls. Not much to base a relationship on, much less a marriage.

"But how can you love Momma when you know her true nature?"

"I see a different Helen than you do. She lashes out mainly because she's afraid. Helen had no control over what happened to her when she was a child in West Virginia. That's why she seeks control of everything and everyone now."

"Momma is from Kentucky. She lied to you about West Virginia just because she wanted your sympathies."

Henry sighed. "I reckon she lied to one of us, Becky." He rose and pushed the stool under the counter. "We need a plan."

"What kind of plan?"

"I want Helen in my life. You and Frank want her out of yours. Right?"

"Right."

"Helen's smart. That's why she can manipulate everyone so well. But we know her better than anyone."

"Do you think we can maneuver her into leaving Sugardale?"

"Yes."

"How?"

In a voice mimicking Helen's, Henry said, "We'll do whatever it takes, Sugar."

I laughed. Now, I understood why Momma loved Henry. But what was it about her that made good men like Papa, Frank, and Henry propose marriage? She must know black magic. Whatever it was — a spell, curse, or hex — I hoped it lasted longer on Henry than it had on Papa and Frank. Otherwise, I'd be stuck with Momma forever.

CHAPTER 22

I returned home from work the next day to find Momma and Henry standing on our front porch.

"You're home early," she said. "Where's Frank?"

"He'll be along. It's such a nice day, I decided to walk home." I climbed the four steps leading to the porch. "Nice to see you, Henry. How you doing?"

"I've been better, Becky."

I headed for the swing at the end of the porch. "You're not coming down with the summer cold that's going around, are you?"

"I wish my illness was that easy to treat. I'm afraid I've come down with a heartache."

Helen frowned. "Don't be so melodramatic, Henry."

"I can't help it, Sweetheart. I learned from the best."

Momma flipped back her hair and giggled. "You're such a card, Henry Nash."

He grinned. "I know, Sweet Pea, but marry me anyway."

She pointed at me. "Becky's listening to every word we say."

"So what?" Henry pulled his shoulders back, looked straight at me. "Becky, do I have your permission to marry your mother and take her to live with me in Palm Beach. We'll lounge around my aunt's pool or go to the beach every day."

"I hate the beach," Helen said. "It's too crowded, too hot."

"It's nice at night," I countered. "The stars come out and it's real romantic."

Momma cast me a sour look. "I guess you and Frank would know about that."

For the sake of our plan, I squelched a sarcastic response and looked to Henry, my partner in a scheme he'd nicknamed HUR, short for Helen's Ultimate Relocation. But to me the letters stood for Helen's Ultimate Removal — removal from Papa's house and removal from my life. With that goal in mind, I'd pledged to help Henry convince Momma that she should move to Palm Beach.

"Don't worry about crowds, Honey Pie. Aunt Velma's property goes to the water's edge. We'll have our own private beach." He leaned closer to her. "Remember the beach scene in *From Here to Eternity*? We'll make Deborah Kerr and Burt Lancaster look like amateurs."

Helen laughed and pushed Henry back a bit. "You are so bad, Mister."

Henry grinned. "That's why you love me. Because I'm almost as bad as you."

They stared at each other. She rubbed her tongue back and forth over her bottom lip. Henry's breathing quickened.

A movie started to play in my head. In it, Momma and Henry ran out of the surf, fell into the sand and proceeded to devour each other, like Deborah and Burt, only Momma and Henry were naked. God help me. I'd seen and heard too much. So had our neighbor across the street. "Mrs. Treadwell is weeding her flowerbeds and watching every move you two make."

Immediately, Henry straightened up. Helen wrapped one hand around a porch column and began fanning herself with her other hand. "It's terribly hot today, isn't it?" she asked as she waved to Mrs. Treadwell.

I pushed the swing higher.

"I'd better go," Henry said. "I don't want to set tongues to wagging. Don't want to damage your stellar reputation, Mrs. Wooten."

Even Momma smiled at the irony of her lover's words. Henry had a better sense of humor than either Papa or Frank. That had to come in handy when dealing with my mother.

He turned toward me, giving Momma his back. "Don't work too hard, Becky." He winked to indicate he was handing off her conversion to becoming a Floridian to me.

"You take care of yourself, Henry Ambrose Nash," Helen said. "Or you'll have me to deal with."

He smiled and gave one of her curls a quick tug. "I will, Peaches. Just promise me you'll think about all we discussed. Remember, I love you."

"I promise."

Henry climbed into his green Impala, waved once, and pulled into the street. The sadness on his face when he left and the fact that he'd told Momma his middle name was Ambrose convinced me he really loved her. I felt sorry for him.

"Love you too," Momma whispered as he drove away. The thumb on her right hand began to twitch.

At our planning session the day before, Henry had assigned me the task of finding out why Momma was afraid to leave Sugardale. The only reason I'd ever known her to do anything was because of pure hate and downright meanness. If Henry thought I could ferret out some hidden motive for her not wanting to marry him, then he'd been sniffing too many permanent wave solutions.

"You could've helped me, Becky." Momma said.

"Helped you with what?"

"Helped me convince Henry not to move to Palm Beach." Momma shook her finger at me. "But no. Instead, you go on and on about how great the beach is." She jerked the screen door open. "Thanks a hell-of-a-lot." From inside the house, she yelled, "You never wanted me to be happy, did you?"

Momma was unhappy. Thus, it had to be my fault. According to her, I'd been the source of all her misery since the day I drew breath. What was it about Henry that made her love him when she couldn't love her own daughter? What secret did he know that I didn't?

For as long as I could remember, I'd told myself it didn't matter. I neither wanted nor needed a mother's love, especially now that I had Frank. But as I watched the dust kicked up by Henry's car settle, I envied his ability to move my mother's rock-hard heart. It made me mad at myself. So mad, I wanted to pull my brain out, scrape off every memory of her, and forget a person named Helen Elizabeth Cooper-Wooten ever existed.

*****

A cool shower had washed away the odor of potting soil and sweat, but had done little to relieve the tension in my neck. I leaned against the mahogany archway to the living room and watched Momma flip through the pages of the latest hairstyle magazine. Her legs were crossed, right over left. The bottom of her sandal popped against her right heel with every swing of her leg. I recognized the behavior. Like a cat lying in wait for a mouse, switching its tail back and forth, readying itself to pounce. Anticipating the kill. My fight or flight instinct warned me to return to the safety of the upstairs. Only once in the three plus years since my return from Havenwood had Momma ventured to the top floor.

Like a blue jay protecting its nest, Frank flew at her, threatening to kick her out of the house if she dared set foot in the sanctuary he'd designed for me. The entire upstairs was my private refuge from the world's turbulence and Momma's storms.

The temptation to flee swelled in me, but I swallowed hard, sucked in a deep breath, and steeled myself for battle. My cause was ambitious, but just. Self-serving, yet altruistic at the same time. If I could succeed in getting Momma to agree to divorce Frank, marry Henry, and move to Florida, then peace, joy, and happiness would reign supreme in my little world of Sugardale. Frank would be ecstatic. Henry delighted. And Momma would have a brand new crop of Picks to work her black magic on.

The rich and powerful folk of Palm Beach would present more of a challenge to her than the citizens of Cascade County, Georgia. But I had complete faith in her ability to rise to the test. She'd zero in on the easy pickin's first, and then work her way up the money chain. Yes, if Henry was willing to take my mother, he could have her with my blessings and my sympathies. My only regret is that his Aunt Velma didn't live in Buenos Aries, Sydney, or Amsterdam. Another country on a different continent would have been better, but I'd take whatever I could get.

"Is Frank home yet, Momma?" I could use backup.

"Do you see him?"

"I thought he might have come in while I was in the shower."

Helen peered over the top of her magazine. "Can't you keep up with your own man? Must I do everything for you?"

I crossed my arms, choked back a retort, and decided to change the subject. "Do you want fried chicken or catfish for supper?"

"I've a taste for meatloaf. Fix a nice meatloaf, please."

Meatloaf had never been a favorite of Momma's. She wanted it now because she knew I didn't like to cook oven meals on hot summer evenings.

"I don't want to heat up the house."

She slammed the magazine against the edge of the coffee table. "Why the hell did you ask me what I wanted for supper if you didn't intend to fix it?"

"I didn't ask you what you wanted for supper. I asked if you preferred chicken or catfish."

Helen stood. "Must I beg in order to get a little meatloaf in my own damn house?"

"I'll fix a meatloaf in the morning, while it's still cool."

"I guess I'll starve until then." She turned on the television, flipped through the channels.

I clenched my teeth and waited for the rage to flow out of me. A victory tonight depended upon my ability to control the two-headed monster of mockery and sarcasm.

"Some of us don't have the luxury of retreating to an air conditioned bedroom like you do, Momma."

"Is it my fault that there's only one air conditioner in this damn house? Frank controls the money. If you can't get him to spring for a lousy window unit, you must not be tickling his fancy properly, girl."

Henry or no Henry, such a nasty remark could not go unchallenged. "Why should Frank buy another unit? I'll take yours when you move to Florida."

She lit a fresh cigarette, inhaled deeply, and blew smoke rings at the actors on the screen. "What makes you think I'm moving to Palm Beach?"

It was the way she asked her question — in her low, slow-down voice — that indicated I'd played my hand too soon.

She turned off the TV, sat down on the blue velvet davenport, and crossed her long legs. The popping of sandal against heel began again. "I didn't hear your answer. Why would I leave such a loving family?"

I slipped down onto the edge of Papa's old recliner. "I thought you loved Henry."

"I do, but that doesn't mean I'm going to run after him." She plucked a piece of tobacco off her bottom lip and flicked it into the air.

"Henry loves you, Momma. If you really love him, you'll go."

Helen rose and walked to the middle of the living room. She twirled in a slow circle, pointing her finger at various objects. "I've spent twenty-three years in this house, in this town. I arrived here with nothing and married into one of the most important families in the county. I've built me a solid place in Sugardale society." She came and stood over me. "Do you really think I'd give everything I've worked for to you and Frank and run off with Henry with nothing to show for it? Are you that stupid, Becky Leigh?"

"How much?" a male voice asked.

Helen turned to find Frank standing behind her. "How long have you been there?"

"Long enough." Frank pulled off his tie, hung it and his jacket on the coat rack in the hall and walked into the living room. "How much, Helen? How much money will it take to get you out of our lives?"

"You think you can buy me off like that?" she asked.

Frank undid the top two buttons of his shirt. "$50,000 cash."

"That money is to finance our wholesale expansion," I said. "You can't give it to her."

"Hush, Becky. This is between me and Helen."

She laughed. "We see how much your opinion counts, Becky. I thought you two were partners."

Frank glanced at me. I didn't try to hide my disappointment.

"Becky and I are partners. It's our future together I'm thinking about."

"And my future? I guess that doesn't matter to either one of you. The fact that the business and house was left to me by Becky's daddy makes no difference, does it?" She fisted her hands on her hips. "If it wasn't for me, neither one of you would have a roof over your head or a pot to pee in."

"There's no need to get vulgar, Helen."

She blew a cloud of smoke toward Frank. "I'm just getting warmed up."

"The hell you are." He pointed to the sofa. "Sit down."

"You can't tell me what to do, Frank. This isn't scared little Becky you're talking to."

Frank's nostrils flared as his breathing quickened; his fingers balled into fists. "I've never believed in hitting a woman, Helen. Don't make me change my mind."

She spun around, stomped across the room, and plopped down on the sofa.

I wrapped my arms around my waist and began to rock.

Frank pushed the ottoman toward the coffee table until it was halfway between Momma and me. "I saw Henry at the post office. He said he'd stopped by today."

"So what?" Helen asked. "I'm allowed to have company, aren't I?"

Frank leaned forward, rested his elbows on his knees and clasped his hands. "He said he was moving to Florida and wants you to go with him. He wants to marry you."

She slid an ashtray across the coffee table and rubbed out her cigarette into the amber glass. "That must have been an interesting conversation. Hi, Frank. How are you?" Momma spoke in a voice meant to mimic Henry's. "By the way, I stopped by your house to ask your wife to marry me. You don't mind, do you?"

Frank straightened. "Henry knows that we haven't lived as man and wife for years. He knows Becky and I are together."

"He knows you and my daughter started an affair behind my back in my own house."

I stood. "That's not the way it happened, Momma."

"Becky, please sit down and let me handle this," Frank said.

Helen nodded. "That's right, Becky. You shut up and let the grownups talk."

Fire burned in my cheeks. I started toward her, but Frank waved me back.

"Pay your mother no mind. She's just trying to cause trouble." He turned to Helen. "Our relationship started long after you began your trysts with Henry, Roy Tate, and who knows how many others."

Helen grinned. "Well, looks like we're all sinners in the same boat bound for Hell."

"Does Henry know you were raising your skirt for Tate at the same time you were bedding him?" Frank asked.

She jumped up. "Shut your mouth, Franklin Wayne Wooten. I haven't been with Roy for years." Momma marched over to the credenza, yanked open the second drawer, took out a new carton of Camels. She unwrapped the cellophane, removed a cigarette, and pulled out her lighter. "Don't you worry any about Henry. He knows everything."

"I'm glad to hear that," Frank said.

She placed the cigarette between her lips, lit it, and then slipped the lighter back into her skirt pocket. "Henry knows everything about me and he stills love me. He's not like you and Becky's daddy. When Henry loves a woman, he loves her unconditionally." Momma pulled hard on her smoke, then blew it out. "He doesn't try to mold her into something she's not or hold back his love as a means of punishing her or trying to control her."

"Papa didn't do that," I said. "Papa loved unconditionally."

"Sure he did, if you were a Cooper by blood. But if you weren't, you'd better stay in your place if you wanted any crumbs of affection from Paul Cooper."

"That's a lie." My hands began to tremble.

Helen shook her smoke at Frank. "You weren't any better."

"You're a liar, Momma. A lying whore, that's what you are." I started toward her, but Frank stepped between us.

She tapped her ashes into the ashtray. "That may be true, Sugar, but then what are you?"

Frank grabbed her arm. "I won't allow you to talk to Becky that way."

Helen pulled away, fled toward the dining end of the room, and slipped between the china cabinet and the formal dining table. "Did you hear that, Becky? Frank won't allow me. Wait until you do something he doesn't like, and then see how fast he turns on you."

He slipped his arm around my shoulder. "I doubt Becky will be beating any children. Besides, we love each other."

Helen grabbed the back of a dining chair with both hands. "Frank loves Becky. Isn't that sweet. Shall we open a bottle of champagne and celebrate?"

Frank's grip on my shoulder tightened. I couldn't tell if the trembling I felt was emanating from him or me. Maybe both.

"Sit down, Becky," he whispered. "I'll take care of this."

I did as I was told.

Frank returned to his seat on the ottoman. "Sit down, Helen."

"I don't feel like sitting."

Momma's legs could've been ready to break off and she wouldn't have sat down. That's her nature — ornery, bull-headed, and just plain disagreeable. For the life of me, I couldn't figure out why a nice man like Henry Nash wanted to be saddled with her. Maybe he was a secret masochist, preferring pain above pleasure, lunacy to common sense, and humiliation in lieu of loving support. If he wanted a dominating crazy woman who knew how to cut a person to the bone, then my mother was the right gal for him. Perhaps the years he spent breathing embalming fluid had mummified his brain cells.

Who knew what the real truth was? No one. That's who. In the sweet sounding world of Sugardale nothing was ever what it seemed, and no one was ever who they pretended to be, including me. Life in Sugardale reminded me of the house of mirrors I visited whenever the fair came to town. There was a different mirror for each kind of person you wanted to be. If you wanted to be skinny or fat, short or tall, round-faced or long-chinned, all you had do was look in the right mirror.

That's what we did everyday of our lives — Frank, Momma, and me. Across the threshold of our front door stood an invisible mirror. Every morning, we lined up in front of it and decided who we needed to be that day — dutiful wife, loving stepdaughter, family man, hard working, church going, pillars of the community. Once we determined what our role for the day should be, we stepped through the mirror and voila! We became that person. At the end of the day, we simply stepped back through the mirror of make-believe and reverted into our real selves.

But the mirror demanded all who used its life-transforming magic pay a fee. Every day, when we stepped back through the mirror, we were required to leave behind a small piece of ourselves, a token of integrity or sliver of truth that we no longer had a right to claim. How long could such payments continue before spiritual bankruptcy occurred? Who knew? Not me. But I feared Frank might have the answer.

Since our return from vacation, I'd observed slight changes in him. Little things, like going to bed without me or not asking me to fix a favorite desert or turning down my offers to wash his back. Our physical relationship had always been very active. We seldom skipped more than two nights making love until now. Frank hadn't touched me in five nights. I told myself he was tired from work, but that was a lie. Our most amazing nights of passion had followed some of our most taxing days at the stores.

Lately, Frank hadn't seemed to need or want me. Something had changed, and I'd decided it was Momma's fault. Without Henry to keep her occupied, she'd interjected her ornery self into our lives again. Her complaining, bickering, and bad temper tainted Frank's and my relationship. She wouldn't stop until I was as alone and miserable as she was. One way or another, Momma had to go. Surely, Frank felt the same way. He had to know our current problems were her fault, not mine.

Helen and Frank stared at each other, neither one willing to blink first.

I sighed. "What do you want, Momma?" Might as well ask. Everything would turn on her desires anyway.

"Well, now that you've asked." She sat down, rested her elbows on the table, and folded her hands neatly under her chin. "Henry has made me a very attractive proposal."

"Are you accepting his offer of marriage?" Frank asked.

Helen grinned. "That would please you and Becky to no end, wouldn't it?"

"We just want you to be happy, Momma. That's all."

She laughed. "You two would ship me to the moon if you could. Wouldn't you?"

"Let's cut the bullshit, Helen," Frank said.

"Is that any way to talk in front of the child, Sugar?"

I stood. "I'm not a child, goddamn you."

Helen shook her head. "Such language. You must have learned that from Frank."

I'd had enough. I headed straight for her.

Frank grabbed my arm. "Calm down, Becky. Can't you see Helen's trying to rile you? She's just playing you."

I jerked my arm free, grabbed two silver candlesticks off the credenza, and flung candles across the floor. Holding up the silver, I said, "And I'm going to play her too. I'm going play the drums using her head."

"Give me those." Frank tried to wrestle the candlesticks from me.

"No. I am tired of her smart-alecky mouth." I tightened my grip on the silver.

Frank pulled harder. "Let go, Becky."

I turned loose of the candlesticks. Frank fell back into the edge of the china cabinet. Antique dishes rattled. Cups and saucers crashed against the glass cabinet doors, followed by a gravy boat and several plates.

Helen swiveled around to survey the damage. "That was your Grandma Cooper's best china. It survived the Civil War."

How many times had Grandpa Eli told me the story of how his grandmother had buried the family valuables, including the silver and good china, in the woods until the war was over. Not one piece got broke. He considered that a tribute to Cooper ingenuity and perseverance. "Even the damn Yankees couldn't get the best of the Coopers," Grandpa often bragged. In an instant, I'd accomplished what Sherman and a regiment of union troops had failed to do — destroy a piece of the Cooper legacy. I wanted to vomit.

Frank got his feet under him, set the candlesticks on the table, rubbed his spine.

"Are you hurt, Frank?" I started to apologize, but he turned his back to me.

"Why do you make Becky crazy like that, Helen?"

Helen shrugged. "Because she lets me, I guess."

I glared at her.

"Don't look at me that way," she said. "I'm not the one who called you crazy."

"Enough!" Frank shouted. "I've had enough of both of you." His eyes bulged, his cheeks puffed out. Quick breaths forced through barred teeth created a wheezing, the tempo of which matched my escalating pulse. He pointed toward the hall. "Since the day I walked through that door eight years ago, you two have put me in the middle. Well, no more. Do you hear me, Helen?"

"The whole neighborhood can hear you, Frank."

"Do you hear me, Becky?" he asked in a softer voice.

"Yes, Darling."

Helen snickered. My term of endearment obviously amused her.

Frank picked up the candlesticks, tossed one to me, and thrust the other into Momma's hand. "If you two *ladies* are so determined to destroy each other, go ahead."

Neither one of us moved.

"How about it, Becky? You've said you wished your mother was dead." He turned to Momma. "And what about you, Helen? You've come close to killing Becky on a number of occasions. Doctor Condray has the x-rays to prove it." Frank slicked back his hair with both hands. "Who wants to strike the first blow?"

At first, neither of us made a move. Then, I placed my candlestick back on the credenza. Momma handed hers to Frank. He set it next to its mate and returned to the ottoman.

"I've done a lot of thinking these past two weeks," he said.

"About what?" Helen asked.

"Let me finish. After I have my say, you and Becky can do whatever you like."

"Sounds good to me. Sound okay to you, Becky?"

My neck muscles tightened. Goosebumps decorated my arms. "I guess."

"I can't go on living this way." Frank ran his hand over his face. "I'm tired of the bickering, fed up with the sarcasm, and worn out by the hate. Most of all, I'm sick to death of the lies." He stood, slipped his hands in his pockets, and rocked back on his heels. "I must be getting old because I can't keep up with all the lies anymore. Don't even want to try. And as far as the sneaking around goes, I'm tired of that too." He walked over and took my hand. "Becky, I love you, and I'm through trying to hide that fact from the world. Do you know what I dream about?"

I shook my head.

"I dream about summer evenings like this. A day's work finished, the distant hills lit by a setting Georgia sun, the anticipation of the coming night's breeze." He rubbed his thumb across the back of my hand. "And you and me sitting in the swing on the front porch, my arm around your shoulders and us waving at all who pass by." Frank patted my arm. "Did you hear what I said, Becky? I said the front porch, in the daylight. Not the glider hidden in the back garden at two o'clock in the morning."

I nodded and blinked back tears.

"I never knew you were such a romantic, Frank," Helen said.

"Reckon it sounds corny to you, but then you never could understand honest emotions."

"Don't get all uppity with me. I went along with our game of charades because it worked best for all of us. You two are the ones who claimed a scandal would hurt business."

"You and Henry believed that too," I said.

"Yes, and we were right. This may be 1971, but Sugardale is still a narrow-minded, stuck-in-the past, old-fashioned community." Helen stopped, pushed her hair behind her ears. "Don't think just because a colored man got elected sheriff, folks here are more accepting of things now days. They're not. No one in this valley will ever accept you two as a couple."

"You're right," Frank said. "They'll never accept us as a couple as long as we're all here together."

"What does that mean?" she asked.

"It means one of us is leaving Sugardale. Either you or me."

The room went silent. I gathered my courage and asked, "What about me, Frank? If you leave, what am I supposed to do?"

"You'll come with me. Wherever I go, I'll want you with me."

"I can't leave Papa's house. You know I promised to take care of it for him."

Frank cocked an eyebrow. "Do you intend to plan the rest of your life around a promise to a dead man?"

"He's not just a dead man. He's Papa, and you're the one who convinced me I had to keep my promise."

"That's when you were at Havenwood and had given up on everything, including living." He grabbed my shoulders. "I would've told you anything to save you. Don't you understand?"

I sunk down into Papa's recliner. The goal for the evening was to get Momma to marry Henry and leave Sugardale. But now, Frank was talking about leaving instead and asking me to choose between him and my promise to Papa. How did things get so twisted so fast?

"Do you have some sort of plan?" Helen asked. "Or should we break out the Monopoly game? Winner takes all."

"Don't do it, Frank. Momma cheats."

She snickered. "Everybody cheats. I need a cigarette."

"I have two plans, Helen. Take your pick." He tossed her a pack of Camels. "As I said before, if you'll marry Henry and move to Florida, I'll give you $50,000 cash."

She flipped back the top of her lighter. "That's not enough."

"It's all the cash I have."

"Cash runs out. I want a percentage of the business, something for my old age."

"You're never going to get old, Helen."

She smiled. "Don't try to sweet talk me, Frank. I want my share. Won't leave without it."

He nodded. "What do you figure your share to be?"

"Since you'd get to keep the house, I think I should get at least half of the profits from the businesses."

"No way," I yelled. "Frank and I built up the stores and did all the work."

"Becky's right. Besides, we can't afford to take that much cash out each month and still keep the stores viable, much less growing."

"Fifty percent of a bankrupt business isn't worth much," I added.

Helen took a puff, held it, then blew it out the side of her mouth. "How much can we take out? And don't try to bullshit me. Remember my decision will affect your futures as much as it will mine. Maybe more."

"Becky's the bookkeeper. You'll have to ask her."

"I can't say without checking the books, last year's taxes, things like that."

"Okay," Helen said. "In plan one, I move to Florida with Henry. In return, you give me $50,000 cash and a mutually agreed upon percentage of the business. You and Becky get the house, the remainder of the business, an eternity of loving bliss, and all the sex a man your age can stand. Is that about right?"

He frowned. "You've got some way with words, Helen."

"Yeah, I know. In my next life, I'm going to be a poet."

"You forgot one thing, Momma."

"What's that?"

"The divorce. You and Frank will need to get a divorce if you marry Henry."

"We're getting a divorce whether she marries Henry or not," Frank said. "That's one thing that's long overdue."

"You don't have to sound so eager. Not after I gave you the best years of my life."

She pointed at the ashtray. "What if I decide not to move? This has been my home for most of my life. I'm comfortable here."

Frank handed her the ashtray. "In that case, we'd split everything. One would take the house and Sugardale store, and the other would get the cash and the business in Kirbyville. I think that's fair."

Helen pushed back her bangs. "Well, I'd want the house and Sugardale store."

"No," I said. "Papa's house is mine."

Helen shook her head. "I'm not moving into that apartment. This was my home first. Frank would still be living in that rundown duplex if it wasn't for marrying me."

"She's right, Becky."

"How can you take her side against me?"

"I'm not taking sides. I'm trying to do what's fair, to do what's best for everyone." He put his arm around me. "Can't you see that?"

I pushed him away and walked into the hall. He followed. "I can't move to Kirbyville."

"We don't have to stay there, Becky. We can sell the damn store, move someplace new, and start another business."

"I'm not giving up Papa's house. I can't."

Frank retreated, the color drained from his face. "And I can't stay. Not if it means living like we have."

I grabbed his shirt. "You promised you'd never leave me."

"I'm not leaving you, Becky. I'm leaving the insanity. This life of lies is killing me."

Frank was right. I'd always known the lies, the sneaking around, and the pretense was harder on him than on Momma and me. For us, living a double life was the norm. No one outside our family, except for Anna and Johnny, knew about the beatings, my broken bones, or Helen's adultery. We were experts at hiding the truth. But Frank had come to us with a code of ethics, a mantle of decency, and a sense of right and wrong. Over the years, Momma had dragged him down to our level. Out of a desire for love and a need for his protection, I'd helped.

"But how can I choose between you and keeping my promise to Papa?" Our eyes met briefly. Frank turned away, but not before I saw the pain in his eyes — pain I'd put there. I grabbed his arm. "Maybe I won't have to choose. Momma might move."

"Yes, perhaps I will." Helen stood in the doorway. "You two can fight and make up later. We've got business to decide on and I don't plan to waste my entire evening on it."

"Helen's right, Becky. You two need to make up your minds about what you're going to do. Why don't you show her the books? Let her see for herself what shape the stores are in. Then she'll know we're not trying to cheat her."

"She won't understand the books. She doesn't know how to read a ledger or a cash flow statement."

"The hell I don't. I worked the store and kept the books before you were born." Helen twisted a curl around her finger. "I help Henry with his bookwork every month."

I frowned. "I don't remember Papa saying you ever worked the store."

"Your daddy didn't tell you everything. And what you don't know about me could fill a library."

"Show her the books," Frank said. "Get this done."

"Aren't you coming with us?" I asked.

"I've made up my mind. Whatever decision you and Helen make, I'll learn to live with. I'll have to." He brushed my cheek with the back of his hand. "I'm going to take a shower and get some supper."

"Chicken or catfish, that's your choices," Helen said. "Don't even think of asking her for meatloaf."

"If you mention meatloaf one more time, Momma, I'll scream."

"You see what I mean, Frank? I've never known a person to get so worked up about a little meatloaf."

He sighed. "Helen, please don't agitate her just because you can."

"I give up." She raised her hands in mock defeat. "I'm going to eat at Henry's. You two lovebirds can have tuna casserole for all I care. But now, let's go check out those financial records. Are you coming, Becky?"

"I . . . I'm not sure . . ."

"She's coming, Helen."

"Good. I'll get my purse." She sashayed out of the hall.

I tugged at Frank's shirtsleeve. "You know I can't handle Momma alone."

"Then it's time you learned." He captured my face in his hands. "Just remember, regardless of what Helen says or does, you remain calm. Can you do that?"

"I'll try."

"You'll need to do more than try." He pulled me to him.

I hugged him. "I can't lose you, Frank."

"Stay calm, Ladybug. If you do that, Helen can't win."

I smiled at him. "You haven't called me Ladybug in years. I've missed it."

"I'll spend the next thirty years making it up to you." Frank kissed the top of my head and worked his way down my face, planting little pecks on my brows, my eyes, my cheeks, and the tip of my nose. In between, his warm breath tickled my ears as he whispered encouraging words and endearments. Frank still wanted me, still loved me.

With that knowledge, I could take on the world. I could even take on my mother.

"You two could sell tickets to this show," Helen said.

I tried to pull out of Frank's embrace. He loosened his grip slightly, but kept his arm around my waist, kept me by his side.

"We didn't see you standing there," he said.

She grinned. "Sugar, y'all wouldn't have seen an elephant enter the room. Not the way you two were welded together."

My face reddened, but not Frank's. There was no apology in his eyes.

"Are you ready to go, Becky? Or is there a second act? If so, I'll pull up a chair." A shameless grin lifted her lips. "I'll wait if you let me watch."

"You're sick, Momma. Plumb sick."

She threw back her head and let loose a wicked laugh. "I'm sick? Sweetheart, you're the one clinging to your mother's husband."

I'd have come right back at her with my own slam, but Frank squeezed my side — his way of reminding me to stay calm.

"Why don't you wait for me in the car, Momma? I'll get the keys to the store and be right out." Her face fell, disappointed because I'd ended our tit-for-tat game.

"Okay." She hooked her purse over her arm and started to leave.

"Helen," Frank called.

She turned around. "What is it now?"

"For the first time and maybe for the last time, we've all got a real chance to be happy. You have a shot at living the grand lifestyle you've always wanted." Frank slid his arm around my shoulder. "Don't throw it away in order to continue this I'll-show-you game we've played for years. I meant what I said. I'm finished playing games."

I leaned into him. "So am I."

Helen sighed. "I might as well move. You two aren't any fun anymore, and Henry is the only one who can fix my hair properly." She opened the front door. "I'll be in the car."

After she left, we stood there in shock and amazement.

"This is really happening, isn't it, Frank? We've got a real chance to get rid of her."

"Looks that way." He handed me his keys. "Go on before she changes her mind."

I hugged him tight. "I'll do a good job for us. I'll negotiate a good deal, I promise."

He drew me close. "Give her whatever it takes to get her out of here and out of our lives."

CHAPTER 23

I tugged at my blindfold. "Is this really necessary?"

"Yes," Frank said. "It's really necessary."

"But I've been here dozens of times before. I've seen the waterfall, the gorge, the pond. I've seen it all."

"Be patient, Becky."

What choice did I have? Frank had insisted we leave work early and drive out to the mountain property of his late friend, Mr. Parr. That wasn't unusual. Frank and I often stopped by to watch the sunset at the gorge or to poke our feet into the cool stream. He'd even talked me into skinny-dipping in the pond a couple of times.

Often, we'd visit Starview Mountain just to soak in the grandeur of the scenery, to be refreshed by the pristine honesty of a land untouched by man or machine. The serenity of Starview served as a counterbalance to the deadlines, financial dickering, and the never-ending lies required to sustain our mock image of the perfect family. For Frank, the natural beauty and unspoiled integrity of the mountain helped repair some of the contamination done to his soul, contamination caused by his collaboration with expert sinners like me and Momma.

"We're here," he said. "You can take off the blindfold."

Eagerly, I removed the cloth. Before me lay the pond, the stream, and the woods. "Everything's the same."

Frank shoved a fist full of papers at me. "Read this. Then tell me this place looks the same to you."

The papers were from some attorneys in Atlanta. The first letter explained how Mr. Edmond J. Parr had passed away two months earlier.

"But we knew your friend died, Frank. You went to his funeral."

"Read the rest of the letter."

"Okay." As I continued reading, my excitement grew. "This is unbelievable. It's too . . ."

"Too incredible," Frank said as he picked me up and twirled me around.

"Why would Mr. Parr leave this wonderful property to you?"

"He wrote me a letter," Frank said, between ragged breaths.

I looked through the papers until I found the letter. In it, Mr. Parr thanked Frank for the years he'd worked for Parr Construction. Mr. Parr also wrote about his love for the mountain property and his fear that, if left to his children, the property would be sold to developers. Thus, he was leaving the land to Frank, the one man who appreciated its natural beauty as much as he did.

"Aren't you pleased, Frank? You've tried to buy this property for years."

"Buying it is one thing. Being given it is another. It just doesn't seem right, Ed leaving something this valuable to me instead of to his kids."

"But he explained his reasons. He knew you loved this land and wouldn't try to make a quick buck off of it."

Frank bent down, rinsed his hands in the clear water, and wiped them on his jeans.

"I was seventeen, just married, and as green as they come when Ed gave me a job. I worked for him until I married Helen and took over the store for her. Almost everything I know about running a business, I learned from Ed Parr." Frank picked up a few pebbles, skipped them across the water. "When April was dying, he gave me time off with full pay so I could be with her. I've never been able to repay him for his kindness."

"This is your chance."

He threw the last of the rocks into the stream and stood. "I always figured parents should leave things to their own children."

"His children are grown, and I'm sure he left them the construction company. It's worth a lot, isn't it?"

"Millions."

"Mr. Parr's children won't exactly starve if you accept his gift. Will they?"

Frank shook his head.

I slipped my arms around his waist. "Then take it. Think of it as a sign that things are turning around for us."

"When Helen called yesterday, did she say when she'd be back?"

"In a week or so. Now that she's got the divorce, Momma and Eva want to visit some of the other islands."

A quiet miracle had occurred in Sugardale three weeks earlier. Helen had agreed to divorce Frank and marry Henry. Despite all odds and without us coming to physical blows, she and I worked out an agreement about the business. After the divorce, she'd receive $50,000 cash and thirty percent of the net profits from the stores, plus any wholesale business we might develop. Afraid that I might manipulate the books against her, Momma had insisted on a guaranteed monthly minimum check of $2,000. Any month her percentage didn't come up to the minimum, Frank and I would have to make up the difference out of our own salaries.

She'd made her position very clear. "No guaranteed minimum, no divorce."

While it galled Frank and me to give into her blackmail, we'd have gladly lived on beans and cornbread if it meant getting her out of our lives.

Henry had done his part. He'd convinced Momma of his undying love and had showed her the detailed business plan he'd developed to assure his success in Palm Beach. Even so, she had *still* insisted on reviewing all of his bank statements, investment portfolio, and the projected revenue from the sale of the Sugardale beauty shop and his ancestral home.

To clinch the negotiations, he'd reminded Helen that he stood to inherit most of his Aunt Velma's fortune. Being a proud man and accustomed to earning his own way, Henry cared little about his aunt's riches. But he believed his "Peaches" would find the possibility of owning a mansion bigger than Eva Whitcomb's too tempting an opportunity to pass up. He knew his woman.

Whenever Helen decided to do something, she wasted no time getting it done. She called Eva, informed her about the move to Florida, and asked her advice on how to obtain a fast divorce. Three days later, the two women boarded a plane for the Dominican Republic where foreigners could obtain a quick divorce as long as both spouses agreed to it.

The gurgle of the stream, the intermittent knocking of a determined woodpecker, and the muted roar of distant thunder rolling toward Starview Mountain serenaded us. Frank and I hugged each other, swaying to the tempo of an accelerating breeze sifting through the cotton-woods.

"You think I should keep the land?" he asked.

"Definitely."

"Okay. I'll go to Atlanta next week and sign the papers."

"Then Starview Mountain will be yours, Frank."

"Ours." He kissed me. "That reminds me, I need to make out a new will, one that leaves everything to you in case something happens to me."

I pushed him away. "Don't say that."

"Everything is in my name, Becky. The stores, the house, this land. I'd sleep better knowing you'd be taken care of in case something unforeseen happened."

"It makes me nervous to talk about wills and such. Do whatever needs doing. Just don't talk to me about it. Okay?"

"Okay." Frank kissed me several times. "I've got something in the back of the truck to show you."

An olive-green tarp covered the truck bed. He untied it, then yanked it off.

"What's all the gear for?"

Frank let down the tailgate. "We're going to camp out on our new land this weekend."

He pulled out two fishing poles, leaned them against the side of the Ranchero. "Tomorrow, I'm going to teach you to drive my truck."

"If I learn to drive, I won't have an excuse to ride with you all the time."

"Soon, we won't need excuses to be together. Will we?"

"Okay. But I'll only drive when we're here. That way the only thing I can run into is a tree."

"Just make sure you don't drive off the cliff."

I laughed. "That's a reassuring thought. By the way, what if we're needed at one of the stores? Won't they wonder where we are?"

"Gordon and Neil are capable of taking care of things, and they'd never question me about our whereabouts." Frank slid a large cooler off the tailgate. "Bring those poles. Let's get camp set up. Looks like it's going to rain."

I laid the fishing rods across the top of a cardboard box filled with metal dishes and a drip coffee maker. "Gordon might not ask, but Reverend Murray will if we miss church on Sunday. What are you going tell him?"

"I'll tell him the truth. We went out of town."

"He'll want more information than that, especially since everyone thinks Momma's visiting a sick friend in Charleston."

Frank plunked the cooler down under a huge oak tree. "I'll tell him we went camping, and that I chased you all around the woods and did you-know-what every time I caught you."

"You can't tell the preacher that. He'd sandblast our names onto his heathen prayer list. Then half the people in Sugardale would be knocking on our door, bent on saving us from the fires of Hell."

"Everyone will eventually find out about the divorce, Becky."

"Do you suppose that we'll lose a lot of customers when word about us gets out?"

Frank shrugged. "They'll be back when it's planting time or when the grass starts tickling their rear ends and they need a new lawn mower."

"Momma thinks we might actually get new customers."

"How does Helen figure that?"

"She says people may hate sin, but they like to see sinners up close. Some people might start a garden so they'll have an excuse to come into the store to see the dirty old man who robbed the cradle and the young hussy who bops her momma's leavings."

"The dirty old man and the young hussy, huh? Helen does have a way with words." Frank took my hand as we walked back to the truck. "She could be right."

"You think so?"

He nodded. "When it comes to sin and sinners, Helen is the world's expert."

That was a true fact.

"Anyway, you've got bigger problems to worry about." Frank heaved a long box up on his shoulder. "You'd better get on your running shoes because as soon as I get this tent up, I'm coming after you."

I snickered. "You know an old man like you can't catch me."

"That's true, but we both know you'll slow down enough so I can."

"Why on earth would I do that?"

Frank grinned. "Aren't you the young hussy who likes to bop her momma's leavings?"

I glared at him. "I have only one response to such a scandalous question."

"What's that?"

"Do you need help setting up that tent . . . Sugar?"

*****

On Monday, Frank came home from work early. Something was on his mind, but he refused to talk about it. When he went to take a shower, I slipped into the bathroom, sat down on the commode lid, and watched his silhouette dance on the plastic shower liner. "Mind if I join you?"

Frank poked his head out. "I'm almost finished."

Not the response I wanted. I tiptoed to the back of the tub, cast off my clothes, slipped into the shower.

Frank swiveled around. "I said I'm about through."

The agitation in his voice surprised me. "Thought I'd wash your back."

"I'm finished." He turned off the water, stepped out of the tub, grabbed a towel and began drying himself off.

"I wasn't finished." I did not attempt to hide my growing aggravation.

Frank looked at me, his face a blank stare as if he'd forgotten I was even in the shower with him. "Sorry about that."He turned the water back on and then walked out of the bathroom into his connecting bedroom.

Anger began to shove my worry aside. I stepped one foot out of the tub, intent on stomping into the bedroom and demanding an explanation for his lousy mood, but my pride stopped me. Instead, I treated myself to a long shower in hopes that it might calm me down and give Frank a little time to unwind. Maybe then, I could get him to clue me in as to what had him so upset.

After my shower, I found Frank lying on his side on the bed. His eyes were closed; his breathing heavy. I lay down on my back on the other side of the bed, trying not to disturb him in case he had fallen asleep.

Frank rolled onto his back and laced his fingers in mine. We lay watching the afternoon shadows crawl across the room.

Turning onto my side, I stroked his brow. "What's the matter?"

"Do you realize how much I love you, Becky?"

"I know."

His blue eyes turned serious. "You couldn't know. I didn't know myself until today."

Frank had spent the day at the Kirbyville store. I'd planned to go with him, but then decided to stay in Sugardale to finish some paperwork. A decision I now regretted.

"What happened? Did something go wrong at the store?"

He kissed my forehead. "We'll talk later."

"Tell me what's wrong. I want to help."

"Later." Frank flopped onto his stomach, rested his head on his arm, and closed his eyes.

"Okay," I whispered. "We'll talk . . . later."

CHAPTER 24

Frank stood in front of the dresser, brushing his hair, wearing a maroon towel tied around his waist. I sat on the edge of the bed, my nakedness covered by the black satin robe he'd bought me when he went to Atlanta to sign the papers on Starview Mountain.

"What's brothering you, Frank?"

He held up his hands. "I think I'm water-logged."

"You promised we'd talk later."

"There's no need. Everything is clear now."

I got up and headed for the door.

"Where're you going?" he asked.

"I'm going to call Neil and ask him what happened today."

"Neil doesn't know anything."

"He's the store manager. He should."

"This has nothing to do with the store."

Now I was truly frightened. It couldn't be Momma that had Frank so upset. She wasn't due back for a couple of days. If it wasn't business and it wasn't Momma, what could it be? I sat down on the bed again. Frank wrapped an afghan around my shoulders, but I threw it off. "I'm not cold."

"You're shaking,"

"I'm shaking because I'm mad at you for treating me like a kid. You're shutting me out. That makes me mad . . . and scared."

Frank bent down and hugged me. "I don't mean to scare you. I just want to protect you."

"Protect me from what?" As soon as the question left my mouth, the answer came. "This has something to do with Donald, doesn't it?"

He nodded and went over to the window, pulled back the curtain, stood staring into the darkness.

Donald. I should've known. After Momma, Donald was our biggest thorn.

"Did he call you today?"

Frank let go of the curtain. "He came by the store."

"Were Charlotte and the girls with him?"

"No. He heard about Neil retiring at the end of the year. Donald wants the job."

"Is he crazy? He knows nothing about the hardware and garden business. Besides, he can't drive all the way from Athens to Kirbyville every day. It's too far."

"He wants to move into the apartment."

"He wants our apartment?"

Frank nodded. "Donald just wants to get Charlotte away from her family. He claims his in-laws are running their lives. I can't say I blame him. Ben Welch is a bit overbearing."

"You gave him our apartment, didn't you? Without even checking with me first."

Frank's jaw tightened. "Do you really believe I'd do that?"

I looked down at my feet. "No, not really."

"We won't need the apartment after Helen moves to Florida. We'll have this house and our cabin. You still want to build a cabin on Starview Mountain, don't you?"

"Yes, but . . ."

"But what, Becky?"

"I can't stand the thought of Donald living in our apartment."

Frank's shoulders sagged. He turned back toward the window. "I know you hate my son.

When I think of what Donald did to you, I could almost kill him." He looked over his shoulder at me. "If any other man hurt you that way, I would kill him. But he's my son, and I'm more to blame for the way he turned out than he is."

"Don't do this to yourself again. A sick wife, two jobs, and a kid. No one could've handled all that alone. You had to send Donald to live with his grandparents."

Frank came and sat next to me. "I promised Donald he'd be at his grandparents a few months, but April didn't get better like I figured she would. The months turned into a year, one turned into two. By the time April died, Donald didn't want to come home." Frank reached for my hand. "When I agreed to let him keep living with his grandparents, I told myself it was for his benefit. His friends were there. He liked his school." He dragged a hand over his hair. "I lied to myself. I was so wrapped up in my loss, so numb from watching his mother slip away that I could barely care for myself. The thought of being responsible for another human being scared me. By the time I got myself together and made Donald come home, he was out of control."

"Because his grandparents spoiled him," I said.

"Because I made a crummy decision and Donald's paid for my mistake all his life."

I jumped to my feet. "Maybe you're to blame in part for some of Donald's actions when he was a boy, but he's a grown man now. It's time he realized the world doesn't owe him everything just because he had a bad childhood. I'd put mine up against his any day."

"I know, and that's what I told him after I spoke with Ben Welch."

"You spoke with Donald's father-in-law?"

"Yes. Something about Donald's story didn't ring true. When he went to the bathroom, I called Charlotte. She'd taken the baby to get her vaccinations, but Ben was there. He'd stopped by to check on Amy and the new babysitter. He told me why Donald is so anxious to quit working for him."

I sat back down. "Why?"

"Ben finally let Donald move up from selling used cars to new ones, even gave him a new Impala to drive as a demonstrator. Last week, Donald wrecked the car."

"Anyone can have an accident."

"Donald was drunk. The accident happened when he pulled out of a motel. Seems he'd been shacked up all day with some gal instead of being in Atlanta at the car show."

"Does Charlotte know?"

"No. The police called Ben. He gave the fellow Donald hit a nice car and some cash in return for his agreeing to keep quiet about everything." Frank rubbed his chest. "This damn indigestion."

"Is that bothering you again?"

"Yeah. Is there any Alka Seltzer left?"

"In the medicine cabinet. I'll get it for you." When I returned, Frank was standing by the window again, still rubbing his chest. Beads of sweat dotted his hairline. I handed him the fizzing drink. "How could you have indigestion? You didn't eat much supper. You should see Doctor Condray."

He drank the medicine and handed me the empty glass. "I'll be fine now. Don't worry about me, Becky."

"Sorry, mister. No can do." I set the glass on the dresser, pulled Frank's head down, and kissed him. He tasted like salt. "At least Mr. Welch didn't fire Donald."

"No, but he put him back to selling used cars. He told Donald that if he ran around on Charlotte again, he'd regret it. Ben is threatening to hire the meanest divorce lawyer in Georgia for Charlotte and he'll take everything from Donald, including the girls."

"Mr. Welch can't stop Donald from seeing his daughters."

"Ben has money and influence. He's not the type to make idle threats. I urged Donald to shape up before he loses his family."

"What did he say?"

"He really wants to get away from Athens."

"He wants to get away from Mr. Welch so he can run around on Charlotte."

"That's kind of harsh, isn't it?"

"Did you give Donald the job as store manager? Is that what you're trying to tell me?"

Frank grabbed my shoulders. "No, Becky. We decided to offer Josh Zagat the position. Gordon's son is great with people, knows the business, and can handle responsibility. He's earned this job, hasn't he?"

"Yes." I placed my hand on Frank's cheek. "What do think about giving Josh the apartment as part of his salary package? The store would get an on-site manager and he'd be downstairs if his wife needed him. She'd like that, especially with their baby coming soon."

Frank pulled me into his arms. "I had the same idea."

For a while, I said nothing, content just to hear Frank's heart beating in my ear.

"What did you end up telling Donald?"

"I explained that the job was filled and offered to set up interviews for him with some companies who are hiring."

"Did he accept your offer?"

"No. I even offered to pay for him to go back and finish college, but he refused." Frank let go and stepped back. "Donald said he wanted to work for me. Claimed he'd like to repair our relationship. I told him there might be an opening on the loading dock at the Kirbyville store."

I sat down on the end of the bed. Frank stared at me, looking like a little boy waiting for his mother to tell him if he could have a piece of candy. "I suppose that would be okay. Since I took over most of the bookkeeping, I'm not at the Kirbyville store everyday now."

Frank collapsed into the chair beside the dresser. "It won't work. I see that now."

"I'm willing to try."

"It won't work because of Donald." Frank rubbed the back of his neck. "When I told him I wanted to check with you first, he started screaming at me, saying I cared more about you than him. He said you belonged . . ."

"Belonged where?"

"He said you belonged back in Havenwood. I told him to shut his mouth."

"Did he?"

Frank ran an open hand over his face. "God, I wish he had."

I blew out a deep breath. "What else did he say about me? Tell me."

"Why? It'll only upset you and it's not true."

"He called me your whore, didn't he?"

"Only once, Becky. Only once."

"Did you two fight?"

"We would have if Neil hadn't come in when he did."

"How did everything end up?"

"Donald gave me an ultimatum. If I don't let him have the manager's job, he won't let me see his girls anymore."

One Sunday each month, Frank drove to Athens to spend the afternoon with his two granddaughters. He looked forward to the visits. I never went for fear of running into Donald, but Helen tagged along sometimes. Frank said his granddaughters were very fond of her and vice versa. I thought it odd at first, especially given how much Momma hated Donald. Then I figured it out. Momma likes children in general. There's just something about me she never cared for.

"Are you giving Donald the job?" I asked, despite my fear.

"That wouldn't be fair to Josh, to our employees, and especially not to you." Frank came and stood over me. "I can't let him get anywhere near you."

"I'm not afraid of him."

Frank captured my face in his hands. "I'm afraid for you. And I'm afraid of what I'd do to him if he hurt you again. Helen will soon be out of our lives and so will Donald."

"But he's your son."

"And I love him. If he ever grows up, he'll see that. Until then, it's you and me."

"I never wanted to come between you two. I only wanted him to leave me alone."

"I know. This is Donald's fault. Donald's and mine."

"Not yours, Frank."

"Yes, mine." He brushed my bangs out of my eyes. "Donald said something else to me. He said I loved you more than I'd loved his mother."

"That's not true. April was the love of your life."

"That's what I'd always thought too." He reached for my hands. "So, when Donald accused me of loving you more than her, I started to argue with him. Then I realized he was right." Frank got down on his knees in front of me, pushed my thighs apart and scooted between them. "You're the love of my life, Becky. I'll do whatever it takes to keep you safe."

"Does that include . . . marriage?" Like most young girls, I'd dreamed of the day some handsome Sir Lancelot would fall on his knees and beg for my hand in marriage, insisting he'd die if I refused. Never in my wildest imagination did I think that when the time came, I'd be one doing the asking. "Will you marry me, Frank?"

"Are you sure you want to marry an old man like me?"

"I'm sure."

Frank rubbed my arms through the black satin. "We'll get married."

"When? Soon?"

"How does week after next sound? Helen should be in Palm Beach by then. Gordon and Neil can handle the stores. We'll take a week off for a honeymoon."

"To where?"

"Where do you want to go?"

I smiled. "I suppose Paris is out of the question, huh?"

"If you're willing to wait a couple of months to get married, I could swing it."

"I don't want to wait."

"Okay," Frank said. "We can go to Ruby Falls for a honeymoon."

"I've a better idea." I wrapped my arms around his neck. "Let's spend the week on Starview Mountain. We can decide where to build our cabin. We can fish, swim, and you can chase me all around those woods."

He grinned. "I'll put a mattress in the back of the truck. We'll lie there each night, count the stars, and plan our life together.''

"I like the sound of that." I brushed the back of my hand across his cheek. "Could you hang a tire swing from the big oak by the pond?"

"I'll hang a swing from every damn tree out there if you like."

"One will do." I pulled his mouth to mine.

CHAPTER 25

It was such a nice dream. Frank and I were on Starview Mountain. Our small, log cabin stood ready. Fireflies came out early in anticipation of the day's amber fading to blue. The splashing of water spilling over stone, the ripple of a trout skimming the pond's surface, and the sound of my own laughter as I urged Frank to push the tire swing higher highlighted my subconscious fantasy. Yes, it was such a nice dream until Momma's voice intruded.

"Wake up, Becky Leigh."

My left eye cracked open a tad to see a manicured hand on my shoulder. I followed it up to find the face of the person shaking me and bolted upright. "What are you doing here?"

"Trying to get you two sleeping beauties awake."

Frank lifted his head. "What's . . . what's the matter?"

"Momma's in our room."

"What?" Frank rolled over and sat up. "Helen, what the hell are you doing? You know you're not allowed upstairs."

"Well, excuse me. I thought you'd want to know the warehouse is on fire."

"What?" Frank and I asked in unison.

"The damn warehouse is on fire. Just look out the window."

Frank jumped out of bed and ran to window. I followed close on his heels.

"Shit," he said. "Call Gordon. Tell him and Josh to meet me —"

"Gordon's the one who called us. Didn't y'all hear the upstairs phone ring?"

"No," we said.

"Too worn out I guess." Helen crossed her arms. "Aren't you two cold? Standing buck naked in front of the window like that."

"Damn it." Frank grabbed his pants, pulled them on without underwear, slipped on his loafers.

I snatched the old afghan off the bed and wrapped it around me. "Do you mind, Momma? We're trying to get dressed."

She leaned against the doorframe. "I don't mind. Go ahead."

"Get out, Helen," Frank shouted.

"Okay, but neither one of you has anything I haven't seen before." She stepped out into the hall.

Frank headed out the door, shirt in hand.

Helen stepped in front of him. "We have fire insurance, don't we?"

"Of course. Now get out of my damn way," he said and pushed her aside.

I zipped up my jeans. "Wait for me, Frank."

"Can't. Get Helen to bring you."

By the time I got to the head of the stairs, he was out the front door. "Will you take me to the store, Momma?"

"Shouldn't you put on your blouse first? Otherwise, the fire fighters will have to turn their water hoses on themselves. And when are you going to learn to drive?"

I yanked a peach and green-striped top down over my head and grabbed my sneakers. "Let's go."

"You didn't put on your brassiere, Becky."

"Haven't you heard? Women are burning their bras these days."

"That's the stupidest thing I've ever heard. A good bra is a woman's best ally. By the way, what are you now? B cup?"

"C cup," I said, rushing past her.

"C cup my ass."

The wail of sirens split the night air. I stopped on the stairs. "Hurry, Momma."

"What's the rush? That old warehouse needed tearing down anyway. We'll build a new one with the insurance money. Is that my old shirt? The one I told you to cut up for cleaning rags?"

"It's a perfectly good work shirt. Now come on!"

At the bottom of the staircase, Momma grabbed my arm. "Is that all you want out of life, Becky? Hand-me-down clothes and a hand-me-down man?"

I jerked my arm free. "You didn't hand Frank down to me. I took him."

"Only after I'd finished with him." An alley cat grin pranced across her face "I never thanked you for carrying out my plan, did I?"

"What are you talking about?"

"My plan for you to seduce Frank, of course." Helen opened the drawer to the hall table pulled out her keys, cigarettes, and lighter. "I recognized the signs. Frank was lonely and getting restless. When a man gets restless, he starts thinking about moving on." She lit her smoke, took a quick drag. "I saw the way you two looked at each other. All I needed to do was get out of the way. Why else would I waste a week of my life listening to some fool preaching about what a wicked world we live in? As if I didn't know."

"You're lying. My getting together with Frank had nothing to do with you."

"I needed him to run the damn business." She stopped to pick a speck of tobacco off her tongue. "I figured once Frank got a taste of you, he'd never leave Sugardale without you. And truth be told, we both know you'll never forsake the Cooper homestead."

"The truth be told? If you ever tried to tell the truth, you'd choke to death."

Helen laughed. "Maybe, but you have to admit, my plan worked out well for everyone. I got Henry. Instead of spending the past two years pining for one another, you and Frank have been bumping bellies. Best of all, the stores have done great."

I pounded the end of the banister. "You can't take this away from me. I came up with the plan to keep him from leaving. It was my idea to seduce Frank."

"So it wasn't true love after all, huh?" Helen grinned. "Goes to show, you're as much my daughter, Becky Leigh, as you are Paul Cooper's."

"I love Frank. We can't wait until you're gone. We're going to throw a party."

She jingled her keys. "Speaking of parties, we'd better go."

I kicked the screen door open and yelled, "I'd rather crawl than ride with you."

*****

Although some people swear our lives are ruled by providence, I'd never believed in destiny, fate, or lady luck. I've found that human beings are quite capable of screwing up their lives on their own. But after last night's fire, I'd started to think maybe there was something to this old divine intervention theory.

For weeks, Frank and I had looked forward to this weekend — Momma's last weekend in Sugardale. Henry had picked Momma and Eva up at the airport on Friday. After taking Eva home, he'd brought his newly divorced fiancée back to Sugardale. She was in a great mood, handing out presents from the islands and going on about how she couldn't wait to start her new life as Mrs. Henry Nash. All she needed was the cash and the settlement agreement, and she'd be out of our lives forever.

Frank had assured her she'd have it all by Monday noon. By suppertime, Momma and Henry would be on their way to Florida. But who would've imagined that the warehouse would burn down over the weekend? If there was some cosmic troll pushing our lives around, he had a depraved sense of humor. Frank had promised to give Helen $50,000 cash. Now, he needed that money to replace equipment and inventory lost in the fire.

I pushed the glider harder and tried to block out Helen's screaming emanating from the house by remembering the stories of how Grandpa Eli built the original store. After returning home from the World War One, he married Grandma Rebecca and went to work in a talc mine near Chatsworth. He worked hard and Grandma saved all she could in order to help him open his own business. The Coopers have a long history of possessing green thumbs so a gardening business was a logical choice. Since you need tools to plant with, he thought a hardware division fit right in.

In early 1930, Grandpa quit his job to peruse his dream of being his own boss. People called him crazy. The stock market crash of the previous year had left many people without a job or a home. But where others saw despair, Grandpa Eli saw opportunity.

He often said to me, "I knew whatever happened, people had to eat. The folks who'd lost their jobs in the city were moving to the country so they could grow their own food. Someone had to sell them seed and supplies. Might as well be the Coopers."

He bought two acres where our house now stood and three lots at what was then the edge of town. Papa was five, too young to be of much help. So every Sunday afternoon, Grandpa Eli went down to the railroad tracks to look over the batch of homeless men who traveled the rails from town to town, looking for work. Some called them hobos, but my grandfather didn't.

"They were just men, Miss Becky," he often said. "Men down on their luck due to no fault of their own. I could've been one of them if your Grandma Rebecca hadn't been such a smart penny-pinching sweetheart."

He'd pick a few fellows and offer them a cot in one of the tents he'd set up on the side lot. Along with a dry bed, they'd get three meals a day, a hot bath, and a two-dollar bill in exchange for a week's hard work. In six weeks time, Grandpa had a store built. In 1952, Papa and Grandpa Eli built a larger store in front of the old structure. The original building became a storage facility for tractors, mowers, and inventory. Last night, the old building burned to the ground.

The ruckus from the house quieted. I heard doors slam and a vehicle leave. Helen's van and Frank's Ranchero were still in the driveway. Henry must have left. Hopefully, he took his fiancée with him.

I'd chosen to sit out this battle between Frank and Helen. He wanted her to let us use the cash to buy the new inventory. When the insurance company reimbursed him for the damages, Frank would give her the $50,000. Sick at heart over what I'd found at the fire, I sought refuge in our backyard glider.

Upon arriving at the fire, I ran around, shoes still in my hand, frantically searching for Frank. I stepped on something hard and round, picked it up, slipped into my pocket, and forgot about it until doing the morning laundry. When I emptied the pockets of my jeans, I found the medallion and recognized it as being the one Donald had showed us at Thanksgiving.

I gave the gilder another push, pulled the medallion out of my pocket, and checked it once more. On one side was a logo and the words Ben Welch Chevrolet, Athens, Georgia.

The flip side read Donald Wooten, Used Car Salesman of the Month, October, 1970.

The backdoor slammed. Frank's familiar footsteps pounded the stone path leading to the glider. I jammed the medallion into my pocket.

"I could've used your help in there, Becky." He plopped down beside me, unwrapped a roll of antacids, and popped a couple in his mouth.

"Heartburn again?" I asked.

"What do you expect? I just went ten more rounds with Helen."

"How did it go?"

"She agreed to wait for her money. At least for part of it."

"How did you get her to do that?"

"I didn't. Henry did. He convinced her to take $5000 now and let us keep the rest to buy inventory." Frank blew out a deep breath. "When the insurance pays off, Helen will get the rest of her money plus an extra $100 a week interest."

"Wouldn't it be cheaper to get a loan from the bank?"

"I want Gordon and Josh to go to the factory first thing tomorrow and pick up mowers and equipment." Frank rubbed his chest and tossed back another antacid. "This arson investigation will make the bank skittish about loaning us money."

"Is Sheriff Hays still insisting that it's arson?"

"Yes, but it's hard for me to believe anyone would do this deliberately."

I got out of the glider. "Maybe he's wrong. He's only been the sheriff a short while."

"Hays might be new to the valley, but he's been in law enforcement for a long time. The man knows his business." Frank stopped the glider, leaned forward, and rested his elbows on his knees. "I hope he catches the bastard who did this and gives me five minutes alone with him. That's all I want. Five minutes."

My neck muscles tightened. What would Frank do it he found out the bastard was his own son? "I think we should let it go. It was probably kids messing around with fireworks left over from last week's Fourth of July celebration."

"Gasoline started the fire. We found an empty can in the debris." Frank got up, stretched, and slicked back his hair. "Who'd do this to us, Becky? The only enemy we have is Helen and burning down the store would be the same as burning her own money. That eliminates her. Who else could've done something so malicious?"

If Frank's mind traveled that road very far, he was bound to think of Donald. I needed to change the subject. "Where are you going to store the new equipment?"

"Henry offered us the use of the big barn behind his house until he and the new owners close their deal next month. We've got to get another building up by then."

"That's not enough time."

"We'll get it done. Neil is sending some fellows from the Kirbyville store over. We'll start hauling off debris as soon as the sheriff gives us the okay." Frank reached for my hand. "I'm meeting with Gordon and Josh to come up with a list of what equipment we need. Do you want to come?"

I sat back down. "No, thanks."

Frank looked at his watch. "I'll be back in a couple of hours."

"What do you want for supper?"

"I'd better not eat. This damn indigestion is bad enough."

"You promised to see Doc Condray about that."

"First chance I get." Frank got up, turned, and squatted down in front of me. "I know you're upset about the fire and about having to deal with Helen, but don't worry. She's going to Palm Beach with Henry tomorrow."

"Are we still getting married next week? What about our honeymoon?"

"The wedding and honeymoon will have to wait until the new building is finished."

"I have a better idea," I said, taking his face in my hands. "You once talked about selling out and moving someplace new. Just you and me. You were right, Frank. Let's do it."

He pulled back, a startled look on his face. "You know you couldn't leave Sugardale. You'd never be able to sell your family home."

"I could. I've worked it all out in my mind."

He stood. "What's come over you?"

I patted the seat beside me. "Sit down. Let's talk a minute."

"I've got to go. Gordon and Josh are both waiting."

"Not yet," I shouted. "Let me explain." I jumped out of the glider, grabbed Frank's arm, pushed him into the seat. "Give me five minutes."

"Okay, Becky," he said. "Calm down."

"I've spent the afternoon thinking about this. Planning it all out." I rubbed the back of my neck. This would be the most important argument I'd ever made. Frank had to see things my way. "We can sell the business to Gordon and Josh."

"They don't have the money to buy it."

"We can sell it to them on contract, the way you bought the Kirbyville store. They can make monthly mortgage payments to us. That would work, wouldn't it?"

"I suppose, but what about the house? What about our plans to build a cabin?"

"Gordon and his family rent a small house now. They could rent Papa's house for the same money. They'd take good care of it." I took hold of Frank's hands. "Starview mountain isn't going anywhere. We can wait on the cabin."

"I don't want to wait, Becky." He got up, paced the stone path, all the time rubbing his arm.

"Look, we've had a setback, but that's all it is. Everything will settle down soon, and Helen will be out of our lives."

"No, she won't. She'll always be here, poking us, jabbing us, hammering at us until we break apart. Are you blind, Frank? Can't you see that?" I avoided mentioning Donald's name in my accusations, even though I now considered him a bigger threat than Momma.

Frank's eyes narrowed. "I'm not blind, but I am confused. Every time I suggested we leave here, you said you couldn't go. Now that I'm committed to making a life together here and am on the threshold of getting us everything we've dreamed of, you want to run away."

"It's not running away. It's escaping before Momma can destroy us."

"No one can come between us unless we let them."

"They're Pickers, Frank. They will find a way."

"They?"

"Momma . . . the preacher . . . neighbors. There's lots of Pickers in this town."

"I don't want to hear any of that Picker nonsense." Frank pulled at his chin. "Perhaps you're having second thoughts about marrying me."

"That's not true." I flung my arms around his waist. "I'm just scared."

Frank lifted my face. "Scared of what? What's got you tied in such a knot? Tell me."

Tell him? Tell him his own son is an arsonist as well as a rapist. Or that out of spite, Donald tried to destroy all his father had worked for over the past eight years? How could I explain to this wonderful man that one day soon he might have to watch his only child be carted off to prison? I couldn't do that anymore than I could convince Frank of the need to leave Sugardale immediately.

For better or worse, we were what we were. Momma and Donald were expert Pickers. Frank wasn't the kind of man to run off when things got tough. And me? I hadn't figured out who or what I was. But I did know two things. I loved Frank, and knew he'd be devastated if he discovered his son had set the fire. What could I do except hide the evidence of Donald's guilt and hope Sheriff Hays wasn't very good at his job?

"I'm tired," I said. "And I feel bad about the store. For over four decades, it stood there. Then in matter of minutes, it was gone. It scares me to think how quickly a person can lose everything."

"Not everything. We're still here. We'll rebuild and make it better." He sighed wearily. "But now, I want you to take a long soak and go to bed. You're exhausted. We both are."

"You're wrong when you say I could never leave Sugardale or this house. I could leave them for you, Frank. I love you that much."

The back of his hand slid slowly down my cheek. "I believe you could." He pulled me into his arms, hugged me tight. "I love you, Becky. Remember that and you'll be fine. You're stronger than you think." His entire body trembled as he planted kisses on the top of my head.

"Don't be gone long," I whispered. "I have trouble sleeping without you."

"I'll hurry." Frank stroked back my hair, kissed me twice, and then let go.

I stood in the middle of the road, watching until the darkness of the encroaching nightfall gobbled up the Ranchero's taillights. The sadness, the feeling of impending doom returned. If Sheriff Hays found Donald's fingerprints on the gasoline can, my hiding the medallion might be for nothing. What if Frank discovered I'd hid evidence of Donald's guilt? Would he be grateful I protected his son? Would he hate me for not telling him the truth? My head ached. I needed two aspirin, a hot bath, and a large miracle.

CHAPTER 26

I placed the pot of chrysanthemums in the box. It was number twenty out of thirty-five plants in need of repotting. Reaching for the next pot, I tried to concentrate on the colors of the flowers — bronzes, golds, creams — instead of on Momma's constant complaining. She and Henry had returned to Sugardale so he could close the sale on his house.

"It's been five weeks since the fire, Becky, and I still haven't received my money or laid eyes on those damn settlement papers. Have you seen them?"

"No, but Frank said he had the papers drawn up when he had his new will made out."

"You took his word for it?"

"Yes."

"Did Frank show you his new will? The one leaving everything to you."

I tapped the bottom of a pot of yellow mums to loosen the dirt. "He knows I don't like to discuss such matters."

"Then how can you be sure he made it out?"

I shook the old dirt off the roots. "Frank wouldn't lie to me."

Helen clapped her hands. "Of course not. Men never lie to women, do they? When are you going to start seeing the world for what it is?"

"If you mean seeing everything like you do, as ugly, conniving, and sinister, then never. I prefer Frank's way of looking at things."

"Frank's way, huh?" Helen folded her arms across her chest. "Tell me, do you need his consent before you pee too."

I jammed the flower into a new clay pot, poured in fresh soil, and patted the dirt down around the roots. "Frank and I respect each other."

"Respect? That's bull. You cling to him because inside you're still a little girl wanting her daddy to protect her from the boogie man." She pushed a fallen strand of hair back up into her French twist. "And Frank? It's no secret why he holds on so tight. Like most middle-aged fools, the only thing he respects is a firm young body."

"One more word and I'm going to throw this pot at your head."

"Don't you need Frank's permission first?"

I picked up the pot, pulled back my arm.

"Calm down, Becky." She walked to the opposite end of the greenhouse. "It's a good thing you have a pretty face and a nice body. You sure don't have a sense of humor."

I threw the pot. It hit a table of mixed greens, rocketing shards of clay, potting soil, and pieces of ivy, philodendron, and Boston fern into the air.

"Now look at the mess you've made for yourself." Helen brushed off the few pieces of soil that had managed to hit her blouse. "Haven't you learned yet not to throw anything unless there's someone else available to clean up after you?"

"When is Henry picking you up?" I asked. "Soon, I hope."

"After he's finished signing the final papers for the sale of his house. Frank had better have all that equipment out of the barn today."

"That's what he's doing now. Gordon, Josh, and Neil are helping Frank move everything into the new building."

"The new building my money paid for." She walked to the front of the hothouse. "Frank said he'd send me a check in two weeks, three at the most. It's been over a month and I still don't have my money. That liar."

"Frank didn't lie, Momma. The insurance company won't pay up until Sheriff Hays has completed his arson investigation."

"Just my luck to have a new sheriff elected and mess up my plans. I can't believe the people of Cascade County were so stupid as to vote for someone other than Roy Tate. He's served this county for twenty years."

"Sheriff Tate ran the county for twenty years. There's a difference between serving the people and running things to suit yourself."

"Well, Miss High and Mighty, consider this. If Roy Tate was still sheriff, I'd have my money and I'd be on my way to Palm Beach tomorrow with Henry. But if I don't get my money, I'm not moving anywhere except right back into that house and right back into you and your lover man's cozy little life."

The slam of a car door saved me from having to respond.

"That better be Frank with my money." Helen stormed out the side door.

It was Josh Zagat who'd interrupted us. Through the greenhouse window, I saw him talking with Momma. I grabbed the broom and a garbage pail and started cleaning up the mess I'd made. Josh burst in with Momma following close on his heels.

"You're too early, Josh. I'm not finished repotting the mums yet."

"I'm not here for the mums." His eyes were wide and wild. "I came to tell you . . ."

"To tell me what?"

Helen pushed Josh out of the way. "I need to tell you something, Becky."

"Tell me what, y'all?" I asked again. Sweat popped out under my arms, along my hairline, across the top my lip.

"It's Frank," Josh said.

"Frank? What about him?" The queasiness I'd been feeling for the past week returned.

Josh took off his hat, wiped his forehead with the back of his sleeve. "He's was loading a small tractor onto a flatbed truck when he fell off."

"Oh, God! Did the tractor run over him? Did it fall on him?" My back muscles tightened.

"No," Josh said. "He . . . he . . ."

"He had a heart attack," Helen said. "Frank had a heart attack and fell off the tractor."

I shook my head. "That's a lie. Frank is too young to have a heart attack." Wrapping my arms around my waist, I leaned back against a table laden with sacks of potting soil and began to rock.

"There's no time for that rocking nonsense, Becky." She turned to Josh. "Where's Frank now?"

"Daddy and Neil rushed him to the hospital in Kirbyville. I thought I should come get y'all."

She patted his shoulder. "You did the right thing. Come on, Becky. We need to get to the hospital. You drive, Josh."

"Yes, ma'am."

Josh and Momma headed for the greenhouse door, but I didn't move. I stood frozen in disbelief.

Helen grabbed my forearm. "Get her other arm, Josh."

Josh did as he was told and they dragged me to the car.

*****

The waiting room at Kirbyville Memorial Hospital was half-full. Bright August sunlight streamed in through the picture window that offered an unremarkable view of the visitor's parking lot. Paintings of various flowers in gold plastic frames hung above the armless black vinyl sofas that hugged two walls. An array of coffee, soda, and snack machines lined a third. Beneath the window, a low bookcase stored crayons and coloring books for use by any child who had the misfortune of being trapped with adults waiting for information that seemed to take forever to get. In the middle of the room, two sets of eight chairs upholstered in a nubby gray fabric sat facing each other, separated by a lacquered, black coffee table cluttered with dog-eared magazines.

A nurse passed by. I blocked her path. "Frank Wooten. Can you tell me how he is? We've been here for an hour."

"The doctor will talk to you as soon as he can, Miss," she said and stepped around me.

"Sit down, Becky," Helen said. "You're driving us crazy."

I looked around the room for support. Gordon, Josh, Neil, and a couple of employees from our Kirbyville store stared at me. Did they agree with Momma? When I was a kid, I often wished God had given me the ability to become invisible. If nobody could see me now, I could float into Frank's room and find out for myself how he was. Maybe if people couldn't see me, I wouldn't be able to see them either. Then I wouldn't have to look into their worried faces or watch their anxious hands fidget around trying to find something to calm the feeling of dread that permeated the room.

A portly man wearing a white coat with a stethoscope hanging around his neck came down the hall. Everyone stood.

"Is Mrs. Frank Wooten here?" he asked.

"Yes," Momma and I replied in unison.

She glared at me, right eyebrow raised, lips pulled thin. "I'm Mrs. Frank Wooten. This is my daughter, Becky Cooper."

Her introduction reminded me that as far as anyone in Sugardale knew, she was still Frank's wife, while I was the dutiful stepdaughter. Her look served as a warning for me to keep my mouth shut.

The man in the white coat extended his hand to her. "I'm Doctor Gibson."

She shook his hand. "How is Frank doing, Doctor?"

The physician studied the clipboard he carried. "Stable for the moment."

"That's good, isn't it?" I asked.

"Yes, but I won't kid you. Mr. Wooten has suffered a massive heart attack."

I grabbed the sleeve of the doctor's lab coat. "What do you mean by massive?"

"Give the man a minute, Becky," Momma said as she pried my hand loose.

"There's been extensive damage to Mr. Wooten's heart," he explained. "Has your husband experienced any sudden chest pains recently? Pains radiating down the arm?"

Helen shook her head. "No, Frank never mentioned anything. He looked fine."

"Indigestion," I said. "Frank has been having a lot of indigestion lately. I told him he should see Doctor Condray, but he never did."

Doctor Gibson lowered the clipboard. "Unfortunately, I see this all the time. The early warning signs of a heart attack often mimic indigestion."

I could feel the panic rising inside of me. "He's going to be okay, isn't he? He has to be. Frank has to get well."

Helen put her arm around my shoulders. "Stay calm, Sugar. Frank's a tough old bird. Can we see him, Doctor?"

"I think you should, Mrs. Wooten. But I want to warn you, he's not conscious at the moment. Come with me, please."

We started down the hall. The doctor stopped, turned to me. "You'll have to wait, Miss. Mr. Wooten is in ICU. I'm only allowing one visitor at this time."

"But Frank would want me there." Panic escalated into desperation. "He'd want to see me!"

"He's unconscious, Becky," Momma said. "He won't know if you're there or not."

I blinked back tears and tried to think of a reason — short of blurting out the truth about our relationship — that would justify my visiting Frank instead of Momma. But logic and speech failed me.

"Come sit with me, Becky," Gordon Zagat said, taking my hand.

Helen handed me a tissue. "That's a good idea. You stay with Gordon. I'll be back as soon as I check on Frank."

Doctor Gibson pointed down the hall. "This way, Mrs. Wooten."

Gordon tried to pull me toward the sofa, but I jerked my hand away. I watched as Momma and the doctor headed for the double doors at the end of the hall. They were halfway there when Momma's knees buckled beneath her. The doctor caught her. She whispered something to him and he led her back to the waiting room.

"Could I have a drink of water, please?" Helen asked as she sat.

"I'll get you some," Gordon said.

She placed the back of her hand to her forehead. "And a cool cloth for my head?"

Gordon nodded.

"Are you okay, Mrs. Wooten?" the doctor asked.

"I will be, but I'm not up to seeing Frank right now." Helen reached for my hand. "You go, Becky. Go check on Frank for me. Okay?"

Mild relief washed over me. "Okay, I'll go."

"Good," she said. "Doctor Gibson, could I get some little something to help steady my nerves? I'll never sleep tonight otherwise."

"Certainly. I'll leave a prescription for you at the desk."

"You're a kind man, sir." Helen gave him one of her tilted-head grins.

He blushed, then cleared his throat. "Follow me, Miss Cooper."

As I trailed after the physician, I glanced back. Momma cast me a quick wink. There was nothing wrong. She'd orchestrated her feigned attack of nerves for my benefit, a ruse to allow me to see Frank. Even here, even now, Momma had to be in control. It was the nicest thing she ever did for me.

CHAPTER 27

Frank died the next morning. So did I. But they only buried Frank. So many people turned out for his funeral, the service had to be moved from Levin's mortuary to the Central Baptist Church. Dozens of our friends, neighbors, and business acquaintances stopped by the house after the service to pay their respects. Gordon and Josh borrowed folding chairs and tables from the fire hall and set them up on the side lawn in an effort to accommodate the crowd. Mountains of casseroles, fried chicken, and desserts were brought by both the sympathetic and the curious.

Since no one but Eva, Henry, and I knew about the divorce, Helen decided to play the grieving widow. "Everyone is upset by Frank's death," she said. "No need to add to their pain or stir up their curiosity by telling them about the divorce now."

Donald and his family came, along with Charlotte's parents. I stayed in the kitchen and in my room as much as possible trying to avoid everyone, especially that despicable arsonist. I fought the urge to confront him. An intense desire to expose the so-called grieving son for the hypocrite he was threatened to overwhelm me. Sensing my impending explosion, Henry spirited me away.

In all honesty, I think Henry needed to get away from the crowd as much as I did. Helen could've won an Oscar for her performance as the grief-stricken widow. The most secure man in the whole world would've had his confidence shaken watching his fiancée carry on so over another man's death, even if it was a lie.

Henry and I didn't return until after dark. A furious Momma met us at the door. "Where the hell have you two been?"

I ignored her and headed for the stairs.

She grabbed my forearm. "I asked you a question."

"Let go of me or I'll —"

Henry intervened. "We just drove around for awhile, Helen." He pried her hand from around my arm.

"Well, you could've told someone." She pushed back her bangs. "We've got a meeting in the morning with Ralph Palmer to go over Frank's will."

"When did Palmer become the attorney for the store?" Henry asked.

"Frank hired him after Mr. Oates died last month."

"Why do we have to do this so soon?" I asked. "We just buried Frank today."

"Mr. Palmer talked to Donald and me while you and Henry were out touring the countryside. We all agreed there was no use in putting it off."

"Donald has no say in the matter," I said.

Helen shrugged. "I guess Frank left him some little something."

"I'm not going. I can't. It's too soon."

"Now you listen to me, Becky Leigh," Momma said. "You're going to be the primary owner of the stores. The employees will look to you for leadership."

I glared at her, hating the truth of her words. "Gordon and Neil are good managers. They can run things for a while."

"Gordon and Neil don't own the stores, you do. Or at least you will when Frank's new will is probated." Helen took a deep drag of her cigarette, blew the smoke out through her nose. "It's time you thought about someone else for a change."

Henry frowned. "Now that's not called for, Helen. Becky needs time to grieve."

She turned to her fiancée. "So you're taking her side against me?"

"Stop it, Momma." I wasn't going to let poor Henry get sucked into a tug-of-war between Momma and me, the way Frank had been. "What time are we supposed to be there?"

"Ten sharp."

"I'll be ready." I started up the stairs.

"Just a minute," she called. "There are dirty dishes in the kitchen. Who is going to clean them up?"

I ignored her.

"Did you hear me, Becky?"

"For God's sake, Helen. Give the girl a break," Henry said. "Come on. I'll wash and you can dry. That way you won't get your nails messed up."

She was still fussing when I closed my bedroom door.

*****

Helen slammed the front door. The etched glass in its oval window rattled.

"You almost broke the glass," Henry said.

She cocked her head to the left, crossed her arms, and in her low, slow-down voice asked, "Are you Donald's property manager now?"

"I'm going to make some coffee." Henry headed for the kitchen.

Helen spun around, tucked her chin in, and squinted her eyes until they were mere slits in a face primed for battle. I was glad Henry had refused to pick up her gauntlet, even though it meant she'd turn on me.

"Where are they, Rebecca Leigh Cooper?" she asked through clenched teeth. "Frank's new will and my goddamn settlement papers? Don't you dare tell me again you don't know."

Our meeting with Lawyer Palmer hadn't gone well. According to the attorney, the only papers he'd found in Frank's office were the divorce papers, Frank's original will, and a $3,000 insurance policy designed to pay burial expenses. The latter two documents had been prepared shortly after Frank's first wife died and years before he and Momma married. In his original will, Frank left everything to Donald, except for a box of old family photographs. Those he left to his sister in Alabama.

Helen explained to Mr. Palmer that at the time Frank made out his first will, he didn't own the stores or the house. She said, "The fact that I deeded the house and business to Frank is just a technicality. Eli Cooper built the house, started the business, and passed it on to my first husband, Paul. When Paul died the property came to me. Becky is the third generation of Coopers. The property rightly belongs to her and to me. After all, I am both Paul's and Frank's widow."

Although he agreed in principle that the property should be ours, Mr. Palmer pointed out that legally — unless we found a copy of the new will — Donald stood to inherit everything. Palmer also informed us we'd face an uphill battle should we decide to contest the will. I wasn't a blood relative of Frank's and since she'd divorced him, Momma wasn't legally Frank's widow.

I told Mr. Palmer that Frank had made a new will and had prepared a settlement agreement for Momma. But when questioned, I admitted I'd never seen the documents.

Over and over, I declared, "Frank would never lie to me."

During the meeting, Donald sat in a corner chair grinning, occasionally laughing. Helen went after him, threatening to knock the smirk off his face. She would've done it if Mr. Palmer and Henry hadn't stopped her.

"I asked you a question, Becky," Momma said. "Where the hell are those papers?"

"They have to be either here or at the Kirbyville store."

On the way home, we'd stopped at the Sugardale store and ransacked Frank's office. We found nothing.

"You're out of coffee," Henry said. "I'm going to get some."

"Hang on a minute," Helen said. "You stay here, Becky, and look for those papers. You rip this house apart. Henry and I are going to Kirbyville to check Frank's office and the apartment."

"You'll need keys." I opened the drawer in the entry hall table and pulled out Frank's keys. Touching his keys — objects he held every day — caused a flood of memories to wash over me. I cradled them in the palms of my hands.

"Give me the goddamn keys," Helen said, snatching them out of my hands. "Let's go, Henry." She yanked the front door open. "You'd better pray that Frank didn't lie to you. If Donald ends up owning everything I've spent a lifetime working for, I'll dig Frank up and kill him again, and I'll throw you in the grave with him."

*****

I felt sick. All weekend, Momma and I hunted for the documents that would give us the right to live in our own home. All weekend, I'd listened to Momma call Frank every low-down name she could think of. She tended to favor words starting with the letter B. Terms such as bastard, bamboozler, backstabbing, broken-down, blood sucking, and boldface liar were repeated with regular frequency. When it came to describing me, any letter would suffice. According to my mother, I was a weak, stupid, foolish, brainless, dim-witted, gullible idiot who could barely find the bathroom by herself.

"Why in the world did I trust the likes of you, Becky, to make sure that bastard Frank lived up to our agreement?" she asked over and over.

I defended Frank. Although I might be stupid, there were some facts I was certain of. The sun rose in the East and set in the West; the ocean's tides rolled in and rolled out; Frank would never lie to me. On that fact alone, I'd staked my heart and my future.

*****

Early Monday morning, Henry left for Palm Beach. He needed to sign the lease for his new hair salon on Tuesday or risk losing the location. He begged Helen to go with him, and assured her that she didn't need her own money. He'd take care of her. But she valued her independence too much to be obliged to any man, even one she professed to love. Sweet Henry even offered me a home and a job as his bookkeeper.

He urged us to, "Think of this as a new beginning, a fresh start. Leave Sugardale and come move to Palm Beach with me. We'll all start over together."

Momma's anger wouldn't let her think about leaving until she had what was rightfully hers. She vowed either to get back the house and business or to see Donald dead. Henry didn't take her threat seriously, but I did.

The notion of moving to Palm Beach didn't register with me either. But then, little did. Numb, lost, dazed and bewildered, I stumbled through a world that looked familiar. The same plaid curtains and matching bedspread. Frank's green toothbrush hanging next to my blue one in the bathroom where we'd shared a bubble bath last Monday evening. Everything looked the same, but felt strange.

It was as if the earth had been knocked off its axis. My world was cockeyed, twisted, skewed by events beyond my control or understanding. If Grandpa Eli were alive, he'd have said my life had gone catawampus.

A catawampus life is one that's out of kilter. It's lopsided, crooked, and bent beyond recognition. A catawampus life is a life devoid of truth.

As I sat on our bed, smelling Frank's favorite blue shirt, the scent of him filling my senses, I realized all I had left was a catawampus life. A world where nothing was the same as it had been seven days prior. My life, which had held such promise a week ago, was now devoid of all truth, as my mind and heart battled over whether or not Frank had betrayed me.

If I could turn back the clock for one week, everything would right itself again. Life would be good again. I'd feel safe. Frank would be alive. He'd hold me, comfort me, and love me once more. He'd show me where the new will was. I'd get him to the doctor's in time. I could save him and myself, if I could go back to last Monday night.

"Please, God," I whispered. "Grant me this one little prayer, and I'll never ask for anything else. I'll never lie or cuss again. I'll be a good girl forever."

"They say only crazy people talk to themselves."

I twisted around to find Donald standing in the doorway, a beer bottle in his hand. "What are you doing here?"

"I came to inspect my property and to give you this." He sailed a piece of paper at me.

"It's an eviction notice. I want you and that know-it-all mother of yours out of my house."

I made no move to pick up the hand-written document. "That's not legal. You've got no say until the will has been probated. A lot can happen before then."

"I saw Helen's van parked at that new lawyer's office. He won't do her any good. She can't afford to pay him, unless she plans to spread her legs for him." Donald stopped to gulp down some beer. "That's her style, but he's young. I heard he has a good-looking wife. Why would he need a worn out bitch like Helen?" A slow smirk spread across Donald's face. "If you made him the same offer, he might be tempted to accept. After all, we guys know that you redheads are always hot and eager for it." He rubbed his hand across his crotch. "You cherry-heads need it on a regular basis. Right?"

Standing up, I pulled my shoulders back and lifted my head high in an attempt to appear taller than my 5 foot 3 inches. "I want you to leave now."

He laughed. "You're confused, moron. This isn't Daddy Wooten standing here. I don't give a shit what you want." He took another swig. "When he came to visit my girls, Daddy would brag that he'd convinced you he loved you. We'd laugh about how gullible and stupid you were to believe he'd ever marry a freak like you."

"You're a damn liar. Frank loved me."

"The only thing he loved about you was the hole between your legs."

I crossed my arms and grinned, determined not to let Donald's vulgar lies upset me.

"You can't stand it because he chose me over you, can you?"

"The hell he did. Daddy left everything to me. If you and that whore Helen weren't such idiots, you'd understand that blood is thicker than pussy."

Somewhere in the back of my brain, a voice whispered, "Walk away, Becky." But I didn't listen. Perhaps, after years of watching Master Picker Momma retaliate and destroy her enemies, I imagined her skills had somehow seeped into my bones. Maybe it was just because I didn't have anywhere else to walk to. For some reason, I didn't back down.

"Frank was ashamed to call you his son. Although it pained him greatly, he finally admitted to himself you were a rapist and murderer of your own unborn children. The only thing Frank didn't know was you're a damn arsonist too. But I know, and I have proof."

Donald's entire face wrinkled. His lips pinched closed making him snort air through his nose like an angry bull. He glared at me.

Realizing I'd struck a nerve, I mustered the courage to continue. "I know Frank loved me. He told me over and over how he loved me more than he'd ever loved anyone, including your mother."

I didn't see Donald's raised hand until it was too late. The beer bottle crashed into the right side of my head. My legs buckled. I fell forward onto my hands and knees. Specks of color floated in the haze before me as I tried to focus. A warm, sticky liquid dripped from my scalp onto the braided rug. I crawled toward the murky outline of the ladderback chair in the corner and used it to pull myself up on my knees.

Donald grabbed a handful of my hair, yanked me to my feet. "You're gonna pay now. You're gonna pay for turning Daddy against me."

He smacked my face so hard I felt it in my legs. Blood gushed from my nose. Still, I managed to rake my fingernails down his cheek.

He grabbed his face. "Damn bitch!" His fist slammed into my jaw.

My teeth sliced my bottom lip. Blood poured from my head, my nose, and my mouth.

Gagging, I spit, then swallowed hard. Blood swirled in my stomach, mixed with gastric juices, then erupted from my throat. A rank mixture of vomit and red spewed across the legs of Donald's khakis.

"Goddamn you," he shouted.

Another whack. This one sent me reeling backwards. My spine slapped the hardwood floor. I screamed. For a moment, I couldn't move. Finally, I rolled onto my right side, pulled my knees into my chest, and waited for Donald's next blow. It's funny the thoughts that flash across your mind when you're in severe pain. Logic would've dictated I consider a plan for escape. But instead, I thought of how odd it was that we begin life in the fetal position and now I was, in all likelihood, going to end my life in the same pose. It was as if my twenty-one years of living had been for naught. Nothing had changed, not even the position of my own body.

Donald jerked one of Grandma Cooper's crocheted doilies off the dresser, sending Frank's bottle of cologne crashing to the floor. The scent of Old Spice mixed with those of blood and vomit. Bile coated the roof of my mouth.

My stepbrother kicked me. "That's for messing up my new pants." He kicked me again. Then twice more. The last kick landed in my lower back. Donald wiped his pants off with the antique scarf. "You're not even worth killing." He grasped my left hand, twisted my wrist, and dragged me across the room to the bed.

"You're breaking . . . breaking my hand," I screamed.

He laughed. "You'll be lucky if that's all I break." Donald picked me up, threw me onto the bed, yanked my pants and underwear off, and tossed them on the floor.

Naked from the waist down, I tried to pull the bedspread over me, but my left hand went limp. My other hand lay firmly wedged behind my back. Donald's fingers gripped my throat.

With his right hand, Donald undid his belt buckle. "There's only one thing a dummy like you is good for." He unzipped his fly. "Do you remember the first time I helped myself to a piece of you? You were nice and tight then. Bet that's not the case now, is it?" Donald started working his slacks down his hips. "Let's see if Daddy taught you anything. If you want, you can close your eyes and pretend I'm him."

I tried to kick him, but he pressed his thighs against my lower legs and tightened his fingers around my throat. I fought for each breath.

He grinned. "Relax, stupid. You're gonna like what I've got for you a lot more than anything my old man ever gave you."

My mind swirled. I saw the ladderback chair rise high into the air behind Donald.

Was my vision real or a hallucination? He pulled back a little. Just as his pants fell around his ankles, the chair crashed down upon his head. He screamed, grabbed his skull with both hands and staggered sideways before tripping over his khakis.

"Hello, Donald," Helen said. "I didn't know you were stopping by today." She looked at me. Her face clouded over.

Donald was the one on his hands and knees now. He shook his shoulders. Pieces of wood fell off his back and onto the floor.

She strolled toward him, stopping to pick up one of the broken chair spindles. "If I'd known you were coming, I would've baked you a cake."

He rose up on his knees. "You fucking bitch. You're dead."

"I don't allow such language in my house, Donald." Helen slammed the piece of wood upside his temple.

He let out a howl and fell sideways, hitting the crown of his head on the edge of the dresser. Holding his head, Donald thrashed around on the floor, kicking his feet, moaning like a dying cow.

Helen walked back to the bed, picked up the edge of the bedspread, tossed it over me. "You should've called before you came over. Becky's not dressed for company."

I tried to sit up, but couldn't put any weight on my left hand. "Momma," I whispered.

She opened her handbag, took out her cigarette case, and lit a smoke. "Stay down, Becky. This isn't over yet." Holding the cigarette between her lips, she reached into her bag and pulled out a white metal object before tossing her purse onto the bed. Not once did she take her eyes off Donald.

He grabbed the dresser for support and staggered to his feet. His pants and underwear circled his ankles. Limp genitalia peeked out through the tail of his shirt.

Helen puckered her lips and blew little smoke rings in his direction. "It's easy to see you didn't inherit any of Frank's best qualities. How did you sire so many kids with that puny thing? Are you sure Kim and Amy are yours?"

"You close your mouth, Helen, or I'll close it for you." He struggled to pull up his pants.

"That's mighty big talk for someone who has so little to offer. Now that I've seen the evidence, I'm sure those girls must belong to Charlotte's lover. She just passed them off as yours." Helen took another drag off her Camel.

What the hell was she doing? My mother could fight and fight dirty, but Donald was six-one, 200 pounds, and so mad his eyes were about to pop out of their sockets. It was her nature to have the last word, but this time I feared Momma's need to win at all cost would get us both killed. Not that I cared much about living anymore. Still, there had to be less painful ways to die.

Donald managed to get his pants pulled up. He didn't bother to fasten his belt. Blood from his head wound trickled down his cheek. He wiped at it, but it continued to ooze down his jaw and drip onto his shirt collar. "I'm through fucking with you. You're both finished."

Momma let loose a laugh so wicked it would've scared the Devil himself. Blonde curls fell across her cheeks, hiding everything except blood-red lips, alley-cat green eyes, and the smoke pouring out her nostrils. "You're through fucking anyone, Donald."

She raised her right hand and touched a button on the side of the white metal object.

A four-inch steel blade popped out. "Can you believe this souvenir from the islands cost only three dollars?" She held the switchblade up for him to see, took a deep drag off her cigarette, and then held up her smoke. The end of it glowed. "What do you want first, Donald? For me to blind you with my cigarette or to geld you with my sweet island keepsake?"

He grinned. "A little knife like that doesn't scare me."

A fiendish smile parted Helen's lips. "It doesn't take a big knife to gut a hog if you know what you're doing. You stick the knife in fast and low, twist it 180 degrees and rip upwards. That hog's guts will fall right out." As she talked, Momma demonstrated her disemboweling technique on an imaginary pig.

The smirk on Donald's face disappeared. "You're both crazy. I'm leaving."

"What's the matter?" she asked. "Don't you like to play with girls who bite back?"

My stepbrother hugged the far wall as he passed in front of my knife-wielding mother. Once out of the room and headed down the stairs, he yelled, "We'll finish this another time, bitch."

Helen ran to the top of the stairs. "I'm ready when you are, jackass."

The front door slammed. I tried to sit up, but a sharp bolt of pain shot through me. I fell back against the mattress. Blood trickled down the side of my head and dripped into my ear. Still in the hallway, Momma was mumbling something. The stench of blood, cigarettes, vomit, and Old Spice blended together. I gagged.

Helen came in carrying a washrag. "Don't you throw up, Becky Leigh." She wiped the damp cloth across my face. "Roy Tate is on his way. You hold on until then."

"Roy Tate?"

"I called him. We need to get you to Doctor Condray's. I can't get you down those stairs by myself." She folded the washrag, laid it across my forehead. "You lie still. We need some fresh air in here." She opened the window, got another washrag, and wiped the blood off my hands. "I'm not going to clean you up too much. I want Roy and Doctor Condray to see what that bastard did to you."

"Is it . . . that . . . that bad?" I asked.

"I wouldn't recommend looking in a mirror anytime soon."

I put my right hand to my face to feel the damage.

She pulled it back down. "Don't touch it. You'll make it worse."

"I can't . . . can't move my left hand or see . . . out my right eye."

"The right side of your face is swelling up. That's what's closing your eye." She picked up my injured hand.

I screamed.

"Damn Donald's hide. I think he broke your wrist." Momma smacked her fists against her thighs, stomped her foot, and started pacing in front of the bed. "Why the hell didn't I kill him? I must be getting soft to let such an opportunity slip by."

"Donald's too big. He's too . . . too mean. He would've killed us."

She folded her arms and glared at me with eyes wild and crazed like those of a trapped bobcat. "I got rid of my daddy when I was fourteen years old. He was bigger and meaner than Donald Wooten could ever . . ." She gasped, slapped her hand over her mouth.

I lay there staring up at my mother. Had I heard her correctly? She killed her own father? The blood in my ear must be interfering with my hearing. Maybe the throbbing in my head had triggered some sort of hallucination. Beatings tended to scramble a brain and produce temporary confusion.

There was a loud knocking.

Helen looked out the window. "There's Roy. I told him to come to the backdoor. You keep your mouth shut and let me do the talking." She started to leave.

"Wait," I whispered.

She spun around. "Don't you dare ask me any questions. Not now. Not ever."

I pointed at her mouth with my good hand. "Your lip . . . lipstick . . . is smeared."

"Damn it. Where'd my purse go?" Momma grabbed her bag, snatched the cloth off my head, and wiped her mouth. She applied a fresh coat of scarlet lipstick, smacked her lips twice.

The knocking grew louder.

"Just a minute, Roy," she yelled. "Do I look presentable?"

I nodded as best I could.

She headed for the door. "Don't you worry, Sugar. Your momma is going to take good care of everything."

Her words didn't reassure me. Who was this woman? All my life, I'd depended upon others to protect me from the demon I knew her to be. But today, she'd risked her life to protect me from Donald. One minute, she's lamenting not killing my attacker. The next, she's fretting over smeared lipstick, while I'm bleeding all over the bedspread. All these years, I thought I knew who and what my mother was. But then, I thought I knew Frank too. Nothing made sense anymore. I closed my eyes and welcomed the darkness of the descending unconsciousness.

CHAPTER 28

When we returned from the doctor's office, Roy
Tate carried me up the backstairs into our house. I
guessed his age to be mid-fifties. His hair had more
gray than black now and the crow's feet around his
eyes were joined by deep wrinkles along the edge
of his tanned face. Despite his age, his body was
still fit, still muscular. My weight seemed no
burden to him.

Momma turned down the covers on my
bed. "Put her in here, Roy."

With an unexpected gentleness, the former
sheriff laid me in my bed. He grabbed a pillow,
lifted my left arm carefully, and slipped the feather
cushion under my wrapped hand and wrist.

"Thanks for taking me to . . . the doctor,
Mr. Tate." My swollen lip made talking difficult.

"Anytime, Becky." He stood looking down
at me, frowning. "Your wrist would heal faster if
it'd been broke instead of just strained so bad."

"Donald did a number on her, didn't he?"
Momma said.

Roy nodded. "He's going to hurt worse than
Becky when I catch up with him."

Momma shoved a couple of pills and a
glass of water at me. "Take these pain pills the
doctor gave you. They'll help you sleep."

I swallowed the medicine. "Donald looked
bad . . . after Momma finished with him."

Roy laughed, reached over and rubbed
momma's shoulders with a familiarity that made
me uncomfortable. "Did you manage to get your
licks in, Helen?"

"You know I did." She flipped back her hair. "If he'd raped Becky, I'd have killed him."

"If Donald had raped her, you'd have a stronger case."

"What do you mean?" I asked. "Momma told Doctor Condray we weren't pressing charges. That's when he got so mad at her."

"We're not pressing charges now," Helen said, "but Roy and a couple of his friends are going to inform Donald that if he tries to kick us out of our house, his ass will end up in jail for assault and battery. That's why Roy took those pictures of you. He'll keep them as evidence to use against that bastard."

"You're using my beating to . . . blackmail Donald into letting us keep the house?"

"I prefer to think of it as leverage." She turned to her friend. "Donald did rape Becky when she was thirteen. Can we use that against him now?"

"Why didn't you tell me about it then?" Tate asked. "We could've burned his ass."

"Momma didn't believe me. It didn't fit . . . her plan . . . at the time."

"Pay her no mind, Roy. Those drugs are starting to work." Momma pulled the blanket up under my chin and whispered, "You be quiet. I'm telling this story." She motioned to the ex-lawman. "Let's talk in the hall. Becky needs her sleep."

They walked toward the bedroom door.

"Wait," I said. "There's something else . . . you need to know . . . about Donald."

Helen crossed her arms. "What?"

"Look in my jewelry box." I pointed at my dresser. "There's a small bag."

Momma retrieved the bag, opened it, and checked the contents. "How did you get this?"

"What is it, Helen?" Tate asked.

"It's a silly medallion Donald won last year for selling the most used cars one month. His name and the date are engraved on it — Donald Wooten, October, 1970." She handed the award to Tate for his inspection.

"And when did Donald give this to you, Becky?" he asked.

"He didn't. I found it in the grass . . . near the warehouse . . . the night it burned down."

Helen frowned. "How did it get there?"

"Wooten must have dropped it when he set the fire," Tate said.

"You think Donald started the fire?" she asked.

He nodded. "Some of my former deputies work for Sheriff Hays. They said Hays suspects Donald of starting the fire, but he doesn't have enough evidence to arrest him."

Momma snatched the medallion out of Tate's hand and stuck in front of my face. "You had this all along and didn't turn the bastard in? Why the hell not?"

I pushed her hand away. "I wanted to protect Frank. It would've killed him . . . to know his son . . . burned down the store."

"That liar Frank died anyway, didn't he? And thanks to you, his no-good son got away with arson and might end up owning everything that's mine." She shook her finger at me. "If you weren't in the bed already, I'd put you there myself."

"Just a minute, Helen," Tate said. "You can still use the medallion to your benefit."

"How?"

"A conviction on assault will send Donald to the county jail for a few months. One for arson will get him years in the state pen." Tate pointed at the medallion. "You couldn't ask for much better leverage against him."

A slow smile crept across her face. "I see your point."

Tate held out his hand. "Maybe I should keep it for you."

"Why's that?" she asked.

"If he believes you or Becky has the evidence against him, Donald might try to force you to give it to him. I'll make sure he knows I'm holding it. The bastard might be brave enough to beat a woman and rape a child, but he's too much of a coward to come after me."

"That's so very true." Helen handed him the evidence. "When you have your talk with Donald, make sure you add a few exclamation points for me."

Tate grinned. "Don't fret, ladies. Wooten will get the message loud and clear. If he bothers either one of you again, he'll be looking at my fist and a short ride to the penitentiary."

*****

Helen yanked back the bedroom curtains. "Let's get some light in here."

"Let's not," I said, pulling the sheet over my head.

Ignoring my wishes, she went right on pushing back curtains, drawing up Venetian blinds and raising windows.

I reached for the blanket at the foot of my bed. "Close the windows. It's cold."

"Don't be silly. It's a beautiful autumn day. The sun is shining. A new school year has begun.

You've been in the bed a week now. It's time you got up."

"I need a pain pill. My hand hurts."

"You need to get out of bed and quit feeling sorry for yourself." Momma pulled a paisley scarf out of her skirt pocket. "I'm going to let you use this designer scarf Eva gave me as a sling for your wrist. The green matches your eyes. It's prettier than that white cotton thing the doctor gave you."

"I'm not getting up today. Where are those pain pills?"

She sat down on the foot of the bed. "Those make you sleep all day."

"That's the idea."

"No medicine is going to stop the pain you're trying to forget. You're not the first woman to be betrayed by some man. Every one of the bastards will swear you're the love of their life, and then double-cross you the first chance they get." She smoothed out a wrinkle in her skirt and sighed. "I'm partly to blame. I knew better than to put my property in Frank's name, but people were beginning to talk about his living at the store. Several old biddies told Betty that it looked like I couldn't keep my man."

"Why should their opinion matter? It'd been a good while since you and Frank had lived together as man and wife."

"Our family's reputation was at stake. The Coopers have always been an important part of Sugardale society. I couldn't let some jealous old crones damage our good name." She twisted a curl around her index finger. "Besides, this house was so quiet, so . . . so lonely with both you and Frank gone. I hadn't lived alone since I left West Virginia."

"West Virginia? You mean Kentucky, don't you, Momma?"

"Did I say West Virginia?" she asked, a note of surprise in her voice.

"Yes, ma'am."

She frowned and tugged at her earlobe. "I meant Kentucky."

I recalled Henry's contention that Momma grew up in West Virginia. I'd concluded she'd lied to him. Was it possible she had lied to Papa and me instead? And what was this talk about being lonely? She had too many gentlemen friends to ever be lonely. "What about Henry, Momma? You had Henry to keep you company, didn't you? And Roy Tate."

"Henry and I were just friends at the time. He liked some gal who lived in Catoosa County. Nadine Tate threatened to leave Roy if he didn't straighten up. He figured it'd be hard for a divorced man to get reelected sheriff." Helen laughed. "Little good it did him. He ended up losing both Nadine and the election anyway."

Experience had taught me that loneliness encompassed a suffering no medicine could ease. But weren't Pickers impervious to all suffering? That simple principle had been one of the cornerstones of my mixed-up life. If champion Pickers could feel pain like us lowly Picks, then it was possible Momma could experience anguish, fear, and heartache like me. Was this revelation an epiphany of some sorts? Or simply mental confusion due to my withdrawal from the pain medication?

I pulled the blanket up higher. "I'm not convinced that Frank would betray me. Maybe I misunderstood him. Perhaps he planned to make out a new will, but didn't get around to it. After the fire, he got busy rebuilding and —"

"And maybe your daddy left me a diamond mine in Africa and forgot to tell me about it." Momma slapped the covers. "Wake up, Becky Leigh. Men are dogs. Frank seemed nice, but in the end, his true nature showed itself. You can't trust any of them."

"Does that include Henry?"

"Henry is better than most."

"Then why don't you go to him?" I pushed myself up against the headboard. "That is him who keeps calling, isn't it?"

She nodded. "He still wants to get married, but I won't go down there empty-handed. If things didn't work out, I'd have nothing. Besides, I won't give Donald the satisfaction of thinking he drove me out of my own home." She pulled the scarf back and forth through her hands. "There is a way to beat Donald, and I'll find it. Come hell or high water, I'll see to it he ends up with nothing or ends up dead. Preferably both."

I lifted my injured arm and laid it across my chest. "Have you . . . done that before? Seen to it that somebody ended up dead?"

She cocked her head, gave me a sideways stare. "There are some questions you should never ask another woman. Her age, for example. Whether she was a virgin on her wedding night." Momma walked over to the dresser, picked up her cigarettes, and tapped the end of one smoke on the wood before lighting it. "And never ask a woman about her past." She took a deep draw, exhaled, and fanned the smoke toward an open window. "I've done what was necessary to survive the bastards who messed with me, and I'll do it again if needed. Let's leave it at that. Shall we?"

I nodded. When it came to my mother's life and her dubious adventures, the less I knew, the better off I was. "I'm going to take a nap."

"The hell you are." Helen pulled a notepad from the pocket of her blouse. "You're going to come downstairs and help me fill these orders."

"Orders? Orders for what?"

"We need money to hire a lawyer to fight Donald. You and I are starting a catering business. I've bought the supplies and have three orders." She flipped open the notebook and began to read, "A chocolate cake to welcome the new music director for the Methodist church. Two lemon pies for Mrs. Treadwell's Daughters of the Confederacy meeting, and one Southern Belle cake and four dozen assorted cookies for Judge Langford's grandchildren."

"Judge Langford's grandkids don't live here."

"No, but now that Harland has retired from the Georgia Supreme Court, he and Ruth are back home in Sugardale fulltime. His daughter and her family are coming to visit this weekend. Ruth wants something special for dessert."

"I can't decorate cakes with one hand."

"Between the two of us, Becky, we've got three good hands. Now get up."

"No." I sank back under the blanket. "I don't feel like cooking."

Momma jerked the covers off me. "I don't give a damn how you feel. You're getting out of that bed and helping me cook or else."

"Or else what?" I yelled. "You gonna hit me? Go ahead." I held out my right arm.

"You want to twist my other arm? Here it is. You've always been good at smashing things — ashtrays, glasses, dreams, lives. Take your best shot, Momma. I don't care."

"You ungrateful little bitch. After all I've done for you."

"You're right, Momma. I should be grateful to you for all the beatings you gave me. They toughened me up enough to survive Donald."

"I covered your ass while you and Frank played house and let you two use my money to build the new building Donald now claims to own." She shook her smoke at me. "You always give up too soon, Becky. No backbone. That's your problem."

"Then why didn't you get rid of me when I was born?" I tugged the covers up, tucked them under my chin, and rolled onto my right side, giving her my back. "You should've stuck me in a burlap bag and drowned me like an unwanted kitten."

Momma grabbed a handful of my hair and yanked.

"Let go," I screamed.

She pulled even harder. "You can say anything to me, except that. Don't you ever talk to me about drowning." She let go of my hair, slid the notebook into her pocket and headed for the door.

I managed to sit up. "You're crazy. You're the one who belongs in Havenwood."

She turned around. "It's the Cooper blood in you that makes you weak."

"You're wrong, Momma. It's the Cooper blood that makes me human."

"Really?" she asked with a snicker. "Well, Miss Cooper, human extraordinaire, you can stay in that bed until you starve to death." She pointed toward the bathroom. "Or if drowning sounds good to you, there's a nice, deep tub across the hall. Either way, I'm sure you'll win Donald's lasting gratitude. But don't worry, when he laughs at your funeral, I'll slap him upside his head in memory of you."

She stomped down the stairs. I listened to the rattle of pots and pans and the muffled cursing emanating from the kitchen. I hated her for all the slaps, kicks, and beatings she'd given me over the years. Hated her for sending me to Havenwood and destroying my baby and the people I loved. And for a lifetime of lies and denying me the one thing every child had a right to claim — a mother's love — I despised her even more. But at that moment, I hated her because she was right. I did give up too soon.

Truth be told, I longed to stay in the quicksand of selfish commiseration. I wanted to wrap myself in a blanket of self-pity and slip quietly out of life's line of fire. That's what any sane person would do, isn't it?

Momma was right about my being weak, but it had nothing to do with my Cooper bloodline. My Cooper ancestors settled in northern Georgia before the Civil War. They fought for the Confederacy, not because they condoned slavery, but to protect their homes and families. They fought, bled, and died. Those left standing picked up the pieces and went back to work, and back to the business of living quiet, honorable lives. No, any weakness in me did not come from Papa's side of the family.

All that was left was Momma. As much as I wanted to blame her for all the evils in my life, I had to admit she'd never exhibited any weakness, other than hating to be alone. She could be as mean as a cur dog, hard as pig iron, and as cold and slick as a frog's belly, but never weak.

I had to be the proverbial black sheep then. Worse than that, I must be a mutation. A weak link in the Cooper chain. Neither Papa nor Grandpa Eli would've ever considered giving in to the likes of Donald. My imaginary friend Claudia wouldn't have either.

I hadn't thought of Claudia in several years. I stopped writing to her shortly after Frank and I became lovers. There was no need to write because Frank had made me happy. But now, there was no more Frank and no more happiness. With my good arm, I wrestled the dresser out from the wall, reached behind it, pulled the dusty journal out of its hiding place. I cleaned it off, retrieved a pen from the nightstand and began to write.

Dear Claudia,

You'll be surprised to hear from me after all this time. Remember Frank, my stepfather? I know you wouldn't approve, but he and I fell in love. We were very happy for the past two years and planned to get married as soon as Momma divorced him. But he died from a sudden heart attack before we could marry. I still can't believe it. He was only 42 and in great shape, or so we thought. Everything was in Frank's name — the stores, Papa's house, the mountain property where Frank and I planned to build a cabin. He told me he had made out a new will leaving everything to me. I reckon that was a lie. The only will we found gave everything to Donald, who is meaner than ever.

A few days after Frank's funeral, Donald came over and beat the tar out of me. He would have raped me again if Momma hadn't stopped him. I've said a lot of nasty things about my mother and they were generally true. But I must admit, she is the most fearless person I've ever known. Too bad I didn't inherit some of her courage. It was amazing to watch her beat Donald down with nothing but a cigarette and a four-inch knife. There I was, flat on my back, rooting for my mother to win a fight. How weird is that?

Stranger still, Roy Tate took me to the doctor and then warned Donald to leave me alone. Momma said it was rumored around town that Donald was hurt in a car accident. But in truth, Momma and Mr. Tate walloped the daylights out of him.

I'm so confused. The man I trusted with my heart, body, and soul betrayed me. My two enemies — Momma and Roy Tate — put themselves at risk to protect me. Nothing makes sense. Is the earth rotating backwards? Will I forever be stuck on this Tilt-A-Whirl, my life going forward, then back, up, then down? Is that the true nature of life, Claudia? Or just my peculiar destiny?

I wish I could be like you. So sure about life and your place in it. You always know what to say and do, what's right and what's wrong. And even when things stray off course, you still have faith in your ability to ride out the storm. How can you cling to hope in a world seemingly devoid of truth? Tell me your secrets, Claudia. Teach me to be like you.

Momma is downstairs. I should go help her. I think that's what you'd do if you were here.

Goodbye for now.

Your best friend,
Becky Leigh Cooper

P.S. Momma wants us to start a catering business. Can you imagine anything more bizarre than Momma and me as partners? Isn't that a recipe for disaster?

CHAPTER 29

By the first week in October, my bruises were gone, but I still couldn't lift anything heavy with my left hand. Doctor Condray gave me a brace designed to help support the wrist, but it made the skin beneath it sweat and itch. Thus, I wore it only when working in the garden or the kitchen.

To my surprise and Momma's delight, our catering business seemed to catch on. At first, most of the requests were for cakes, pies, and cookies. But then folks started asking if I could rustle up a batch of chili, some chicken and dumplings, or a pot of stew for their club meeting or unexpected company. My cheese soup served with fresh-baked nut bread was especially popular.

Whatever a customer ordered, Momma would always suggest something more. "A cherry cobbler would taste wonderful with chickens and dumplings," she would advise. "You'll want a nice strawberry whipped pie or a fresh apple crisp to compliment that soup, won't you, Sugar?"

In addition to talking the customers into ordering extra goodies, Momma charged such high prices, it embarrassed me. But not her. "People expect to pay more for quality and convenience," she said. "Give your customers both in one product and they'll pay whatever price you ask. Besides, good lawyers don't come cheap."

It's hard to argue with success and harder still to argue with Momma. Big smiles dotted our patrons' faces as they forked over their hard-earned money. By the end of September, we had a number of standing orders. It surprised me to learn that I enjoyed cooking more than gardening. Momma got me some cookbooks from the library, including one with recipes developed at the famous Le Cordon Bleu cooking school in Paris. On slow afternoons, I'd try out new recipes and pretend I was a student at Le Cordon Bleu. I knew such pretense was childish, but it was the only time I forgot the pain of Frank's betrayal.

Customers always sneaked one cookie for the road or asked for a taste of whatever aromatic concoction simmered on the stove. They'd also ask about the bruises on my head and the wrap on my wrist. The old story about falling down the stairs came in handy once again.

I hadn't left the house since Donald's attack. But the first Friday in October brought with it the grand opening of the discount store, Save-U-More. Betty Powell called and convinced Momma she needed to be there. Momma didn't view herself as a discount store shopper, but the grand opening included a drawing for a free trip for two to Las Vegas, a city she'd always dreamed of visiting. I didn't want to go, but she insisted.

"If we both enter, Becky, we'll double my chances of seeing Las Vegas."

I noticed she hadn't said *our* chances, but that suited me just fine. The idea of spending a week with her in a city that Reverend Murray referred to as the sin capital of the world gave me a chill. So, we compromised. After registering for the drawing, I'd go to the library's annual book sale.

It seemed we did a lot of compromising in the six weeks following Frank's death. Momma pointed out that all we had left was each other, a fading chance of contesting Frank's will, and her plots for revenge against Donald — plots that ran the gamut from the feasible to the ridiculous to some so brutal, they would've made Geronimo wince.

When we could find no compromise, we did what we always had done. We did it Momma's way. Between the injuries inflicted by Donald and a chronic stomach flu that had plagued me since shortly before Frank's death, I seldom cared about what went on around me. I tried not to think of Frank. When I did, I waffled between missing him and hating him for leaving me with nothing except my mother.

After registering for the drawing, I left Momma and Betty debating on where to go for lunch and headed to the library. I purchased a thick reference book, *The Complete Encyclopedia of North American Plants*. A sudden craving prompted me to stop at Ferrell's drugstore for a vanilla coke and a double order of fries. Mrs. Ferrell remarked that I'd never be able to eat so many French fries, but I surprised us both by polishing them off, along with an ample amount of catsup.

The weather was perfect. A temperature in the high sixties, a clear sky, and a modest breeze muffled by leaves dressed in their autumn finery. I decided to walk home the long way, via the back roads. Hopefully, the exercise and fresh air might help settle the revolt of my stomach against all the French fries I'd crammed into it. I'd just turned onto Bragg Road when Mrs. Treadwell stopped and offered me a ride.

"No, thank you. It's a fine day for walking."

My elderly neighbor agreed. "Did Helen tell you I needed three dozen cookies to hand out on Halloween?"

"Yes, ma'am. I can decorate them to look like pumpkins and ghosts if you'd like."

"In that case, make it four dozen, two of each design." She started fumbling with her purse. "Should I pay you now?"

"No need, Mrs. Treadwell. I know where you live."

She gave me a quizzical stare and then laughed. "Sure you do. I've lived across the street from you all your life."

"Yes, ma'am. That's what I meant."

Mrs. Treadwell laughed again. "You must be patient with me. It takes awhile for me to catch on to things now days. Did you hear Anna Santo's boy moved back?"

"Johnny? Who told you that?"

Her wrinkled fingers brushed across the top of snow-white hair. "I can't rightly remember. Maybe it wasn't the Santo boy. It may have been the youngest Sanders kid instead. What's his name?"

"Jimmy. It couldn't have been Johnny Santo, Mrs. Treadwell. He got married and moved to Texas when he finished his military service. If he'd moved back, he'd have come by or at least called. We were very good friends."

"That's right. His mother worked for your family for eleven years, didn't she?"

"Thirteen."

Mrs. Treadwell shook her head. "It's hard when you get old, Becky. Things get so mixed up. It's like your entire brain becomes a Mulligan stew."

I smiled, reached in, and gave her a pat on the shoulder. "Don't you worry about that, ma'am.

I'm only twenty-one and I stay mixed up most of the time too."

We shared a laugh. I offered to deliver her cookies early on Halloween and help her decorate her front porch. As she drove off, I wondered if being lonely was harder on the young or the old. The young had fewer memories to draw upon for comfort. But the elderly must face the regrets of plans not carried out, dreams never realized, and friends and family members gone to soon. Did anyone ever get to the end of life and feel content? Feel satisfied with what they'd accomplished in their life? Saw everything they wanted to see? Loved and were loved in return? Based upon my experiences, I didn't think so.

*****

It's such a little word, the word *if.*

Who'd ever think that two letters pushed together could make such a difference? Could change joy into pain or life into death.

If I had stayed home that day. If I'd went to lunch with Momma and Betty. If I'd accepted Mrs. Treadwell's offer of a ride home, then I wouldn't have been walking down Bragg Road when Donald came along in Frank's old truck.

Four weeks prior, Donald had moved his family to Sugardale and had taken over managing the stores. Charlotte didn't like being away from her parents. After forcing me into the Ranchero, Donald told me how she and the girls had slipped out during the night and gone back to Athens. She'd left a note saying she was filing for divorce and wanted full custody of the children. From Donald's ranting, I surmised he'd come home drunk the night before. Apparently, Charlotte had confronted him about his drinking and about an affair he'd started with the new secretary at the Kirbyville store, Wanda somebody.

"I'll be damn if that bitch, Charlotte, is going to tell me what I can do," he said as he drove toward Starview Mountain.

Every pore in my body seeped. The flutter in my stomach matched the quiver of my chin, but I was determined not to let Donald see how scared I was. No matter what happened, I wouldn't let the bastard make me cry. With trembling hands, I opened my book and pretended to read. Perhaps if I said nothing, he'd ignore me.

Donald grabbed my book and threw it on the dash. "Are you listening to me? I asked if you were the one who told Charlotte about Wanda."

"I didn't know you hired a new secretary. What happened to Mrs. Compton?"

"I got tired of looking at that scowling old warthog. I fired her. What do you think about that, dummy?"

Jacqueline Compton had been an excellent secretary and loyal employee for nine years. A fact I decided not to point out to Donald given his agitated state.

"When you're running a business, you need a secretary you can feel at ease with."

"You're damn right. I'm the boss. I can hire and fire anyone I please."

I nodded. My unwillingness to confront him seemed to settle him down some. Hopefully, Roy Tate's threats about what would happen to him if he hurt me again had registered in his depraved mind. If I controlled my mouth, maybe I could avoid another beating.

Donald pointed to five long rolls of white paper lying on the seat between us. "Do you know what these are?"

"No."

"They're blueprints and my secret to making it big. I'm going to be richer and more important than my daddy or Charlotte's old man ever thought about being."

"How's that?" I asked, trying to sound interested.

"This real estate company from South Carolina approached me about building a resort on the mountain property Daddy had."

"Mr. Parr gave Starview to Frank because he didn't want the property developed."

Donald cast me a sour look. "Who cares? Raw land doesn't make money. Besides, I'm not selling to the realty company."

"That's good."

"Those jerks treated me like crap. Planned to pay me chump change, build a fancy resort, and make millions off the rich hot-shots." Donald patted the rolls of paper. "I'll show them. I'll build the damn resort myself. What do you think about my idea, moron?"

In truth, it was an excellent idea. The county's growing popularity as a weekend retreat, and the increase in the number of vacation homes had helped our stores prosper. Still, I doubted any reputable bank would loan Donald the money to build a doghouse, much less a resort — an opinion I kept to myself. "Sounds good. Those well-heeled professionals in Atlanta could use a place to unwind."

"You bet they could." He grinned at me. "If you're nice to me, pea-brain, I'll give you a job as groundskeeper."

I gave a small nod, tugged at the neck of my pullover, and focused my attention on finding a way out of my predicament.

As he drove, Donald's rhetoric fluctuated between his grand plans for the resort and the malicious strategies he'd concocted to use against Charlotte. As his subject changed, so did his mood, from excited to menacing.

When we arrived at the entrance to the property, Donald jumped out to unlock the gate. For a moment, I had the truck to myself. I could slide to the driver's side, throw the truck in reverse, whip it around, and leave Donald to walk home. It'd been a while since I drove Frank's truck, but I still remembered how, didn't I? If I failed, I'd get the living daylights beat out of me or worse.

"Take a chance, Becky," I whispered. "Do it. Do it now." But I'd waited too long.

Donald climbed back into the truck. "Did you say something?"

"I was talk . . . talking to myself." If Momma had been in my place, she would have hijacked the truck and run over the bastard. Unlike me, she had guts. She had a backbone.

He laughed, rolled down his window, and gave me a hard thump on my temple. "That proves you're crazy." He didn't bother to close the gate.

When we arrived at the bluff overlooking Cascade Canyon, Donald swung the truck around so the tailgate faced the edge of the cliff. "Get out."

"Aren't you going to turn the engine off?"

"If I do, we'll walk home. This piece of junk won't start without a jump." He slid out and stood by the driver's door. "That bitch wife of mine took my car."

I decided not to remind him that Charlotte's daddy had given them the car.

Donald reached in, gathered up the blueprints, and tucked them under his arms. "Get out of the damn truck, stupid. You're not going anywhere."

I did as I was told.

My stepbrother slammed his door, walked to the back of the truck, and let down the tailgate. He unrolled the blueprints and began studying them.

"I'm going to walk down to the pond." I waited for his reaction.

Donald stared at me for a moment. "If you fall in, don't yell for me. One less idiot in the world suits me fine."

I clenched my teeth, pivoted, and marched off toward the pond. How could that creature spring from Frank Wooten's loins?

*****

I wasn't prepared for the memories my visit to the pond conjured up. I'd never been to Starview Mountain without Frank. On our last trip, he'd driven four stakes in the ground to mark the corners of the cabin we planned to build. Three still stood, but one had toppled over. The giant oak that stood sentinel over the meadow, looked smaller without its full uniform of leaves.

A light breeze jostled the swing hanging from the oak. I closed my eyes. In my mind I could hear the laughter again — Frank's and mine — as he pushed me higher in the old tire swing. My senses vibrated with the echoes of my giggles and his teasing as we chased each other around the meadow. It was as if I could feel his arms around me. Once more, I could taste his lips, smell his cologne, and hear his whispers of love. And if I kept my eyes closed and stood perfectly still, I could see him smiling and reaching for me again. If — that damn two-letter word.

I opened my eyes and sucked in a deep breath as reality assaulted my senses. I'd come to the pond to get away from Donald, not to refresh my heartaches. If I cut through the woods and made it down the mountain to the main highway, I could hitch a ride home. But the highway was miles away and I didn't know these woods. People had got lost in them before. Some had been found in time. Others had not.

If I didn't come home, Momma would start hunting me. She'd call Roy Tate for help and maybe the new county sheriff too. Donald would be her prime suspect in my disappearance, but he'd bite his tongue off before telling them where to search for me.

Maybe that's why he hadn't objected to my walking down to the pond. Perhaps he figured I'd head off through the woods, get lost, and die from exposure or be set upon by a pack of wild dogs. Was this his scheme to get rid of me so I couldn't testify against him for the crimes he'd committed?

My head ached. Half-digested French fries practiced jumping jacks in my stomach. I needed an escape plan. If I made my way along the edge of woods, staying low so Donald wouldn't see me, I might be able to sneak past him. The clearing where he'd parked the truck contained few trees big enough to hide behind. Still, it seemed a better plan than just taking off through unfamiliar woods.

If I made it past the clearing, I knew Donald would never be able to catch me.

When I approached the line of cottonwoods, I heard shouting. I hid behind the biggest tree, peeked out to see who Donald was arguing with, and recognized the tan Rambler station wagon as belonging to Gordon Zagat.

I'd never heard Mr. Zagat so much as raise his voice before. He hollered at Donald and my stepbrother yelled something back at his store manager. I couldn't understand their words because they were shouting at the same time.

Donald threw a punch, but Mr. Zagat ducked, and all Donald's fist hit was air. Then Gordon swung. He didn't miss. My stepbrother went down and stayed there.

Mr. Zagat headed for the Rambler, staggering slightly. If it'd been anyone else, I'd have sworn he was drunk. Mr. Zagat got in his car, started the engine, and began backing up. He was leaving, and so was my best chance to get away from Donald.

I ran toward the Rambler, shouting for Gordon to wait for me, but he didn't stop. The engine noises of the two vehicles, the rolled-up windows of the station wagon, and the curtain of dust kicked up by its hasty departure drowned out my pleas.

"Damn." I grabbed my side with one hand and fanned the dust out of face with my other.

"I'm going to kill that son-of-a-bitch," Donald said, rising to his feet.

"What were you two arguing about?"

Blood trickled from Donald's lower lip. "If that bastard thinks he can tell me what to do, he's crazier than you."

"What have you done now, Donald?"

My stepbrother wiped the blood off his chin with the sleeve of his shirt. "I did what I should've done weeks ago. I fired his ass."

"You fired him? Why on earth would you do something so stupid?"

"Watch your mouth, bitch." He brushed the dirt off his khakis. "That old man thinks he knows everything about running the business."

"He does know everything about running our business."

Donald gripped my shoulders. "It's my business now, moron."

I pulled away. "You won't be happy until you ruin it all, will you? You're going to destroy everything Grandpa Eli, Papa, Frank, and I worked hard to build. Aren't you?"

Donald raised his right hand. I ducked to avoid his slap. His hand slammed against the back of my head and I fell on my hands and knees.

"Get up, slut."

I didn't move except to shake my head in an effort to clear my mind.

"I said get up." Donald grabbed a handful of my hair and lifted me to my feet. "Some idiots never learn. Guess you need another lesson."

I tried to pull free, but couldn't. "Roy Tate warned you. You'll go to prison."

He laughed. "No, I won't. Haven't you figured it out yet, dimwit? The chain that binds me, binds you too. If I go to jail, you and Helen end up on the street. You'd never risk losing the old homestead regardless of what I do to you. I can have you anytime I want."

"Let me go," I screamed.

Donald threw me to the ground. He stood over me. "I'd planned to go to Kirbyville this evening to see Wanda. That apartment above the store comes in handy, doesn't it?" A bloody, merciless grin snaked its way across his acne-scarred face. "Thanks to Helen's interference, we didn't have a chance to finish our party that day at the house. Might as well do it now." He pointed to the truck. "There's a blanket behind the seat. Get it. Spread it out under that clump of trees over there, unless you prefer to do it in the dirt. Then take off your clothes. All of them."

I didn't move.

My stepbrother hooked his hands under my armpits, yanked me to my feet, and shook his fist in my face. "You do as I say or so help me I'll throw you off this mountain."

"All right," I cried. "Okay." A sudden breeze ruffled the trees. I motioned toward the back of the truck. "Your blueprints are blowing away."

Donald turned. Resort blueprints drifted toward the edge of the cliff. He ran to catch them. Over his shoulder, he yelled, "Get the damn blanket, bitch."

I staggered to the truck.

CHAPTER 30

The last lemon pie was in the oven when someone knocked at the front door. Above the stove, a clock shaped like the face of a black cat read half-past eleven. I pushed open the swinging door between the kitchen and living room. "Can you get that, Momma? I'm cooking."

"I'm trying to watch my soap opera. It's probably Rudy with the groceries."

"His name is Randy."

"I don't care what his name is, and stop giving him free food every time he comes by."

"Then stop asking him to do chores for you. His job is delivering groceries, not changing light bulbs and hanging curtains."

She waved her hand as if shooing away a pesky fly.

I pulled off my oven mitts, threw them on the kitchen table, and headed for the front door. I turned the doorknob and pulled.

For a moment, the world paused. The wind stopped tickling the scarlet leaves of the Japanese maple. A gray-tailed squirrel halted its hunt for a noonday meal in a lawn bounded by pink Confederate roses and flowerbeds filled with summer bulbs waiting to be dug up. The earth seemed to stop in a show of solidarity with the stillness of my heart and the lack of air in my lungs. A rock-hard quince fruit fell from its thorny bush. The thud of the aromatic fruit hitting the ground bought my world back to life and started my heart beating again.

"Who is it?" Momma asked.

I swallowed hard, licked my lips, swallowed again. I wrapped my arms around my waist, leaned against the doorjamb, and stared at the man on the other side of the screen door. "It's Johnny. Johnny Santo."

Johnny took off his gray Stetson. "They call me John now, Rebecca."

I smiled. *Rebecca.* The name sounded almost foreign to me. Nobody had called me that in five years, not since Johnny had been sent away. Now here he was standing on my front porch, knocking on my door. But something was different. His faded jeans and dark tee shirt — his trademark attire in the sixties — had been replaced by a crisp, gray uniform. "You still in the military, Johnny?"

He pointed to a man standing behind him. "Not exactly."

Behind Johnny stood a black man dressed in a similar uniform. He was older, early fifties I guessed. A thick mustache hid his upper lip.

"Good morning, ma'am. I'm Sheriff Nathan Hays." He took off his hat and stepped up even with the younger man. "Sorry to bother you like this, Miss Cooper."

A small gasp escaped my lips. "You're a cop, Johnny?"

He laughed. "I guess I'm the last person you'd expect to become a law officer considering my history with Sheriff Tate. But things change, Rebecca. People change."

I studied Johnny. His hair was shorter, but still thick and black. Even through the uniform, I could tell the hardened muscles of a man had replaced the gangly legs of an eighteen-year-old. His hands were weathered some. Were they still as gentle? I wondered.

"May we come in?" the sheriff asked.

Nathan Hays stood at least six-two. Broad shoulders topped a lean, muscular frame. The color of his skin reminded me of the way I liked my morning coffee — half coffee, half milk, all stirred together.

"I heard how you beat out Roy Tate for sheriff."

"Yes, ma'am. I guess everyone in Georgia heard about a black man being elected sheriff." Hays ran his fingers alone the edge of his Stetson. "I reckon it didn't set well with some folks."

I grinned. "Reckon not." I turned my attention back to Johnny. His brown eyes still had that twinkle. A mixture of mischief and mystery.

"What the hell does that damn Mexican boy want?" Momma yelled.

Heat rose in my cheeks as I pushed open the screen. "Some people never change."

Once inside the living room, I introduced Momma to Sheriff Hays and held my breath. But she surprised me by being polite. "You remember Johnny, don't you, Momma?"

"I remember Sheriff Tate telling him he'd best not set foot here again."

Johnny took a deep breath, squared his shoulders, exhaled. "That was five years ago, Mrs. Wooten. Like I told Rebecca, things change."

"Not where you're concerned. Sheriff Tate warned you what he'd do if you came around here bothering us again."

"Roy Tate isn't sheriff anymore," I shouted at Momma. "Mr. Hays is sheriff now, and Johnny is his deputy." The room went silent as all eyes focused on me. "I'm sorry. I didn't mean to yell."

Sheriff Hays sniffed the air. "Something's burning."

"My pie!" I ran to the kitchen.

Spirals of smoke seeped out the sides of the oven door. I yanked the door open. A thick cloud enveloped me. I started coughing and waving my arms in a frenzied attempt to breathe.

"I'll open the backdoor," Johnny shouted as he entered the kitchen.

Fresh air cleared the fog enough for me to see the burned pie. I foolishly grabbed the hot pan. "Dammit!"

"Get out of the way." Johnny wrapped a dishtowel around the pie pan and deposited it in the sink. "Let me see your hands."

I offered no resistance as he inspected my burned fingers. He led me to the sink and turned on the faucet. "Cold water will ease the pain. Do you still keep an aloe vera plant on the back porch?" He didn't wait for an answer before heading outside.

The water ran across my fingers, fell on the burned pie, and disappeared down the dark drain, carrying clumps of yellow pie filling and blackened meringue with it. The squeak of the screen door announced Johnny's return.

He laid his hat on the table, then walked over and opened the second drawer in the cabinet and pulled out a fresh dishtowel. "I guess you're right" he said, clutching three pieces of aloe vera in one hand and the cloth in the other. "Some things don't change. Hold out your hands."

I did as I was told.

Johnny squeezed the gel from the plant onto my fingers, taking care to make sure every patch of burned skin was covered with a thick layer of the healing balm. I closed my eyes, content to trade burned fingers for his touch. The tender, circling motion of Johnny's fingertips against my own stirred a deep-buried pain and a long forgotten need.

"Johnny," I whispered as I opened my eyes.

He looked up. His eyes widened as if surprised by what he read in the green eyes watching him. He pulled away, walked over to the sink, and washed his hands. "That should help, but you should call your doctor. You might need an ointment or something."

"I'll be fine."

Johnny dried his hands on the dishtowel. "Shame about the pie."

I pointed to the Hoosier cabinet that stood against the far wall of the kitchen. "I've got another one. I'll give it to Randy."

He wadded up the dishtowel, threw it across the hall. It landed in an empty clothes basket in the laundry room. He grinned. "Haven't lost my touch." He turned his attention to the Hoosier. "Don't see many of these anymore." He rubbed his hand over the white porcelain countertop that pulled out for rolling dough or holding home-baked goodies in need of cooling. "This pie sure looks good. By the way, who's Randy?"

The kitchen door swung open. "Everything okay in here?" Sheriff Hays asked.

Johnny pointed to the sink. "I'm afraid our visit interrupted Miss Cooper's baking."

The sheriff walked over and looked into the sink. "Too bad. Lemon is my favorite."

"She has another one, but it's for Randy, whoever he is."

I frowned. Sarcasm was not a trait I remembered Johnny possessing.

Hays picked up the flattened aloe vera leaves. "Someone get hurt?"

"I burned my fingers a little."

"I told her she should call a doctor."

"And I told you, Deputy Santo, I'll be fine."

"I remember just exactly what you said, Rebecca. I just didn't realize you'd got a medical degree since the last time I saw you."

"Are you sure you're okay?" Hays asked.

"I'm sure." I thought Johnny might argue the point, but he didn't. Instead, he leaned against the Hoosier, crossed his arms, and focused his dark eyes on me.

Sheriff Hays cleared his throat. "You're probably wondering why we dropped by."

I nodded.

The sheriff pushed open the swinging door. "Let's go back in here. Shall we?"

In the living room, I gave Momma a brief report on the ruined pie.

She pointed at Johnny. "Trouble always did follow you."

"For God's sake, Momma, I burned the pie. Not Johnny."

"Don't you use the Lord's name like that in my house."

"I'll do whatever I please. I'm not sixteen"

"Excuse me, ladies," Sheriff Hays interrupted. "I've got some bad news for you."

"What kind of bad news?" Momma asked.

"I afraid your stepson, Donald, is missing."

Momma frowned. "What do you mean by missing?"

"My office got a call this morning from Sy Lambert. He is the assistant manager of Cooper's Hardware. Neither Mr. Wooten nor Gordon Zagat, the store manager, have reported to work since last Friday morning."

"I know who Gordon Zagat is," Helen said. "My first husband, Becky's daddy, hired him. I never trusted the man much."

"How can you say such a thing, Momma? Mr. Zagat has worked for us for twenty years. Papa trusted him completely."

"Your daddy was a fool when it came to running a business."

It wasn't Momma's words that surprised me. I'd endured her spiteful slurs against Papa all of my life. But for her to make such a remark in front of others was a betrayal. A betrayal of those nasty secrets families keep hidden behind pulled curtains and locked doors. Secrets spoken to torment someone society tells us we're suppose to love.

Johnny Santo had returned. Not for me, but nevertheless, he was here. Standing in front of me, talking to me, touching me. For the first time since Frank's death, I felt a flutter of joy. But Momma still hated Johnny and needed to destroy my moment of happiness.

Sheriff Hays pointed at the sofa. "Maybe you'd best sit down, Miss Cooper."

Grateful for his intervention, I did as he suggested.

The sheriff began again. "According to Mr. Lambert, your stepson and Zagat got into a heated argument last Friday. Nobody at the store in Sugardale or Kirbyville has seen or heard from either man since."

"Did they call Mr. Zagat at home?" I asked.

Sheriff Hays nodded. "Deputy Santo and I went by his home earlier. No one was there. Neither the mail nor the newspapers have been picked up for several days."

Momma turned off the television, lit a cigarette, sat back down. "Did you talk to Gordon's son, Josh? He works at the Kirbyville store."

"He did," Johnny said. "He walked off the job late last Friday after he got a phone call from his mother. Didn't give a reason. Just said he wouldn't be back. He and his wife are missing too."

My scalp began to tinkle. "Gordon's wife has family in Mississippi. Perhaps they had a family emergency and had to go out of town suddenly."

The sheriff shrugged. "You've worked with Mr. Zagat before, Miss Cooper. Is he the type of man who'd miss work without calling in?"

I shook my head.

Johnny removed a small notebook from his shirt pocket, flipped it open. "Donald told his secretary, a Miss Wanda Gimmer, he'd be in Kirbyville Friday afternoon, but then called to say he had problems with his truck."

Helen pulled at the top of her turtleneck. "Did you check with his wife, Charlotte?"

"We haven't been able to contact her yet," the sheriff said. "She and her daughters are visiting her parents in Athens. I left a message for her to call my office as soon as possible." Sheriff Hays patted the back of a blue striped wingback chair. "Mind if I sit, Mrs. Wooten?"

She frowned. "You can sit down, but not there. Sit in the rocker."

"The sheriff can sit anywhere he likes, Momma."

"It's much harder to get sweat stains off upholstery than wood, Becky Leigh."

"Your mother is right, Miss Cooper," Hays said. "My wife tells me the same thing. You'd think I'd know better by now."

I couldn't tell if the lawman was telling the truth or being polite. I glanced at Johnny. His lean form rested against the mahogany molding that framed the opening between the living room and front hall. He studied his boots, shook his head, tried not to laugh. Some things may have changed in the past five years, but not Momma. I knew that. So did Johnny.

Sheriff Hays settled himself in the rocker. "When was the last time you saw your stepson, Mrs. Wooten?"

"At church a couple of weeks ago."

"And you, Miss Cooper? Is that the last time you saw him?"

"Becky hasn't been to church in awhile," Momma said. "She's been a bit under the weather. She hasn't seen Donald since the week of his daddy's funeral."

Sheriff Hays twisted to look at me. "Is that right, Miss?"

Momma slapped her hands hard against the arms of her recliner. "I just told you she hasn't seen him. Do you need a hearing aid, boy?"

Johnny snapped to attention. He took two steps forward, his face set in battle mode.

The sheriff waved him back. "Deputy." Hay's voice was soft and controlled, but he gave Johnny a look that signaled he wouldn't allow any interference, even on his own behalf.

Johnny resumed his former position in the doorway. I wrapped my arms around my waist, held my breath, and waited for the explosion.

Sheriff Hays rose from the rocking chair. He strolled over to the dining table, pulled a Queen Ann dining chair out from beneath the table, and placed it next to Momma's recliner. The big man sat down and leaned forward, bringing his dark, brawny frame closer to her. "You know, Mrs. Wooten, my wife asks me the same question a couple of times a week. She claims men don't know how to listen."

Helen pulled the lever on the side of her chair until it reclined a notch. "I agree."

Sheriff Hays straightened and let out a husky laugh that resonated throughout the living room. "I do too, ma'am."

I started breathing normal again.

"Does Donald come around here very much?" Johnny asked.

"No." I knew the concern on Johnny's face had more to do with my safety than with my stepbrother's disappearance.

"After Frank's funeral, everyone came back here, including Donald and his family," Helen said. "Donald visited a little, but spent most of his time in his room."

"His room?" Hays asked.

I motioned toward the stairs. "He still has a room here from when he was in high school. I've being meaning to clean it out for years, but I don't like going in there."

"Why's that?" Hays asked.

"Donald never liked anyone touching his stuff." I glanced at Johnny. His jaw tightened; his hands balled into fists.

Sheriff Hays stood. "May I see the room?"

"Why do you need to see Donald's room?" Helen asked.

"We might find a clue as to what's happened to him." The big man returned the dining chair to its proper place. "I promise I won't touch a thing."

"I'll show you, Sheriff." At the bottom of the stairs, I stopped to wait for him. He whispered something to his deputy. Johnny shrugged, then nodded at his boss.

Hays joined me at the foot of the staircase. "Deputy Santo will stay with your mother if that's okay, Miss Cooper."

I grasped the implication of his words. In Sugardale, Georgia, a young woman didn't go upstairs alone with a man unless he was a relative or a repairman hired to fix a broken window or leaky pipe. A white woman never went upstairs with a black man. But I liked Sheriff Hays. Momma had not intimidated him one bit. By exercising restraint, he had refused to let her get the best of him. Such self-control fascinated me.

"Okay, but you know Momma and Johnny hate each other, don't you?"

"I figured as much. Don't worry, Deputy Santo is a professional."

"That may be true," I said as I started my climb. "But Momma's not."

*****

Slipping the skeleton key into the lock, I rotated it until I heard a click. I pushed open the door to Donald's room and stepped aside to allow the lawman to enter. I stayed perched in the doorway. "I'm sorry about the dust. We had to let our housekeeper go after Frank died. And like I said, I don't come into this room."

Sheriff Hays didn't reply. His eyes scanned the room in a slow, deliberate manner, stopping whenever some particular item caught his attention.

Pictures of famous sports figures decorated the walls of Donald's room, along with calendars of young women clad in skimpy clothes, lying in provocative poses.

Sweat broke out around my hairline. I pulled my hair up into a ponytail in an effort to cool off.

"Is this room always locked, Miss?"

"I've babysat Donald's girls a couple of times since he and Charlotte moved to Sugardale. I didn't want them coming in here."

"That's understandable. Do you pick the girls up or does Mr. Wooten drop them off?"

I shifted my weight from one foot to the other. Momma had told him I hadn't seen Donald. Clearly, he didn't believe her. "Charlotte dropped them off. I don't drive."

"You don't drive?" he asked, making no attempt to hide his surprise.

"No. I never took driver's training or got a driver's license."

"May I ask why not?"

I hesitated briefly before relating the lie I'd told others who'd asked me the same questions over the past five years. "When I was sixteen, I moved to Alabama to help care for Frank's sister who was ill. When I returned home, we didn't see the need for another car. Frank or Momma took me places or I walked." I wondered if it was a crime to lie to a law officer if you weren't under oath.

A quick smile indicated he'd heard me. His attention focused on Donald's dresser. Wedged between the glass and the oak frame of the mirror were five photos of teenage girls, former high school classmates of Donald. The sheriff pulled out three of the pictures, turned them over, read the inscriptions out loud. "To Donald with love, Sue. To Donnie. Thanks for the good times. Love, Janette. To a great lover, Angie." The sheriff slid the pictures back into the frame. "Seems your stepbrother was quite a ladies' man."

"Donald was popular in school."

Hays picked up the picture of Donald in his University of Georgia football uniform. "Wasn't there some talk about him being drafted by the pros? Too bad about the accident."

I stared at Donald's picture. He was holding the game ball given to him by his teammates after a close victory over their archrivals, Georgia Tech. A drunken joyride with his friends two nights later ended in an accident that left Donald with a broken leg, a concussion and a couple of fractured ribs. By the time his injuries healed, the scouts had lost interest.

"Playing pro football was his dream." I preferred not to think of Donald as being a person who could dream and suffer the anguish of having those dreams crushed. He was a taker. A Picker who hurt people just because he could.

Sheriff Hays sat the picture back on the desk. "You and your stepbrother aren't very close are you?"

"No. Are you about through in here?"

"Almost." He pulled a piece of paper from his shirt pocket, showed it to me. "Is this Mr. Wooten's handwriting?"

I examined the note. ATLANTIC REALTY INVESTMENTS, INC., HILTON HEAD, SOUTH CAROLINA — $250,000. "It looks like Donald's writing."

"I found this note on Mr. Wooten's desk at the store. Do you know if he had any business dealings with this company?"

I shrugged. "I don't know. Like Momma said, I haven't seen Donald since shortly after Frank's funeral. It's taken me some time to heal after my accident."

"Accident? I thought your mother said that you'd been ill."

I faked a cough in order to have a moment to recall Momma's exact words. "She said I've been under the weather, but it's because I fell down the stairs."

"Is that why you haven't worked at the store since Donald took over?"

Before I could answer him, a commotion erupted below.

*****

Sheriff Hays and I entered the living room just in time to see Momma throw her ashtray at Johnny's head. She missed, but not by much.

"Deputy Santo, what's going on here?" The sheriff's voice boomed across the room.

Helen pointed a crimson-painted nail at Johnny. "I want this man out of my house. Now!" Her cheeks glowed firebrick red. Her green eyes — squinted slits at first — began to widen, like a female vampire getting ready to chomp down on the jugular of her victim.

Hays frowned. "I think you'd better wait outside, Deputy."

"No," I shouted. The thought of Johnny leaving so soon was unbearable. "You . . . you can't go without your hat. You left it in the kitchen. Let's get it."

Johnny looked to his boss for an okay. The older man gave a curt nod and Johnny headed for the kitchen. I followed.

Once in the kitchen, I asked, "What did you say to Momma to get her so riled up?"

"I told her she was a bigger bitch now than she was before."

"You didn't say that."

"The hell I didn't." He gripped the back of one of the dinette chairs. "She started talking about how I ruined your life and hers too. She went on and on, but I held my tongue. Then she accused my mother of stealing from her. I had to speak up."

"I see." The scorched pie pan was still in the sink. I picked it up, carried it to the trashcan, and scrapped the crust into the garbage.

"You don't seem surprised."

I put the stopper in the sink, squirted some dishwashing liquid in it, and turned on the faucet. "I've heard it all before."

"Has Helen been spreading lies about my family?"

I glanced at Johnny. He stood there, arms crossed, teeth clenched, eyes narrowed. In the sink, a cloud of bubbles was cascading over the sides of the pie pan. The foam spread across the bottom of the sink and started sneaking up the sides of the porcelain basin. I had to stop the source feeding the rising tide before it spilled over and ruined everything.

I cut off the water and twisted to look at him. "You know Momma. She hasn't changed. She still talks about everybody." Johnny's mouth relaxed a bit, but his body remained tense. "According to her, your mother is a thief, Frank married her to get her property, you're a born troublemaker, and I'm . . . I'm nothing."

I turned back to the sink, scooped up a fist full of suds. One by one, the bubbles disappeared from my hand. Just like the years of my life, they vanished, leaving nothing behind to indicate they'd ever existed. I felt Johnny's hands on my shoulders.

"That's not true, Rebecca."

He spun me around to face him. His eyes were softer now. Placing my hand on his chest, directly over his heart, I found the courage to ask the ultimate question. "Why didn't you come back for me?"

Johnny licked his lips as if his mouth had suddenly gone dry. His pulse quickened.

The door swung open. "John, I think we need to be going." Sheriff Hays stopped in the middle of the doorway. He stepped out of the way of the swinging door at the same time Johnny pulled away from me. The two men almost collided.

The sheriff walked over to the Hoosier. Johnny stepped back next to the stove. I stayed by the sink. No one uttered a word. We watched the door swing back and forth, getting ever slower before finally coming to a complete stop.

Johnny cleared his throat. "Rebecca . . . Miss Cooper and I were discussing the case."

"Really?" Hays asked, lifting a brow.

Johnny and I exchanged glances.

The sheriff extended his right hand. "Thank you, Miss Cooper, for your cooperation. I'll get back to you as soon as we know something."

I shook his hand and also apologized for Momma's behavior.

"Don't worry about it. I've been dealing with people like her all my life."

Johnny snorted. "There is nobody like Helen Wooten. Thank God."

His boss cast him a firm look. "I'll wait for you in the car, Deputy."

"He's mad at you, Johnny," I whispered, as the door closed behind Johnny's boss. "He's mad at you and it's my fault."

Johnny laughed. "Nathan's not mad. A little ticked off maybe. He wasn't sure I should come, given my history with your family."

"Why did you come?"

"Because I wanted to see you, Twig." He reached down and gave my nose a little tweak the way he often did when we were children.

I smiled, pleased to discover he remembered the nickname he and Papa had given me.

"Mrs. Treadwell said she heard a rumor you were back, but I didn't believe her. At her age, she tends to get things mixed up. Besides, I knew if you were here, you'd come by or at least call. How long have you been back, Johnny?"

"A little while."

"How long is a little while?"

"It's been crazy at the station. Half the deputies either quit because they didn't want to work for a black man or were fired by Nathan for being corrupt."

"How long have you been back?"

"I started right after Labor Day," he said, averting his eyes from mine.

"Labor Day was over a month ago. You've been here a month and haven't called?"

He reached for the Stetson, smoothed back his hair, slipped on his hat. "Between work and trying to get the old Baxter place livable, I haven't had any free time."

"The old Baxter place? You're living at the old Baxter place?"

"I made a deal with Mr. Baxter. I'd fix the place up in exchange for free rent."

"Damn you, Johnny. The Baxter house is only about three miles from here." I spun around, grabbed a SOS pad and started scrubbing the pan.

"I've been meaning to stop by, Twig."

"Meaning to stop by. What the hell does that mean?" I asked without turning around.

"I know I should've come by sooner, but I wanted to get settled first. I thought I'd run into you in town. Nathan insisted all his deputies go through an orientation program. That kept me busy the first two weeks."

The more lame excuses Johnny offered, the harder I scrubbed.

"Please, please say something, Rebecca," he pleaded in a small voice.

I rinsed off the pan, placed it in the dish drainer, and started scrubbing the sink. "You need to leave now, Deputy Santo. Sheriff Hays is waiting for you."

"Rebecca," Johnny whispered.

His hand brushed the back of my head. "Don't touch me," I said, irritated at the quiver in my voice. All motion ceased.

"May I come back, Twig? We need to talk."

I wanted to say, "Yes." Wanted to scream, "Yes." But my wounded pride was on a rampage. Keeping my back to him, I said, "I'll check my calendar. Maybe I can squeeze you in sometime next month."

Johnny's boots clicked across the linoleum. The door banged the back wall.

I glanced around the kitchen. The swinging door and the flattened aloe vera leaves were proof that his visit had been real and not a daydream. "Wait, Johnny," I yelled.

Helen stood at the front door, screaming at Johnny, warning him not to come back. I tried to squeeze past her, but she blocked me.

"You're not running after that Mexican boy again, Becky Leigh."

"I'm not sixteen anymore. You can't tell me what to do."

She grabbed my arm. "You'd best remember all the trouble he caused you."

I jerked my arm free and pushed her hard. She stumbled back and hit the wall. She almost fell, but Momma has too much cat in her not to land on her feet.

"I'm warning you, Becky, that boy is a lot of trouble."

"He's not a boy, Momma. He's a man. A lawman." I stepped closer to her. "And you arranged for the death of his unborn child. You'd do well to remember that."

The gleam in her eyes turned from hate to fear. "You can't tell him that."

"Then stay out of my way." I pushed open the screen door.

Johnny opened the door to the police car. I yelled for him to stop. He turned, tramped back up the sidewalk, and met me halfway between the street and the house.

"Momma goes to bed downstairs after the late night news. Frank built some stairs from the backyard up to the veranda. Come by around eleven."

"I'm busy tonight."

"Busy?"

"Yeah, busy."

"I thought you wanted to talk."

"I do. How about tomorrow night? I'll pick you up at half past seven and we can go to my place." He looked over my shoulder. "We won't be interrupted by Queen Bitch."

I knew Momma was watching us, straining her ears to hear our conversation. "Okay. I'll be outside so you won't have to come to the door."

"Great. I'll fix supper, unless you want to go out to eat."

"No, but . . . but . . ."

"But what, Twig?"

"I heard you got married. Your wife might not appreciate you asking me to supper."

Johnny sighed. "She's in Texas. We're divorced."

"I'm sorry to hear that," I said, trying not to sound too cheerful. I reckon there's some of Momma in me after all.

Johnny pointed at the car. "I'd better go. See you tomorrow." He walked back to the patrol car, got in, and waved once before they drove off.

I practically skipped back to the house.

Helen was in the front hall smoking a cigarette. She didn't say anything until I started upstairs. "What do you think happened to Donald? Do you think he's dead?"

"Why ask me?"

"I wondered if you'd killed him."

"That's funny. I thought about asking you the same question." At the top of the stairs, I looked down. She stood there, staring up at me. "Did you, Momma? Did you kill Donald?"

She shrugged, flashed a little grin, and walked back into the living room.

CHAPTER 31

I sat in the front porch swing waiting for Johnny to pick me up for our...our whatever. Reunion? Dinner with a friend? Under no circumstances would I allow myself to think of the evening's activity as a date. We were two friends getting together for supper and a chance to catch up after being parted for five years. There would be no romance tonight. None. There couldn't be. There shouldn't be. Johnny was fresh from a divorce, and I couldn't make any sense out of my mixed feelings for Frank. Still, I'd changed my clothes four times, brushed my teeth twice, and gone through half a pack of Dentyne gum. I needed to focus on what had occurred today instead of brooding over what was not going to happen tonight.

Upon receiving the message that Donald was missing, Charlotte, accompanied by her father, returned to Sugardale. The girls stayed in Athens with their grandmother. Charlotte and Mr. Welch stopped by our house around noon to ask if Momma or I had any new information on Donald's whereabouts. We didn't at the time, but a couple of hours later Sheriff Hays came by to let us know that both Gordon Zagat and Frank's truck had been located.

The Zagats were in Mississippi as I had suggested. Upset about being fired, Gordon had fled to his wife's relatives to visit and to look for a new job. The entire family, including Josh and his wife had accompanied Gordon in a show of solidarity.

Donald — or what the authorities suspected were his charred remains — had been found in the cab of a burned-out Ford truck at the bottom of Cascade Canyon. A startled fisherman, intent on trying his luck at Lazy Rock Creek, made the gruesome discovery shortly after sunrise and called the county sheriff's office. A license plate found in the surrounding rocks proved the vehicle was Frank's Ranchero.

The body was burned beyond recognition so they couldn't be sure the deceased was Donald until an autopsy was done. Sheriff Hays cautioned us against being optimistic that the body wasn't Donald. Obviously, Johnny hadn't informed his boss of the true nature of our feelings toward my stepbrother.

As soon as the sheriff left, Momma decided we should go comfort Charlotte. I reminded her I'd been invited to Johnny's for supper. She threw a hissy fit when I refused to change my plans.

Momma's reasons for visiting Charlotte were three-fold. First, if Donald was dead, then Charlotte could end up owning our home. As far as I knew, my mother had no spicy tidbits that she could use to blackmail Charlotte. Thus, she'd have to charm her step-daughter-in-law into letting us keep our house.

Then there was the matter of Mr. Welch. A short, wiry man with thinning hair and a bald spot the size of a silver dollar, Ben Welch wasn't Momma's type at all. But he had three qualities my mother admired. He was rich, powerful, and could exert considerable influence over his daughter. So before going over to comfort poor Charlotte, Momma fixed her hair, polished her nails, and cracked open a fresh bottle of White Shoulders.

Whenever my mother splashed on White Shoulders, she had some man in her sights.

"Men hate heavy perfumes," Helen said. "They like a delicate scent. Something sweet, yet enticing to arouse their interest. Something like White Shoulders."

Helen regarded Ben Welch as a potential ally, a man she could use to get what she wanted. He was also a man in some emotional turmoil due to his worry over Charlotte, and a man whose wife was miles away — two factors that could help render him easy pickin's for Momma.

I saw Charlotte's father as a painful memory. I'd watched Mr. Welch's attempts to comfort his daughter. His soft voice, the reassuring pats on her back, and the spontaneous hugs reminded me of Papa and reminded me of how much I missed him. I preferred not to have my feelings of loss rekindled again tonight. I certainly didn't want to watch Momma use Mr. Welch's fatherly concern as a tool to help her play him as she'd done so many times to Papa.

The third reason Momma wanted me to accompany her was easy to figure. If I were with her, I wouldn't be with Johnny.

I checked my watch: 7:43. Johnny had said he'd pick me up at half past seven. No need to worry yet. Johnny had been habitually late when he was a kid. No reason to figure he'd changed. Still, if I'd been smart enough to get his phone number, I could've called him to make sure everything was okay. There it was again, that infuriating two-letter word — if.

*****

Johnny rinsed off the head of lettuce, plunked it down on the stained pine table.

"Why don't you let me fix the salad for us, Johnny? You watch the pizza."

"Okay."

"How's Anna doing?" I asked. "I lost track of her when she moved to Texas."

"Mother's fine. She remarried in '68." Johnny handed me two fat tomatoes, a cucumber, and a red bell pepper. "Rueben, the man she married, invented this gasket for appliances. Two years ago, this big company paid him three million dollars for the patent."

I dropped the tomato. "What! Three million dollars?"

Johnny laughed. "Yeah. Mom and Rueben bought a Winnebago. They spend half the year touring the country. They're in New England now on one of those fall foliage tours, but they'll be here for Thanksgiving. Then, they'll head back to Texas for the winter."

"Three million dollars," I repeated. "You should've told Momma that when she accused Anna of stealing from her. That would've shut her up."

We both laughed. It felt good. It felt like old times.

When Johnny first picked me up, it'd been a bit awkward between us. He spent the entire ride to his house apologizing for the frozen pizza he bought for our supper. After a couple glasses of wine, we loosened up enough to give each other a brief rundown of the past five years.

I lied to Johnny, telling him I'd moved to Alabama for sixteen months to care for Frank's ailing sister. That's what everybody in Sugardale believed, and I'd told the story so many times it seemed like the truth, except at night. At night, in the darkness of the bedroom, I'd remember Havenwood. Sometimes the creaks and moans whispered by the old house startled me awake and for a long moment, I'd think the Pickers-in-white were coming for me again. When Frank was alive, he'd hold me close, tell me it was only a bad dream, and promise me he'd never let anyone or anything hurt me ever again. He lied to me. I lied to Johnny. Everybody lies to everybody.

Johnny's career in the military had gotten off to a rocky start. "I was so damn angry about being forced to leave you and join the Army, I got into a lot of fights and spent a good deal of time in the brig." He explained how his commanding officer had suggested that since Johnny enjoyed fighting and seemed determined to homestead the brig, he should join the military police. That's how he'd ended up in law enforcement.

When Johnny told me he was wounded in Vietnam, I actually cringed, imagining the enemy ambushing him. Then he described how he'd been shot while trying to break up a fight in a Saigon bar. A Marine and a sailor were at odds over which man would spend the evening with a certain Asian exotic beauty. According to Johnny, the most embarrassing part of the whole scenario was that, while he was struggling with the servicemen, the prostitute wrestled his own gun out of his holster and shot him in the leg for interfering in her business transactions. We laughed until our sides ached.

After the laughter, I found the courage to ask Johnny about his marriage. He'd been sent to Tripler Army Hospital in Honolulu for surgery on his leg. That's where he'd met Justine. They married three months later. Johnny accepted an offer to get out of the service early and he and his wife moved to Austin, Texas to be near Anna and the rest of his family. He worked nights and weekends as a part-time deputy sheriff while getting a degree in criminology. Before his divorce, he'd planned to go to law school. Now, he wasn't sure what he wanted to do.

Justine. Her name sounded clean, honorable, and full of truth. I drew a fork down the sides of the cucumber so when I sliced it, the cucumber would have pretty serrated edges. Anna had taught me that.

"Why did you move back here, Johnny?" I asked, knowing it had nothing to do with me. Still, a girl could hope.

"I came to Sugardale last May for my cousin's wedding and met Nathan at the reception. He'd just been elected sheriff and I'd gotten my degree and my divorce from Justine the week before." Johnny opened the oven and checked the pizza. "I needed a change. Needed to get out of Texas. Nathan told me if I decided to move back to Cascade County, I should see him about a job. In August, I called to see if he was serious about his offer. He was and so here I am." Johnny checked the pizza again. "It's ready."

I tossed the salad, filled our bowls, and shook the bottle of Italian dressing. Johnny sliced the pizza, and then offered me the first piece. We barely spoke. I think we were about talked out. Johnny hadn't said anything about the discovery of Frank's truck and the body in it. I was grateful. Donald and death were the last things I wanted to discuss. After supper, we did the dishes together. I washed, he dried.

"Why didn't you call or come by when you were here in May, Johnny?"

"I came by your house, but no one was home. I telephoned the store and asked for you. Someone told me that your family had gone on vacation."

"Frank took me to see the Atlantic Ocean as a present for graduating from junior college. We rented a house on the beach for a week. It was the best time of my life."

Johnny frowned. "I think being stuck with Helen for a week would've been hell."

"Momma stayed at her rich friend's house in Atlanta. You remember Eva, don't you?"

He nodded. "You and Frank spent the week together? Just the two of you?"

Something in Johnny's voice caused a warning bell to ring in my head. I'd omitted telling him Frank and I had been lovers and planned to marry. Momma often employed a diversionary tactic whenever she got backed into a corner. She'd pretend to be insulted and then put her attacker on the defensive. I decided to try it.

"What do you mean by that remark? Frank and I were family and as you said, having Momma along would've been hell. She hates the beach."

"I didn't mean anything. I just said —"

"If it hadn't been for Frank, I would've never got to see or do anything. He's the one who insisted I go to college, the one who looked out for me. You of all people should understand that." I threw down the dishcloth and marched off to the living room.

Johnny trailed after me, offering his apology.

I accepted it and changed the subject to his work on the Baxter house. It was really more of a cabin than a house. It consisted of a kitchen, a bath, a storage room, and a large front room that had a fireplace on the north wall. That end of the main room served as the living area, while the opposite end of the room contained a beat-up knotty pine bedroom set. Johnny explained his plans for fixing up the place and I offered to help. Then he brought up the subject of Donald.

"Did Sheriff Hays tell you and Helen about the body we found?"

"Yes. He said they'd do an autopsy, but he was pretty sure it was Donald."

"It was definitely Frank's old truck. The big question is how did it end up sailing off the cliff?"

"What makes you think it went off the cliff? Maybe Donald drove the truck in. There's a bunch of old logging roads leading down to the bottom of the canyon."

"It went off the cliff all right. We spotted pieces of the truck up in the rocks. Looked like it hit the wall a couple of times before landing on the canyon floor."

I sat down on the arm of an overstuffed chair. "Can you tell when it happened?"

"We're pretty sure it happened last Friday. We interviewed a couple who were camping downstream. They heard an explosion and saw smoke rising out of the canyon that afternoon."

"Why didn't they call the sheriff?"

"They figured someone was clearing land by blowing up a stump and burning brush."

I played with my hair — twisting it, braiding it, unbraiding it — while Johnny gave me an unsolicited explanation on how the investigation would likely proceed. All possibilities would be considered. Murder. Accident. Even suicide would be mulled over, despite the fact that Donald was too much of a son-of-a-bitch to do the world a favor and kill himself.

Every person close to Donald would be investigated for motive and opportunity. Gordon Zagat, the fired employee. Charlotte, the wife wanting a divorce. Sheriff Hays and Johnny had heard the rumor that Donald was having an affair with Wanda Gimmer and that Wanda's brother, Mitch, wasn't too happy about it. They'd both be checked out and so would Momma. Her dispute with Donald over Frank's will wasn't exactly a secret.

"Why did Helen sign her property over to Frank in the first place?" Johnny asked.

"While I was living in Alabama, Frank left Momma. People starting talking. Rumors began flying. Momma desperately wanted him to move back into the house, even if it was strictly for appearances. She offered to put things in his name if he'd move back."

Johnny scratched his head. "I never thought of Frank as being the type of man to take advantage of a woman, even one like Helen."

"Frank didn't want to accept it, but I talked him into it. He wanted a divorce, but went back because I begged him to. I couldn't bear losing both you and him." I grabbed Johnny's hand, squeezed it. "Can we talk about something more pleasant? Your cousin, Emelda, told me your wife was expecting a baby. Did you have a boy or a girl?"

Johnny pulled away, walked over to the fireplace, and stoked the fire he'd started earlier.

"Maybe I misunderstood Emelda," I said.

"No, you understood right. We had a baby in December of '69. A son."

"What's his name?"

"We named him Robert Earl, after my dad and hers, but everyone called him Robbie." Johnny smiled. "You should have seen him, Twig. He had a grin that would melt your heart. When I'd come home, he'd hear my voice and squeal like a piglet until I picked him up."

I could picture Johnny with a son. Playing with him. Hugging him. Loving him. "You must miss him a lot, with you here in Georgia and him in Texas."

"Yeah, I do. I miss him." Johnny plunked down on the cracked leather sofa. He stared into the fire, sucked in a deep breath, held it for a moment before exhaling. The air came out of him in a sluggish, whistling flow, like when you remove the plug from a kid's blow-up toy.

"I'm sorry. I didn't mean to make you feel sad," I said.

"He's gone. Robbie's gone." Johnny leaned forward, rested his elbows on his knees, and covered his face with his hands.

I got down on my knees in front of him. "You'll see him again. I'm sure you'll visit —"

"You don't understand." Johnny grabbed my shoulders. "He's dead. Robbie died last year, two days before Thanksgiving. He got sick all of a sudden. A problem with his heart. The doctors did their best, but they couldn't save him."

I hugged Johnny tight and let him cry until the heat from the fireplace began to burn my back. I sat down at the end of the couch and motioned for him to lay his head in my lap. My mind searched for something comforting to say, but words seemed so trivial. I wanted to tell him I understood the pain of losing a child, the pain of losing his child, but couldn't. I vowed never to tell Johnny about Havenwood or the child we'd made and lost.

He rested in my lap for a good hour before getting up. The fire had died down and the radiance of the smoldering embers cast a muted, dreamlike glow across the room. He pulled me up. My feet were asleep and I wobbled a bit. Johnny drew me into his arms and kissed me. It wasn't a light kiss, nor overly passionate. I judged it to be just right.

He nuzzled my neck and murmured, "Stay with me, Twig. I need you."

My toes tingled as warm blood began circulating through them, chasing away the numbness. My body trembled as Johnny's warm breath tickled my skin, awakening my dead heart. "Don't worry," I whispered. "I'm not going anywhere."

*****

It was almost dawn by the time Johnny and I got around to making love. The soothing touch of skin upon skin helped keep us calm as we made our way back to each other, stumbling at times through the debris that cluttered the past five years of our lives.

I lay on Johnny's bed, naked except for my panties, and felt no shame. The shy, frightened sixteen-year-old who had shared his bed in a flooded Tennessee fishing camp no longer existed. Gone too was the clumsy young man who'd claimed me as his common-law bride in a marriage sanctioned by no one except us and perhaps, the Lord Almighty.

Johnny slipped off his briefs and stood nude at the foot of the bed — so handsome, so erect, so ready. He bent over, pulled off my white, cotton underpants, tossed them on the pile of clothes we'd shed earlier. "You're beautiful, Rebecca."

I smiled at him, pleased by the way he slipped back and forth between calling me Twig and Rebecca. It made me feel like some sort of sophisticated woman, a woman too complicated to have only one name.

He pressed his knees on the mattress. The silence of the room amplified his heavy breathing and the crackling of the rekindled fire. Dark, widening eyes inspected my body as he crawled toward me in cautious anticipation.

My chin quivered, a reflection of my body's own eagerness. Pulling him close, I pressed him into me, urging him to deposit his pain and suffering deep inside of me.

He cried out my name twice. "Rebecca . . . Re-bec-ca." Then all movement ceased.

The intensity of our mating surprised me. Though brief, it lasted long enough to produce the shuddered relief our bodies craved. Johnny rolled off me and onto his back.

We lay side-by-side, our fingers intertwined.

"Damn, Twig . . . damn."

"Are you okay, Johnny?"

"I'm not sure yet," he said, a touch of amusement in his voice.

I rolled toward him. "We've both learned a few things since that fishing camp."

He grinned at the ceiling. "Who taught you all that . . . that stuff?"

"Do you really want to start exchanging names, Johnny?"

"Forget I asked."

I kissed his shoulder. "We should each be allowed some secrets, shouldn't we?"

He nodded. "I'm whipped."

"Yeah, me too."

Johnny kissed me goodnight, turned over and fell right to sleep.

I snuggled up close to his back, taking in its musky scent and warmth. My fingers skimmed his body — a light touch so as not to awaken him, yet firm enough that even the deepest recesses of my brain acknowledged the reality of him. This time, the dream was real.

Satisfied that Johnny was not an apparition, I turned over and fitted my back to his so we could sleep cheek-to-cheek, in a manner of speaking. I thought myself content. Yet when I closed my eyes, I didn't see Johnny's face. I saw Frank's.

CHAPTER 32

Three days later, the dead man found in Frank's burned-out truck was officially identified as being Donald Wooten. Even so, it was the middle of the next week before they released the body for burial.

Donald's funeral didn't draw the number of mourners Frank's had. Still, the chapel at Levin's Funeral Home was standing room only. Most attendees were either friends of Charlotte's or people who'd gone to high school with Donald. A decent number of employees from Cooper's Hardware and Garden turned out, including Gordon Zagat, Wanda Gimmer, and her brother, Mitch. Everyone asked if I was going to run the stores again. I gave the stock reply, "We'll see."

In addition to mourners, family, and several local reporters, a contingent of law officers, including Sheriff Hays attended the service. The inquiry into Donald's demise had been designated a suspicious death investigation and would be treated as a murder case until the evidence proved otherwise. Johnny explained how deputies often go to funerals to watch the reaction of family and friends because it's usually one of them who committed the murder. According to Momma's unofficial, but reliable source — Roy Tate — there were at least five people who had both motive and opportunity to kill Donald.

Gordon Zagat admitted fighting with Donald over being fired. He claimed he had nothing to hide because Donald was alive when he left Starview Mountain. No one could verify his claim except me, and I wasn't talking.

When Donald called Wanda Gimmer that Friday to say he had to cancel their tryst because of truck problems, she figured he'd lined up another girlfriend for the evening. Claiming a family emergency, she and brother Mitch left work. Later that afternoon, they showed up at the Sugardale store demanding to see Donald. When she discovered he'd left for the day, Wanda started cursing, knocking over displays and screaming, "That bastard is going to regret two-timing me." Neither she nor Mitch had a good alibi for the afternoon Donald died.

Charlotte told Sheriff Hays she'd been in Athens all day Friday. But her neighbor reported seeing her and a large, good-looking man entering her Sugardale apartment late that Friday morning. When caught in the lie, Charlotte claimed she'd been so upset by the news of her husband's disappearance, she'd forgotten about returning to Sugardale to get extra clothes for the girls. Her gentleman friend had supposedly come along to protect her from Donald.

Momma enjoyed telling me Johnny had been taken off the case because he too was a suspect in Donald's death. One of his fellow sheriff officers remembered that Johnny had at one time threatened to kill my stepbrother. I reminded Momma that Johnny made the threat eight years ago because Donald had raped me. She replied, "Maybe so, but some folks think it's a mite strange that Johnny returns to Sugardale and a month later Donald is dead."

The fifth suspect lived in our house. Momma had no alibi from the time she finished an early lunch with Betty Powell until 6 p.m. when her Sunday school teacher, Sue Atwood, called to brag about winning the trip to Las Vegas. Momma never could take defeat very well. The next day, I caught her spitting into the batter of a pineapple upside-down cake Mrs. Atwood had ordered.

Momma told Sheriff Hays she'd been home all Friday afternoon. When he mentioned that Mrs. Treadwell hadn't seen our van in the driveway, Momma claimed she'd put it in the garage to keep leaves from falling on it. The only time I remembered her putting the van in the garage was once when I inadvertently discovered her and Henry going at in the folded down back seat. She claimed they were trying to recapture the days of their youth.

People talked of nothing except Donald's strange death. The demand for my baked goods doubled, mainly because customers wanted to drop by, pick up their order, and pump us for information on the investigation. By mid-October, we stopped letting folks pick up their orders and hired a high school boy to deliver them.

I now seldom went anywhere except to Johnny's. The whispering and stares bothered me. I wondered if the glue holding the veneer of lies that concealed our true lives could withstand the heat of such scrutiny.

Charlotte wouldn't comment about her plans for Papa's house. Momma said I shouldn't worry because she knew how to handle airheads like Charlotte. Fighting Donald for Frank's estate would've been a cakewalk compared to going against a sympathetic widow, her two fatherless children, and her daddy's big-time lawyers. Momma accused me of sabotaging her efforts because I'd refused Charlotte's request to run the stores until the estate was settled. As soon as the law permitted, Charlotte planned to sell the stores and the Starview Mountain property. Atlantic Realty Investments, Inc. offered her half-a-million dollars for Starview.

When she heard how much money would be going to Charlotte instead of to us, Momma took to her bed. She claimed she had the flu, but I knew she needed time to regroup and devise a new scheme to wangle total control of the estate from Charlotte.

Johnny and I spent much of our free time together working on the Baxter house. I painted walls and hung pretty curtains, while he caulked windows, repaired the roof, and replaced rotted boards. In order to avoid Momma, we always stayed at his place. Even so, she made her presence known.

Whenever I spent the night at Johnny's, Momma would call at all hours. Sometimes she'd hang up as soon as he answered. Twice, she insisted prowlers had broken in. The intruders turned out to be squirrels in the attic and an overgrown limb slapping an upstairs window. She'd drive by Johnny's house just to see if we were there.

It was ironic. Now, Momma was the one alone, while I had someone to care about, someone to laugh with, and someone who could help shoo away the loneliness. And in my new career as a caterer, I could set my own work hours. That gave me more time with Johnny, and I had Momma to thank for that.

I thought our role reversal funny. Funny, but a little sad for Momma. I hadn't a clue why I should care about her feelings. She never cared about mine. I tried to will away the kernel of sympathy my heart felt for her, but discovered the heart has a mind of its own.

CHAPTER 33

Momma came through the front door just as I set out the last tray of caramel apples.

She pointed to the rolls of orange and black crepe paper. "What's this?"

"I thought we'd decorate for Halloween."

She threw her purse on the sofa. "Did you fill all those orders? We need money."

"Everything's done, every cookie delivered." I picked up a bag of angel hair and a handful of plastic spiders. "Let's hang some spider webs before the trick-or-treaters come. Where's that witch's costume you used to wear?"

Momma yanked opened the top drawer of the buffet. "Shit, I'm out of cigarettes."

"This might be a good time to start cutting back. We could save some money."

"Don't tell me what to do," she shouted. "Don't you dare." She pushed her hair off her face with both hands. "Why don't you go to Johnny's?"

"It's Halloween. He's working tonight." I went to the kitchen and returned with a half-pack of Camels. "I found these earlier."

Momma snatched the smokes out of my hand, lit one, and inhaled. Her hands trembled as she tried to light a second cigarette off the first.

"You want some help?"

"I don't need your goddamn help to light my own cigarette." She tried again, finally succeeding on her fourth attempt. "I don't need anyone's help. Not now. Not ever."

"What's wrong, Momma? Did something happen to Henry? Is that why you're upset?"

"Screw Henry and you too." She pointed at the candy apples. "Take those out on the porch. I don't want a bunch of painted brats running in and out of my house." She tapped her ashes into the creamer of her prized silver tea set. "My house. That's a laugh."

"What's happened, Momma?"

She pointed to her purse. "Read the letter."

A pink envelope stuck halfway out of the side pocket of Momma's genuine alligator purse. I opened the letter. A picture of spring flowers mixed with green ivy trailed across the top of the page. I caught the faint whiff of lavender.

"That bitch," Momma yelled. "That goddamn bitch didn't have the nerve to tell me to my face. Sent me a letter on scented stationary."

The letter was from Charlotte. She'd moved back to Athens to stay with her parents. Before leaving, she'd told us her daddy had convinced her that letting us keep our home was the decent thing to do. I guess Donald's widow decided she didn't want to be that decent because the letter stated her intention of selling the house as soon as the lawyers settled the estate. But Charlotte wasn't totally devoid of sympathy for our plight. In a postscript, she offered to sell us our own home at a ten percent discount.

"I drove all the way to Athens to talk some sense into her. The bitch wouldn't even open her damn door." Momma lit a third cigarette. "But that's okay, I'll come up with something special for that whore. She'll regret messing with me."

I eased down onto the edge of Papa's old recliner. In the ten weeks since Frank's death, I'd never really believed we could lose our house. Suddenly, the reality of our precarious situation slammed into me like a locomotive rolling over a plastic doll. I found it difficult to breathe. The air grew thick; afternoon shadows crept across the room. I swallowed the wail forming in the back of my throat.

Momma flicked her cigarette ashes into the fireplace. "I wanted the authorities to blame Charlotte for Donald's death instead of charging Gordon."

"What are you talking about?"

"Roy's source in the sheriff's office told him they're going to arrest Gordon Zagat for Donald's murder."

I shot out of the chair. "They can't do that. He didn't kill Donald."

"People heard Donald fire him, and others saw Gordon drinking at Mike's Tavern around lunchtime." Momma shook her head. "I can't believe he admitted to fighting with Donald on Starview Mountain. What an idiot."

"He's not an idiot. Mr. Zagat believes in telling the truth."

"That proves he's an idiot. If he goes to prison for murder, it'll be his own fault."

"Gordon Zagat didn't kill Donald. There's no evidence he did."

She shrugged. "Roy did say all the evidence against Gordon was circumstantial. A good lawyer should be able to get him off."

I rubbed my scalp, trying to massage my throbbing head. "This isn't right."

"You bet it isn't right. If I had my way, they'd arrest Charlotte."

I wiped the sweat off my upper lip. "We have to help Mr. Zagat."

"Let me think a minute." Momma stood staring into the mirror above the buffet. A spiteful grin eased across her face. "I've got a solution."

"What?"

"I know a fellow who lives across from Starview Mountain Road. He owes me a favor."

"For what?" Before she could answer, I added, "Never mind. It's none of my business."

"You're learning, Becky." She rubbed out her half-smoked cigarette and slipped it back into the pack. "If my friend said he saw Charlotte's car come speeding down Starview Mountain Road the afternoon Donald died, then it would look like she and her male friend had been on the mountain too. Charlotte had more to gain from killing Donald than Gordon did." Momma let out a wicked laugh. In her low, slow-down voice she said, "With any luck, Frank's granddaughters will be visiting their slut of a mother in prison."

"But that would be a lie."

She finger-combed her hair toward her face. "So what?"

"It's wrong, Momma. Can't you see that?"

"You're the one who wants to help Gordon. If we throw some suspicion on Charlotte, there'd be grounds for reasonable doubt. Then his attorney will have no trouble getting an acquittal."

"You've been watching too many Perry Mason reruns, Momma. These are real people with real lives. We can't manipulate them this way."

"Relax, Becky. I don't expect them to convict Charlotte. That would be too much to hope for." Momma ran her finger across the top of one of the apples. "I just want a little revenge, and want to force Charlotte to waste lots of money on attorney's fees. Are there any cookies left? Caramel sticks to my teeth."

I sank down onto the ottoman, wrapped my arms around my waist and began to rock.

"Don't start that rocking nonsense." She headed for the kitchen. "I hope you saved me some of those frosted Halloween cookies."

I jumped up and shrieked, "Fuck the cookies, Momma. Fuck the cookies." Over and over I yelled, "Fuck the cookies." But it wasn't really me. I was calmly floating near the ceiling, watching a young woman with my face and voice act like a fool. She ran around the living room flailing her arms, pounding her fist against the walls, and screaming, "Fuck the cookies." Finally, she collapsed on the sofa. I drifted closer and gazed into her green eyes. Stunned and bewildered, I recognized the sobbing female as being Becky Leigh Cooper. Me. I was the crying fool.

"Calm down, Becky," Momma ordered. "What's got into you? A little payback now and then is good for the soul."

"What soul, Momma? You don't have a soul. Neither do I. We traded them for the power to manipulate, the talent to deceive, and the zeal for revenge." I picked up a linen doily off the coffee table and wiped away my tears. "We did this to ourselves. It's our fault we've lost everything Papa and Grandpa Eli spent their lifetimes building."

She crossed her arms. "You're talking nonsense. Frank did this to us when he left everything to Donald."

"You signed everything over to Frank to manipulate him into moving back home because you needed him. He hated living here. He accepted your offer because I begged him to. I wanted to take everything from you just as you had taken everything from me. I craved revenge and used Frank to help me get it."

Helen ran her hand back and forth over her forehead. "That drive to Athens wore me out. I'm going to take a nap."

"You're not going anywhere until we settle this matter."

"What matter are you talking about? Charlotte? Gordon Zagat?"

"Our lives, Momma. Our lives and the mess we've made of them." I walked over to the front window, pulled back the lace curtain, and watched the cars pass by. "The people of Sugardale believe our family grows beautiful flowers and delicious vegetables. But that's not what we do, is it?"

I released the curtain and turned to face her. "We take seeds of truth and spit on them. We stomp them and smother them with vindictiveness and cruelty until they sprout as lies. That's what we grow, Momma — lies. From a seed of truth, we grow acres of lies. We feed the deceit to our friends and neighbors, all the while eating it ourselves. We eat so much, we forget they're lies. How many lies does it take to cover up one truth?"

"Shut up, Becky Leigh." Momma slammed her fist against the fireplace mantel. "I'm sick and tired of hearing you spout off about the truth, like it was something fine and noble. It's not." She shook her finger at me. "I'll tell you what the truth is. It's dirty, ugly, and nothing to be cherished or prized. Truth is simply another name for the filth he pours over you, for the pain he inflicts, and for the shame that never goes away."

"Who, Momma? Who is he?"

Momma stared at the dying embers in the fireplace. "You don't want to know."

"You didn't grow up on a thoroughbred ranch in Kentucky, did you?"

She didn't answer.

"You're father wasn't a major in the army, was he? You didn't go to a private girl's school, and you never had a pony named Coal, did you? It's just more of your lies."

She remained silent.

"Tell me the truth," I yelled. "There was no Coal was there?"

Momma whipped around. "There was coal all right. Every day the mine where my daddy worked dumped its waste, a mix of shale and coal. And every day, I stood poised at the base of the coal bank ready to launch an attack the moment the scraps were dumped. I'd claw my way up the bank, fending off older, stronger gleaners, to meet the avalanche of waste head on. The challenge was to fill your pail with coal, slide down the bank, pour it into a wheelbarrow, and return to the top before the others." She stopped, took three ragged breaths and pointed to herself. "I always won. I always got the most. The only reason my family didn't freeze to death during the long West Virginia winters was because of me."

"Why did you keep that a secret from Papa and me? That's nothing to be ashamed of."

She let out a laugh that bordered on hysteria. "You haven't heard the best parts yet, Becky. Don't you want to know the whole truth and nothing but the truth?"

"Yes," I said, ignoring her sarcasm.

"Belmar Ridge, in West Virginia was a company town. Everything and everyone belonged to the Belmar Mining Company. Every night, my daddy would stop by the only bar in town, spend half his day's pay, then stagger home to our two room shack." Momma stopped to light a cigarette. "Some nights he'd pass out right away. Other nights, he'd beat the hell out of Ma, me, and Laurel too if he could catch her."

"Who's Laurel?"

"My baby sister. Laurel was eight years younger than me. I tried to protect her."

"I don't understand. You never mentioned having a sister. Why didn't your mother protect you and Laurel?"

Momma laughed again. "Daddy beat her down so hard and so often, she couldn't save a mosquito, much less us. She finally had enough. One afternoon Ma took Laurel and me down to the pond back of our shack. She told us she'd found a better place for us. A place filled with food, warm clothes, and no more beatings. She grabbed our hands and led us out into the pond. The water was up to Laurel's neck when I realized Ma intended on drowning all of us."

She stopped, rubbed her hand across her forehead again. "I fought my own mother to prevent her from drowning my sister and me, but I won. I carried Laurel back to the bank. When we turned around, Ma was gone."

Momma sat down on the sofa and I plunked down on the ottoman. Now I knew why she'd gotten so angry when I suggested she should've drowned me when I was a baby.

She finished her cigarette and lit another. The thumb on her right hand twitched — a sign she was telling the truth.

"What happened after that?" I asked.

"They found her body the next day. There was a funeral. The neighbors brought us food." She grinned. "I'd never seen so much food. Laurel and I pigged out." Then her smile faded. "My sister and I slept on make-shift beds in the main room. That night after Laurel went to sleep, Daddy called me into his bedroom. He said I'd have to take over the wifely duties."

"He meant the cooking and cleaning, right? And taking care of your sister?"

All the color drained from Momma's face. "Yes, that and . . . and everything else that goes with being a wife."

I felt a chill flow across my chest as if someone had poured cold rubbing alcohol on it. "What do you mean when you say. . . everything?"

Momma stared at her hands. Her right thumb twitched so hard, she had difficulty holding her cigarette. She looked at me with eyes as empty as a corpse's. "I was thirteen when my daddy made me his whore. By my fourteenth birthday, I was carrying his child."

The foul, bitter taste of bile crawled up my throat and coated my tongue. I slapped my hand over my mouth, choked back the sludge, and willed myself not to throw up. We sat in silence. I did the math in my head. Papa and Momma married in July of '48. I was born in May of '50. Did I have an older brother or sister somewhere? "What happened to your baby?"

She didn't answer. Momma looked lost, as if she'd gone to sleep during a long trip and woke up in a strange town. She glanced around the room as if trying to get her bearings.

We needed time to compose our thoughts. "I saved some of the frosted cookies, Momma.

Would you like a cup of coffee or hot tea to go with them?"

"What . . . what did you say?"

"Would you like a cup of tea and some frosted cookies?"

"That would be nice," she said. "We can have tea and cookies and pretend we're as good as the Queen of England. Can't we, Becky?"

I blinked back a tear. "Of course we can, Momma. We're good at pretending."

*****

I placed a platter of cookies decorated to resemble ghosts, witches, and pumpkins on the kitchen table. In our house, even the cookies pretended to be something they weren't.

Momma played with her teacup, spinning it around on its matching china saucer. She picked it up, put it down, and ran her finger around the rim. As she did, she told me about growing up in West Virginia.

She'd traded her most cherished possession — a barrette decorated with imitation pearls — to the local midwife for an abortion. When her father staggered home the next evening, Momma met him at the front door and slammed a two-by-four across his skull. The blow knocked him backwards, causing him to fall and bust his head open on the steps. She told the neighbors he'd gotten drunk and fallen.

"Did you kill him?" I asked, hoping in a way she had.

"No, although that was my intention. The bastard lived, but lost all memory. He didn't recognize Laurel or me. He didn't remember what he'd done to us . . . done to me." Momma shook her head. "I ended up doing the jackass a favor.

Some Christian folks took him in, fed him, and gave him a warm bed. He never did another day's work."

"What happened to you and Laurel?"

"They sent us to an orphanage. The food tasted terrible, but there was plenty of it. We each had a bed and the work was easier than hauling coal. The woman who ran the place tried to whip Laurel once. I snatched the belt from the biddy's hand, told her I'd wrap it around her neck if she hurt my sister. The old crone never bothered us again."

I handed Momma a tea bag. "What became of Laurel?"

"A nice couple adopted her. She didn't want to leave me, but it was for the best. The couple had a new car and the woman wore a mink stole. I knew they'd give my sister a nice home. After Laurel left, I borrowed money from the grocery fund and caught the bus to Atlanta."

I filled our cups with hot water. "You borrowed the money?"

"It's not really stealing if you intend on paying it back, is it?"

I returned the kettle to the stove, sat down across from her, began dunking my teabag. "Did you pay it back?"

She shrugged. "They owed me money for the work I did."

As we drank our tea and ate the cookies, she told me how she'd met Eva Whitcomb soon after arriving in Atlanta. She helped Momma get a job, a room in a boarding house, and a fake birth certificate that said Momma was eighteen instead of fifteen.

"There wasn't anything Eva couldn't get, except your father."

"What do you mean?"

"Our boss, Mr. Gillespie, built a big house outside of Atlanta. He invited us out for a weekend party. The Coopers had done the landscaping and Paul Cooper came to the party."

"I remember Papa saying he met you at a fancy party. He said you were the prettiest girl there. That's why he took you home to Sugardale with him."

She grinned. "All the girls wanted Paul, but I snatched him away from everybody, including Eva. Your daddy had everything I wanted in man. Good looks, money, a nice house, and the respect of important people like Mr. Gillespie." She reached for another cookie. "Before Paul knew what hit him, I'd lassoed him and had a ring on my finger."

"What about love, Momma? Did you ever love Papa?"

She lowered her cup. "In time, I came to love your daddy more than any smart woman should ever love a man. He treated me like a queen. When he found out I was pregnant, he hired Anna to cook and keep house. I wasn't allowed to lift a finger."

"So Papa's the one who spoiled you so rotten?"

Momma didn't laugh. "Until you came along. After that, everything changed."

"How?"

"After you were born, Paul practically forgot about me. Everything he'd given me, he now gave to you — his attention, his presents, his love. I couldn't compete against you."

"It was never a competition, Momma."

"Everything in life is a competition. And there can be only one winner." She pointed at me. "I'd married into the Cooper clan, but you were a Cooper by blood. There was no way I could ever be first in Paul's eyes again."

Throughout my childhood, I'd tried to figure out why my mother hated me. I'd never dreamed such a beautiful, polished, and confident woman like her could be jealous of a clumsy kid like me.

I took a sip of tea. "There are different kinds of love. Papa loved us both."

She pushed back her chair and stood. "He loved you best, Becky Leigh. I got his leftovers. Leftovers and hand-me-downs were good enough for Myrtle Odetta Mott, but not for Helen Elizabeth Cooper."

"Who's Myrtle Odetta . . . Odetta . . .?"

"Myrtle Odetta Mott," she repeated. "That's the name my folks stuck me with. But everyone called me 'Myrtle the Turtle,' including my daddy. He'd say, 'Come warm me up, Myrtle the Turtle. You're sure a pretty thing, Myrtle the Turtle. Don't make me hurt you, Myrtle the Turtle.' He'd say . . ." Momma sank down into her chair, grabbed a cookie decorated to resemble a ghost and bit off its head.

If only we could devour the ghosts haunting our lives as easily. It seemed strange to think of Momma as being her father's Pick, the way I'd been hers and Donald's. I felt an odd bond with her, like we were both survivors of the same tragedy. I reached for her hand.

She yanked it away. "I don't need your goddamn pity, Becky Leigh. What I need now is my cigarettes." She got up, marched into the living room, and left me to clean up the dishes.

As I rinsed out our cups, I thought about her real name. Myrtle Odetta Mott. Little wonder she hated it. It dawned on me her initials were M.O.M. Life can be such a sarcastic brute.

*****

I finished the dishes and returned to the living room. Momma's purse dangled from her arm; keys jingled in her hand. "Where are you going?"

"I'm going to get some cigarettes before the little ghouls and goblins clog the road."

"But I've got something important to tell you. A secret."

"Been too many secrets shared tonight. By the way, if you ever repeat what I've told you, I'll strangle you with your own hair." She headed for the entry hall.

"Wait. I've got to tell you something."

She waved goodbye, turned the doorknob, and opened the front door.

"I am the one. I killed Donald." The words rushed out of me.

Momma stopped, but didn't turn around. The grandfather clock in the hallway counted the silence between us — twenty seconds, forty seconds, a full minute.

"We need milk. I'll get some while I'm out." She swung the door open wide, pushed back the screen, took one step onto the porch.

"Didn't you hear me?" I shouted. "I killed Donald."

She flew back into the house, slamming the front door so hard the glass rattled. "Shut up before the neighbors hear you."

"I didn't mean to kill Donald. It was an accident."

She arched her left eyebrow and folded her arms. "How do you accidentally kill a bastard like Donald?"

"He saw me walking home from the library and forced me to go to Starview Mountain with him." I told Momma about Donald's problems with the truck, about his anger at Charlotte, and of his plans to build a resort. I explained how my stepbrother and Gordon Zagat fought, and how I'd failed to catch a ride home with Mr. Zagat.

"Donald must have been mad after Gordon left," she said.

I nodded.

"Did the bastard hit you, Becky? Did he rape you again?"

I didn't answer.

"Did you kill him before he hurt you or afterwards?"

"It was an accident."

"An accident, huh?" Momma dropped her purse and keys on the coffee table and sat. "Okay, I'm listening. Just how did you accidentally kill Donald?"

"I asked him to take me home, but he wanted to study the blueprints for the resort some more. He suggested I get a blanket out of the truck, spread it under a tree, and read my gardening book until he finished."

Momma snickered. "Donald never suggested anything in his life. Demanded, but never just suggested." She retrieved her last cigarette, lit it, and crumpled up the empty package. "Come on, Becky. Tell me the rest of this fairy tale."

"Like I explained, Donald had left the Ranchero running because he'd had problems getting it to start. I opened the truck door and reached in for my book. It was very heavy. When I picked it up off the dash, my injured wrist buckled, and the book fell. It hit the gearshift, knocked the truck out of park and into reverse, and landed on the accelerator."

Momma rolled her eyes and waved the smoke out of her face. "Then what?"

"The pickup jerked backwards. The driver's door hit me, spun me to the ground, and the truck rolled slowly down the hill in the direction of the cliff. I yelled at Donald to get out of its way, but instead he ran toward the truck. He grabbed the door and managed to swing up into the cab. I guess he thought he could save the pickup."

"Apparently, he couldn't," she said.

"No, ma'am. When the truck finally stopped, it came to rest halfway over the ledge. It teetered there like a seesaw and then slipped over the cliff. I ran to the edge of the overhang. When the truck hit the canyon floor, it exploded and burned. I knew Donald had to be dead."

"What did you do then?"

"I ran. Past the Lambert's horse pasture, through the thicket, across Lost Mule Bog —"

"Lost Mule Bog? Were you trying to get yourself snake bit, girl?"

"I wasn't thinking straight."

"I wondered why you were as white as sugar when you got home. You went straight to bed. Didn't even fix my supper." Momma snuffed out her cigarette. "When Donald came up missing, I figured you had something to do with it."

"Why didn't you say something to me?"

"I didn't want to risk getting that Cooper conscience of yours stirred up. Didn't want you to do something stupid like turning yourself in."

"That's just what I'm going to do, Momma. First thing Monday morning."

"You're not going to do anything, Becky Leigh, except keep your mouth shut."

"I can't let Mr. Zagat go to prison for something I did."

"He hasn't even been arrested yet. If he goes to trial, he'll get off. I guarantee it."

"You can't guarantee that."

She stood. "They need twelve people for a jury. I'm bound to have something on a couple of them. Something that'll convince them to see things our way."

"Are you crazy, Momma? You can't blackmail a juror."

"I said convince. There's a difference."

"I don't think a judge would see it that way."

"You have no imagination, Becky Leigh. You never did."

I dropped down onto the ottoman. "I can imagine us in adjoining jail cells. Me for killing Donald and you for jury tampering."

Helen snickered. "That wouldn't be very pleasant, would it?"

"It'd be hell, Momma."

She pulled off her pearl clip earrings, laid them on the credenza. "Just how did Donald really die?"

"I told you."

"I didn't believe that story for a minute. I think Donald either raped you or threatened to rape you and somehow you managed to knock him out."

"How would I've done that?"

"With a rock. Once Donald was unconscious, you could've stuffed him into the pickup and sent it sailing over the cliff." Momma massaged her earlobes. "That's what I would've done and you're more like me, Becky, than you think."

"Donald weighed 200 pounds. How could I've lifted him into the truck by myself?"

She parked herself on the coffee table. "Did someone help you kill him? Johnny, perhaps?"

"Maybe Donald told me to get that blanket out of the truck because he was going to rape me again. Perhaps, I pretended I couldn't find it so he'd have to come hunt it himself. When he leaned in to get it, I could've knocked him out with the tire iron and then pulled him into the cab. He'd left the Ranchero running. It would've been easy enough to put the truck in reverse and drop the book on the accelerator right before I jumped out."

Momma stared at me stone-faced.

"What about it? Would that have worked?"

She grinned. "That would have done the trick."

I went to the front window and pulled back the curtain. The pinkish glow of a dying sun tinted the sky behind Mrs. Treadwell's red brick colonial. Next to the front steps, a four-foot plywood Frankenstein stood ready to test the courage of the anticipated trick-or-treaters. Ghosts cut from sheets and tethered by thin, silver wires fluttered beneath the porch ceiling.

I released the curtain, rubbed the back of my neck, then turned to face Momma. "Donald's death was truly an accident. But you can believe whatever you want."

She shrugged. "People believe what they want or need to believe. The truth seldom matters."

"Grandpa Eli once told me something like that."

"Eli Cooper was a smart man." Momma stood, stretched, and then walked over to stand in front of the mirror above the credenza. "Some folks might claim I'm Myrtle the Turtle, but she died the moment I stepped on that bus to Atlanta. I'm Helen Elizabeth. Named for a woman whose beauty was so great, it started a war, and for a young princess who became the Queen of England. I am Helen Elizabeth, and that's the gospel truth."

"And you're the one who said I should show more backbone."

"I didn't mean you should stand up and tell the world you killed a man." Momma pushed her bangs up off her forehead. "How about starting with something simple like declaring you'll do the laundry only twice a week, or vowing not to fix supper on Sunday nights?"

"I can't let Gordon and his family suffer the embarrassment and expense of a trial. I've got to tell the truth."

"You need to take care of yourself first. If you can do that and still help others, then that's fine. The biggest truth in life, Becky, is you must put yourself first because others will degrade, disappoint, or destroy you if given half a chance."

"That's your truth, Momma. Not mine."

"Oh? And just what is your truth?"

"I don't know yet, but it's definitely not letting someone suffer because of what I've done. Can't you understand that?"

Momma walked over and raised her hand. I thought she was going to slap me. Instead, she pushed my hair behind my ears. "You have such pretty cheekbones. You should wear your hair back to show them off." She sighed. "You are your daddy's daughter. Just as I am, in my own way, my father's child." She patted my cheek, walked over to the phone table, and pulled out the directory. "If you insist on turning yourself in, you'll need a good attorney."

"I can't afford one."

"I'd be surprised if Judge Langford charged you anything."

Judge Harland Langford had been Grandpa Eli's best friend. He'd begun his law practice the same year my grandfather started Cooper's Hardware and Garden. They often joked about passing the same five-dollar bill back and forth between them. Grandpa would pay his friend five dollars for legal work. Then Harland's wife, Ruth, would spend the money on garden supplies.

"But he's retired," I said.

"Ruth told me Harland was going stir crazy from not having enough to do. You'll be doing him a favor." Momma flipped through the phone book. "He's been a defense attorney, county prosecutor, and Georgia Supreme Court Judge." She picked up the receiver and started dialing. "Besides, the judge always did like you. He taught you how to play checkers. If he can do that, he can get you out of a murder charge."

The logic of my mother's last statement might have eluded someone else, but I understood. I'd been allowed a glimpse at Myrtle the Turtle, a vulnerable young girl, a girl like me in so many ways. Momma's unflattering critique on my ability to learn a simple board game was her way of warning me that Helen Elizabeth was back to stay.

CHAPTER 34

The Cascade County courthouse stood in the center of town. Like many small towns in the South, Sugardale had grown outward from the courthouse square. By the time Judge Langford and I arrived most of the parking spots around the square were taken. We parked across the street in front of Ferrell's drugstore.

"The first Monday of the month is always a busy time at the courthouse," he said.

I nodded and unbuttoned my sweater. "Is it me, or is it unusually warm for November?"

"Relax, Becky. Everything will be fine."

"I'm so nervous, I threw up this morning. I keep thinking someone's calling my name."

"Someone is. Looks like Helen to me."

"Wait up, Becky Leigh." Momma headed straight toward us, waving a red scarf like a crazy woman.

"What are you doing here?" I asked as she approached. "Your note said you were going to the beauty parlor."

"I changed my mind. Hold this."

She handed me her purse, slipped off her ruby pumps, and picked grass blades off her heels. "I hate walking across wet grass." She pushed her feet into her shoes, retrieved her purse, and tied her stylish scarf over her hair. "How are you, Judge Langford?"

"I'm fine, Helen."

"What are you doing here, Momma? The judge and I have business to take care of. We don't have time to visit."

"I'm not here to get my shoes dirty." Momma pushed the strap of her purse onto her shoulder. "I stopped by to have a word with the county attorney, Cordell Varner. It's a good thing I did. That rascal has gone fishing and left his new assistant, Gerald Wilkes, in charge. Do you know him, Harland?"

"We've met a couple of times. Seems like a bright fellow. A little eager."

"A little eager? I've spent the last half-hour watching him trying to get poor old Mr. Boyle locked away. Everyone in town knows that when Mr. Boyle gets his retirement check each month, he gets drunk at Mike's Tavern and wails over his late wife until Mike calls the sheriff. Roy Tate always let the old fellow sleep it off in a cell and then took him home." She shoved a stray curl under her scarf. "Wilkes is a barracuda. He'll see Becky's case as a way of making a name for himself."

"You let me worry about Wilkes. Becky's my client. I'll take good care of her."

"She may be your client, but she's my daughter. I know what she's capable of handling. Wilkes will gobble her up." Momma turned to me. "If you insist on carrying out this foolishness, you should wait until county attorney Varner is here. Cordell and your daddy grew up together. He's known you all your life. I can reason with Cordell."

That's all I needed, Momma reasoning with the county attorney. In her dictionary, the term *to reason with* was synonymous with the term *to blackmail*. No telling what information she had on him. "I'm not going home, Momma. But you are."

"Can't you talk some common sense into her, Harland?"

"Becky, would you rather come back when Cordell is here?"

"I'd like to settle the matter today."

The judge patted my back. "That's fine. Helen, go home. I'll call you when we're finished."

She rubbed her forehead. "I might as well go. Becky's not going to listen to me."

Judge Langford and I watched Momma get into her van and leave.

"Are you ready, Becky?" he asked.

"Reckon so. I wonder where Momma is going now."

"Helen said she was going home."

"Yes, sir. But home's the other direction."

*****

For once in my life, I wished I'd listened to Momma. Gerald Wilkes looked amiable enough. A short, slim fellow in his late twenties with light brown hair and gray eyes, he had a quick smile. Too quick. The kind of smile someone gives you when he doesn't believe a word you're saying. And it was clear from his questions that he didn't believe me when I said Donald's death was an accident.

"That would've had to been a heavy book to knock the truck out of gear as you claim," he said.

"I told you three times. It's *The Complete Encyclopedia of North American Plants.*"

Wilkes pulled his pocket watch from his vest and checked the time again.

"Are we keeping you from something?" Judge Langford asked.

Wilkes grinned, snapped the watch closed, poked it back into his pocket. "Not at all, Mr. Langford. It's just I hate wasting time, and this story your client is telling me is nothing but a waste of my time and yours." The young lawyer sat on the edge of a large mahogany desk. "Frankly, Miss Cooper, my four-year-old can spin a better yarn than the one you're telling me."

I didn't know how to respond to Mr. Wilkes' insinuation. All I could think of was how much pleasure Momma would get saying, "I told you so, Becky Leigh." I wondered if prisoners could refuse visits from relatives.

The office door swung open. A middle-aged man of average height and weight, dressed in khakis, a faded denim shirt, and an olive green vest tramped in. His rubber boots stopped at mid-calf and a dozen fishing lures decorated his Georgia Tech ball cap.

"Howdy, folks. What's going on here?" he asked.

Wilkes immediately slid to his feet. "What are you doing here?"

Ignoring his assistant, Cordell Varner walked over to where my attorney and I were sitting. "Judge Langford," he said, extending his right hand. "This is a real pleasure, sir. How are you today, Becky?"

"I've had better days, sir."

He smiled. "I bet you have."

"What are you doing here?" Wilkes asked again.

Varner turned to his assistant. "Someone told me you were sitting on my desk. No one sits on this desk. Not even me."

With the sleeve of his suit, Wilkes wiped off the spot where he'd been sitting. He mumbled an apology and stepped back.

Mr. Varner ran his hand across the dark wood. "I had this shipped up from Key West. An antiques dealer told me it once belonged to Ernest Hemming-way. I don't know if that's true or not, but I like to think it is."

Everyone, except Gerald Wilkes, laughed.

"You'll have to excuse my appearance, Judge Langford. When I left home this morning, I was on vacation." The county attorney slipped off his hat and vest and hung them on a coat rack. "I was down at Minnow Creek, about a mile above where it feeds into Hammond's Dam, and you'll never guess who I ran into, Becky."

"Who?"

"Your mother." Varner pulled off his boots and retrieved a pair of oxblood-colored loafers from the bottom drawer of a file cabinet. "I couldn't believe it. Helen always hated the outdoors. But there she was, tromping through the woods in a pair of red high heels."

Judge Langford laughed.

Before Papa died, our family and the Varners would get together sometimes for picnics, barbeques, and rides in Mr. Varner's boat. He tried to teach me and his twin girls how to ski. Jo Nell and Janet Fay were natural water babies, but I never could get the hang of it. The Varners and Papa talked about taking us camping in the Smoky Mountain National Park, but Momma didn't like camping. Too much dirt, too many mosquitoes, and no decent place to get her hair fixed.

"I don't know how she found me," Varner said as he stepped into the loafers. "But Helen always was a resourceful woman."

"I'm sorry she interrupted your fishing. We told her to go home."

"Don't worry about it." The county attorney sat down at his desk. "What was it Paul used to say about giving Helen orders?"

"Papa said trying to tell Momma what to do was like trying to dictate to the sun when it should rise and set."

Varner chuckled. "Yeah, and Paul was right on the money."

Wilkes cleared his throat. "Excuse me, Cordell, but you won't believe the stories Miss Cooper and Mr. Langford have been telling me."

"Mr. Langford? Gerald, do you know who this man is?"

"Sure. He's Harland Langford."

"No, he's Judge Harland Langford." Mr. Varner pointed at my attorney. "He's been a judge for thirty years. Half of them years spent on the Georgia Supreme Court. I'd appreciate it if my staff showed him the proper respect."

"I apologize, Judge Langford," Wilkes said. "I didn't mean any disrespect."

The judge gave Wilkes a curt nod.

"I'll take over from here," Mr. Varner said.

"But I've already got her statement. I've made notes about —"

"I see you have. Leave them, and on your way out tell my secretary to hold my calls."

"But Cordell," Wilkes protested, "you're on vacation."

"Thanks for reminding me. Ask Tressie to cancel the rest of my vacation too. And close the door behind you."

Gerald Wilkes' face puffed up. He stomped out of the room and slammed the door.

"That boy is a little over zealous, isn't he?" Judge Langford asked.

"Yes, sir. But we were all like that in the beginning, weren't we, Harland?"

"I suppose."

Mr. Varner smiled at me. "Becky, I hear you've got something to tell me."

"Yes, sir, I do."

The county attorney picked up the yellow legal pad, tore off the pages filled with Wilkes' notes. "I like to draw my own conclusions." He wadded up the paper and threw it in the trash. "Okay, Miss Becky. Tell me your story."

I took a deep breath, blew it out, and again recited the tale of how I'd accidentally killed Donald. Mr. Varner kept his eyes focused on me and made notes at the same time. When I finished speaking, he leaned back in his chair, folded his hands across his stomach, smiled, but said nothing.

His silence increased my apprehension. "That's all I have to say, unless you have some questions, Mr. Varner."

He leaned forward and reviewed his notes. "I do have a few, if you don't mind."

"I don't mind. I have a question for you."

"Go ahead. Ask."

I pointed at the legal pad. "How do you take notes without looking at your hand?"

He grinned. "Practice. I've had years of practice. Any more questions?"

I shook my head.

"Okay, my turn." The prosecutor pulled at the skin on his throat. "You said Donald was afraid to turn off the truck because he'd been having problems getting it to start. But I recall Frank talking about how he kept his truck in tip-top shape."

"Frank did. The minute something starting going wrong, he'd take it over to Roger at Hunt's Garage. But Donald didn't take care of it. Frank would jump out of his grave if he saw how filthy his son let the Ranchero get."

"Reckon so," Varner said. "Was Helen there when you got home?"

"Yes, Momma was there."

"She didn't notice anything wrong with you?"

"Could I have some water, Mr. Varner?"

"Sure, Becky." He got a glass down from a row of cabinets and disappeared into the bathroom.

Judge Langford patted my hand. "You're doing fine, Becky. Just fine."

Mr. Varner returned with the water. I drank half of it before continuing. "Momma was mad because I'd been gone so long. She screamed at me because her supper wasn't fixed, but I ignored her and went upstairs."

Varner scratched his head. "How can you ignore Helen when she's yelling at you?"

"Practice, Mr. Varner. I've had years of practice."

Both of the attorneys laughed. Then Mr. Varner's questions resumed. "Becky, you said when you got home you took some medicine, went to sleep, and didn't wake up until the next morning. What kind of medicine did you take?"

"A few days after Frank's funeral, I fell down the stairs and hurt my wrist. Doctor Condray gave me some pain medicine. I'm supposed to take one every eight hours as needed. But I was in such a state that afternoon, I —"

"You were in shock, Becky," offered Judge Langford. "Anyone would be after seeing someone plummet off a cliff."

"You're right, sir. My head hurt something fierce and my heart pounded in my ears. I couldn't stop shaking so I took the pain medication and went to bed."

"How much did you take?" Varner asked.

"Two tablets at first, but it didn't help, so I took a couple more. Four altogether."

"That would explain why you were groggy and confused the next day," the judge said.

"I thought it all a nightmare until Sheriff Hays and Deputy Santo informed me of Donald's disappearance."

Mr. Varner threw down his pen. "But why didn't you come forward then?"

"Because she was scared," Judge Langford said. "Hell, Cordell, you've got two girls close to her age. Can't you imagine how they'd feel if the same thing happened to them?"

"Yes, I can. But you have to admit Judge, her not coming forward until now looks real bad."

"We've both been in this business long enough to know things are seldom what they look like on the surface." The judge tapped his index finger on the desk. "Remember what this child had been through. Her mother had divorced her stepfather. The family business half burned down by an arsonist your office has never caught, and Frank's death. He was more than a business partner and stepdad to her. She tells me he ran interference for her with Helen. Now Helen is a nice woman, but she can be more than a little overbearing."

"You don't have to convince me. I had a taste of Helen's persuasive nature this morning at

Minnow Creek. That woman should've been a lawyer." He picked up his pen, began twirling it through his fingers. "I didn't know Helen divorced Frank."

"About a month before Frank died," I said. "Momma planned to move to Palm Beach and marry Henry Nash after she got her divorce settlement. That got delayed because we needed the money to rebuild the storehouse and buy inventory. She agreed to wait until the insurance check came, but then Frank died and left everything to Donald."

"Helen is going to marry Henry Nash?" Varner asked.

"She was. I don't know what's going on between them now."

"I'd heard Donald got everything," Varner said. "How did Frank talk Helen out of the store and the house?"

"Momma signed them over to him in '67." I decided it best to fill the county attorney and Judge Langford in on some of our family history and long-kept secrets. I didn't want them thinking bad things about Frank and I didn't want to go to jail.

I told how Frank only accepted the property because I'd begged him to, and how Momma and Frank's marriage had been a sham for over five years. I even told them I'd had been in Havenwood instead of in Alabama caring for Frank's sister. Maybe if they didn't believe Donald's death was an accident, they'd think me innocent by reason of insanity. I didn't tell them about Frank and me, or about my getting pregnant and Momma's part in the illegal abortion. Some wounds never heal. Some truths can never be told.

Neither man spoke for a long time. It was lot to absorb. The shock on their faces served as proof that all the time and energy Frank, Momma, and I spent pretending to be the perfect family had been worth the effort. We'd fooled everyone.

"Why did Helen send you to Havenwood?" Mr. Varner asked.

Judge Langford reached for my hand. "That's privileged medical information, Becky. You don't have to answer that."

"I'll tell him if he promises not to tell anyone else."

Judge Langford turned to the prosecutor. "Off the record, Cordell?"

"Okay."

"Do you remember making Johnny Santo choose between joining the military and going to prison, Mr. Varner?"

"I remember you and the Santo boy ran off to Tennessee and Helen had Roy Tate bring you back. She filed charges against Santo, which was her right to do. He was an adult and you were a minor. She dropped the charges on the condition he join the service."

"I went into a deep depression after that. So Momma sent me to Havenwood. She and Frank fought about it. He moved out after she committed me."

"I heard a rumor Frank had moved into the store." Mr. Varner rubbed his chin. "I've visited Havenwood. It's hard to imagine you in such a place."

"I would've died if it hadn't been for Frank. He came to see me every week."

Harland Langford and Cordell Varner had no doubt seen and heard many stories in their careers. I figured it must take quite a bit to move them. But I'd done it. The faces of both men became a mask of sympathy for me. Normally, I don't like people feeling sorry for me, but if it helped keep me out of prison, so be it.

"Please don't tell Momma I told you this. I'd never hear the last of it."

Both men pledged their silence.

Varner checked his watch for the time. "I've got a few more questions, Becky. You said Frank had settlement papers drawn up that gave Helen some cash and a percentage of the business. He also made out a new will that left everything else to you. Is that correct?"

"That's what Frank told me. But after his death, no one could find the papers. Momma believes Frank lied to us, and that he always intended to give everything to Donald."

"Do you believe he lied?" the judge asked.

I took a drink of water. "In all the years I knew Frank, he never lied to me. But the fact is there isn't a new will to be found. I don't know what to believe anymore."

The county attorney picked up the legal pad. "I have one last question, Becky."

The judge leaned forward. "She told you it was an accident, Cordell."

"And I want to believe her, Harland. But I have to ask the question."

"What question?" I asked.

"Your stepbrother would have ended up owning everything that rightfully should've gone to you and your mother." Varner stopped to slick down a wayward cowlick. "Becky, did you murder Donald out of revenge because he took everything from you?"

"No, sir. It was an accident. Donald wanted to try to run the stores, to see if he could do the job. That suited me fine because it was too painful for me to go down there. Everyone I've ever loved and lost is associated with the stores." I stopped, took another sip of water. "As far as the house is concerned, we had an arrangement. Momma and I agreed to take care of it and the greenhouse. In return, Donald let us live there. Now that he's gone, Charlotte has informed us she's selling the house as soon as Donald's estate is settled.

Harland Langford pulled off his glasses, rubbed the bridge of his nose. "So you see, Cordell, it was to my client's benefit that Donald Wooten stay alive."

The county attorney nodded.

"What happens now? Am I going to jail, Judge Langford?"

"That won't be necessary. Will it, Cordell?"

"You're not planning on leaving the county anytime soon are you, Becky?"

"No, sir."

"In that case, I think you will be more comfortable at home." Mr. Varner stood. "I'll have to conduct an investigation. Talk to Roger about the truck and to Doctor Condray about the injury to your hand."

The judge nodded. "I'll tell him he has Becky's permission to discuss that part of her medical record."

"Thank you, Harland. I'll have Sheriff Hays search the canyon for Becky's book. I need to see how heavy it is. The library can order us another one if Hays doesn't find it." Varner came around the desk. "How often did you drive Frank's pickup, Becky?"

"I never learned to drive a car." Technically that wasn't a lie. I'd never driven a car.

Varner cocked his head. "You don't have a driver's license?"

"No, sir. My friends learned to drive while I was at Havenwood. The mental hospital doesn't offer driver education classes. Whenever I need to go someplace, I always just walk or catch a ride." My explanation seemed to satisfy him. Momma would've been proud of the way I'd sidestepped his question.

We headed for the outer office. Mr. Varner assured Judge Langford he'd let him know as soon as possible if charges would be brought against me.

"Let's go to Ferrell's for lunch, Becky," Judge Langford said.

"Patsy's House of Pies has a better blue plate special. All their cream pies are now made by my daughter." Helen walked over and put her arm around me. "Everyone knows Becky makes the best pies in the county."

"Momma, what are you doing here?"

"Waiting. I've been waiting all this time. Tressie wouldn't let me in, Cordell."

"Blame me for that, Helen. I gave her strict orders not to disturb us."

"Since I interrupted your fishing, I'll let you slide this time, but I don't like being excluded when it comes to my daughter's welfare. You will do right by her, won't you?"

Mr. Varner took hold of Momma's right hand. "You bet, but I've got to conduct an investigation. The taxpayers insist I at least pretend to earn my money."

She laughed.

He patted her hand. "How do you like being a free woman, Helen?"

"I like it, but it can be a little lonely. You let me know if that wife of yours doesn't treat you right. A good man is hard to find." She gave him one of her teasing, tilted-head grins. "Come to lunch with us, Cordell."

A smidgen of rose decorated the county attorney's face as he returned Helen's smile.

"I'd better not. I promised Becky I'd get this mess straightened out as soon as possible."

"I'll give you a rain check this time." She hooked her hand around Judge Langford's arm. "Come on, Harland. You can buy me lunch."

"It would be my pleasure, ma'am." They headed for the door.

They say fish got to swim and birds have to fly. And if my mother couldn't flirt, she'd probably lie down and just plain die. Even then, I'd wager she'd find a way to flirt with the undertaker.

CHAPTER 35

County attorney Varner's office appeared smaller today than it had eight days prior when I confessed to accidentally killing my stepbrother. It wasn't, of course. But thoughts of being locked in a prison cell had made me acutely aware of room sizes and dimensions.

Judge Langford called the night before to say Cordell Varner had finished his investigation and wanted us at his office at 9 a.m. today. Momma ached to come, but the judge convinced her to stay home. It was now half past nine and the prosecutor still hadn't showed up.

Varner's secretary, Tressie Grant, entered carrying a tray containing cups, ice water, and coffee. "Thought you folks might be thirsty."

"I could use some coffee," the judge said. "How about you, Becky?"

"No, thanks. I'm not feeling well. I threw up twice this morning."

Tressie handed the judge his coffee. "We get that a lot. I can't tell you how many times we've had to clean this carpet after Cordell got through with a suspect."

"Is there a rocking chair around here?" I asked.

"Nope," Tressie said. "Why?"

I sighed. "No reason."

"You're looking tired, Becky. Have you been getting any sleep?" the judge asked.

"Not really. A week before Frank died, I caught a bug I can't seem to shake. One day I'm fine. The next, I'm sick to my stomach and dog-tired."

"Maybe you need more fluids." Tressie handed me a cup of water. "Drink this."

I did as I was told.

Judge Langford stirred his coffee. "When we leave, maybe you should go see the doctor."

I hoped and prayed I'd be allowed to leave. "Do you think Mr. Varner forgot?"

"This isn't like Cordell," Tressie said. "I can't imagine what's keeping him."

"I'll give him another ten minutes. Then I'm taking my client home."

The secretary's eyes widened. "You can't just up and leave."

Judge Langford put down his cup. "Are you trying to teach me the law, Tressie?"

Her face turned red. "No, sir. I'd never presume to do that. I just meant —"

The door to the office swung open and the county attorney walked in.

"And where have you been, Cordell?" she asked. "These people have been waiting on you for a half hour."

"Something unexpected came up."

"Tell them, not me." Tressie tramped out of the room and slammed the door behind her.

Mr. Varner hung his suit jacket on the back of his chair. "Right there's a prime example why you shouldn't hire your wife's relatives. I'm sorry I kept —"

"I'd expect a cheap trick like this from a first year lawyer, Cordell," the judge said. "But not from you."

Varner sat down opposite us. "This isn't what you're thinking, Judge Langford. I've got too much respect for you to pull something like that here."

"Something like what?" I asked.

Judge Langford looked at me. "It's an old lawyer's trick, Becky. The prosecutor tells you to be here, and then he doesn't show up. In the meantime, the client gets nervous and is more likely to blurt out incriminating information. It's a mind game."

Varner shook his head. "That's not the situation here. I received a last minute phone call from Atlanta that had a direct bearing on this case."

"How's that?" the judge asked.

"We'll get to the call in a minute." The county attorney placed a large manila envelope on his desk. "I found answers to my questions, Becky, but every answer brought more questions. There's a lot more going on here than you led me to believe."

"Just what are you referring to?" the judge asked.

"I don't know how much Becky told you about her history with the victim, but I'd urge you to consult with her before we get started." Varner stood. "I'll give you two some privacy."

A weird, hollow-sounding laugh penetrated the room. It took several seconds before I realized the laughter was coming from me.

Judge Langford reached for my hand. "Are you okay?"

"I'm sorry," I said, while trying to stifle another laugh. "It just struck me as funny. Donald . . . a victim?"

County Attorney Varner loosened his tie. "Donald Wooten is the one who's deceased."

I stood, grabbed the edge of the desk with both hands and leaned in. "He's dead, but he was never a victim. Don't you understand that?"

Varner frowned. "I'm not sure I do."

Judge Langford put his arm around my shoulders and pulled me back into my chair. "Relax, Becky. It's going to be okay."

"I don't feel well, Judge. Can we get this over with?"

"Sure. Cordell, why don't you show me your hand, one card at a time? If things stray too far off course, I'll stop you."

"Yes, sir." Varner picked up his pen. "I checked with Roger at Hunt's Garage about the condition of the Ranchero. Frank told him the truck was getting hard to start and the transmission seemed to be slipping a bit. Your stepfather had an appointment to drop his pickup off for repairs, but didn't keep it because of his heart attack. Donald never brought it in either. As far as Roger knows, the repairs were never made."

"You just confirmed my client's testimony that there were problems with the truck."

Varner nodded. "Sheriff Hays couldn't find your book. It probably burned up in the fire. But the county librarian remembered you buying it. She ordered me a copy." The prosecutor walked over to the bookcase, picked out a thick book, and laid it in front of the judge. "It's heavy."

Judge Langford examined the book, and then handed it back to his adversary. "This helps to corroborate Miss Becky's statement about what happened."

"It does up to a point." Varner slipped the book into his desk drawer. "I asked Roger to conduct an experiment for me."

"What kind of experiment?" I asked.

"You said you picked the book up off the dash with your left hand. Because of your previous injury, your wrist gave way under the book's weight causing you to drop it. It hit the gearshift knocking the pickup out of park and into reverse." As he talked, Cordell drew a diagram of the inside of a truck on his notepad. "The book then landed on the accelerator. The truck pitched backwards and rolled down the hill toward the cliff."

"That's correct," I said.

Mr. Varner drew a circle around his drawing. "I had Roger recreate the accident with a truck similar to Frank's. He repeated the test 58 times. Only once did he get a scenario similar to the one you claim took place on the mountain."

"Thank you, Cordell," the judge said. "You just made my case for me."

The county attorney rapped his knuckles against the desk. "Come on, Harland. One time out of fifty-eight tries."

"It could be one time out of a 158 tries. If it happened once, then it's a possibility. If it's a possibility, then there's reasonable doubt." The jurist leaned back in his chair. "You're too good an attorney not to know that. What are you up to?"

I twisted around to see my lawyer. "Mr. Varner doesn't believe me. He wants to lock me away like Momma did. I bet he didn't even talk to Doctor Condray."

"Yes, I did," Varner said. "The doctor said your wrist had been severely strained. When I showed him the book, he confirmed you'd have a hard time holding anything that heavy with your left hand."

Judge Langford pounded the desk. "I say again, where are you going with this, Varner?"

The two lawyers glared at one another and then Cordell said, "It's not what Doctor Condray said, it's what he didn't say that got me to turning over rocks you should've told me about, Becky."

I shook my head. "Doctor Condray didn't tell you anything more than that. He couldn't, not without my permission."

"That's right, he can't. But Roy Tate can . . . and did."

"What's Roy Tate have to do with this?" the judge asked. "He's no longer sheriff."

"No, but he is a friend of Helen's." The county attorney opened the manila envelope and took out some photographs. "Do you want to tell Judge Langford about these pictures, Becky, or should I?"

My lips moved, but no words came out. I scooted to the edge of the black leather chair, wrapped my arms around my waist, and started rocking. I wanted to rock myself into another place, into another universe where the knot of lies that held my twisted world together was not being untangled right in front of me.

"Show me what you've got here," said the Judge.

The county attorney placed six photographs on the desk. "Roy took these at Doctor Condray's office a few days after Frank Wooten's funeral."

The photos were of a bruised and battered me. I felt nauseous.

The judge studied each picture. "My word, Becky, you really had a fall, didn't you?"

"She didn't fall down the stairs," Varner said. "Donald Wooten beat her."

Judge Langford's head jerked back. He reviewed the photos again before turning to me.

"Is this true, young lady? Did Wooten do this to you?"

Both men stared at me. "Mr. Tate had no right to give you those pictures. Momma is going to be so mad at him."

"What's Helen got to do with this?" the judge asked.

"Roy said Helen called him and asked for his help in getting Becky to the doctor's."

The prosecutor rested his elbows on the desk. "Apparently, Helen had come home and found Donald in her daughter's bedroom. He'd beaten Becky senseless and was about to rape her again when Helen interrupted him."

"Rape her again?" the jurist asked. "What do you mean by that?"

Varner's eyes sought mine. "This might sound better coming from you."

I turned to the judge. How could I discuss Donald's vile act with a man I respected so much? I covered my face with my hands.

"Cordell, I need some time alone with my client."

He stood. "Of course, Judge Langford. I'll wait in the outer office."

"Wait, Mr. Varner," I said. "Is it necessary to go into all of this now? It happened so long ago. What does it matter now?"

Judge Langford reached for my hand. "I need to know about anything that might have influenced your relationship with your stepbrother. I can't adequately defend you if you don't trust me enough to tell me the truth, all of it."

"I trust you. I just can't say the words. I'm too ashamed."

"You have nothing to be ashamed of," Varner said. "You were a child, unable to defend yourself. It wasn't your fault." He sank back down into his chair. "Would you prefer I tell Harland what happened the day of President Kennedy's funeral?"

I nodded, folded my hands in my lap, and stared at them while Papa's boyhood pal described Donald's assault against me to my grandfather's best friend. If only I could disappear, fade into the blackness of the leather chair, or melt into the worn fibers of the mottled gray carpet.

Judge Langford took off his glasses, rubbed the bridge of his nose, then put them back on.

"Thirteen-years-old. My God, Cordell. Eli would've shot the bastard, and I would not have blamed him."

"I'd feel the same if someone hurt one of my girls." The county attorney took a white plastic bag from the folder, opened it, and laid its round contents in front of me.

"Momma and I told Mr. Tate things in confidence. She'll kill him for betraying us."

"Roy wanted to help you," Varner said.

Anger flashed through me. "He's never did anything to help me. He brought Johnny and me back from Tennessee and let his deputies hurt Johnny. He's Momma's friend, not mine."

"I know Roy had his own way of doing things when he was sheriff. He and I went round and round about his roughshod methods." Varner rubbed his lower lip. "But in the thirty years I've known him, there has been one thing he couldn't abide. And that's a man hurting a woman or a child."

Judge Langford picked up the medallion and examined it. "What's this?"

"As you may know, the fire that destroyed Cooper's warehouse was deliberately set." Varner locked his hands behind his head and leaned back. "Sheriff Hay's investigation turned up one viable suspect. Neil Abbott, the manager of the Cooper's Kirbyville store, informed my office that Frank had almost come to blows with a fellow a few days before the fire. When the sheriff interviewed the suspect, he gave a bogus alibi."

"Did you arrest him?" the judge asked.

"No, sir. Although Sheriff Hays and I were convinced we had the right suspect, we had no concrete evidence against him at the time." The prosecutor unlocked his hands. "There was another factor that caused us to proceed with caution."

"What was that, Cordell?"

"The man was Frank Wooten's son."

The judge leaned forward. "You suspect Donald Wooten committed arson against his own father?"

"Not anymore. Now, I'm certain he started the fire." Varner picked up the medallion.

"Ben Welch was Donald Wooten's father-in-law and employer. Every month, Welch gives one of these to the salesman who sold the most vehicles the previous month. As you can see, it's engraved with the salesman's name and the date." Varner turned the medallion over in his hand and read the inscription. "Donald Wooten. October, 1970."

"What does this have to do with my client?" the elder attorney asked.

Mr. Varner focused on me. "Roy said you gave him this medallion, Becky. He said you found it in the grass near the warehouse the night it burned down, but you never told anyone about it. Is this true?"

"Don't answer that." Judge Langford stood. "Are we looking at an obstruction of justice or a tampering with evidence indictment here?"

Varner shook his head. "No, sir. Please sit down, Harland."

"I'll sit down when you convince me the office I devoted twelve years of my life to has not sunk so low as to heap more pain upon this young woman. She's been through enough because of Donald Wooten."

"I can't prosecute a dead man, and I have neither the time nor the budget to bring charges against anyone in a case that'll never be filed." Mr. Varner loosened his tie some more. "I'm not trying to hurt Becky. I'm just trying to get at the truth."

Judge Langford sat down. "I'll hold you to that, Cordell."

He nodded. "I did wonder why she would elect to protect Donald."

I remained quiet.

"If you would've turned Wooten in to the sheriff, then he would've been in jail instead of free to hurt you, Becky."

"Do I have to answer that, sir?"

"No, you don't." My attorney eyed the prosecutor. "Where do we go from here?"

The county attorney scratched the back of his head. "The way I see it, there are three possible scenarios as to what could've happened that day on Starview Mountain. It's possible Wooten's death was an accident as Becky claims. Possible, but not probable."

"If we go to trial, possible is all I need for an acquittal," the judge said.

"What are the other two scenarios, sir?" I asked.

Varner rubbed his chin against the back of his hand. "I'd be remiss in my duties if I didn't at least consider the beating, the arson, and the rape as motives for murder."

"And I can use those same three points as grounds for self defense." The judge yanked off his glasses and shook them at Varner. "All I'd have to do is show those pictures and that medallion to a jury and tell them what kind of man Donald Wooten was. A man who'd destroy his father's business and beat a young woman half to death. The kind of man who'd rape a child. No jury in this county would convict Becky." The judge pushed a lock of gray hair back into place. "You're a damn good lawyer, Cordell, but I'm better."

"I don't dispute that fact for one minute, sir. But you've sat in this same chair, and you know regardless of how I feel personally, my job is to uncover the truth."

I jumped to my feet. "The truth? You don't want to hear the truth. No one wants to hear the truth."

"Sit down, Becky," the judge said.

"No, sirree. Mr. Varner wants to know the truth, and I'm going to tell him."

Judge Langford stood. "As your attorney, I'm advising you to keep quiet."

"I used to think the truth was important too, Mr. Varner. But then I realized —"

"Don't say another word," the judge said. "Just calm down."

"Dammit, don't say that," I yelled. "All my life, people have told me to calm down. I'm tired of it. I've been waiting for years to find someone who really wanted to hear the truth."

The judge stepped back, his eyes wide with surprise. He sighed, ran his hands through his hair, and then slumped into to his chair.

"Neil Abbott told the truth about Donald and Frank almost fighting. They were arguing over me." I stopped, pushed my hair behind my ears. "Donald asked his daddy for the manager's job at our Kirbyville store. Frank refused. He didn't want me around Donald that much."

"Did Frank think his son would hurt you?" the prosecutor asked.

"Yes. In the past three years, I've only seen Donald a few times, and Frank was always there. The day of the argument, Donald insisted his daddy choose between him and me. Frank chose me." I eased down into my chair. "You're both fathers, so you should be able to appreciate the pain such a decision caused him."

Both men nodded.

"Did Frank and Helen know about the rape?" the judge asked.

"I told them about the rape the day it happened, but they didn't believe me. Frank believed his son, which was natural since we hardly knew each other then. When he realized I'd told the truth, Frank was heartbroken."

"I bet." The county attorney leaned forward. "Why didn't Helen believe you?"

"She and Frank had been married for only three weeks. It wasn't convenient for her to believe me. Like I said, nobody wants to hear the truth, especially if it's inconvenient."

Judge Langford tugged at his earlobe. "Unfortunately, that's often the case."

I nodded. "Frank always tried to protect me. When I found the medallion the night of the fire, I saw my chance to protect him. He loved Donald and hoped his son would change. Hope was all Frank had left. I would've taken a dozen beatings before killing that hope."

Mr. Varner rubbed his temple. "I understand your desire to hide the truth from Frank. But then Donald never had to face the consequences of his crime. We're all responsible for our actions, regardless of what our intentions are."

"Does that include you too, Mr. Varner?" I asked.

"Of course, Becky."

"You came up with the idea of making Johnny choose between joining the military and going to jail, didn't you?"

"I wanted to give the boy a second chance."

"I thought your job was to find the truth," I said.

"It is."

"You never found the truth in Johnny's case. If you'd talked to me or to Frank, we'd have told you that I begged Johnny to run away with me." I looked at Judge Langford. "Frank wouldn't have had to worry about me if I got married and moved to Texas. He could've left Sugardale and made a good life for himself someplace." I gripped the desk. "You have no idea the disastrous events your decision set in motion, Mr. Varner."

"Like I said, Helen had a right to bring charges against Santo. You were a minor."

"So the truth can be discarded if the person is under eighteen?" I asked.

The prosecutor pulled his chair closer to the desk. "That's not what I'm saying. But Helen insisted on filing charges. In a way, my hands were tied."

I shook my head. "No, my hands were the ones that were tied, Mr. Varner. Tied to a hospital bed after Doctor Nixon killed mine and Johnny's baby and almost killed me."

Cordell Varner's chin dropped. He sat there, silent, his mouth open.

Judge Langford cleared his throat. "Nixon. Isn't he that Brockton dentist who went to prison last year for performing illegal abortions?"

"Yes," Varner said softly. "He did one on a fourteen-year-old from Lumpkin County. The girl died."

"Dr. Nixon put me to sleep to supposedly pull a bad tooth. I woke up in the Brockton hospital. I still had my tooth, but not my baby." I wiped the sweat off my top lip. "The doctors believed I'd killed my baby and had tried to kill myself. Frank told them the truth, that Dr. Nixon had done it. But as I explained before, no one really wants to hear the truth." My throat went dry. I picked up the pitcher of water, but my hand shook so I set it back down.

"Let me help you, Becky." The judge filled a cup and handed it to me.

"Thank you, sir." I gulped down the drink, wiped my mouth with a napkin, and returned the cup to the tray. "Those damn doctors refused to acknowledge the ugly truth. Because of that, I spent sixteen months locked up in Hell and a young girl died. So you see, Mr. Varner, it's hard for me to believe you're only after the truth."

Varner stared at me for a time. Then he got up and walked to the window. He stood, hands in his pockets, staring out the window. "I didn't know you were pregnant."

"Would it have made any difference?" I asked.

He looked over his shoulder at me. "I don't know, Becky. I honestly don't know."

Judge Langford poured me another glass of water and one for himself too. Cordell Varner stood gazing out the window. For a time, no one spoke.

"None of us are perfect, Becky," the judge said. "We all make mistakes. We make bad decisions regardless of how well informed or well intentioned we happened to be. But that doesn't mean we should stop striving to discover the truth."

I shrugged. "In your business, Judge Langford, you must assume that telling the truth is always the best thing."

"I've found that's usually the case."

"Where's the line, sir?"

"What line?" the jurist asked.

"The line that divides the good truths from the bad ones. I've been looking for it all of my life. I've never found it."

Mr. Varner walked back to his desk. "There are no bad truths, Becky."

"Really? Are you sure?"

He nodded, pulled out his chair, and sat back down.

"Johnny got wounded while in Vietnam and ended up in a Honolulu hospital. He married a girl, and they had a little boy. Last year, the baby died. His death almost killed Johnny. It did kill his marriage." I rolled my chair up to the edge of the desk. "Johnny doesn't know anything about my being in Havenwood or about our baby. Should he be told the truth?"

The county attorney offered no reply.

"Johnny's right downstairs in the sheriff's office. Shall we call him and tell him to come here?" I picked up the receiver of the phone and held it out to the prosecutor. "In the name of truth, Mr. Varner, shall we tell Johnny that he's lost not one child, but two?"

At first, the county attorney didn't move. Then finally, Varner took the receiver from me and returned it to its cradle.

Judge Langford rested his hand on my shoulder. "No one can make that decision, Becky, except you."

"But I'm not very good at making these decisions. I never was." I turned to face the judge. "Do you remember Grandpa Eli bringing me with him when he visited you?"

"Yes, I remember."

"You sometimes played a game with me. You would show me both fists and tell me if I picked the correct hand, I'd get a piece of candy or a nickel. Remember?"

The judge nodded.

"I always . . . always picked the wrong hand. You'd give me the candy anyway, but it doesn't work like that in real life. All my life, I've picked the wrong hand. I've always chosen the wrong people and the wrong truths to believe in." I stopped, took another sip of water. "Grandpa Eli told me if I'd listen to my heart, it'd tell me the right thing to do. But that's not true. The heart lies. It plays tricks on you."

"Your grandfather was right," the judge said. "It's incumbent upon us all to heed the messages of our hearts. But the heart doesn't scream; it doesn't yell or shout out its warnings. The heart whispers to us. Too often, I'm afraid we let the noise of the world drown out what it's trying to tell us. That's when we get into trouble." Judge Langford gently squeezed my hand. "To hear what your heart is saying, Becky, you need to find a quiet place. And you must believe in yourself enough to trust the whisperings of your heart."

"I listened when my heart told me to trust Frank. I listened when it said he loved me and would never hurt me, never lie to me. But in the end, he did. He lied about the new will." I looked at the county attorney. "You asked me if I wanted revenge against Donald. His beating didn't hurt me half as much as Frank's deceit did."

Varner rose from his chair. "Perhaps this is the time to show you the other evidence we found concerning this case."

A wave of panic washed over me. My neck muscles tightened. My scalp tingled.

"What are you up to now?" my attorney asked.

"Give me just a second, Harland." Varner opened a cabinet door to reveal a wall safe. He unlocked the safe, took out a metal box, returned to his desk. "This holds the answers to a lot of questions."

Judge Langford removed his glasses and laid them on the desk. "Say what you have to, Cordell. If it's possible, I'd like to get home sometime today."

I was thinking the same thing. But the current actions of the prosecutor seem to indicate that possibility was growing more remote by the minute.

Varner placed the box on the desk and sat. "Becky, do you know Dora Sikes?"

"Yes. She's the manger of the floral department at the Kirbyville store."

The county attorney nodded. "During our investigation, Sheriff Hays interviewed her. She told him Donald came rushing into the store at closing time the day Frank had his heart attack. He claimed he needed to get into his father's office. Dora had just returned from maternity leave and didn't know about the trouble between Frank and his son. So, she let him in."

"She never told me about that," I said.

"Dora figured Donald needed insurance papers for the hospital. No big deal." Varner opened the lid of the metal container. "Sheriff Hays also discovered that Donald rented a safety deposit box at the Citizen's Bank in Marietta the very next day."

"Why would Wooten drive all that way to rent a deposit box?" the judge asked.

"We wondered the same thing. I got a court order to open it and we found some interesting items. Things Donald apparently found in Frank's office. Stuff he didn't want anyone to see." The county attorney handed some papers to the judge. "Frank took out this $50,000 life insurance policy two days after the birth of his first grandchild. Upon his death, half the money went to Donald. The other half went into a trust fund for his granddaughter and any future grandchildren. The policy names Becky as executor of the trust fund."

Judge Langford slipped on his glasses and reviewed the policy. "This doesn't make any dang sense. Why didn't Donald cash the policy in when Frank died?"

"Upon learning about Frank's death, the insurance company would've checked their records and found that Frank had bought a second life insurance policy at the same time." The prosecutor handed the judge another stack of papers. "This policy is for $250,000 and goes entirely to one beneficiary, Miss Rebecca Cooper."

"Say what! Frank left me $250,000 in life insurance?"

"He never told you about the policies?" Varner asked.

"No. I returned home from Havenwood a few days before the baby was born. Frank knew I didn't like to talk about anything connected with death."

The prosecutor nodded. "I'm sure he didn't want to upset you."

Judge Langford threw the policy down on the desk. "In order to deny Becky what was hers, Donald deliberately cheated his own daughters out of their inheritance. What a sick bastard. Excuse my language, Becky."

"There's more." Varner retrieved an envelope from the box, slid it over to me.

"What's this?" I asked.

"It's the divorce settlement Helen's been looking for," he said.

I yanked the document out of the envelope, glanced at it, and handed it to the judge. "Is that right, sir? Is this Momma's divorce settlement from Frank?"

Judge Langford scanned the papers. "That is indeed what it is."

"You'll find this interesting, Becky." Mr. Varner pushed a stack of papers across his desk.

All the papers were stapled together and neatly folded twice. I tried to undo them, but my hands trembled too much.

"Would you like me to help you?" the judge asked.

"Please."

Judge Langford opened the document, read each page.

I rubbed the back of my neck. "What is it?"

"This is the last will and testament of Franklin Wayne Wooten." My attorney looked at me over the top of his wire-framed glasses. "It's dated June 28, 1971."

For a moment, I stopped breathing. An involuntary gulp started the air surging through my lungs again. Had I heard correctly? Or had hope tricked my ears into fabricating falsehoods to heal my wounded heart? "I didn't hear you correctly."

"You heard me just fine," Judge Langford said. "Here, read it for yourself."

As I reviewed the document, Mr. Varner described the phone call he'd received earlier from a law firm in Atlanta. When Frank visited the firm to sign the papers for Starview Mountain, he'd hired them to prepare his new will and Momma's settlement papers. The new attorneys didn't know about Frank's death until Mr. Varner contacted them concerning the will he'd found in Donald's safety deposit box.

"Do you know what this means, Becky?" Varner asked.

"Yes," I said, hating the quiver in my voice. "It means Frank didn't betray me. It means he really loved me." A tear slipped out. Another one followed. Then a rush.

Mr. Varner gave me his handkerchief. "It also means you're a wealthy young lady."

"That's not important. Is it, Judge?"

The jurist smiled. "No, Becky. That's not important at all. The thing that matters is that you realize your heart whispered the truth when it told you to trust Frank."

I closed my eyes and waited for my mind and heart to settle down, waited for them to restore order to the turmoil of emotions threatening to overwhelm me. In a few brief minutes, my world had once again spun 180 degrees. At first glance, it looked as though life had righted itself, that fate had finally grown tired of tormenting me and moved on to its next victim. But then again, perhaps this was but another trick, another irony played out at my expense. Now that I had it all — the business, Papa's house, proof of Frank's love — would I have to enjoy them from the confines of a prison cell?

I opened my eyes, laid the will on the desk, and silently ordered my pounding heart to slow. "Mr. Varner, you said there were three scenarios as to what might have happened on the mountain the day Donald died. One premise said his death was an accident as I claim. A second possibility is murder. You never told us your last theory."

"Sheriff Hays and I talked to folks around town who remembered seeing you at the grand opening, the drugstore, and the library." Cordell stretched his arms across the desk. "Mrs. Treadwell told us she saw you walking down Bragg Road and offered you a ride home, but you declined."

"I like walking when the weather's nice."

He nodded. "I believe Donald came along and forced you to go with him. I say forced because you're too smart to go anywhere alone with him. If he'd beat and rape you in your own house, what would he do to you on an isolated mountain top?"

"That's a good point, Cordell," the judge said.

"Thank you, sir." Varner ran his hands through his hair. "We know Wooten was angry. His wife had left him. She'd taken his children and his car with her. Because of the problems with the Ranchero, Donald had to cancel his regular Friday night rendezvous with his mistress, Wanda Gimmer. In addition, he'd fired Gordon Zagat that morning after a heated argument. To top it off, several employees heard him complaining about how his land deal had gone sour."

The judge reached for more water. "Sounds like his day wasn't going very well."

"And it got worse when Zagat showed up on Starview Mountain. Zagat remembered that Frank's truck was running, but he didn't recall seeing Becky." The prosecutor focused on me. "Did you witness the argument between Gordon and Donald?"

"Yes. I'd walked to the pond, but I came back when I heard shouting. I hid in a grove of cottonwoods." A flutter in my stomach surprised me. I scooted back in my chair before continuing. "The two men were arguing. Donald threw a punch, but Mr. Zagat ducked and then threw one of his own. He didn't miss. Donald fell to the ground."

"How many times did Zagat hit Wooten?" the prosecutor asked.

"Only once. Then Gordon got in his car and left."

"Wooten must have been madder than a cat dunked in turpentine," Harland said.

The county attorney nodded. "And with nobody to vent his anger on, I figure he turned it on you. Did Donald rape you, Becky? Did he try to, and you killed him in self-defense?"

I didn't answer.

He leaned in. "You know you have a right to defend yourself, don't you?"

"It was an accident," I said.

Varner frowned. "Harland, please tell her that she had every right to defend herself."

"Cordell's right, Becky. A person in fear for her life has a legal right to protect herself." Judge Langford patted my hand. "But don't let us put words in your mouth."

I studied the two attorneys. Both were good men, good fathers. "Frank's granddaughters are little now, but one day they'll ask about what kind of man their daddy was. How would your girls feel, Mr. Varner, if they discovered you had committed arson and rape?"

"They'd be devastated," he said. "I can appreciate how you'd want to protect Donald's children, Becky, but I need to know what really happened."

"I have told you. Donald's death was an accident. It happened like I said it did."

The county attorney locked his fingers behind his head, leaned back in his chair, and blew out a deep breath. "How long do you plan on sticking to that story?"

"Until I die, I reckon."

"The next move is yours, Cordell." Judge Langford cleaned his glasses with the end of his tie. "I'd hate for the hardworking folks of Cascade County to hear you squandered their tax dollars on a case you knew you couldn't win."

Varner grinned. "Would you tell them that about me, Harland?"

The judge smiled back. "I wouldn't have to. Helen would take care of that."

"Let's not bring her into the mix," Varner said. "When she found me at Minnow Creek, Helen insisted I come back to my office. I didn't want to give up my fishing, but I finally had to concede defeat. She came at me like a grizzly sow bent on protecting her cub."

I laughed. "I always thought of Momma as being more like one of those animals who eat their young." Mr. Varner and Judge Langford stared at me. They didn't know the real Momma enough to appreciate my point, but Frank would've agreed.

Varner's face turned serious. "Only you, Becky, know the truth about what happened on Starview Mountain. But regardless of what went down, an accident or self defense, I've got a feeling justice was served." Varner pointed at the judge. "I'm sure Harland will agree when I say that in our business, that's the best we can hope for."

The judge nodded.

"What does that mean?" I asked.

Mr. Varner placed the medallion and the pictures Roy Tate had given him back into the manila envelope, closed the flap, and placed it in his desk drawer. "As far as my office is concerned, Donald Wooten's death was the result of an unfortunate accident."

I blew out a deep breath. Muscles in my shoulders went limp as relief poured over me.

"You've made the right decision, Cordell," Judge Langford said.

The county attorney smiled.

"Thank you, Mr. Varner. How can I ever repay your kindness?"

"As a matter of fact, there are a couple of things you could do for me."

"Just name it," I said.

Cordell pulled off his tie. "I'm planning on trying my luck at Minnow Creek later this afternoon. If you could keep Helen away from there, I'd appreciate it."

"I can handle that. What's the other favor?"

"I'd like to be there when you tell her we found the new will and her settlement papers. I'd like to see her face."

"The whole town will hear Momma scream when she realizes she's getting her money."

Varner grinned. "I'm surprised Helen didn't come with you."

"I told her to wait at home for us," the judge said.

"You *told* Helen?" Varner picked up the phone, pushed a button. "Tressie, is Helen Wooten sitting out there? She is. Arrived about ten minutes after I did. Been waiting all this time, huh? Don't send her in yet. I'll let you know when."

Harland Langford scratched his head. "I should know better than to give Helen orders."

Mr. Varner nodded and then turned to me. "Becky, I'm keeping your mother waiting because there were two other items in the safety deposit box. Items of a personal nature."

"What were they?" I asked.

The county attorney reached into the metal box, retrieved another envelope and a gray, velvet-covered box. He opened the tiny gift and sat it in front of me. "I think Frank intended you to have this."

I stared at the contents. My hands trembled. I dared not pick it up for fear of dropping the treasure inside. Three rings. The one in front — a diamond solitaire mounted on a band of gold. The other rings were a matched pair of wedding bands. A spiral of silver inlay wrapped around a band of gold. Embedded into the silver were seven small diamonds. I started crying again.

Judge Langford handed me his handkerchief. "Do you think you're up to seeing what's in the envelope? Are would you rather wait?"

I wiped my faced and nodded. "I'd like to see everything now, please."

"Sure." Mr. Varner pulled a couple of thin booklets from the envelope. "We have here two round-trip airline tickets from Atlanta to Paris, France. One for Mr. Franklin W. Wooten and the other for Mrs. Rebecca L. Wooten." He handed me the tickets.

I read the names five times before my mind convinced my heart it was true. Frank had planned to take me to Paris for our honeymoon. I could feel the eyes of the two gentlemen staring at me. How could I explain my intimate relationship with Frank to those who had always thought of us as stepfather and stepdaughter? I decided to break with tradition and tell the truth.

"Frank and I fell in love a couple of years ago. We were very happy together and planned to get married after his divorce."

"Did Helen know?" Varner asked.

"Momma knew. As I said, their marriage was over before I was sent to Havenwood. She's been in love with Henry for years. They'd planned a big wedding."

"Really, then why didn't Helen move to Palm Beach?" the judge asked.

"Henry tried to get her to go. But Momma couldn't just walk off and leave everything to Donald. She's been trying to find a way to nullify Frank's first will."

"Well, she won't have to worry about that anymore," Varner said. "The Atlanta law firm will get everything straightened out for you. I gave them our phone numbers, Harland, in case they need any assistance on this end."

"Good. I'd like to get this mess cleaned up for Becky as soon as possible."

"I appreciate your help, Judge Langford," I said. "Yours too, Mr. Varner."

"What are you going to do now, Becky?" the prosecutor asked.

"I have no idea." I thumbed through the airline tickets. "Frank tried to get me to leave Sugardale. He wanted me to get more education and to see more of world." I placed my elbows on the desk, rested my head in my hands. "How could I've ever doubted Frank's love for me? I didn't deserve him."

Judge Langford softly patted my shoulders. "Now Frank wouldn't like you running yourself down like that. Under the circumstances, anyone would've had their doubts. Life is full of twist and turns. All we can do is navigate the best course we can and try to learn as we go."

I looked up. "By learning to listen to the whispers of our hearts?"

"Yes, and by trusting your own instincts," the jurist said.

"And you need to remember to forgive yourself for the mistakes you make," Varner added. "Otherwise, you'll drive yourself crazy."

"Listen to Cordell, Becky. He's the voice of experience talking."

The county attorney frowned. "I'm not sure that was a compliment, Harland."

We all laughed.

I picked up the tickets. "When would I have to use these, Mr. Varner?"

"Frank left the dates open. You call the airlines, see when a seat is available, and you're on your way to Paris."

"I've never flown before. Is it scary?"

The judge smiled. "Everything's scary the first time. Even riding a bike. But it's worth the effort."

Cordell undid the top button on his shirt. "I'm telling you, Becky, you should give serious consideration to using one of those tickets."

"I will. I have a habit of doing what I'm told."

Judge Langford smiled. "That's one habit you should try to break."

Varner reached for the phone. "Are we ready to invite Helen to this party?"

"I have one more question, sir."

"What's that, Becky?" Cordell asked.

"Does anyone have a pair of earplugs?"

CHAPTER 36

I'd never seen my mother so happy. When Mr. Varner told her she would be getting her divorce settlement, Momma had two requests. First, she wanted to call Henry and tell him she could marry him now. Second, she wanted to be the one to tell Charlotte that all she'd be receiving was the $25,000 in life insurance meant for Donald. The only thing Momma likes better than good sex is twisting the knife into her enemies. It took Judge Langford's considerable skills as a negotiator to convince her it was the county attorney's job to inform Charlotte about the final outcome of the investigation.

Over the next few days, I felt like Sleeping Beauty waking up in the middle of a five-ring circus. The first ring concerned the businesses. Gordon and the employees wondered if I'd sell the stores. If I didn't, who'd run them? Could the House of Pies still count on me for their cream pies?

Attorneys from Atlanta called or came by almost every day with papers to sign, forms to fill out, and requests for copies of various legal documents dating back to when Grandpa Eli built the house and started his garden business. Judge Langford's help proved invaluable.

Atlantic Realty Investment, Inc. sent three men — a lawyer, architect, and banker — to try to convince me to sell them Starview Mountain. Momma let them in, served them ice tea and pecan pie, and begged me to listen to their proposal.

I told them I wasn't interested in selling the property to developers, but I don't think they believed me. Probably because Momma kept asking how much they were willing to pay. When they offered the same $500,000 they'd offered Charlotte, Momma showed them the door. I asked them not to come back. Momma told them not to come back until they were ready to double their offer. She and I went more than a few rounds over the whole mess.

In addition to her harping at me to sell Starview Mountain, Momma kept nagging me to commit to going to Palm Beach with her to help with the wedding arrangements. According to her plan, she would invite Henry to come for the Thanksgiving holiday. After a big traditional dinner — prepared by me — we'd go back to Palm Beach with him. Momma envisioned a Christmas wedding with her wearing a tea-length designer dress in whisper pink with matching mink accents around the cuffs, hem, and a neckline cut to show a hint of cleavage. She wanted me to be her bridesmaid. I suggested she ask her friend Eva.

She liked the idea. "That way Eva has to come to the wedding. She can see firsthand how much bigger my mansion is than hers."

I pointed out that Henry's aunt was still very much alive.

That didn't worry Momma none. "She's eighty-six, Becky. How much longer can she last?"

Momma decided she and Henry would save a considerable amount of money if I'd do the cooking and all the flower arrangements for their wedding. I suggested she double up on her Valium and offered to buy her a first-class plane ticket to Palm Beach if she would leave immediately. She pretended I was kidding.

I'd told Johnny about my part in Donald's death the night before I turned myself in. Upset because I hadn't told him earlier, he accused me of not trusting him. It took a week for him to calm down enough to realize I'd been trying to shield him. If he'd known I'd killed Donald, he would've been forced to choose between his duty as a deputy sheriff and his desire to protect me. We didn't make up until the day before the county attorney announced no charges would be filed against me.

*****

I stepped out onto the porch of Doctor Condray's office, pulled the door closed behind me, and eased down onto the cast iron bench beside the entrance. The physician's words churned in my mind, making me oblivious to all around me. A tapping on my shoulder brought my attention back to the present.

"Becky, did you hear me?" Ruth Langford asked.

"Hello, Mrs. Langford. I didn't see you there."

"You were in another world." She joined me on the bench. "Are you all right?"

"I . . . I'm fine. How are you, ma'am?"

"I'm okay. Just here to get my arthritis prescription renewed before Harland and I take off to Savannah. We're visiting my sister for a few days."

"Savannah's nice. Frank and I spent a week at the beach last May. He took me to Savannah to . . . to . . ."

"It's okay, Becky," she said. "I hope you don't mind, but Harland told me about you and Frank."

I felt blood rush to my face. "I know people think it's wrong, but we loved each other."

"We don't get to pick who we fall in love with, Becky. If we did, I certainly wouldn't have chosen a judge."

"I thought you and Judge Langford were happy."

"We are." She leaned in close. "Sometimes Harland forgets that black robe of his doesn't carry much weight around the house. I have to remind him."

We laughed and she asked me about my trip to the beach.

"It was the first time I'd ever seen the ocean. Frank always wanted me to see new places, to try different things, to learn more about the world. It was the best time of my life." I started to cry. "I'm sorry, Mrs. Langford. I'm not myself today."

"With all the stress you've been under, it's a wonder you're not bald." She retrieved a monogram-med hankie from her purse and handed to me. "Harland told me you'd picked up some kind of virus. Are you still feeling poorly?"

"The nausea is better, but I'm tired a lot. Doctor Condray said it wasn't a virus."

"What is it then?"

I shrugged. "Nothing that won't pass in time. The doctor recommended I get more rest, take some vitamins, and try not to worry so much."

"Sounds like good advice."

"I've got so many decisions to make. About the stores, the mountain property. Momma wants me to go to Palm Beach with her, and I'm not sure where Johnny and I are headed. We always figured we'd end up married. We've loved each other since we were kids, but . . ."

"But what, Becky?"

"My mind is filled with Frank. I miss him so much I ache for him. Is that crazy?"

"Not at all. You haven't had time to grieve for him, much less figure out the mess that's been dropped into your lap." She gave me a hug. "I have an idea. You need some time to yourself and some time away from here. We own a cabin on Tybee Island. Do you know where that is?"

"It's near Savannah, isn't it?"

She nodded. "Why don't you ride out to the coast with us? We can drop you off at our cabin and pick you up when we start home. The cabin is right on the beach, not far from the Tybee Island Lighthouse."

"I couldn't impose on you and the judge."

"We'd love for you to use it. The house is fully furnished and all the stores are within walking distance. If you want to rent a car or book a local tour, my niece, Robin, owns a travel agency and could arrange it."

"I don't drive, but I'd like to visit the lighthouse." I returned the handkerchief. "Has your niece ever been to France?"

"She lived there for three years when she first got out of college. She studied art restoration, traveled around Europe, and took cooking lessons at Le Cordon Bleu in Paris. She goes back every year for a visit."

"Does she go alone?" I asked.

"Usually."

"Isn't she afraid?"

"She was in the beginning, but not now."

"I've always dreamed of visiting Europe, especially Paris, but the thought of traveling alone terrifies me. How did Robin get over her fear?"

"She claims the hardest part is getting on the airplane. After that, everything falls into place." Mrs. Langford tucked her handkerchief into the side pocket of her purse. "Harland said Frank bought you a ticket to Paris. You are planning on using it, aren't you?"

"I don't know. I've never been anywhere by myself."

"Then Tybee Island is a good place to start. You'll have time to sort out your thoughts and decide what you want to do." She stood. "I'll introduce you to Robin. She can answer all your questions about Paris and traveling abroad."

"I'd like to hear about Le Cordon Bleu." I smoothed out a wrinkle in my skirt. "Is there a rocking chair at the cabin?"

"Several, and a hammock on the screened porch." She leaned down and gave me another hug. "It's settled then. We'll pick you up at 7 a.m. day-after-tomorrow. Don't let anyone talk you out of going."

"I won't."

After Mrs. Langford entered the doctor's office, I lingered there on the porch for awhile, contemplating the flutter in my stomach. Was it due to Ruth's encouraging words? Or was it due to Doctor Condray's news? Perhaps, it was a little of both.

CHAPTER 37

Henry placed the roaster pan on the top pantry shelf. "Is that the last one?"

I nodded. Henry had insisted on helping me clean up after our Thanksgiving dinner. A sudden headache struck Momma as soon as our feast was over. She had to lie down.

"Thanks for your help, Henry."

"Thank you for a fine meal. The chefs in Palm Beach could take lessons from you."

"I enjoy cooking." I hung my apron on the hook behind the door. "I might like to open a restaurant one day."

"Did you decide that while visiting Tybee Island last week?"

"I thought about lots of things last week."

Henry hung his apron next to mine. "Helen said you'd made some plans, but you'd refused to tell her what they were."

"I needed to take care of some business first."

"Patience has never been one of your mother's virtues."

"It must be one of yours if you're willing to marry her."

He laughed. "Helen's a challenge for sure, but I always liked a good challenge. Besides, I'm crazy about her."

There must be something good in Momma to make a fine man like Henry fall in love with her. Something down deep — real deep.

"I hope she realizes how lucky she is to have you, Henry."

He blushed.

I opened the refrigerator. "How about some tea?"

Henry got two glasses from the cupboard and sat down at the kitchen table.

As I poured our tea, I recalled our earlier conversations about pursuing dreams and standing up for those dreams against family members like his father. My heart told me this man could be trusted. I took the seat across from him. "I got some news a couple of weeks ago."

"Hope it was good news."

"It came as a surprise, but it was definitely good news." I cleared my throat. "I haven't told anyone yet, but I'd like to tell you, Henry."

"Sure, Becky. You can tell me anything good or bad."

I took a sip of tea and gathered my courage. "Before I do, you must promise not to tell anyone, especially Momma."

Henry lowered his eyes. "Then you'd better not tell me."

"Can't you keep a secret from her?"

"Yes, but I don't want to." He squared his shoulders. "On the drive up here, I thought about how Helen's and my courtship has been shrouded in secrets."

"You didn't have a choice. Neither did Frank and I considering the circumstances."

"That's what we told ourselves at the time. But Becky, we always have more control over our circumstances than we think. It's just easier to pretend that we don't. It's less work for us, less responsibility." He took a sip of tea. "I don't want there to be any secrets or lies between Helen and me. I'm determined to have an honest marriage, at least on my part."

"I hope you're not expecting that same honesty from Momma."

Henry chuckled. "I expect Helen to be Helen. It wouldn't be fair to tell her I love her and then insist she change who she is. What kind of love would that be?"

I'd never envied my mother as much as I did at that moment. She had found the rarest gem — someone who loved her unconditionally. I prayed she'd be worthy of Henry's love.

"What about Johnny? Can't you tell him your secret?"

"I will eventually. But right now it would only complicate matters between us."

"Are you two having problems?"

"Not really. We had a long talk and got everything straightened out. Johnny had wanted to get married."

Henry frowned. "From what Helen told me, I thought that's what you've always wanted."

"I thought so too, but the timing is all wrong. If we married now, it'd be more out of loneliness and heartache than out of love." I grabbed a couple of napkins, handed one to Henry, placed the other under my glass. "While at the beach, I realized Johnny needs more time to grieve for his son and his broken marriage. And I still miss Frank something fierce."

"Frank adored you. It's too bad he can't be with you."

I slipped my hand under the table and rested it on my stomach. "A part of Frank is with me wherever I go."

"I'm really sorry if I've disappointed you, Becky."

"On the contrary, I think you're an amazing human being."

"Me?" He laughed. "I've been called a lot of things, but never amazing."

"Trust me, you are. And don't worry about me. My little secret will keep for now." I got out a tin of assorted holiday cookies and placed them on the table.

Henry refilled our drinks. "So you've made some plans. Right?"

"Right."

"I wish to hell you'd tell us what they were." Momma stood in the doorway leading from the kitchen into the back hall.

"How long have you been there, Momma?"

"Just a minute. Why? Are you two telling secrets?"

Henry grinned. "Come join us, Peaches."

Momma got a glass, settled in the chair between Henry and me, and poured herself some tea. "Okay, Becky. What's this big decision you keep hinting at?"

"First off, I'm not selling Starview Mountain."

Momma slapped the tabletop with her open hand. "They've upped their offer to $700,000. You're a damn fool if you don't accept."

"Mr. Parr gave us the land because he wanted to keep it natural. Frank vowed to do so, and I'm honoring his wish."

Her jaw tightened. "I'd think you'd be happy to get rid of it after what happened with Donald."

"Are you selling the house or business?" Henry asked.

"No. I'm not as courageous as you."

"Holding on to the family home and business doesn't mean you lack courage. It just means you haven't found your dream yet." He reached for a cookie. "When you do, you might discover they're part of it."

"Are you going to run the stores?" Helen asked.

"I'm going to use the ticket Frank bought me and go to France."

She frowned. "I suppose Johnny's going with you."

"I'm going alone."

"You can't go alone," she said. "You don't speak French."

"I'm learning it. Mrs. Langford's niece, Robin, gave me a book. I can order from a menu and ask for directions to the bathroom."

Henry laughed. "Sounds to me like you've got both ends covered."

I laughed too, but Momma didn't.

"Who's going to take care of the house and the business while you are gallivanting all around Europe?" she asked.

"Johnny's going to live here. He'll take care of the house and garden."

"No way," Momma said. "I won't have him living here, rummaging through my things."

I gripped my glass with both hands. "I need someone I can trust to take care of Papa's house, and Johnny needs to save money for law school. He's going to live here."

"So Johnny's going to study law," Henry said. "That's nice."

Helen stared at her fiancé. "You're just happy for everybody, aren't you?"

Henry grinned and pushed the tin of sweets toward her. "Have a cookie, Sweetheart. You'll feel better."

"Before I leave for Palm Beach, I'm putting a padlock on my bedroom door. And what about the stores, Becky Leigh? I'd better get my monthly check."

"You will. I've worked it all out. Neil Abbott will train Josh Zagat to be the new store manager in Kirbyville. Sy Lambert will supervise the Sugardale store, and Gordon will be the general manager. He'll have the same authority Frank did."

Henry nodded. "That's a good plan."

"You were right about Judge Langford finding retirement boring. He's decided to take on a few clients, including me. He'll have my power of attorney. He and Gordon will send me reports every quarter."

Momma frowned. "Every quarter? Just how long is this visit to France?"

"I'm not just visiting France, I'm moving there."

She shot up out of her chair. "The hell you are!"

"I'll be gone at least a year, maybe more. I'm taking cooking lessons at Le Cordon Bleu. Robin has friends living in Paris. She's arranged for them to meet my plane. They'll help me find an apartment and show me around town."

"You've certainly done your homework," Henry said.

"Don't encourage her." Momma pushed her bangs off her forehead. "This is the most ridiculous idea I've ever heard. Moving to a foreign country when you've barely been out of the valley. Why don't you move to Atlanta? Or Palm Beach? Somewhere that makes sense."

"I've always wanted to go to France. That's been the one constant in my life. Besides, I need to get far away from here."

She shook her finger at me. "What you mean is that you need to get far away from me. Do you hate me so much you can't stand being in the same country?"

"This isn't about you, Momma."

"The hell it isn't." She headed for the living room. "I need my cigarettes."

I trailed after her. Henry followed and took a seat in the corner.

"Frank once accused me of using him and my pledge to care for Papa's house as excuses to hide from the world. He was right." I waited until she smoked half a Camel before continuing. "I'm going far away so if things get hard, I won't be able to run back home. I need to learn to solve my own problems and to depend upon my own judgment. That's what you did when you left West Virginia."

"I didn't have a family or a home to go to. But you do." She snuffed out the cigarette and reached for another. "Granted, it hasn't been a picnic around here, but you've always had plenty to eat, a warm bed, and people who loved you. Your daddy, Frank, Eli. Even Anna and Johnny loved you."

"Yes," I said. "Everyone except you."

She whirled around to face me. "I never said I didn't love you, Becky Leigh."

"You never said you did."

"I never said I didn't."

Henry stood. "Maybe I should go for a walk while you two talk."

"Sit down and be quiet," Momma ordered.

He did as he was told.

I stepped closer to her. "The night I told you about Donald's death, you asked me what my truth was. I didn't know. Still don't. But I'm going to find out."

"You have to move to France to do that?"

"I believe so."

She sashayed over to the front windows. "You're doing this so you won't have to attend my wedding."

"That's not true. I've been the one encouraging you to marry Henry."

"So you could be rid of me." She blew smoke rings toward the ceiling. "Can't you move to Paris after my wedding? I need your help."

"Everything has been arranged, Momma. I'm leaving December 6th. Le Cordon Bleu is offering classes in holiday desserts the next week. I plan to take them."

"The last thing you need is to dabble in holiday desserts."

"What do you mean?"

"Since we started the catering business, you've gained weight. You're supposed to sell your products, Becky, not eat them." She pulled back the curtain and stared out the window.

Henry touched my shoulder. A question flickered in his eyes.

I looked away. Had he guessed my secret?

He walked over to Momma. "I've got a surprise for you, Helen."

"Henry!" I yelled.

"It's okay, Becky."

Momma's eyes darted back and forth from her fiancé to me. "What kind of surprise?"

"As her wedding gift to us, Aunt Velma is paying for everything. She'll hire the best people in Palm Beach. You won't have to lift a finger except to point to what you want."

Helen squealed, put out her smoke, and threw her arms around Henry's neck.

Breathing a sigh of relief, I slipped out of the room and returned moments later with a box wrapped in silver paper with white ribbon. "Here's my wedding gift to you." I handed the box to Henry.

"Oh let me open it, Bumblebee." Momma snatched the present out of Henry's hands, ripped off the wrapping, and lifted the lid. A puzzled expression clouded her face as she retrieved an envelope from the box. "What's this? My eviction notice?"

I laughed. "Open it, but be careful not to tear it."

She handed the envelope to Henry. "You open it."

With great care, he tore back the flap, pulled out the papers and reviewed them carefullly. He grinned. "Becky, you shouldn't have done this."

"What's she done now?" Momma asked. "What do those papers say, Henry?"

"They're roundtrip airline tickets from Palm Beach to Las Vegas."

Her eyes grew big. "Las Vegas?"

"That's right," I said. "And there's also a voucher for a week's stay at Caesar's Palace."

More squeals from Momma. More hugs for Henry.

"Save a few hugs for Becky, Lovebug," he said.

She looked at me. "We save our hugs for the men in our lives. Don't we?"

"Whatever you say, Momma."

Henry mouthed a silent apology. I gave him my best don't-worry-about-it smile. "If you plan to go to Las Vegas for your honeymoon, Robin suggested you make your reservations soon. It gets busy around New Year's."

"New Year's Eve in Las Vegas," Helen said. "I can't wait. Let's call Robin."

"It's a holiday, Doodlebug. Her office is closed."

"We'll call her at home then. You have her number, don't you, Becky?"

"Robin is having Thanksgiving dinner with her family. I'm not going to bother them."

Helen reached for the phone. "They're finished by now. What's her number?"

Henry walked over, slipped his arm around Momma's waist. "Why don't I call the hotel and airlines direct, Butterfly?"

She handed him the phone. "That's a great idea, Bedbug."

Having had my fill of insect endearments, I decided to retreat to the kitchen.

"Wait a minute, Becky. We haven't settled the matter of you missing my wedding. What am I going to tell people when they ask why my own daughter didn't attend?"

"Is that what you're worried about?"

"People will think you and I don't get along."

"You and I not get along? How absurd!"

"Don't be cute. This is serious. It concerns my reputation and my good name."

I shrugged. "Tell them I couldn't get a plane home, it being the holidays."

"That's not a good enough excuse. Eva had to cancel a trip once because she couldn't fly due to an ear infection. We'll tell everyone you've got a terrible ear infection." She rubbed her bottom lip. "Better make that both ears, okay?"

Henry and I nodded. Once more, Momma had pulled us into her web of lies.

I made it as far as the kitchen door before she hollered for me to stop.

"When you get to France, you need to remember two things. First, watch out for those French bedbugs. I've heard they can be very charming with their French accents and fancy berets."

"I'm not looking to find a man, Momma."

"Nonsense. Every woman is looking to find a man." She grinned at Henry. "Unless she's lucky enough to have already found him."

"And what's the second thing I need to remember?" I steeled myself for yet another of her lectures on the sexual proclivities of men.

She walked over to me and pushed my hair behind my ears. "You have an advantage I never had, Becky."

"What's that, Momma?"

"You can always come home." She hugged me. Only a quick squeeze, but a definite hug.

CHAPTER 38

Flashes of light cut the early darkness of the chilly December night. The strobe atop the Atlanta airport tower reminded me of the beacon from the Tybee Island Lighthouse. Both signaled a warning and a welcome to the adventurous and the weary. I stood at the huge glass window watching the planes come and go.

"It's too bad it's nighttime," Johnny said. "You won't be able to see the ground when you take off."

I laughed. "That's probably a good thing."

"Are you nervous, Twig?"

"Terrified, but excited too."

"Just think, Twig, you'll have breakfast in Paris."

"And I know just what I want."

"What?" he asked. "A croissant? Perhaps an éclair?"

"Nope. I've had this craving for a big bowl of chocolate ice cream."

"But you don't eat ice cream. Not since —"

"Not since Papa's accident. But I think it's time for ice cream again. Don't you?"

He slipped his arm around my shoulders. "Yeah, Twig. I do."

"Ever since Frank died, I've felt like I've been lost in a giant labyrinth with every twist and turn leading me deeper into some bizarre pit."

Johnny pointed toward the giant window. "Imagine those red runway lights are there to guide you out and you'll be fine. You're stronger than you think."

"Frank used to tell me that, but I could never bring myself to believe it."

"Believe it now." Johnny had worn his uniform. After seeing me off, he planned to transport a prisoner from the Fulton County jail back to Sugardale.

We sat down on a gray vinyl bench and Johnny talked about the work he planned to do on Papa's house. Clean out the gutters, scrape and paint it in the spring, reattach several shutters that had fallen off. All the things Frank had planned on doing.

As I listened to Johnny rattle off his list of fix-it jobs, I thought of Frank. All the plans we'd made, all the dreams we'd shared. Plans and dreams that seemed so unimportant now. All that is except for one. I rested my hand on my fluttering abdomen.

If Frank was here, if he knew my secret, he'd be overjoyed. Maybe he did know. Surely, he's watching me from wherever he is because I hear him whispering to me, "You can do this, Ladybug. You can get on that plane, leave Johnny and the only world you've ever known behind, and make a better life for yourself and our child. You're stronger than you think. Trust me, Ladybug. Trust the whispers of your heart."

Lost in my thoughts of Frank, I hadn't noticed when Johnny stopped talking. When I did, I found his eyes fixed on a little boy playing on the bench across from us.

The boy looked about two, maybe three years old. About the age of Johnny's son if he'd lived. This youngster had a stuffed palomino pony with flaxen mane. As he galloped his pony back and forth over the vinyl bench, the boy clicked his tongue to imitate the sound of a horse's hooves on stone. His mother looked up from her magazine, ruffled his chestnut hair, and returned to her reading.

I watched the expression on my friend's face change from sadness to delight to sadness again. I knew he was thinking about the son he'd lost. How tall would he be now? What would his laughter sound like? How many times had I stared at a baby and wondered what our child would've looked like? Would it have been a boy? A girl? Dark hair like Johnny's? Green eyes like mine? Such questions can drive you crazy if you dwell on them too long.

I reached for Johnny's hand. "I'm glad your mother came for Thanksgiving. Anna and Ruben make a nice couple, don't they?"

He nodded. "When I told mother we were seeing each other again, she started picking out names for our kids."

"Do you think I would be a good mother? Considering Momma's legacy and all."

"You'd be a great mother, Twig. You're not anything like Helen."

I shrugged. "I've seen flashes of her in myself. I wanted revenge against Donald."

"You wanted justice. There's a difference." He squeezed my hand. "When you do have a kid, the best thing you could do for it would be to move as far away from Helen as possible."

"Funny you should say that. I recently came to the same conclusion."

"Are you sure you can't wait until after Christmas to leave?" he asked.

"I'm sure."

"But why the rush?"

"I have a good reason."

"Care to share it with me?"

"Our first night together, didn't we agree we'd each be allowed to keep a few secrets?"

"I suppose."

"I'll tell you about it one day, Johnny. Just trust me for now."

He stroked my cheek with the back of his hand. "I thought it'd work out for us this time."

"It's too soon. I need time and so do you."

"Yeah, I know. But I'd hoped . . ." He stood, turned and stared out the window.

I unzipped my carry-on bag and checked the contents again.

"What's the notebook for?" Johnny asked.

"It's a journal." I pulled it from my bag and handed it to him. "Frank used to give them to me so I could write down my experiences, my feelings . . . whatever."

"Did you ever write things about me?"

"Sure."

He flipped through the journal. "All the pages are blank."

"I wanted to start fresh."

Johnny handed it back. "I can't believe Helen put a padlock on her door. Does she really think I'm a thief?"

I tucked the journal into my bag. "You know how she loves to aggravate people."

"Especially me. What was it your grandfather called people like her?"

"Grandpa Eli called them Pickers because they like to hurt and manipulate others. They're always looking for easy pickin's."

"Yeah, and Helen's the queen. Queen Bitch if you ask me."

"Momma's not all bad. She and I talked and —"

"Helen's a monster. I can't believe you'd forgive her for the stuff she did to you."

"I used to think it was my fault Momma didn't love me. Now I know better. She couldn't love me because when she was a child, no one loved her. You can't give another person something you never had." I rubbed my forehead, trying to find a way to explain the unexplainable to Johnny. "I'll never forgive Momma for some of the things she did to me and to the people I loved, but at least now, I understand why. And that's enough for me."

"You're too soft hearted." Johnny kissed my cheek. "That's one of the things I love most about you."

A woman's voice came over the intercom. "Delta flight 122 to Paris is now boarding at gate nine. Delta flight 122 to Paris boarding at gate nine."

I jumped up. "That's me, isn't it? That's my flight?"

"Calm down, Rebecca. They won't leave without you." Johnny picked up my small carry-on bag and handed me my purse. "Better hold on to this."

A nervous laugh slipped out. "I'll write as soon as I get settled. On second thought, I'll call. Just don't give my address or phone number to Momma."

"I thought you promised her you'd write."

"I promised to write her, but didn't say anything about including a return address. I don't want any surprise visits from her the first time she gets mad at Henry."

"You're not going to tell Helen where you live?"

"Eventually. If there's an emergency, you can call me."

"Good thinking," Johnny said as we walked toward the gate.

The ticket agent stood by the counter. I joined my fellow passengers in line. Johnny held my hand, gently squeezing it now and then for encouragement. When my turn came, I handed the petite blonde my boarding pass. Johnny started to walk the half-dozen steps to the gate with me.

The agent stopped him. "Only passengers are allowed beyond this point, sir."

Johnny pointed at his badge. "I'm Deputy Sheriff John Santo, ma'am, and I have strict orders to personally escort this pretty lady to the gate."

The agent studied the badge and cast me a suspicious glance.

Johnny bent closer to her and pointed at me. "Miss Cooper was a witness in a recent murder trial." He straightened to his full six feet and with great authority settled the Stetson over his dark hair. "We felt she should go abroad for a time. Understand, Miss?"

I faked a cough in an effort to stifle a giggle.

The woman's eyes widen. She nodded and waved him through.

"You should be very ashamed of yourself, Johnny."

"Yeah, but I bet you get great service all the way to Paris."

We stood by the gate, talking softly as one by one my fellow travelers passed by. Johnny spoke of his plans to start law school the following

September. As I listened to him talk about his future — a future without me — a barrage of emotions assailed my heart and mind. I felt an escalating desire to confess all leftover secrets to this man who'd been my best friend and first love. I wanted to tell Johnny about the small miracle growing inside of me so he'd understand why I had to leave now. Loose clothing wouldn't hide my expanding abdomen much longer. Would he understand about the baby? About Frank? About my need for some time alone? I had to know, but there was no time for true confessions now. Still, I silently vowed not to let our destiny be ruled by the fickle whims of fate any longer.

I cleared my throat. "According to Robin, many Parisians go to the shore in August to escape the summer heat. She said if I wanted to rent a house on the French coast for the month, she could arrange it. What do you think, Johnny? Should I?"

"A whole month at the beach sounds like Heaven."

Without the slightest nod to subtlety, I declared, "Before you begin law school, you really should take a nice vacation too. Get some sun and fresh air."

"Good idea." He lifted my chin, forcing my eyes to meet his. "Do you think you could stand my company for a month?"

My spirits soared. "Of course, silly. I'd love for you to come."

Johnny's face brightened. He brushed back my bangs, kissed the small scar at my hairline. "Maybe by then you'll be ready to tell me your secret."

"You can count on it."

My baby would be born in May. In August, Johnny would visit and I'd tell him everything. All about the tragedies and the triumphs. All about the loneliness, the lies, and the love that had enriched my life forever. Yes, I'd tell Johnny the whole story. Where we went from there would be up to us. We alone would decide our future. What a heady thought, and one chockfull of possibilities.

"I'm going to have to close the door in a minute, sir," the ticket agent said as the last of the passengers filed by.

Johnny nodded, handed me my bag, and kissed me one last time. "I love you, Twig. Always have. Always will."

"Love you, too." I hugged Johnny, concentrating on the feel of him, the smell of him. Things I wanted to remember. Finally, I let go and started to walk away.

"Can I ask you one thing before you leave?"

I turned to face him. "Sure, Johnny, you can ask me anything."

"Donald's death. Was it honestly just an accident?"

Finally, Johnny had found the courage to ask the one question I knew he'd been silently struggling with for weeks.

"Who's asking?" I queried. "Deputy Santo? Or my friend, Johnny?"

He pulled off his Stetson, kneaded the brim with both hands for a long moment before answering. "Never mind, Twig. I think I know the truth."

I smiled, then turned and walked toward the plane.

Grandpa Eli had been right all along. We all filter the realities of life through our own personal fears, individual experiences, and the human need to cling to hope despite the circumstances, regardless of the odds. And in doing so, we each determine our own truth.

Reading Group Questions
and Topics for Discussion
(Spoiler Alert: Questions may contain spoilers)

1. What was your response to Breaking TWIG? What did you like best about it?

2. What was unique about the setting of the book? How did it enhance or take away from the story?

3. Describe the characters and plot. How do the characters change or evolve throughout the course of the story? Did the plot pull you in?

4. What specific themes did the author explore? Did certain parts of the book make you feel uncomfortable? If so, why did you feel that way?

5. Frank felt guilty for sending Donald to live with his grandparents and blamed himself for Donald's actions. How much responsibility (if any) does a parent bare for the actions of their grown children?

6. A major theme in Breaking TWIG is surviving abuse. Becky, Helen, and even Henry were victims of emotional and/or physical abuse as a child. How does each character deal with the abuse? How are their personalities shaped by it? In your opinion, who suffered the greater abuse?

7. Becky said having one person who loves and believes in you is all a person needs to keep hope alive. She had her grandpa, Dad, Frank, Johnny, and Anna. Henry had his mother, while Helen had nobody. How influential a role was this love or

lack of love on how each character developed as an adult?

8. Does Becky change her feelings about her mother after she learns the truth about Helen's childhood? Were your feelings or opinions changed toward Helen? Is it possible to have understanding without forgiveness?

9. Did Helen love Becky at all? Does Becky's struggle exemplify the strength of the human spirit? When forced to go to Starview Mountain with Donald, Becky makes a critical choice with moral implications. Would you have made the same choice?

10. Did the book end the way you expected? Did Becky make the right decision? Do you believe Grandpa Eli was right — do we each determine our own truth?

To schedule a conversation with your book club or reading group, contact me at:

breakingtwig@hotmail.com

About the Author

Born and raised in the Deep South, Deborah Epperson grew up during the era of the Civil Rights Movement, integration, and Vietnam. She received a BS degree in biology and English in Texas, and later moved to Atlanta to work and pursue post graduate work at Georgia Tech. After working in the scientific field for twenty years, she turned her talents to writing fiction and nonfiction. Her award winning nonfiction and poetry have been published in newspapers and magazines locally and nationally.

Through her storytelling, Deborah tackles issues most people, especially Southerners, can identify with and, like her, may have struggled to understand. She enjoys writing stories and characters steeped in the lyrical traditions and mystical surroundings of the Deep South where she grew up.

A transplanted Texan, Deborah lives in Montana with her husband and children. When not working on her next novel or article, she enjoys doing pet therapy work with her golden retriever, and volunteering in animal rescue.

14566335R00243

Made in the USA
Charleston, SC
18 September 2012